TEN
DIRECTIONS

By

Samuel Winburn

Ten Directions

Samuel Winburn

Address enquiries to:
Samuel Winburn
c/o Pleiades Perspectives
PO Box 1081, West Leederville Western Australia 6023

www.samuelwinburn.net
www.facebook.com/directions10

For information about special discounts available for bulk purchases, sales promotions, fund-raising and educational needs, contact Sales at +61-400244438 or sales@samuelwinburn.net

Table of Contents

PREFACE

This story began in an unusual way. That is to say, it was unusual compared to my preconceptions of how your average work of fiction begins – with a central concept, a plot summary and outline, followed by the methodical execution of that plan. This story didn't happen that way. This is what happened.

Whilst taking a shower 20 years ago, an artistic vision arose from one of my daydreams. The vision regarded a teaching by the Buddha on generating compassion through the visualization of breathing in the suffering of the world, dissolving one's own suffering in that, and breathing out liberation from suffering for oneself and all beings. In this daydream, I imagined a monk on a remote planet breathing in the suffering of the universe in the form of a black hole, the densest and darkest phenomenon known to science, and breathing out compassion in the form of light. Inspired by the clarity of this vision, I wrote a short story, which is still my introduction to the character Kalsang in Chapter 4.

Thereafter, the whole book gradually and organically grew from this seed of a vision. Providing soil for that seed was an early decision to set the scene in a world where, somehow, humanity has managed to survive the fall-out from our current ecological overshoot. This choice came as a natural consequence of my career helping develop the profession of environmental accounting, an important piece in the puzzle of achieving a sustainable future from out of our current mess. The climate and sky into which in this seed grew was a commitment to exploring the spiritual evolution of my characters, in an open way, as they navigated their way through the plot. In the process, the narrative became a mirror in which to reflect on my own Path, and many of the struggles of the characters became improvisations on my own inner struggles.

The final ingredient bringing this book to fruition was magic. In my case, magic only occurred once I had become properly lost. Truthfully, I have been lost since the beginning, but I'd been too busy showing everyone that I knew where I was going to notice. However, at some point it became difficult to pretend anymore, and it was only then that magic had a chance to happen.

The magic began at a barbecue. A friend, Akiko, had invited my family over for lunch. While shopping in our neighbourhood shopping centre in suburban Western Australia, she had randomly met her old roommate from the California Institute of Integral Studies in San Francisco whom she hadn't seen for over a decade. When we arrived at the barbecue, I recognized that Akiko's friend was the renown Buddhist female lay master Khandro Thrinlay Chodon whose teaching I had attended earlier that week. Over the course of that afternoon, I learned that Khandro Rinpoche was the widow of the ninth Shabdrung Ngawang Jigme Rinpoche of Bhutan, and also carried the wisdom lineage of her great grandfather Tokden Shakya Shri, an important spiritual reformer in the Himalayan Buddhist yogic tradition. Khandro Rinpoche was the only female Buddhist Master I had met at that time, other than the fictional Lama Wangmo, Kalsang's Guru, who I had invented for this novel. Later that afternoon Khandro Rinpoche's brother, Sey Jigme Dorje, came to the barbecue with his daughter, Seymo Yeshe. Learning that Sey Jigme also lived in Perth, I asked where he lived and he replied with an address only a few houses down the street from my own. Magic.

Thus, began a new era in my life. For 30 years prior to this meeting I had been diligently attending my local meditation centre, struggling to learn a spiritual tradition with a history and culture, which was distant from my own. Perhaps part of the attraction to Tibetan Buddhism was this distance, which cast the shortcomings of our unsustainable and frenetic modern Western culture into sharp relief. In this regard, the moral high ground of the Tibetans "turning the other cheek" to the loss of their homeland was unassailable. However, this conceptual approach to learning Buddhism had done little to settle my crazy emotions, which was what I had been longing for.

With Sey Jigme steering me towards authenticity in following the spiritual direction Khandro Rinpoche has lain down, I have since been learning that meditation practice is much more than sitting in a room doggedly trying to apply some formula learned from ancient, often esoteric, texts. Instead, Khandro Rinpoche teaches that wisdom manifests humbly and organically in ordinary daily life through realizing that we are not separate from the flow of our world. Rather than becoming defensive and remote from our chaotic and turbulent times, we can transform ourselves and our world from within those conditions, which are not separate from ourselves. Through practicing these teachings, it is slowly, painstakingly, becoming clearer to me that expanding insight comes only through the process of becoming more genuine.

This book has had a 20-year gestation period because, for most of that time, my creative well often ran dry. Without the inspiration and direction from Khandro Rinpoche and Sey Jigme, which flowed from that magical barbecue, perhaps I would have never have had the confidence and persistence to complete it. Perhaps I would never have had the courage to release it into your care. In any case, out of gratitude to my Teachers, I offer my book towards the goal of attaining the magic potential within each of us. May our lives become ever more peaceful and productive.

Em ah ho!

THE MEASURE OF HEAVEN

*'May the mind of compassionate awakening
grow where it has now grown,
and where it has grown purely
may it increase forever more'*

~Shantideva, 8th Century India

CHAPTER 1

d'Jang

No one, not even his mother, had responded to his calls in many tides.

d'Jang couldn't fault them now that all tides were being consumed into one. Time itself was being swallowed by that horrible hole in the sky, so maybe there was no longer any point in repeating tearful farewells.

All of this was his fault; there was no getting around it. It would be a conceit to take full credit, but there had been a moment when he had at least a chance to say something. He had not - so few had even tried, and now it was too late.

Here he sat, in relative if temporary safety, on a remote satellite while the planet of the Mother Ocean was being swallowed. He longed to indulge his self-pity by hailing someone, if only to relieve his loneliness, but what would that accomplish?

It would all be over soon enough anyway.

Feeling hungry, d'Jang reached out with his lower left octopodal arm and wrapped his tentacles around some feed swimming past. His catch, dangling over the mouth of his fifth head, was rescued by a thought. This one, so common in the Mother Ocean, would soon be among the last of his species. d'Jang looked at it kindly and decided to spare it. The hole should swallow his ship before he died of hunger. The feed wriggled free and slipped behind the pilot's console. d'Jang waited, disappointed when the creature did not re-emerge. This was what had come of him, having his heart broken by feed.

d'Jang thought of his lovely daughter d'Song. As the future died the past was becoming everything.

He once again scanned the logs for the last transmissions received from his Home Reef, including mnemes, computer encoded packets of feelings and memories, sent from the children of his Pod, although the youngest would not understand their significance. Right now, much effort would be expended to shelter them from what was going on. If adults with full melding could not comprehend the sudden finality that had interrupted the busy constancy of their lives, how could they explain it to children? d'Jang savored these last echoes of pleasure as their mnemes stirred in his heart, the excited potential and clever associations from the new minds, even in these final moments.

d'Song again appeared before him, or at least an echo of her. What he saw was a computer augmented mental image, but enough had flowed between them over the tides that she was able to manifest in his mind as an independent presence. She was maturing so beautifully. Her faces had all emerged from their buds, each revealing different facets of her loveliness. He longed to enfold her in his tendrils, but in trying to, her image drew away.

"Do not worry, Melded One." She said that as if there were anything else left to do.

One of her brothers struggled against her attentive grip, the unmelded personalities of two of his heads fighting with each other again, and d'Song released him with a sigh. There was too much resignation there for eyes so young.

She had already grown stronger than her father. d'Song was one who had spoken out after d'Jang had told her about the instabilities in the Channel Between Planets when they had first been observed in his telescope - the ones that everyone else had busied themselves in explaining away. She was a kid, and so had been ignored. Perhaps together, a kid and a low rank male like himself, they could have prevailed with someone of significance - someone like her mother, queen of a high caste pod. That was fantasy. Important people rarely listened, and especially not queens to their daughters. And as for him, d'Song's mother had enjoyed her concubine and then forgotten him. He was no Alpha. So, he had stayed silent; even then d'Song had not given up on him.

"I miss you d'Jang."

"My lovely d'Song, beyond my depth."

His concentration was middling, and her image began to fade as his words completed. He struggled to keep her fresh in his mind, but her dissolution into sadness and memory could not be stopped. Then there was nothing to do but wait. And watch.

d'Jang caught himself feeling bored with the slow progress of the terrible thing growing outside his portal, wishing it would just finish what it was destined to do and end his misery. Objectively it appeared completely benign, a nothing edged with a blur and growing at an imperceptible rate. Yet this nothing would soon erase all beauty from the universe.

d'Jang's body blackened with shame. Was he not a villain to wish away any of the few precious hours remaining for his people and their world? Was the pain of knowing so great that it called for shortening, by even an instant, the billions of years of evolution and tens of thousands of culture and knowledge, or accelerating away even one hopeful laugh of the children who in their youth could not comprehend the small number of their remaining days?

A sharp flash of light from the blurred edge told him that some celestial fragment, an asteroid or comet, had vanished beyond the event horizon of the black hole.

d'Jang tightened the tendrils on his lower third left hand to access the recording of the event by the space telescope array of which he was now the lone operator. Always the scientist. Who was going to be around to analyse the results? Still it gave him some small peace to have a job to do. He ordered a different spectral image for ten of his eleven faces; the eyes of his main face too smeared with tear mucus to focus on anything useful.

Scientist. The word had lost all nobility. Endless procedural meetings and meaningless debate and pride masquerading as humility. Too proud to break things down for the masses. Dithering in the name of truth while the other side felt no such qualms. "All Oceans Will Become One." Such an inane inversion of the simple spiritual truth, that they were all connected by the ocean they shared. Those idiot prophets, growing fat dishing out self-serving delusion to the Alphas. Like c'Virm, the worst of that despicable lot. How did he feel now, d'Jang wondered, facing compaction into his Great Ocean, completing his fantasy of everyone becoming One?

Then again, who was he, d'Jang, to fault anyone else for cowardice? He might be able to convince himself otherwise if he alone had not stayed behind while his colleagues had shifted out. Still hiding behind his investigations as a distraction from the approaching cataclysm. Scientist.

d'Jang's main face looked past their dying planet into the infinite night and the lights that would outlive them. Which one of those was home to the demon responsible for inviting his world into oblivion? He wanted to focus all his helpless anger on that single light - to focus it on the owner of that horrendous face, imprinted upon all podlings in history lessons, with that strange thatch of threads sprouting from its crown and obscuring its singular face. The one who had introduced the instructions for building this, this thing? There were no words to describe the horror that his other faces were intently dissecting with the telescope. There was no way to get to the bottom of it or of his grief, or of his shame at the depths of his complicity. Wasn't the telescope that he had been so proudly manning the very one which had received the instructions for building the damn thing in the first place?

His anger was misplaced. What possible benefit could those strange beings derive from destroying the Mother Ocean? They were much too far away. So, they likely did not know. They probably thought they were doing everyone a favor by sharing their wonderful technology. Maybe they had been swallowed up by it too. The scientist in d'Jang would not let him diffuse responsibility across the waves of stars so easily.

No, his people had done this to themselves. d'Jang could remember the excitement the Channel Between Planets wormhole had engendered, as short ago as 20 moons, before it had decayed into a channel to their doom. The hopeful Surge out into the waiting Oceans of the cosmos. How were they to know that it would suddenly produce the end of everything? The sister planet, m'Hoomuun, now within reach of his people eager to escape the fouling waters of their Mother Ocean, had already been eaten. With blinding flashes even pieces that had ripped away early had disappeared into emptiness.

Nothing remained of a billion people and all the creatures of that world.

And today would be the final moment of the Mother Ocean, of everything that had ever been or could ever be. And he, d'Jang, would watch it all. The simple geometry of his cowardice dictated that this would be so.

There were no words for the sadness that seeped away his being. It was a blackness of greater depth than the hole in the heavens. Nothing would remain.

Precious time ran past.

As the monstrosity bore down on the Mother Ocean, d'Jang launched a probe back to his Home Reef. By what insanity had he done that? As the probe fell away beneath the shaking waters of the Mother Ocean his mind's eye had travelled with it.

Even before the probe camera located the glowing phosphorescent layers of his Home Reef, he could hear their Singing, millions of voices, in a communal celebration of grief, clicked and boomed and trilled through the ocean, vibrating the view. As the probe approached the Home Reef, d'Jang noticed its glow was brighter than usual; overwhelming the usual dull green and red of the coral were pulsating electric rainbow hues. Focusing the probe lens, d'Jang realised that their reef was gleaming with people, lined across the ledges, their chromataphore skin aflame with every color imaginable.

The probe hovered close enough to resolve individual faces. Perhaps he would see d'Song. The improbability of that did not diminish his hope. His search was unsuccessful, but in scrutinising faces d'Jang noticed a strange commonality in their expression. They were all staring the same direction, towards the West, and all their faces were blossoming with individual variations of hope. How could this be? It was as if each found confidence in the sense that through their solidarity they could yet survive. Their courage ennobled them and included him. d'Jang turned the probe to join them in facing the darkness ominously growing on the horizon. He would stand with them, his people, in their proudest hour. They sang out their hearts as one, and their collective song became one current, rushing back against the approaching darkness. The black mass that swooped in upon them was not the black hole. It was the hardening of water.

Oh!

What d'Jang then witnessed, in footage which lasted only minutes but never ended, was terror beyond imagining and left him ruined. The last screams merged with the water's roar as the last tide ran out. The Ocean drained. Even the echoes of his loved ones were silent.

She was gone.

d'Jang's heart cherished suicide in the tideless time that followed, as visions from the probe invaded his dreams and when he replayed the footage for no reason other than to torture himself with loss. This desire went unrequited, for who was he to put an end to the last remnant of being remaining from their world?

"d'Jang. What about the others?"

"d'Song?"

At that moment, the pardoned feed ventured out from behind the console and hung in the water before d'Jang, fearless. It was beautiful.

"The others."

"The others?"

This last thought d'Song had given him, and which the feed had seconded, slowly built in d'Jang's mind and would not leave. Was it possible that in the short time left he might redeem a small fragment of who they had been and could have become?

"What about the others?"

The others out there in the endless thin waters, others like their kind. Even the ones who sent the message. Perhaps there was still time to warn them. The conviction grew. No one else should EVER experience this tragedy, this bottomless pain.

He would send them a final mneme from his people to theirs, a warning, and more, an embrace.

It was almost too late.

Great urgency flowed into him. His computer contained a reflection of most of the knowledge from the Surge. d'Jang searched frantically as the void pulled him into it. The transmission would need to occur before the insatiable appetite of the black hole captured even his radio waves.

What could he send in the short time left? The probe footage. The last moments of his Reef. Only that would show the true horror of the thing. No one could watch that and contemplate ever creating a Star Channel. He queued it for broadcast.

How could people make sense of what was being warned against? He needed to tie the warning to the wormhole technology. Then d'Jang happened upon the original transmission from the aliens to his people containing the instructions for building the Channel Between Worlds. What better way to explain to other aliens the intricate technology he was warning them about? It had already been packaged for that purpose. Of course, he had to take out the explicit instructions for building it, otherwise he might only be exposing others to a horrible fate. Scanning the mneme file d'Jang was confused by the complexity of the Star Channel transmission. The complex physics and engineering, expressed in the unfamiliar notation of the aliens, would have been impossible for him to decode even if he had the time. When it had first arrived, unravelling the alien message had taken the best minds of the Mother Ocean months. d'Jang struggled to find a separation between the description of the technology, and the specifications for building it. Frustrated, d'Jang decided to delete random chunks only to find out that a security setting on the file rendered it un-editable.

His ship shook violently, a loud crack echoing through the cabin. The water envelope in the cockpit began to retract, indicating a breech. Alarms were flashing. Time was the one thing he didn't have. d'Jang queued the whole aliem mneme. Surely, having seen it's distructive capability, no thinking being would seek to build it. Surely. Anyway, there was no going back on his decision.

The ship buckled again. The Tide was running out. It was almost too late. One final thing left to do. d'Jang faced the recorder and flowed his whole being out to the people of the other worlds. They would need to absorb the fullness of the tragedy and, although this was a selfish motive, perhaps something of his kids might yet survive. Of d'Song, his beautiful girl. All his faces cried out as he transmitted the last record of his people out into the fabric of the Universe.

An uneasy sense of fulfilment grew in d'Jang - a feeling that in acting on his responsibility to the cosmos he had connected himself to everything - a bittersweet compassion for all who had come before them and all who remained.

His beloved feed swam up beside d'Jang and waited with him.

All channels joined in the one Ocean. d'Jang glowed. And then his light was swallowed, and he became no more.

ONE HALF OF KNOWING

'My children, your toys ,... bullock-carts, goat-carts, deer-carts, which are so pretty, nice, dear, and precious to you, have all been put by me outside the house-door for you to play with. Come, run out, leave the house; to each of you I shall give what he wants.... And the boys, on hearing the names mentioned of such playthings as they like and desire, so agreeable to their taste, so pretty, dear, and delightful, quickly rush out from the burning house, with eager effort and great alacrity.'

~Shakyamuni Buddha, Lotus Sutra

The planet Earth

Suffering through escalating ecological and economic systems collapses, the citizens of planet Earth eventually became serious. The Ecolution occurred.

Instigated by activist Revs and emanating from South Asia, where climate change posed the most existential threat, a new world order emerged based on united local community Hubs and their Nets, social business networks, which empowered them. Money was replaced by Ecos, a universal currency based on the intrinsic shared value of repairing Gaia, the living Earth. Ecos were estimated and validated by new global scientific institutions, the Sys, who matched local projects to natural planetary cycles. The guiding political philosophy for this revolution was Parnarchy, where each citizen's loyalty to Hub and Net jurisdictions is a free choice liberated from geography, but where local loyalties are balanced by sacred oaths sworn to protect Gaia.

The Ecolution was fiercely resisted by the declining world-order of transnational corporation Coms and the Govs, their client nation states, and eventually these battles ground to a détente, the Peace. The Panarchists now rule the Earth, while the Capitalist Coms are free to develop the Heavens. This deal has not turned out as well for the Coms as they had hoped. Despite a century of concerted effort, known as The Second Wave, only a handful of humans live elsewhere in the Solar System, far fewer than the Coms had envisioned.

CHAPTER 2

August

What variety of demon chases the soul of a man out from his own private eternity?

Is it the echo of unformed pain resounding within the flesh of his ambition? The ticking clock of incremental regrets counting out the remainder of his days? The shattering of darkness complicating even the grandest oblivion? Or the involuntary cry for help unanswered?

All of these and none, wearing his own face, looking back though his own eyes with an inescapable vacuity present in even the most steadied outward gaze. The daily competing crises, the unending task of personal resurrection, the monotony of intoxication, the confining shallows of narcissism. The man, once confident striding out upon the familiar shifting of this terrain, is now uncertain. He senses something watching him from beneath this ceaseless swamp, a familiar presence without a name. The demon waits for him patiently, outside the passage of hours. It stalks him relentlessly, immune to distance or circumstance. It may destroy him in an instant, although lacking the force of the slightest breeze.

The man spends his days not hearing this faint whisper he cannot afford to ignore, becoming a constant refugee from the omnipresence of an unrecognized foe. He may conquer the universe, yet this will not deliver him. For, though as insubstantial as a dream within a dream, the demon holds a devastating advantage. It is this.

The demon is only as real as the man is false.

Only in these morning hours of interrupted dreams, rare moments of wakefulness, exposed nerves played by a ragged wind - only now can the man hear the demon call his name.

This time the man answers back.

* * * * * * * * * * * * *

"Illya!"

The man's cry, which could not travel through the vacuum beyond his helmet, felt as though it travelled all the long way back home to an intimate place on the vivid blue world balanced above the horizon. Mesmerised by the planet's beauty, he had been drawn out here, sleepwalking out of a morning dream, yet in some way more awake than he had been in a long time. The contrast between the living Earth and the strange country of light and darkness, which he currently inhabited, mirrored this inner dichotomy. Shadows retreating from the merciless brilliance of the rising Sun on the surrounding regolith plains were jet black. The man padded himself through his suit for reassurance that he was still alive against the evidence of his eyes that life, in this place, was never intended.

The man's name was August Bridges, but the fact of this name and the history of circumstance attaching it to the wealthiest person in the solar system were irrelevant at the moment. At the moment he was simply a man in pain, as he had been long before the name had outgrown its owner. The dream, which had inspired this morning's exodus, was from that time. From before his ambition had replaced friendships. From before isolation and loneliness had become his last refuge.

The indicator blinking in August's neuroview told him that his oxygen was running low. How long had he been out here? He reluctantly turned back, and then panicked when he realised how far he had walked away from the station. He must be kilometers away from safety. Puffing as he bounded back, steadily sucking in the remaining air in his tanks, August realised this time he had gone too far. As his stride fell into a slow trudge, and his lungs shrunk, August tripped and fell on his side, staring back at the angelic Earth and praying for deliverance. His eyelids began to narrow, focusing on a path homewards into the safety offered by his dream.

He struggled against their fall. Unwilling to surrender his life with all his sacrifices, feeling its fragility in each labored breath. It was impossible that August Bridges, the legend he had become, could die so easily and so stupidly. Like a moth lured into a flame. It simply was not possible.

There had to be another way. There must be. It was to this flicker of possibility that August committed his survival. Having decided to continue at this moment only one thing was sure. It was time for August Bridges to wake up.

"August. August. Respond to me please."

"I'm here Dmitri," August thought back to the voice in his mind.

"I'm here."

Even his thoughts became whispers. Was answering a mistake? Surely it was better to just let go.

"I hear you my friend. Thank God. I have locked on your coordinates."

August attempted to stand, but his muscles demanded too much oxygen and he swooned again, falling back into his dream, promising himself it was only for a moment.

"Illya."

The alarm in his helmet, a mosquito's buzz, pried its way into the recurring dream until he could ignore it no more. August swatted it away. The action rolled him off his side onto his back. He lapped at the residual air in his suit, extracting what life was left in it.

Where was he? August wasn't sure anymore. His eyes rested on the cooling blue and white circle hanging alone in a field of infinite blackness above.

"Mom? Is that where you are?"

"Who are you talking to August? Is there someone with you?"

Then August remembered. They had chased him away from there. His own people. All he had wanted to do was save them. Ignoring Dmitri's question, August closed his eyes and did not answer, leaving the pain to burrow back into another time when he had been happy. To the point where Anya's eyes had first left his.

Was this where it had all begun to go wrong?

"August. This is Dmitri. You've gone Out okay? Don't do anything stupid. Your head is screwed up. I'm on your trail - I'm coming for you."

Dmitri's voice forced August's eyes back open. Why wouldn't they just leave him alone? August rolled off the mound where he had fallen and onto his stomach. He groggily lifted his helmet out of the talcum soil and suspiciously regarded twin lights rolling towards his location. Sweat dripped into his eyes, turning the view into mirage. The indicator panel floating in his mind's eye warned him that the cooling system circulation in his suit was beginning to slow. If he didn't get back inside soon he would fry like an egg out here if he didn't suffocate first. The lights winked out as the rover went down into some riffle in the terrain; August panicked for a moment at the thought that his pursuer had disappeared.

Couldn't they hurry up and catch him? He was too exhausted to run, and he wasn't sure anymore who he had run from, only that he had crimes enough to answer for. And then he wasn't sure even of that. Nothing made sense. August huddled into himself, clinging to all that was left to him, his dream, his future, his past.

"Augustus Mishen'ka, I see you. I see you. I'm coming."

August reacted to Dmitri's entreaty by curling tighter into himself. Whatever they did to him when they caught him, whatever uncertain terrors had driven him from the protection of the station to certain death where he lay - for a short while more he had a hiding place they could not reach.

This was the place in his dream August wanted to stay in, a place far away from the exposed conscious part of his mind, which was busy ignoring the red blinking indicators that his neurovisor projected into it.

"August? August? Can you hear me? Shit. Please don't be dead."

"Give me some sign. Move."

Insistent tugging jerked August up to his feet and back into what was left of his life. A familiar presence linked into the unsecured part of his mind, flipping through the life support monitors floating in his imagination. They quickly changed color from red through yellow towards green as energy and oxygen were injected into his suit.

"Thank God you are still alive. You lucky shit. You stupid, stupid ass of a man."

Dmitri was weeping. Such a good friend.

Energised by the injection of oxygen, August flailed his arms, kicking, twisting, and offering what resistance he was able offer, kicking up a cloud of dust that launched away into the vacuum with unbroken momentum.

"Leave me be," he whimpered.

"Slow down idiot. I'm trying to save you."

The infusion of energy quickly exhausted, August went limp and felt his body being lifted, feather-light, off the ground and over a shoulder. A spasm of paranoia tightened his heart. This was it. They had caught up with him, and he was even grateful it would soon all be over. August fell once more into sleep, protected by the truth that there was nothing real in his fear.

His dream ran out into darkness.

Later, out of a fog and unsure where he was, August wrestled to pull a tube out from his nose. Achieving his purpose, he rubbed his nosebleed across his face and wondered why he was here in the infirmary. The acrid smell of burnt charcoal reminded him that he was still on the Moon. When he reached for the bed rail he was given another reminder as a painful jolt of static electricity fired through his body. August leaned over the railing and puked, watching the vomit arc lackadaisically out across the room and skid lightly across the floor into a corner where it began to evaporate into the parched artificial atmosphere. Hanging over the rail, August noticed where the ground wire on the bed had not been attached. There was the source of his nausea. Not only that, the therapeutic vibrator in the bed base that helped bones and flesh retain their mass in lunar gravity wasn't even hooked up. Someone was going to lose their job over that.

At that point, August recovered himself and who and where he was. He remembered he had fired almost everyone. Damn Gudanko and his pedantic pencil sharpening. August had sent them home to make a point. As if the safety of the Mirtopik Com CEO was as luxury. No unnecessary expense would be needed to support his exile on the Moon, and Gudanko could go shove that up his tight ass.

That was basically what he said at the time, although the other reason, which August wouldn't admit to, was that he felt safer without so many potential assassins wandering about. With numbers down to a very short list of people he still believed he could trust, and the crater walls of Plato separating him from the shift workers in the helium-3 mines down South in the Sea of Rains, August felt almost safe. Almost.

Except that he didn't. And time was running out.

Which brought him back to the question of why he was wasting time here in the infirmary. August coughed uncontrollably as he attempted to leave the bed. He reflexively reached for the vaporizer that simultaneously countered a litany of symptoms of living on the Moon: sinus passages continually overfilled with gravitationally liberated body fluids, constant heartburn as stomach acids lifted off into his oesophagus, throat and mouth lining scalded away by a parsimonious atmospheric pressure, and a host of other irritations. At least this was working. After a few drags he was able to settle himself enough to climb out of bed. His dehydrated body ached as he made his way to the sink for a drink.

There he was confronted by an army of Augusts reflected endlessly in wrap around mirrors, each reflection as dishevelled as the rest, only from a slightly different angle.

"My God," August recoiled, "the hair."

The static standoff occurring on his scalp exaggerated the one aspect of August's appearance with which he felt wholly unsatisfied. An exploded fault line of a cowlick jagged across his head from mid-brow to the crest of his spine. Hair fell indiscriminately about the rift like a forest knocked down in a windstorm. The condition could be easily corrected, if only he had not let it become his signature. In earlier days the "hair bomb," as Gregori had named it, had given August a rangy, boyish appearance that endeared him to others and encouraged trust. So, August had kept it, cultivated it in truth, cutting it jagged, scrambling his fingers through the golden thatch, letting it fly in the wind.

Time had removed the charm. Middle-aged grey and a general hardening of his features should have accentuated what he was, a man in the prime of life at the crest of his powers. Instead he was crowned like an eccentric mad scientist. The only thing that would look more ridiculous now would be getting rid of it. The vanity of an aging man was not something August was ready to admit to the world, and besides no one would recognize him. If they were to mint a coin with August Bridges' head on it, half of it would be this hair.

"Impossible."

August pushed his dripping locks carefully in place, appreciating the temporary order enforced by a rapidly evaporating dampness.

"August?" It was Dmitri.

Startled, August turned to escape only to slip on vomit and drop slowly to the floor. Dmitri caught him halfway. Recovering, August pushed Dmitri back and drew himself to full height, struggling to enact some semblance of dignity.

"What, what am I doing here?"

Dmitri laughed his disbelief. "Staying alive for a start."

August flattened his hair again with frustrated brushes of his hand.

"This is no joke Dmitri."

"No, no, no my friend. No, it isn't." Dmitri smiled and shook his head and embraced August tightly. "Death is no joke, at least we never see the humor in our own. On the other hand, our life? Hmm."

August struggled, reluctantly, to free himself from Dmitri's steady support.

"What are you crapping on about? We have things to do. I don't understand."

"Is okay. You are confused, no? Not so surprising. I found you out there with only enough oxygen to fill your tiny prick. A few minutes more, world loses its favorite pain in ass."

August attempted to stare his friend back into place, but Dmitri responded with the casual insolence of long familiarity. It did not matter how far August had come, Dmitri had been with him the whole way.

"I saved your ridiculous life. Don't be such peacock."

August raked his hair and it flicked back into disorder. "Okay. Tell me what happened."

"What happened? I come all way up here to kick your head out of the clouds. What happens? You are nowhere to be found. I thought you were hiding in the Station somewhere. Instead you are laying on ass five kilometers out towards the crater wall."

"But I called you up?"

"Why else am I here? Am I rich enough to come as tourist?"

August smiled. "Actually, you are."

Dmitri frowned, "Actually, you don't watch our share price."

"What would be the point in that?"

August gave his leave before Dmitri could respond to the provocation. "When I am dressed and more myself, and we each have a few drinks behind us, better you tell me then."

"Better I stay with you."

"You want to hold my dick while I piss?"

Dmitri regarded August with exasperation. "You are going crazy out here."

"If it makes you happy, I'll give you access to the ComSec cams in my eyes."

"It would make me happy."

August focused his attention through a series of menus in his imagination and linked over to Dmitri's neuroview to transfer the relevant permissions.

August watched Dmitri's eyes twitch as his mind's eye linked into August's perspective looking back at his own face.

"So that is how you look at me." Satisfied, Dmitri shrugged. "Okay Boss. Call me."

On his way back to his cabin, August pushed away a curious impulse to turn back towards the airlocks instead. Entering the room, he checked the corners for hidden assailants and, finding none, welcomed his loneliness back like an embrace. Loneliness had become his refuge. It was the backdrop against which everything else in his life came to be. Wasn't his greatness the product of his abandonment? People would not follow those who followed others, and he had still to lead them a very long way.

August thought open the skylight and gazed past the Earth out to the stars. The Earth might have rejected him, but the stars were where his destiny lay. Even in the early days, those stars had called out to him, if only in a metaphoric sense. These days, of course, August had the ability to pick up the phone and listen to their conversations. One day, not too distant in the future, they would call him home.

Reclining into his webbing, a hammock like chair he had mentally commanded to descend from a portal in the ceiling, August extracted his neurovisor from his skull and waited for it to cycle through its repair and cleaning algorithms. The neurovisor looked like a pair of spectacles without lenses, the cross-bridge instead merging into a stem leading to a writhing mass of almost imperceptible silver threads that, when positioned correctly, would feel their way to the center of his forehead and into a network of pore sized portals that had been drilled through his skull. There they would merge with the neurons in his brain and link his mind to the neuronet. It seemed almost too creepy to work, but it did.

After removing the device, the room felt expansive. August breathed easier. It seemed contradictory that extraction of a technology that expanded his senses into an endless virtual panorama would contribute to his claustrophobia. Removing it made him feel vulnerable, as if most of his senses had been suddenly blinded. Still, without it his thoughts were also completely his own.

What, August wondered, had happened to him out there? How had he ended up nearly dying so far out on the edge? Why would he have wanted to run from Dmitri, of all people? These were all bad signs, indicators of the inexorable degradation of sanity that visited whoever left the Earth for too long. Of course, the Moon was supposedly close enough to avoid the more extreme symptoms of that condition. Then again, he was in the process of setting some kind of record given the length of his exile. The lunar miners that those studies were based on were all one month on, two months off shifts. August had been here much longer than that.

There was a knock on his door, a sound that had become unfamiliar to August. Why hadn't Dmitri mentally telegraphed his request to enter? Looking down at his neurovisor, August remembered why. He walked over to the door and searched awkwardly for the manual latch.

"Are you there August?"

"Yes, just a moment."

The door slid open as August mastered the switch.

"Your neurocams?"

August motioned to the table and his neurovisor.

"You took it off?"

"I needed to think. Come sit."

Dmitri casually summoned another webbing from the ceiling with a twitch of his eye. A beverage tube descended between the seats.

"Vodka tonic?" Dmitri asked as August seated himself first.

"What else?"

August picked up the suppressed tension in Dmitri's motions as he carefully poured the drinks. "Why are you here Dmitri?"

"Not this. Are you going to run out on me again?"

"No. Seriously. Why?"

"You called me up. Remember?"

"I've called you up before. Many times. You didn't come then. No, there must be a reason."

Dmitri's posture tightened, and he exhaled audibly. "Do you have to ask, or are you trying to make some kind of point?"

"The other Directors. Gudanko?"

"No. No, of course not him."

"Then who?"

Dmitri scowled. "Are you being obtuse? This is me."

It was as August feared. "They got to you."

"I am here for my own reasons August. What? Do you think I went to all this trouble to climb up someone's asshole? I would have had a much shorter trip back in LA."

19

"Then why?"

Dmitri set his drink aside and stiffened. "They're dead, August."

August tugged at his hair, composing his features to best express his sympathy.

"Sacha, Gennadiya, Irina."

"Anya?"

Dmitri shook his head. "I haven't heard."

August released his breath. "Dmitri, we've been over this. What do you know?"

"Sacha. My brother. Definitely. Mama told me."

"I'm so sorry Dmitri, Sacha. Such a terrible sacrifice."

"Sacrifice? Sacrifice? You think he died for some cause? It was senseless. He was shot leading a group trying to break into a Com warehouse trying to help widows and children survive the famine. He died fighting us. Fighting me."

"That's incredible Dmitri, and so senseless. Why didn't he just ask for your help instead? This is what comes of siding with Revs."

"Revs? You know better. We used to be on their side remember?"

"Yes Dmitri. I remember. But..."

"But? But what? You think this has nothing to do with you? You bring down the economy of whole countries and it is nothing to do with you?"

August smoothed his hair and sipped his drink intently. "Dmitri, this was never what we wanted. Things will get better."

"No August. We didn't intend. It all went too far too long ago. Let our Hubs out of their contracts, it is time. Let them go back to Ecos. For the love of God."

August swirled the alcohol in his mouth. "At least now I know, Dmitri. You didn't come from the Board."

Dmitri's expression hardened, and he shook his head. "Tell me August, when you make a whole society dependent on the share price of the Com that you head, don't you have some responsibility to that society?"

August widened his eyes in sympathy. "You know the answer already Dmitri. Would we be here without those contracts? Do you think we would have developed the moon with a 'gratitude economy'? How do you thank someone for the favour of freedom? We needed capital, upfront not after the fact. Where would all the energy come from for society, for geo-engineering to repair Gaia? Packaging up all the plastic floating in the Pacific in reflective wrapping to increase the Earth's albedo. A million micro-pipelines in Siberia intercepting melting methane. Absorcrete dry reefs. This all takes power. Where do we get it? Look out the window man, from our helium-3 mines on the Moon. And then, when the aliens have told us how to conquer Space."

Dmitri scowled. "That's where you have to stop August. Space? Listen to yourself. This capital doesn't come from nowhere. This isn't a hundred years ago, before we strip-mined the planet. It doesn't take much to destabilise Gaia these days."

"Hey, hey, my friend. Sit and drink. Calm yourself. We both know where this leads. The reason we came back to the moon, the reason we abandoned the Ecolution. The damage was too deep to lead anywhere but a long decline. Humanity deserves better. We made this decision together."

Dmitri tentatively returned to his seat, tears welling. "August, I don't know anymore. The price has been too high."

August's hair bristled. "Do I believe what I am hearing? Dmitri - my Dmitri - throwing up his hands. Such crap. The exergy imported from the moon, helium-3 fusion is even creating Ecos, because the eco balance is positive. And when we have Space, Mars, the Solar System?"

"Stop August. Can you hear yourself? The Moon, it has begun to pay off, almost, a little bit. But these other adventures besides?"

"This is unbelievable. You want to quit now when everything is nearly in place? The lunar mines, the Mercury antimatter factory, MASO, the deep space listening stations already tuning in on extra-terrestrials. Even the monks that man them have been prepaid. These are sunk costs."

"You think Mirtopik isn't bleeding, August. Do you think there are no on costs? Do you think the world even still needs our exergy, with all the gaiatech development happening down there? The Board has had it. The shareholders, whole countries, have been cut from food distribution through the Nets because you got them to trade their Eco rights for shares in your mad dream. They gave you everything you wanted. And what return have they seen from these exorbitant projects? The aliens have told us nothing."

"Of course, they have. We've already heard from five alien civilisations. We've opened the galaxy. We know we are not alone. We know it is possible."

Dmitri pressed his temple. "August. The promise was space travel. Cheap and affordable space travel. Myself, I thought you were mad but went along because things looked differently then. Now I know."

August was rolling now. "Have I not delivered? Five times."

"What? Five ETs with less tech than us. What kind of payback is that? People aren't eating August."

"Why are you doing this Dmitri? You know the deal. The Sys and the Hubs control the Earth, mostly. All our Coms have left, besides Russia and a few Free Cities, is Space. That is the Peace that we ourselves negotiated for the continuation of the Free Markets. If we back down?"

"It's time to reconsider, August. People, people we love are starving. Isn't the Moon enough? The AGM is a chance to step back, to reconsider, to be reasonable."

"Reasonable? Get out of here." August wrestled his friend from his webbing and towards the door.

"What? You are insane."

Exhausted, August stalled on the way and drooped pathetically. "You betray everything. Go back to Gudanko and tell him he can stick his numbers up his ass. If I tuck in my tail and give in, who will lead Mirtopik Com? Who?"

"August, I'm not..."

"You came here to kill me."

August saw Dmitri flinch, which revealed an unexpected truth in his asinine accusation.

"You are. You give yourself away. I see it in your face. You've come to finish what Gudanko is too pristine to dirty his hands with."

Dmitri shook August roughly. "You are the most ridiculous man. Should I have spared myself the trouble by not saving you in the first place. Go to hell."

The door snapped shut behind Dmitri as he left August slumping to the floor.

"The shareholders will still believe in me," August shouted after him. "You'll see. You all will."

Weary, August pulled himself back up using his webbing and held his cleaned neurovisor to his forehead, waiting for the tendrils to squirm their way back into his brain. He would show Dmitri, that coward. August Bridges fail? Traitor.

Following a thought command, a new reality painted over August's third eye as the room faded into the background, retaining only enough substantiality for August to maintain his balance and to keep him from walking into walls.

August strode out into his ComSyn, a projected stylized map of the world where three-dimensional icons indicated the offices and operations of Mirtopik's myriad empire and alliances. Graphs and executive summaries floated about the heavens like majestic flocks of birds. Pulsing red pointed out current Rev flash points. Green sinew connected these attacks to flesh out the bodies of declared Campaigns. The sabotaged launch pad connected to the class action suit connected to the coordinated supply chain disrupts connected to the Hub boycott.

Divining the strategies and affiliations of the ramble of enemies and allies that lurked behind these divergent flat facts employed an army of Syns. The writhing, world-embracing creatures projected live from the intertwined brains of thousands of people, computer systems, satellites and nanoid sensors into August's virtual domain were wondrous to behold.

A large green thicket ran wildly around and over Papua New Guinea and surrounding islands. The bleeding beast at its core BilongMeCom, a Mirtopik Com subsidiary, was facing a hostile ecoversion takeover coordinated by Rev activists. Although structurally no different, most of the company's stock was now held and traded within a close-knit tribe of local Hubs, their affiliate web of Net businesses, and the ecology-governing Sys to which they were integrated. The Board of the Com would now be replaced or otherwise intimidated until they fell into line with their new masters.

August would have, in his previous life, cheered news of a big ecoversion together with the rest. Ecoversion meant power and wealth being shared more democratically, or rather, and more importantly, that someone else wasn't enjoying your birth-right. At the root Ecoversion was ultimately about jealousy. They'd all been raised on the propaganda - about how the Ecolution had saved the planet, about how people had finally risen up over the century to claim their rightful share of diminishing ecological resources and in so doing had stopped disaster, about how nearly all the Coms now included the Earth in their balance sheet, with the Ecos from their realignment being 'recycled' to the services supporting the poorest and most vulnerable.

Crap. All gone to shit.

Take Ecos for instance. A good idea. Give economic value to efforts to reduce greenhouse gases by making that the basis of money. It gave everyone something to do after automation had taken most of the jobs away. A good idea. But what had they done with the Eco once it became the new God? To begin with the formula had been straight forward. Everyone understood it. Any physicist could calculate it. But by now they had complicated it to fit some religious idiocy about a living planet. And once the high priests had taken over GEO, the lunatics were in charge of the asylum. Now the formulae changed every year, chasing this mysterious goal of Alignment, that elusive point where all the sins of the Fathers would be paid out.

And what would that accomplish? Intergenerational equity. What a crock. Had our forebears given a shit about us when they cranked the thermostat on the planet to just below survivable and flooded the cities and salted the Earth. So why was everyone eager for Mirtopik Com to pay out on the bad bets of the long dead? This kind of thinking only killed the ambition and creativity need to clean up the awful mess. It wasn't like people were going to suddenly start doing the right thing for no reward. Since when had human beings been wired for altruism?

That's the world Dmitri wanted to latch back onto - back to sucking off the tit of a worn-out Mother Earth. Was that a manly thing to do? How disappointing.

Viva the Ecolution. A toast to the beautiful memory it had become. What was it now? This sad, long unwinding of human potential. The Earth was no place to look to live a life. Only Space could deliver true abundance and new wealth. Goddamn Dmitri. Now it would only be himself, August Bridges alone, who would ultimately save the cause everyone thought he had betrayed. One day they would understand.

August grimaced at the problems on display before him, specifically the screw up in PNG. Someone had been asleep at the wheel here with this ecoversion and he knew who it was.

With a thought he materialised in Duoshi's office, or rather in Duoshi's office as it existed in the idiot's brain. Too clean, especially for someone whose responsibilities so clearly exceeded the hapless salary man's capability. It would have given August pleasure for the shock of his unannounced entrance to throw at least the wall hangings into disarray, but the Mirtopik Head of East Asian Integration responded with the well-practiced placidity that never failed to infuriate August.

He spent a fruitless hour of grilling Duoshi over his failure, which was inevitable given the decay of relations with the Nets over the usual complaints on local control over ecological benefits. August left the meeting with a frustrated sense of his increasing irrelevance. In the old days he would have handed Duoshi his ass. He stopped short sensing that it would might look like he was lashing out, which might be perceived as a sign of weakness to the Board. Too much had happened today anyway, and he didn't have the energy.

As August strode back across the Pacific towards California, one of the Rev alerts, impatiently swooping up and down over Fiji caught August's attention - a display window containing a stylized chalk outline of a body. When he looked at it the summary indicated an assassination attempt at Mirtopik Com headquarters in Los Angeles. August clutched his hair. All his nightmares and paranoia came at once to the fore.

Who was it? Many of August's key allies were based out of LA and a loss of any of them could have a critical impact on the outcome of the Annual General Meeting. The thought sent August into a rage. Why the hell hadn't ComSec briefed him? Did they think that because the boss was locked away on the Moon that they didn't have to do their jobs? Someone was going to pay for this screw up. His angry stare told the alert box to swoosh over to meet him out near the coast of Hawaii.

He read the summary with trepidation and, as he did, his hair bristled. The lack of information was ridiculous. To begin with there was no name, just the fact that the victim was a member of the Com executive. Not even his position was included. For all August knew it was just some assistant vice president, but it could be bad. Dmitri? It couldn't be Dmitri. Dmitri was here. What was going on with his memory? Frustrated, August was about to discard the alert box and head over to ComSec when he noticed the location and date details of the death. The date was in the future, a few days' time, and the place was …the Moon? An icon near the location details offered pictures. August ordered them up.

A single photo appeared containing a dimly lit tall figure with a prominent thatch of hair that August recognized instantly. The face in the picture was his.

The caption read "AUGUST BRIDGES. Struck down in the prime of his time."

What the hell?

A wall pressing against his back stopped August from backing away and contained his urge to run and hide. This was the realisation of every fear that had chased him to the Moon, which had left him cowering in the most remote of exiles, and which, at the arrival of a ship purportedly carrying his trusted deputy, had driven him out to almost certain death.

But, for some reason, this validation of the threat that had driven him to the edge of madness and death had a calming effect. Phantoms could not be fought, but a flesh and blood adversary? August had a long history of overcoming many of these. August's mind, stimulated by a real challenge, became clearer as he considered the possibilities.

Apparently, he wasn't dead, so what was this? Some Hax prank? "In the prime of his time?" For pity's sake. But of course, August knew who it was.

"Calvin30," August commanded, but the neurolink rang through to a message bank. "Pick up, damn you."

Whatever shit Calvin30 got up to on his behalf August was sure he didn't want to know, but he was always off line at the worst time, even on the most urgent channels. Times like this he'd love to fire the little bastard. The problem with owning people was that you simply couldn't get rid of them.

August thought through the situation. Classic Calvin30 to leave things out in the breeze, trailing breadcrumbs leading through mazes within mazes. Smart-ass.

Although it pissed him off, August had to accept the logic. Following the tracks as Calvin30 left them made August sniff the wind and touch the soil in which they were embedded. And far more critical, in these days of exile, this engaged August instead of isolating him.

So, what was going on here?

August's attention moved to the green Campaign lines creeping out from the Alert to the Four Corners.

"Pull links to Alert 827E." August thought.

A mad mob of images flapped down, perching in green branches sprouting up underneath the named Alert. August followed the thickest branch down to a report detailing a few small Alignment account transfers from the Directors' discretionary funds to several Pacific Island Orgs having something to do with reef stabilization and humanitarian services for Islanders displaced by rising sea levels due to the greenhouse effect.

Nothing was out of the ordinary there. It was standard practice for Coms to 'donate' Alignments, documented improvements of ecological performance, to the Orgs. It was by this 'donation' process that the Alignments could be converted into Ecos to be paid out to those working for the Orgs and the Hubs they serviced. The Coms routinely made these payments to strengthen strategic relationships or for public relations reasons.

The next branch sideways up from the Alignment account transfers made more of an impact on August.

The Orgs involved in most of these transfers had possible links with *Kaliyuga* Rev. Just reading the name gave August an involuntary urge to look over his shoulder, as would be the case with most Com executives. Most Revs were steadfastly committed to the non-violent ideals of the Ecolution and the gradual capture of target Coms, as they had done to BiLongMeCom, through relentless globally coordinated and targeted Campaigns. *Kaliyuga* was not one of these. They were extremists, lethal terrorists who went straight for the top so-to-speak. They considered space travel to be the principal heresy of humanity. Mirtopik, and August Bridges especially, were not high on their love list.

Which brought August down the next branch, the subsequent arrival from Fiji to L.A., a few days prior, of a suspected high-level Kaliyuga operative. The branch back from here traced to Moscow, the last known location of this woman, where, as the next branch revealed, a scan of her apartment had revealed the presence of tracer nanoids released during an earlier criminal investigation by Euro Gov authorities. A web of dun lines emanated from this last Alert like roots disappearing into disparate ends of the Earth, containing odd facts from seemingly disconnected events. He followed each root as far as he could before they disappeared into the ground. Money transfers, travel itineraries, names and faces, histories and relationships.

It was a grind working through this morass of data; hours passed as August's interest waned. He stopped several times to rest his eyes and attempt to tame the static building up in his hair. During one of these breaks he became aware of the time and resolved to abandon the search after one last attempt.

It was then that a jumble of roots finally gathered again beneath a new, minor stem growing upward to a new thicket of Alerts. These involved a police report regarding a theft from a decommissioned military research institute that had once specialized in the development of nanoweapons. Invisible, invasive, intelligent and capable of unending combinations of lethal terrors.

Nanoweapons. August read the word several times as if questioning its meaning. The word related to every paranoid fantasy that had plagued him since the terrible events that had brought him into power. It was the circularity of fate implicit in the word that terrified him. A man must reap what he has sown.

August read the Alerts with renewed intensity but failed to uncover any description of the items that had been stolen. This was a surprising omission for a police report; although less surprising when one considered the potential political messiness involved for a Gov to admit possession of technology that had been illegal throughout Gaia for nearly a quarter century.

He tried Calvin30's neurolink again. "Listen you insolent shit," he left his message in a stony voice, "if I die today because of information you have failed to provide, I will not be the only one with a problem." The threat only increased his feelings of impotence. Threatening Calvin30 was like threatening the dirt beneath his feet, because both were simultaneously inconsequential and irreplaceable.

An unseen and unexpected hand touched him lightly on the shoulder. "Sir?"

"Shit!"

The neuroview blinked out and August nearly lost his balance with the abrupt change of perspective. "Don't ever do that again," he gasped at the slight woman standing beside him, "Do you understand? Shit."

Linda, his new admin assistant, bit her lip while smoothing the skirt of a smart, corporate cut sari. "Sir," she pressed valiantly on, "Terribly sorry to startle you. We couldn't reach you otherwise. The Director's ferry has confirmed that they have left Earth's orbit and are on their way."

"Of course. Of course," August recovered his breath. "That's okay Linda."

"Thank you, sir."

August ran his fingers through his hair, preening it as he thought. He had to think quickly. In a short time, he would walk into a room containing the few people in the universe capable of determining his fate. One of them, perhaps several, could be holding an imperceptible loaded gun to his head. Of course, Calvin30's trail of evidence was entirely circumstantial, the rough skeleton of a conspiracy theory. Still it wasn't implausible, and Calvin30's imprimatur on it made more than plausible.

Why? Perhaps it was Gudanko's cold actuarial style of management. Certainly, the businessman would have dealt with other enemies this way, with as much passion as signing off on an annual return. But if that were the case, surely Gudanko would have many years ago eliminated the extreme outlier to the Com risk model that August represented. And besides, wasn't time on the accountant's side? Besides, the thought that *Kaliyuga* and Gudanko would conspire on anything was a theory that stretched the bounds of the believable. Their mutual contempt outweighed any animosity they harbored towards him, which was saying something. Besides, murder was a horrible way to do business. August's tangential involvement in one still gave him nightmares such as the one this morning. It was possible that Calvin30 took care of such things on his behalf, but he didn't want to know.

"Linda," he spoke evenly, "this is absolutely critical. One. Transfer this mneme I'm sending to you by neurolink over to ComSec." August switched back on his neurovisor to transfer the access codes. "Have them take care of it. I don't want to be interrupted. Two. Prepare the kitchen for a full nanoid scan. We have a possible contamination that ComSec will be investigating. It doesn't matter if the process delays greeting our visitors with food," he added with a grin, "it'll be good to keep Gudanko off balance, his blood sugar is a weak point. Three," he paused, but there was nothing else she could do for him, "three, do whatever needs to be done."

Linda turned on a delicate heel and vanished in a brisk and competent manner leaving August with racing thoughts. The faces of each participant of the upcoming Board meeting flashed before his eyes, challenging him to guess who might try to end his life. His immediate thoughts were on the unjust inconvenience of it all. This was just insane. He had more important things to be thinking about than staying alive.

What lunacy. August grinned despite himself. His life on the line and it was all just too much of a pain in the ass. When he thought about it there was some logic there. Who was he, after all, besides the greatness of his dream? Having recreated his self in its image, what would be left if the dream were subtracted?

Underappreciated and over-accumulated wealth, the unreliable vagaries of power, iconic hair on an aging body. No loves, few friendships, no enjoyment of time's passage. Who was he indeed, if not for this all-consuming, all inspiring, all demanding master? His dream. Until now August had assumed his dream was something possessed by him, but now he could see that he was just as possessed by it. Or rather, that both he and the dream had arisen naturally together, from some primordial source.

Dmitri had it wrong. There was no speculation in August's assurance that the message from the aliens would come. It was certain. It was as if he had sent it to himself, simple cause and effect, and in that reality, there was no other choice but to see his dream through. Consequently, what was there to fear?

"Destiny drives history, not the other way around," August shouted at the crescent Earth hanging in his skylight.

The Earth did not answer, and August felt fatigue overtake him. He replaced the wad of bloody tissue from his nose and then lay down in his bed and tried to work through why he had almost died today. His memory of specific events was sketchy. Most of what was alive in his mind today were details from a strange dream, which had entranced him while he was in the process of dying. Like a ghost it had haunted his thoughts since.

Even now he could remember almost every detail, as he yawned and closed his eyes and surrendered back into it.

The Earth hanging in the skylight above faded, replaced by the full moon casting long shadows across a Russian winter and into a grey bar room with many mirrors, which reflected the moonlight and the gas flame in the fireplace. Both were a vain attempt to shut out the frost and the day long night. The deep brown of Anya's eyes surreptitiously met his while Gregori, her husband and August's most loyal friend, played the clown for the cheering locals.

The slumping black spruce forest outside the windows gave no hint of specific location - only a typical Siberian village, the local Hubs incredulous at the discovery of unclaimed ecos buried in the drab swamp that surrounded their home. August and his friends had been to this same place, bearing different names but populated with the same hopeful expressions, many times. Always the same bar.

All was as it had once been, a possibility only in dream. Laughter spilled freely, untainted by the betrayals yet to come. The future was still sensitive in its unfolding to the small events of life. The sense of sharing fate over a drink and a prayer was a particularly bittersweet emotion that held August's attention most profoundly. The memory of what true friendship had felt like.

They toasted with the bar. "To warm friends and cold winters. To Mother Russia and God's Earth. To the Generations!"

Gregori and August, locked arm in arm, spun to some hectic ballad as the sweat spun down off their flailing arms into the cheers of the crowd and under the spotlight of Anya's admiring eyes. Even this flirtation, a first of many betrayals to find a home in August's soul, was still innocent.

The waiter visiting their table, a passing detail in August and Gregori's whirling rapture, was oddly attired - threadbare robes and an odd moon-shaped mitre perched atop a broad Mongolian face. The waiter refilled August's glass and retreated into shadow.

Contrasting with the grey moon cast hues pervading the other players and props, the liquid in his glass glowed warmly. August again drank the nectar and relived it rolling back, sweet flavor encasing his tongue, pulling his awareness down his throat to his heart. For only an instant he felt completely at home in himself and in this place.

And then the dream betrayed him. Abruptly the longing in Anya's eyes for his began to fade, to pass through him to Gregori, now the sole recipient of the crowd's adulation, and beyond. This sudden departure of his substance was disconcerting. August called over to his friends, who reacted at first by turning slightly as if hearing their name mentioned in conversation, and then not at all.

August floated through the room and its inhabitants, his anxiety steadily mounting. This was not possible. He could forget them, but they were not allowed to forget him. After all, it was he who had betrayed them - how could they ever forget? The music and singing continued unabated. Anya's eyes engaged Gregori's with a meaningful glance before roaming off to greet the patient stares of other men waiting their turn for acknowledgement. August waited with them, hungry to glimpse even a hint of memory remaining in her eyes.

Heedless of his agitation, the laughter continued, tormenting August as he circled the bar, straining for recognition from even the most obscure figures in the dream - shouting at them. A gust of wind slammed open the door and August slipped out the exit, pulled by a vacuum of moonlight that he was helpless to fight against.

Illya was there standing broad-legged at the edge of a slough, urinating. As the great bear-man hummed contentedly in his moody baritone, an immense wave of anxiety engulfed August. He could not abide this. August the wraith, the phantom, pleading to be seen by a dead man. Illya: his friend, his mentor, his father, his victim. Illya, whose ghost would haunt him forever.

Illya beamed beneficently as the swamp swelled and over spilled with his magnificent discharge. Opulently dyed with tannins and Earth, the deluge overcame August in a swirling rush. As the rising torrent drowned him, August reached out for the hand of a man who wasn't there.

31

CHAPTER 3

Aurora

Settle down. Just sit where you are girls. Now, I'm gonna tell you lot about the two beginnings. Not one but two of them. How is it there are two beginnings? You never had a dream inside another one? That's how it all started.

See those stars up there around? Those are my sisters. They are the sisters of all of us. Whitefellahs call them the Pleiades. And they're trying to get away from those brothers over there. You know the story, don't you?

So, this is the beginning and there are two dreams you see. One for the brothers and one for the sisters. They both ended up different places before going back up to the sky there.

Back in the Dreamtime there were two worlds, this one here Yulbrada, she's the Earth we live on and another Waijungari, the planet Mars, who had a bad habit of sleeping around with other fellahs' wives so he's painted up in red ochre, so people would know it.

Well the brothers and sisters, the Sun gave them different jobs. The brothers, they're good at lifting things and moving stuff. That's why we keep them around, you know? Don't laugh - it's true. Okay, maybe there are some other things.

So, the brothers, they came to Yulbrada and dug out the ocean, and stacked up all that rock to make the land, and they drew in the rivers with their fingers but that was as far as it goes. And then they left it only half done so it was up to the sisters to finish it off. You know how it goes. So, then our sisters, they made the Earth a good place to live in, brought in all the trees and plants to eat and flowers to look pretty and all that. And then they invited the animals in to come share everything with us.

So that's the one beginning of the Earth, the world we come from. The other beginning you can't see. That's Waijungari, the planet Mars, the dirty old man. The brothers, they went to his camp and they did all the same as here, mountains and oceans and valleys and such. And they liked Waijungari because he filled their heads with all sorts of nonsense. They sat around the fire waiting for the sisters to show up. You think they ever did? No, they weren't that stupid. So Waijungari, he got older and dried up into stone and you can still see him up there waiting, and the brothers went to chase the sisters in the sky where they'd had a good head start.

And that's where things stood until another one of our sisters went back up to Mars to try to join the Dreaming there. That's another story.

* * * * * * * * * * * * *

Aurora Davidson, Wheatbelt Wallaby, sprang softly from the rock where she had been perched while listening as Auntie Munya told her the story of this place and how a wayward star-girl might fit into the landscape. It was all in Aurora's head of course. One of the star sisters coming down to sing the first songs here - that much was true.

The long shadows of midsummer's evening were darkening the yellow sky and airbrushed blue clouds gathered around the summit of Elysium Mons on the horizon. As she wandered towards the drilling rig Aurora stooped to examine an interesting specimen. A round, crusty rock lay on the shores of an ancient, sublimated sea.

Cracking it open with a hammer she noted the distinctive layering of the yellow crystals and rust in the rock. Sulfides, she guessed, from the primordial Martian thermal vent she had been tracking. The rock spoke from an age unreachable on the Earth, where flowing rain and ice and tectonic plates had worn the deep past to dust. On Mars the Dreamtime lay naked to the fingertips. Aurora shivered, merging respectful awe with biting cold.

To warm up, Wheatbelt Wallaby plunged into the boiling mineral waters for a well-deserved soak.

Singing the songs of rocks, one of the few things Dad had left to her from his long ramblings out on the songlines, in his intermittent and only long-term job as a bioflora prospector. According to her father, Aurora's Wallaby song began with her first kick. He marked the spot with a stick. A visiting Law Man, an old mate, scanned the horizon and then walked out to a nearby rocky outcrop.

"A Wallaby. Said that's who you are Ror. What d'ya think of that?"

Dad would play this story up wherever he had a few drinks in him, which wasn't as infrequent as the family would have liked. Of course, Dad, with his sandy hair and freckled, sunburnt skin, was as Aboriginal as the next Highlands Scot. It was Mum's side that was indigenous, the source of Aurora's copper skin, which protected her to a degree from the unfiltered

Martian sun. Of course, Dad had claimed Mum's portion of Aboriginality for himself, to his wife's discomfort, but with enough good nature and genuine respect thrown in to be acceptable to a few Uncles and Aunties.

Dad was always a helpless bullshitter, even after Mum sent him packing and he might have learnt better. Poor Dad. Aurora continued on Mars the stories he and his Wheatbelt Wallaby girl had started whenever she'd accompanied him out Bush. Every large rock, every dry riverbed became an actor in the new songline of Wheatbelt Wallaby on a new world. Those stories helped her see the life latent in Mars, helped her find her place here, even more so than her career spent scrutinizing geochemistry, morphology and maps.

Rinsing the stain of red fines from her pelt, Wheatbelt Wallaby splashed the tranquil, pregnant sea covering the new land in all directions. Keeping her head above water by balancing on her thrashing tail, she cracked the thin crust of sediments further increasing the luxuriously hot upwelling of mineral waters. Steam from her breath condensed as fog and hung within the walls of the half-inundated gorge of Elysium Chasma, whose striated far walls peaked up over the rise behind her. Tracks of her tail dragging along as she came and left had become the rocky folds leading out from the fossilized springs. Following her own footprints, she'd come to this spot.

Noticing the angle of the sun, Aurora returned to her tasks with renewed urgency. With numb fingers she unfolded a neurocam, placed the sample within where its structure was recorded in a flash of laser light.

Focusing her thoughts through her neurovisor, Aurora flew over the projected surface of the rock. In and out of hairline cracks that spread open before her like wide valleys, down the thermal gradients revealed by the changing crystal sizes of the sulfites and other salts. Aurora was familiar with the terrain. She knew where to look. Not too hot where the heat would scramble the proteins. Nor too cold where easy energy sources would not be found. Just right, at that thin edge between hot and cold, between order and disorder, where life could begin. Something caught her attention and she swooped in to investigate.

Little friends, bulbous bodies standing out against the sharp edges of the crystalline landscape. Ticks left by Wheatbelt Wallaby, guarding the site, awaiting her return for their next blood meal.

Aurora examined the bacterial ancestors respectfully. Good specimens these. Colony formers gathered together in a ring configuration, whip-like cilia tails waving in the ancient percolations of the vent just like their cousins back on Earth continued doing to the present day. Therein lay her problem. Were these fellows indigenous or merely emigrants, like her? Pieces of Earth, jettisoned into space by asteroid collisions, had been making the journey between worlds for eons and there was no way of knowing, from looking at their fossils, where the life on early Mars had come from.

Aurora switched off her neuroview and spent a few minutes relaxing her eyes on the endless vista around her. She was disappointed, but no more so than she had expected. Thermal vents were the principal suspects in the search for the origin of life. Tiny vortices of heat in the surrounding mud and mineral gases given off by the hot rocks gave birth to exotic chemistries and cell-like structures that, in the laboratory at least, they'd managed to turn into life. But, of course, the simple bacteria in Aurora's sample had evolved far beyond that point leaving no indications of a possible spontaneous generation from the stuff of Mars. Life evolved fast. No one had yet found any traces of the initial spark of life, even given the absence of tectonic turnover on Mars.

Placing the sample in a collection bag, Aurora rechecked her position and pencilled some notes in her field book.

The drilling rig robot fed another stem into the ground. The friction thawed water, which had existed as a frozen solid for nearly as long as the rock surrounding it, came out in puffs of sublimated steam, leaving a ring of frost on the rig outlet. Besides small aliquots taken as samples, the bulk of the ancient water evaporated without trace into the desiccated Martian air.

Cupping her hands in the upwelling spring, Wheatbelt Wallaby brought the water to her lips and sucked it down. The cool water flowed down her throat, slaking the terrible thirst of a drought lasting billions of years. Her eyes grew bright as liquid life leaked past her stomach lining to flush the dust from her veins. Long withered muscles miraculously filled with hydraulic power. Wheatbelt Wallaby stood up on creaking knees and shook the sediments off her back.

Aurora unlocked a side panel on the rig and pulled out a tray of square plastic containers filled with bronze ice. After loading them into an esky, she downloaded the sample manifest from the rig into her neurovisor. She rested a moment as the nanoprocessors in her neurovisor charged up from standby using her body's chemical energy. Then she dragged the esky over to her sled and winched it aboard.

Aurora examined her day's catch with mixed feelings. The Holy Grail of Martian micropaleontology that she had come to Mars searching for were bacterial spores, living ancestral organisms that might one day be resuscitated. Only by decoding the DNA, or whatever had developed here in its place, for these resurrected survivors would they be able to determine whether Mars had ever given birth. But Aurora understood the chances of that happening, with these samples, was two-fifths of bugger all.

She looked around her, and then back in the direction of her base camp. The rusty plain of Daedalia sloped down West from her position on the beach of the ancient ocean that circled the wide base of the Elysium volcanic highlands. Yardangs and other wind sculpted depressions and scalds created a menagerie of Dreamtime characters out of the broken crater rims down below. Their long shadows began to walk in the twilight. North and South were covered in endless undulating dunes with sunlight slithering up and down them like a thousand snakes.

The steep cliffs of the Elysium and Hybleaus Chasma canyons bordered her position to the East. The rock layers along their walls provided an invaluable peek into the brief history of life on the planet since Elysium had risen in the middle of what was then a Martian ocean. Aurora had spent many happy days rappelling down their sides with rock hammer and pick. To top it off, a fortuitous concentration of permafrost ice provided a source of drinking water. There was no doubt this was the best place to locate the only research station on Mars.

But Aurora looked longingly eastward across the great gulf of the Chasma, a minor canyon on Mars but still as large as the greatest in Europe, towards a minute knob on the horizon. Elysium Mons, the fifth largest volcano on Mars, and still twice the height of Everest. It was a month's sled journey too far.

Satellite imagery and robotic explorers suggested that the embers of the volcano still glowed near the surface. Even now faint rumblings tickled the seismometers. Perhaps geo-thermally heated liquid ground waters there may have kept Mars' children alive much longer. Perhaps long enough. And it was there that the greatest unexplained mystery of Mars was found, an emission of methane that could possibly have a biological source. It was so tantalisingly close, her dream mission, to spelunk down into a cavern in the Fossae, rifts along the walls of the volcano, and discover that life in the solar system had two homes instead of just one.

Then again, she would not be the one to find them, and all evidence pointed to the possibility that no one would. Planetary missions, especially basic science, were of declining interest to the public. Now that E.T. had come calling from myriad rich and exotic worlds, who would still be interested in such lesser sparks of Life as her bacterial Martians?

A persistent red flashing drew Aurora's attention to her wrist. Drawn out of her reverie she suddenly realized that her neurolink back to Base had been switched off. How long ago had that happened? She switched it on.

Her neuroview crackled to life. A wiry woman with a crooked grease streaked nose, tightly cropped hair and an anxious expression abruptly appeared.

"You right darl?"

"Yeah, sorry for that Terry. Must have been lost in my thoughts." Aurora looked back over her shoulder towards the encroaching sunset. "You weren't worried?"

"Too right we were. Lost in your thoughts? Where d'you think you are, Byron bloody Bay? It's only been half a day. We were just about to come looking. Thought you'd gone Outers on us." Terry's voice cracked revealing honest concern.

Aurora flushed with embarrassment. "Look, I'm sorry about that. I didn't realize the neurolink was stuffed until just now."

"No shit?"

"True. What did you think, I'd go Out without taking you with me?"

Terry smiled, an indulgence Aurora was sure she didn't deserve right now. "Maybe . . . One less mouth around here to feed I was thinking. D'you reckon you'll still be in for a share of the pudding?"

"Nah, I'll load mine on the compost heap when I get back."

"Shit mate, that's a sin."

Aurora laughed. Terry was the archetypal Queenslander, irreverent as a rule but pious about the important things. "Just processed the last batch of samples. Should be back by 20 hundred. Bit worried about the power levels in the rig."

"Ah she'll be right. Get in before your tits freeze. Take too long and I mightn't be able to restrain myself when it comes to dessert."

"I'm sure you'll do your best. See you soon Terry."

The conversation closed to static. Aurora tapped the neurolink panel woven into the cloth on her wrist a few times, but it refused to come back to life. Best hurry home now. She walked back to the rig and initiated the fail-safe mode and sent out a few radio whistles to Denali.

Aurora grinned as the tail of her sidekick came weaving in and out of the ejecta field of a nearby crater. A moment later his familiar white flash came bounding across the fines, weaving contrails of red dust in his wake.

Denali was the newest, you beaut artificial intelligence unit around. By the late 21st Century scientists had finally been able to translate the real-world intelligence of a dog into a computer or, more correctly, into an organic quantum molecular matrix. He was quite remarkable. Denali didn't just act like a dog. He was a dog. Maybe he heard radio signals through his fur and maybe his nose was a sophisticated ion spectrometer, but his eyes looked adoringly into Aurora's as she stroked his fur.

The secret, she had been told, was in his development. Denali's brain and body had grown together through some miracle of nano-molecular engineering. He had been raised among other dogs where he had been accepted by the pack. His human masters had painstakingly trained his neural net as they would train an ordinary dog. He even seemed to dream and have nightmares. Aurora was certain that Denali thought he was a dog, or rather a person lodged in the body of a dog that was a robot under the hood. Scientists could debate self-awareness in robots all they liked - Aurora reckoned Denali didn't mind.

Denali had been scouting the area, marking rocks with artificial pheromones, and making millions of observations that would later be downloaded from his head for inspection back at the station. His white, solar cell fur was rusty with fines. Aurora scratched behind his ears as she attached the sled harness to him. She gave the sled one more once over and then stood on the back skids signalling Denali to mush them back home. No wind blew against her face, safely enclosed in a pressurized buckeyball helmet, and the wind at fifteen millibars would have been a scarcely perceptible breeze - the one missing element to an otherwise exhilarating journey home.

Wheatbelt Wallaby ran alongside, her toes thumping into the sand alongside Denali's paws. The sands of today and the waters of Dreamtime crested and sank into lengthening shadows as she bounded across them. Each step covered a million years. Memories of past atmospheres billeted her face. Old mates, twin moons Diemos and Phobos, tracked her progress as they chased one another through the twilight. She waved goodnight to her old friend Elysium Mons as the great Goanna man ducked into his hole down under the horizon. Behind her, crimson dust bled into clear air from the scratches her paws cut in the skin of the land. Far to the North beyond the range of her eyes though not of her Dreams, the orange and white inter-bedded ice and dust terraces of the Great Termite Mound covering the Northern Pole pulsated in the setting sun. The Termites there held greedily to the water they had stolen from the rest of Mars and Wheatbelt Wallaby still bore a grudge. When she raised her paw to cut the glare, it was not a salutation.

The slapping of a loose harness caught Aurora's attention as she leaned wide to balance the sled behind Denali's undomesticated dance down a scree slope. She nearly slipped from the sled as she bent over to catch it, a dangerous moment as the slightest rip in her squeeze suit would leave her exposed to bone gripping frostbite and depressurization. The shock tightened her senses. She was not as invulnerable as the beings in her Dreaming, and she would never be part of this place. The ever-present radiation alone would limit her stay to a mere four years. It was an impossible love affair. After so many years of bloody-minded pursuit, Mars the seducer would abandon her. What she'd do after she returned to the life she'd always run from, she had no idea.

Perhaps she could freeze into the landscape, together with other explorers of Mars who had lost their lives here. Her training activated like a slap in the face, and Aurora shivered as she discarded the thought. Romantic and suicidal notions of dying unprotected in Space were a classic early symptom of Outlanders.

Outlanders, going Out, over the limit, heading home in your bones, returned to sender, eyes on the skies, Blue Heels (there's no place like home), Fixed on the Far Side, toxic prox, under the ox, not to mention the obvious acronym. All were names for Proximity Malaise Syndrome, an unexplained malady afflicting space explorers. The effect seemed to increase with one's distance from Earth. The first signs were unpredictable. People could wig out in all sorts of creative ways. Then they would freeze up until finally their hearts stopped beating if they hadn't managed a more effective way to achieve the same. Entire expeditions thus stricken had either perished in psychotic fits or simply withered away. Humans, it turned out, were congenitally bound to their home world.

No one really knew why. Numerous medical Orgs had grown up around the subject to no avail. Some people seemed to be resistant, a handful of women, far fewer men, and intriguingly, a small number of Tibetan monks from some high-altitude areas and a few other odds and sods who were apparently almost immune. All their genetic profiles were under intense scrutiny back home - huge rewards awaited discovery of a treatment derived from their genes.

Nowadays all candidates for astronaut duty were carefully screened and were not expected to remain away from home for lengthy periods of time.

They all watched each other carefully for signs. All supply shuttles contained specially fitted passenger pods to facilitate emergency evacuation. Out of Aurora's original contingent of twenty, only three, the Australian mission remained, including herself and Terry and Cath. All the rest, except for Paola, were safely back Earth-side. Paola had opted to go for a walk outside one day without wearing a squeeze suit.

Most people who came to Mars did not stay more than a year and Aurora had been here for two and a half, making her the senior scientist, in terms of Mars time, on the planet since Terry and Cath were in logistic support. Some might argue that she had not been as productive as others. She had not submitted a single paper in her tenure here, but with a world waiting to be explored Aurora felt an urgency to collect as much data on the ground as she could. There would be plenty of time to reflect on her findings later. She felt it was more to her testament that, while she had not published, neither had she perished.

In this moment Mars was the home Aurora had never found elsewhere. A cramped world of expectation and obligation completely left behind, millions of kilometers away, literally. Even Antarctica had been stuffed with an entrenched and ossified bureaucracy. The Earth was full. Mars was empty.

Aurora was not lonely amidst this titanic desolation. She could spend the day out, pursuing a variety of projects, on her own time, free in the infinite now. Tonight, she would return to the warm embrace of her family of co-workers, sharing the intimacy of their mutual isolation.

The hours passed cleanly, interrupted by very few thoughts other than wonder. At last Aurora and Denali rounded a familiar rise and descended towards a group of cylinders near the edge of a great cliff, attached to one another at various points like a hamster habitat. The accidental looking complex was the solitary inhabited outpost on the entire planet, the Mars Alliance Scientific Org Research Station 1, or MASO 1. The Australian contingent had nicknamed the station "Mawson Mars" after the Australian Antarctic station and in keeping with the proud, if somewhat slack, Aussie tradition of recycling names.

The walls of Mawson Mars sported a United Nations of Gov and Sys flags along with a peppering of various Com, Org and Net logos. Aurora's eyes targeted the most recently added green and gold of the Confederated Sys of Australia bordering the Southern Cross of the old Gov. Her eyes purposely skipped past the large banners proclaiming the new operators, slapped on the axis and other high-profile spots, but the effort only highlighted the oppressiveness of Mirtopik Com's unwelcome presence.

A squeeze-suited figure exited one of the out sheds and walked on a course to intersect hers.

"Hi Aurora." The high, delicate voice chiming through the neurolink brought a smile to Aurora's face. It belonged to Xiao Li, her best mate. Xiao Li had shipped out to Mars with the Many Sys One China expedition, which arrived soon after the Australians had. Before Mars, Aurora and Xiao Li had remotely collaborated on the same scientific proposals to MASO and, until recently, they'd worked those projects together. Before Phillipa had gone and mucked things up, that is.

"G'day Shel."

"We became worried when you didn't respond to the radio check." There was strain in Xiao Li's voice as she delivered the admonition.

"Yeah. Terry's already belted me round the ears for that," Aurora admitted sheepishly.

"I should have gone out with you on this Away. It was too dangerous."

"Well Shel, you've been given your own projects now." Aurora could almost hear Xiao Li roll her eyes.

"Those are not my projects Aurora. Anyway, you must tell me, did you find any more sulfanogens?"

"Just where you said they'd be." The familiar cadence of shoptalk accompanied them back to the shed where they unloaded the sled.

Aurora unbuckled Denali and released him to prowl the night and mark off the boundary of his lonely territory against the universe. He would later let himself in, download his data, and collapse into shutdown mode at the foot of her bunk tube. Aurora watched him weave out into the dunes.

"Denali looks after me Shel."

Xiao Li tightly gripped Aurora's hand as they walked back to the airlock of the main station.

"Denali does not have hands."

These unselfconscious gestures of endearment were what Aurora valued most about her friend.

As they removed their helmets the soothing sounds of Freya's guitar and the rambling buzz of evening conversation issuing from the main cabin welcomed them. Aurora and Xiao Li stowed their buckeygel outer layers of the squeeze suits and helped each other strip off the constricting body stockings that compensated for the weak atmospheric pressure of Mars.

"You must go first," Xiao Li directed Aurora to the shower stall.

Aurora eagerly embraced the penetrating warmth of the hot shower - lukewarm in truth but as hot as anything could be on Mars. Invasive red fines fizzed as the water found them. The stuff was corrosive – loaded with hydrogen peroxide and other nasties. The first experiments on Mars brought on board the Viking lander had mistaken this chemical reactivity for signs of life. What they were really seeing was the long-term effect of a planet with no ozone layer.

She inspected her body, tracing the overlapping scars on her bronzed skin from where the fines had worked into her squeeze suit. Aurora noted a new area of rawness and applied some nanosorb and noted with relief that a dark patch under her left breast had receded indicating that it was at less risk for becoming a melanoma. Her hands worked around her breasts, completing the routine check. Their voluptuousness seemed so excessive, so out of place on this barren world, that Aurora lately felt embarrassed for them. She preferred them flattened down underneath the squeeze suit. Perversely Mars accentuated them, where the gravity of Earth would have pulled them down to more modest dimensions, here they floated out unrestrained. She worked the soap expeditiously over the remainder of the curves of a body that was plainly from another world.

Flipping off the shower in response to the ration meter, she turned to the mirror. The face that reflected in it utterly betrayed the body that it was attached to. A tight grin beamed from a thin face, and the yellow highlights in hazel eyes glinted with the remainder of joy from so much time alone out in the field. Whereas the other girls would condition and dye theirs, Aurora had let the peroxide sap the color from her red hair and left it to frizz. The lines etching up to the corners of her eyes mirrored the crags and jags of the planet she loved.

As Aurora stepped out Xiao Li filled her in on the latest gossip.

" …and so Phillipa reduced computer time for Ramibai's Org. She says the modelling work is slowing down her neurolink to the Mirtopik office."

"How's that? Phillipa using her neurovisor to virtually attend meetings Earth-side again is she? The time lag would have to be awful. What did Ramibai say?"

"That is just what Ramibai says. She recommended to Phillipa that she must use the 2D conferencing or e-mail. And then Phillipa put in a notation against IndraSys's mission time."

Each person's time left on Mars was dictated by a points system designed to predict the risk of team members developing Outlanders. Notations from authorized persons, such as Freya as medical officer or Phillipa as chief scientist, could add up to a costly early departure for an entire mission. Aurora suspected that it had the opposite effect, causing crew members to mask their symptoms instead of reporting them. She was doing it herself. Aussies seemed better at this subterfuge than most, which likely accounted for them still being here.

"I don't believe it. What was the note?"

"Phillipa marked her as Irrationally Combative. Ramibai doesn't contest it. Chandra put in a counter diagnosis as psychology officer, but Ramibai was angry."

Aurora had a hard time imagining Ramibai getting angry about anything. The eldest crewmember and head of the IndraSys mission, Ramibai was like a wise older sister to everyone. She suspected that what Ramibai really objected to was the dangerous precedent set by Phillipa playing politics with Notations.

"Ramibai never gets angry. You'd think by now Terry would have picked up enough Notes for all of us."

"That is how Phillipa justified it, an uncharacteristic change in personality."

"Because she knew Ramibai would put up and shut up. No chance of that with Terry. Plus, Ramibai's scientific, more of a threat. Terry's just logistics."

"Probably. Devi is developing some interesting scenarios on Martian prehistory. She told me yesterday, she linked one causal chain through 213 distinct Syns, cross-audited. Can you believe it?"

"Yeah?" Aurora scratched her head, struggling to keep up with the casual pace with which her friend flitted between topics, never an easy task for her, but particularly so after a long time in the field.

"Yes. It seems that Boreal Vastis Ocean could have lasted several hundred million years longer than previously thought."

Give or take a few, thought Aurora, and that was over a billion years ago. The idea that it could once again come to life filled with water from redirected comets or by some other absurd fantasy, was the official fiction for which they all were required now to feign enthusiasm.

"I wonder how that finding will affect our share price today?" remarked Aurora cynically.

Few things got under her skin like the charade forced upon them by Mirtopik's "rescue" of the MASO mission. In return for free energy and space transport they were now beholden to twist every minute scientific finding into corporate propaganda supporting August Bridges' grand plans for the human race. It was sickening. Ramibai's team from IndraSys were the best planetary systems modellers out. Their time on Mars was precious. Here they were being forced to beg resources behind Phillipa's marketing of Cloud Cuckooland. Aurora's own excursions to find life on Mars had to be constantly justified in these fraudulent terms.

"Julia?" Aurora asked guiltily as Xiao Li passed her a towel.

Xiao Li looked down as she took Aurora's place in the shower.

"Shel?"

"She is not doing well."

"Shit." Aurora wrestled into her tracksuit.

"It is definitely the Outlanders, Freya and Chandra both agree. Everyone can tell by now, it's coming on very rapidly. She needs to be evacuated very soon."

"How long until the next shuttle?"

"Two months."

"Jesus."

"Yes Ror, I've been praying to God every day."

And there was nothing more to say. Aurora felt a silent prayer of her own stick in her throat as she dressed and headed for the door.

"Oh, Aurora," Xiao Li called out, "I really need to warn you."

The door slid opened and Terry stuck her head in, close-cropped ginger hair, oil stained from daily rounds keeping the wheels from falling off the station. "What're you two lessies getting up to in here?"

Xiao Li stepped quickly back into the shower.

"Wishful thinking, Terry?" Aurora punched playfully at Terry's shoulder. "Xiao Li was just..."

"I can see," Terry aimed an exaggerated leer towards the quickly drawn shower curtain. "Come on, we're waiting up for you."

Aurora followed Terry's lead down to the toroidal main node of the station that housed the mess. The remaining population of Mars, all twelve of them, were waiting as they entered.

"Where have you been Aurora?" Chandra, always the shrink, never asked a question that didn't come off as loaded.

"Out near Hyblaeus Catena."

Terry whistled, "Now that's a way beyond the black stump."

A small, defeated voice whispered from the alcove near the doorway to the mess hall. "I thought you were dead."

It was Julia. She had lost a startling amount of weight in just these few days. Her eyes had bored back into their sockets and her hands lay slack at her sides. It was a far cry from the hilarious and vivacious character that had kept them all in stitches since the day she had first arrived on Mars. It didn't seem possible that a person could undergo this drastic a change in her personal presence, virtually overnight.

"Hey Jules, I'm sorry mate. Neurolink went on the blink." It felt like a lie. Aurora went over to lay her arm across the stooped shoulders, which felt disturbingly fragile. Aurora cradled the deflated woman and Julia collapsed into her.

"Terry ate your pudding," Xiao Li chimed, abruptly challenging the mood as she entered the room. This was customary. It didn't do to dwell on how close to the edge they all really were. Julia smiled and quietly slipped into the seat up next to Aurora, seeming to take some strength by contributing to the groups shared denial. "Terry's a pig," she said with considerable effort, and laughed.

"Terry, you bastard."

"Dob me in why don't ya?" Terry aimed a sharp look at Julia, "It was getting cold."

"And I wasn't? –75 C. Not exactly balmy." Aurora protested.

Cath intervened unnecessarily, "They're j-just winding you up Rory, it'll be in the pantry with the roast."

"Oh yeah, the roast, now won't that be delish?" The comment evoked sympathetic sniggers. Tucker at Mawson Mars was not the best. Freeze-dried, shrivelled or powdered, just add Martian water and hope.

"Well, myself, I did not find the roast to be that bad," Ramibai offered, "Vegetarian as well." This observation was met with a collective groan.

"Ramibai, with all due respect you'd eat a dag off a sheep's bum and make out it was better than fillet."

"It always pays to make the best of the situation Terry. But, in any case, please, now you must satisfy our curiosity and explain. What is a dag Terry?"

"Wool balled up in poo."

"How gross," Julia whispered timidly, pulling one of her bizarre faces and then collapsing back from the effort. Everyone laughed a bit too hard.

"Aurora, what did you find out there? Any little red men?" Alice asked as Aurora warmed up supper.

"Yah, because we could use some of them. Men, that is," Freya weighed in.

"Explored that geo thermal vent scald. I think I identified some archaebacteria fossils in a fissure. I'll need to get Nyi Song to cut some slides for me."

"You mean when she's not doing any more important work," Phillipa offered. Phillipa. Phillipa had the most annoying "quirks," which was as charitable a way as Aurora could put it. Aurora disliked almost everything about the Mirtopik installed Chief Scientist, whose credentials were more in public relations than science. She'd tried to separate her feelings about the role from her feeling about the person, but with Phillipa there didn't seem to be a difference. Phillipa had arrived with the most recent rotation. She kept her cards close to her chest and mostly spoke in that annoying tone she used when filming those horrid infomercials for Mirtopik. She'd interfered with everyone's projects and had even tried to turn the mission into some kind of voyeuristic freak show by installing 25-hour neurocams around the place. Thankfully, Chandra had argued against that on psychological grounds. The tight confinement was bad enough without turning the place into a fishbowl.

To be generous, she was not as bad as all that, not nearly as bad as some at Mirtopik. But that was being generous. The fact was everyone hated her, except maybe Xiao Li who couldn't hate anyone.

"Well, when Nyi Song has some time to spare from investigating the extraordinary economic potential of this rock, I'd appreciate it." Aurora regretted letting Phillipa get to her as she followed the microware buzz to her steaming meal and made her way over to sit next to Julia. She was not in a mood to exchange blows with Phillipa just now. However, their exchange had provided an opportunity for Terry to engage her new favorite pastime - getting up Phillipa's nose.

"Too right. Listen Pippa, mining water and oxygen's a fine idea, but where you going to send it? Earth? Even the asteroids have more water than we've got, and it's accessible. In case you hadn't noticed we're on a planet and it's really cheap to launch stuff out from here."

"A planet, that's right, we're on a planet Terry, and the planet is going to need to know where its reserves are to develop." Phillipa sighed as if her answer was too self-evident to warrant voicing it.

Terry rolled her eyes right back. "Yeah, true Pip, they're gonna terraform Mars. This place is an UV baked, dried up, hard ball of shit in the middle of bloody nowhere. They can't afford to keep us here let alone emigrate. We'd be dead in the space of months without a regular care package from Earth."

"You have to think more strategically, over the long term," replied Phillipa, as if explaining the color of the sky to a three-year-old.

Intentionally avoiding the confrontation, Aurora stroked Julia's hair. The distance between the group's argy-bargy and her being seemed to stretch. Her hand seemed to take forever traveling the length of the hair, which seemed to grow longer as her hand progressed. It began to flow like water, like water within water. Aurora licked her parched lips, where chap had overlain chapped. Lifetimes of dryness. The urge to join the stream overpowered her mind and she followed her fingers into the stream, pulled by an irresistible tide. The current hardened around her and she was being dragged into a waterfall of hair, being crushed underneath it, dropping into a bottomless well.

Wheatbelt Wallaby put her foot down, hard into the ground to anchor herself against the upwelling, but the force was too strong, and she began to dissolve into the current. Pebbles broke off from her leg in odd places and were carried away.

"Aurora, what is going on?"

There was a long moment before Aurora understood what was said, and a longer one where everyone turned to watch her carefully.

"Sorry Chandra, spaced out I guess."

It was the wrong choice of words.

47

"Just tired, that's all," Aurora waved off the concerned looks.

After a pause that lasted too long, the argument resumed its flow around familiar contours, although Aurora lacked the concentration to follow much. She keyed in on important bits. One way or the other, August Bridges was going to bring many others to Mars. Not enough to make any difference to life on Earth, not in any way that would change Mars as a planet, but enough of the wrong sort of people that quarantine protocols would fail. That enough bacteria from the Earth would invade, seeking out any survivable niche and pushing out of the way any surviving indigenous Martian microbes, was inevitable. An imperceptible genocide launched into motion by predictable carelessness, which would finish off the Natives of this planet more surely than the crashing comets of the terraformers wet dreams. Before anyone even found them, they would be gone. Stopping this catastrophe from happening was the main reason behind her prolonged outings and faking her mental health to squeeze one more mission day out of Chandra.

"I don't find this amateur political speculation useful at all," Phillipa reasserted herself. "Politics are not your problem."

What other source of problems was there?

"In any case, I think what Aurora really needs to know here is that these developments have implications for the Australian mission." The tone was self-satisfied.

Aurora looked blearily to Terry for confirmation.

"Yeah Ror. With the Yanks offside, the PM's put us up for the chop with the next budget. Him and all you Sandies mob down Perth-side even managed to push it through the Tropo Sys up in Queensland, useless yobs that we are."

Terry reported the facts glumly, and even her colorful way of saying them failed to take the edge off.

The air thickened again around Aurora's chest. Her hands clenched on her chair against the feeling that she was being picked up in a rushing flood out into the night. The force of the current was pulling her apart. She shrugged away from Julia so that the feeling would not be passed on. Julia leaned to close the gap, lightly grasping Aurora's arm like a nearly drowned child, as if the slightest movement would send her drifting off in the current. Aurora sucked in the resulting wave of fear and tried not to let it show.

Phillipa brightened as she cut to the chase. "So, Aurora, now we all know that there is still some interesting science left in the Life question. I do recognize that. However, resources are limited and, with this kind of pressure, well, we will need to keep the focus on the strategic priorities of our mission, no matter what fun it must assuredly be to go gallivanting about the planet in search of hypothetical bugs."

They were cutting her off. They didn't want to even know what was out there because then they might have to care. Because then they couldn't bulldoze Mars, which was an insane dream to begin with, unless August Bridges' luck improved with the aliens. Aurora didn't even want to think where that might lead.

An inverted whirlpool, screwing upward into the sky, dissolving the stars and emptying space of light. Her limbs rapidly melting into the whirlpool, Wheatbelt Wallaby pushed off towards the eye of the tempest. Great tremors gripped the land, her body, as a circle of sky pulled back overhead. As she reached the center of the gyre the currents cancelled each other, and she drifted soundlessly upwards into the dark.

More words.

"Strategic priorities Pip?" Pip. Priorities. "Like Aurora said, Terry. There are expanding markets." Said. Terry. Expanding. "Yeah darl, a lot to sell us Martians." Us. Martians." Yanks are falling over themselves to swap some peanut butter for a jar of Vegemite. Whatta ya say Alice?" Say. Falling over. "Fifty years on Mars and we're all they've got to show for it." Fifty years. All show. "Terry, you can be as cynical as you like, but people have invested a lot of money to pay for you to fix lorries on another planet." Money. Another planet.

As Aurora's body slumped into the vacuum left by her departing thoughts, Julia lost her tenuous grip and slipped towards the floor. The motion as Chandra ducked in to catch Julia momentarily brought Aurora's attention back. Chandra looked into her eyes with concern, "Aurora, you do not look so well."

"No. Nothing. I'm tired that's all."

"Yeah, we'll give it a rest Ror. Sorry to hit you with all the bullshit straight up."

Thanks. Terry. Good. Night. Somehow, more mechanically than intentionally, Aurora found her way back to her bunkroom. She leaned on the doorframe to catch her balance. In her neuroview an idle thought had switched on the news when she meant to power it off. She was about to give the annoying stream of babble the flick, but paused on her recognition of an unwelcome and familiar face.

49

August Bridges, king idiot of the universe, going off on his latest bright idea for the masses. She'd met him once, as unlikely as that seemed. The Aussie Mars mission had been trucked up from Antarctica to Tokyo when the Japanese unexpectedly handed over their mission spots to them. Mirtopik Com had just bought into MASO and there was a press event on.

Aurora remembered not making any sense of what he was going on about up there on the stage but noticing that he still managed to make an impression. If nothing else, the man had charisma.

Then for some reason she never could figure other than that she was trying to keep her head down and that he was an old school charmer who felt compelled to make everyone's business his own, he had chatted her up during the after drinks. He was a good-looking bloke who could draw people out, and soon she was telling him about her mission. The end of the conversation was the only thing that had stuck with her.

"That's very important work you're doing. If we don't document Martian bacteria, we won't be able to preserve some before the bacteria we bring over during settlement overwhelms it."

"Maybe that would be a good argument for slowing things down," she'd suggested, realizing at the same time she had knocked him back.

He'd looked at her sympathetically, as if this was the most profound thing he'd ever heard.

"Exactly. My worry is that after the aliens tell us how to make space travel cheap, Mars will be the main place people will want to go. That's why we have to work together to open things up the right way."

She couldn't figure out if that last bit was a line, but she'd felt somewhat invaded.

What he'd said had, over the years, added urgency to her work, as if she were the only one working to protect billions of years of unique evolution. Up to a point Aurora had played with a fiction that he might be an ace up her sleeve, that her feminine wiles - that was a stretch - might have bought her extra time. Until now, when it was clear as glass he had no such honorable intentions.

She was being screwed and it almost seemed personal. Everything she had worked for. It was too much. The breakdown in front of Chandra, Julia, and everything she'd worked for going out the window. What was the point? It was getting hard to breathe, more so than was ordinary with the rationed air pressure. Aurora needed to talk to someone. Someone who couldn't dob her in to Chandra, or who wasn't already sick of the politics, or worse, like Pip and Terry, who thrived on it. Dad was dead and was never good at listening when he wasn't.

That left the least pretentious person she knew, who listened so well that it felt like she'd known him for lifetimes, who always told her to never give up. Through her neurovisor Aurora thought up a link to Kalsang, even though it took eight hours for the message to reach him out at Neptune and she couldn't pretend it was a conversation. Even though he rarely replied, when he did it was always to the point and lovely. How Kalsang managed out there doing solitary on the edge of nowhere was beyond her reckoning. She was sure he must take some solace in her messages, in playing the role of her diary. She couldn't imagine the monk taking much badly.

Aurora let loose a rant. One word pulled behind the other like they were tied by string, by her passion. She was aware that some of what she said might be thought beautiful. The reasons she had come to Mars. What the desolate and rarefied country had come to mean to her. The stories that the place held, perhaps under the silent witness of life. Of the privilege she felt trying to give voice to the sole survivors of a once vibrant planet. What was at stake? Billions of years of evolution hanging in the balance, and it wasn't worth the bother. What was the rush? Mars would always be here. Wasn't it their duty to preserve the most interesting bits of it?

When it had all drained out of her, for a moment Aurora almost felt better. God she was tired. Then, as she dwelt numbly on the newsfeed still hanging in her neuroview, August's face reminded her of someone else. Her Dad telling Mum some new wild fancy to explain why they'd all soon be pulling up stumps once again to follow him on some mad trip. She felt the ghost of that stab of guilt, secretly looking forward to the adventure that Mum and Jesse dreaded. When the strain of it all finally broke the marriage, Aurora blamed herself for encouraging him. But it was just Dad being a dickhead, same as her now, nearing 40 and chasing microbes across Mars without a shred of family to hold her back.

August's talking head disappeared as Aurora extracted her neurovisor and stumbled into her bunk. August Bridges, desperately selling the universe to the world when it was all too big for one man to handle. As much as she resented him for this, for a tired moment she almost felt sorry for him.

Aurora's mind reclined, not on the softness of her pillow, but into the empty spaces and still sands of Mars. But even as she settled down into this comfortable obscurity, she was kept awake by a troublesome feeling that she was being watched. As if billions of eyes had somehow made their way across the great void of the solar system to find her hiding place and were peering in on her. Aurora turned and stretched and yawned and rolled over and turned and turned. The eyes would not take the hint and remained, scrutinizing the molecules of her motions, calculating their sum by equations that left little room for emptiness or for freedom.

This was how it was going to be, Aurora thought. Fine then. She turned over once more, cradled her head in her hands, and wept. As Phobos dropped like a spent flare over the horizon, Aurora's tears trailed off into a dreamless sleep.

CHAPTER 4

Kalsang

Light loses the race against the expansion of the universe, resulting in the daily withering away at the edges of the knowable into an impossibly distant past, until nothing remains but the fizz of iron dissolving into itself and the phantom echoes of memory. Reality is information, the symphony of existence. Whatever is beyond knowing no longer exists - thus life cries out for recognition across the void.

A string of pearls nests in orbit around a lapis lazuli planet, glimmering in the pale light of a brilliant star, threaded in an invisible, parabolic net of radio waves that converges on a coral pink moon. As the pearls rotate in obedient synchrony with the moon, the invisible strands vibrate to a billion frequencies overlain - a celestial harp. Beautiful voices sing within this marvellous instrument. The birth and deaths of stars and galaxies and of the creation, the music of the spheres, the gentle lapping waves of cosmic radiation echoing through the Milky Way.

Every now and again a fleeting whisper of something else enters the net - a momentary challenge to the universal unravelling. A spike in complexity - a proclamation of identity standing out against the selfless void. Here we are, we have lived, we have died, you should know, please acknowledge. And finally, after a long journey of centuries and eons, at last someone is listening. A patient ear waits, comparing each new vibration in the net against the cacophony of the cosmos, waiting for the infinite improbabilities to collapse into an actuality, another member of the neighborhood, the new kid on the block. But the ear is deaf to meaning. It is mechanical. It has no heart, and so it passes the message on to someone who does.

* * * * * * * * * * * * *

On Kalsang's world Neptune was rising.

Slowly the fine lines emanating from the corners of twin golden eyelids parted. The universe abruptly encountered two wide, dark orbs and slowly sank into a deep pool of consciousness. A broad grin spread at an imperceptible rate across a previously solemn face. A young man extended his hand from maroon robes and selected a pungent, rough looking piece of granitic cheese from a bowl, tossed it casually a few times into the air, rolled it mindfully in the palm of his hand, and popped it into his mouth.

Crunch, crackle, and crunch.

Kalsang's neurovisor issued an electric hum and vibrated off the edge of the ledge where it had been carefully placed. Behind the ledge, beyond the clear buckeyball insulated portal it was snowing, a light dust of pink nitrogen and methane ice, falling lightly against the carbon alloy walls of a small half sphere resting snugly in the middle of that absolute nowhere that was Neptune's moon, Triton.

This was how it was today and how it had been for a seemingly unending sequence of days since Kalsang had first arrived on this distant, dim world.

Crack, crunch, crunch.

Kalsang's smile grew wider as he reflected on the rough hands of Amala, his mother, in a felt tent in the mountains of western Tibet five planets away, who had somehow rolled her heart and love into this jaw-breaking ball of cheese delivered as an offering to her son who now resided in a land further from her imagination than death.

Crunch, crunch.

Finished.

In this way his mother's love transcended the lonely distance more efficiently and directly than the radio waves he was charged with monitoring.

Kalsang Jampa, full time Buddhist monk and part time radio telescope operator responsible for picking up the phone whenever ET called. That was his job description. Nearly a year had passed since his posting to the Mirtopik Neptune Extra-terrestrial Listening Array Triton Station, travelling twice again as far away from the Earth than any human had managed, to a place so cold that his unprotected flesh would freeze into stone. There was no point dwelling on that though, since really, he was just where he was, and dead was dead no matter how it happened and any fame that might have attached to his name through the feat was meaningless in that context. Anyway, the peace this reality enforced was something he cherished.

His neurovisor buzzed again, which reminded him that the cost of his seclusion, and for the generous endowment by Mirtopik Com to many monasteries and charities, was for him to perform certain duties a few times a year. It took some effort to shift his concentration from his meditation and to bring those duties back to mind.

Scattered through light years of inter-meshing gears of interstellar gas, most alien radio broadcasts managed to converge in the radio telescope he was manning for the space of a few hours - a brief debut in which entire civilizations announced their existence and presented their message.

Reconnecting was problematic. Given the strength of most radio transmissions, it could be decades before chance alignments in the heavens produced a clean signal again. This interstellar *"twinkling"* effect was like the bending of radio signals in the ionosphere experienced historically by short wave radio operators at the dawn of radio communications. Reception time was short, transmissions episodic, and decisions had to be made on a much shorter time frame than was allowed by the eight hours round trip required for light to travel from Neptune to the Earth and back.

For these reasons the telescope had to be manned and it was Kalsang's honor to be the first monk assigned to the new station. In a year he would leave to trade places with one of the other monks on Europa, and from there rotate back to Earth. That was a long time away.

Having shifted his attention to the task, he carefully picked up the neurovisor, holding it above his forehead while the groping spider-silk tendrils at the device's base felt their way through the nano-pores in his skull and into his brain. Once the neurovisor was in place he focused his imagination into it and the air around him suddenly sprang to life with a whirl of images and symbols. He surveyed the day's catch.

"*Ai*, so many today."

The transmission field looked like the contents of a kaleidoscope caught in a whirlwind. The other transmissions he had processed before were much smaller than this one, and not as clear. Someone out there wanted to make an impression.

Kalsang noted a promising diagram dancing in the air just above head height as he turned around. He focused his eyes on the desk before him and the diagram followed his thoughts down from the surrounding constellations and hovered at a comfortable viewing distance. He swivelled his attention back and forth drawing a collection of other images down into his reading range.

One diagram was the most telling - two circular objects floating in space near two planets, a tube of twisted space-time connecting them, and small ships travelling through a tunnel between worlds.

"How good. This is exactly the sort of thing they are looking for."

Kalsang turned and ordered a search of the relevant frequencies. He worked for a while cataloguing the remaining images. Some revealed the beings who had sent the transmissions. They were very strange beings, tall and slender, so many heads, which was something he had not seen before in the other alien transmissions, and many tentacles like an octopus but with the tips of the many arms branching out into tentacle fingers. They looked frog-like in their expression, with wide eyes, and seemed to live mostly underwater. They were, by any standard, the strangest looking creatures he had ever seen, but their faces expressed familiar emotions and Kalsang felt himself immediately drawn to them, almost as if they were old friends. How odd.

The signal went dead. While he waited for the connection to re-establish Kalsang resumed his latest project. He turned carefully around in the pantry that doubled as his kitchen, library, altar, bedroom, toilet, office, dining room, and gym.

The robust smell of roasting barley joined the constant juniper and sandalwood incense that filled every crevice of his compact abode. The smell originated from a pile of whole barley, which Kalsang had poured onto a pan lain over the hot plate built into his desk.

The barley was carefully measured - one hundred grams for this week's real meals. It had arrived with the chirpee cheese the other day, the other week, the other month? Time was almost meaningless here. Five kilos to last the next six months. In any case it was a welcome treat, thoughtfully supplied by his mother's cousin, Thubten Lodi. The alternative fare was a textureless paste, with an assortment of flavors all equally indistinguishable, reconstituted from a self-sufficient blend of skin cells from the cabin air, yesterday's cough, last week's bowel movement, and a brew of organic molecules harvested from sediments outside.

Kalsang listened to the continual and comforting scuttles issuing from the walls around him. His tiny friends were busy, keeping life going in this self-contained world. He glanced through the clear panels that revealed the activity occurring within his Terrapod, which was one of the newest Luna bred extra-terrestrial ecosystems. Nanodroids, like molecule-sized farmers and veterinarians, roamed about selectively catalyzing reactions, recycling nutrients, harvesting products essential for the balanced functioning of all the inhabitants of the Terrapod of which Kalsang was the least essential member. Kalsang was happy to return whatever contribution he could as the nanodroids clambered about his veins and digestive tract harvesting compounds required by the others.

Kalsang noticed another incoming message, this one coming from a friend.

"Aurora. . . Rora bora dora. He He."

Kalsang welcomed the transmission into his mind and smiled as Aurora materialised before him like a goddess in a dream. For some reason she always seemed young, even though she was older than he. Why would it be? Then he concentrated to hear her talk.

"Oh Kalsang. Mate, I need to unload."

Oh dear. She looked too stressed. Kalsang invoked visualisations of the Buddhas to accompany Aurora in her sadness.

"I don't know what to do. No one seems to care. There is an entire potential world of life here and it is just too inconvenient to know. They're sending me home Kalsang, when I am so close."

And then she let her emotions flow, like rain. Letting herself release. Telling the truth. Kalsang enjoyed her messages, and even though they couldn't have a real conversation because of the lag he felt like they were keeping him from falling off the edge of loneliness.

Rocket capsules of hot barley cracked open all at once and jetted through the air in wild, twisting arcs. Oh, what to do?

Releasing the ghost of Aurora from his attention, Kalsang yanked a magnetized plastic waste bin from the wall and held it patiently over the hot plate to contain the swarm. He grimaced as his hand brushed the hot pan and he pulled faces at his reflection in the portal.

The barley dance ceased. A few erratic puffs and those grains not electrostatically attached to the walls of the bin slowly settled into the pan. Kalsang switched off the heat and searched for his grinding tool, a hand-held fire extinguisher. He then relaxed into the rhythmic motion of crushing the roasted cereal into flour.

"May all beings find happiness and its causes."

Kalsang switched off Aurora with the intent to give her full attention later. His eyes narrowed contentedly as he concentrated on grinding the barley.

"May they be free of suffering and its causes."

Kalsang stared out the portals at the frozen panorama where single flecks of pink snow, dropped one by one by scant winds, landed atop inch high drifts about the base of his retreat. In the pale light of the distant Sun, diminished to a thirtieth of its familiar glory, the snow reflected an eerie spectrum of strangely coordinated colors. Triton was a land that had been still since the beginning and a place perfectly suited for meditation, far from the endless dance of Samsara on a crowded Earth. He was growing accustomed to this place and he felt that it would be difficult to leave.

"May they find the happiness that never ends."

Steam whistled from a hole in the wall.

"May they dwell in equanimity free from extremes of craving and hatred."

Time for tea.

Kalsang mentally summoned a hose from the ceiling. Hot steam and water gurgled forth and settled gingerly on the bottom of a rough, ornately carved, and colorfully painted wooden tube. In went a few cubes of what one might, for want of a better word, call butter. Close enough. The tea was real. Kalsang pulled a black, crumbling brick of Indian Darjeeling from a storage bin, and broke off a mindfully rationed bit into the mouth of the churn.

Pumping the handle of the churn with one hand, his other hand fingering his mala beads, Kalsang began another round of mantras.

He meditated, relaxing into the repetitive actions of his churning with one hand and the incremental rotation of his mala through the other.

An alarm beeped on the monitor indicating that the frequency search had returned some more results. Kalsang let go of the churn handle and adjusted his neurovisor. His imagination began to flicker in anticipation, ready to receive whatever image was to be painted onto it.

This time the customary ghosts of images attempting to be borne did not appear and instead a subtle darkness enveloped his mind. Kalsang leaned over and fiddled with cables on the console to restart the transmission to his neurovisor, which had apparently gone dead.

Without warning the wall to his left dissolved into a yawning chasm, a deeply unsettling absence of light.

Kalsang recoiled, tripping over his robe and losing his balance. In the reduced gravity he propelled into the air until the tubes connecting his body stocking to the Terrapod ecosystem yanked him back. He rebounded slowly back onto his tea-drenched cushion.

As Kalsang regained his balance, he turned and inspected the void now sharing the room with him. He checked his mind carefully. Was he hallucinating, lost in some mistaken nihilistic twist in his meditation? He narrowed the focus of the neuroview, shrinking the hole to harmless dimensions and embedding it in the palm of his hand. He studied it warily before releasing it back into the room.

Moving his attention from side to side, he probed its depths, looking for something substantial upon which to attach any frame of reference beyond the occasional static. He found nothing other than a blurry edge, which framed the blackness from a more palpable darkness around it that was peppered with stars.

The focus of the image began to back away, carrying his viewpoint through a portal and into the interior of an aquarium of sorts. A small fish swam about without obvious vertical orientation. One of the alien beings, with a deep sadness recognizable in his many eyes, floated before Kalsang and addressed him in a sonorous whale-song language. The being pointed out several technical schematics and mathematical formulae as they drifted by. When this demonstration had finished the being jabbed a tentacle finger back out of the portal and towards the dreadful void.

Kalsang registered a movement to his right. A large, round shimmer of blue drifted into the view. It was a world. Not Earth, but as alive, dangling in a halo of translucent rings. Serene and majestic, almost wholly covered by ocean, a vast field of blue flecked with white. Red and green aurorae danced about the top pole. Bands of cloud wrapped around the globe.

Beneath them Kalsang could make out some disturbance, a web of lines ricocheting about, each traversing the whole visible hemisphere of the planet. The pattern of what were evidently gigantic waves on the surface seemed to converge in the direction of the void as the planet rotated making it apparent that a tremendous gravitational pull was being exerted upon it.

Black hole. Kalsang knew the theory, the puncturing of the walls of the universe when a massive star, the atomic fires in its heart no longer able to support its weight, collapsed into a point of mass so dense that even light could not escape it. This one was in the process of eating a planet.

"How horrible."

Kalsang shuddered at the monster's uncompromising pull.

The focus moved back to the being who closed his eyes in grief. Abruptly Kalsang's perspective was flung into space, perhaps riding on a robotic probe that had launched out of the being's spacecraft, although it seemed to have been dropped from some other satellite in a closer orbit. As he fell towards the planet's surface, the dark scar in the sky fell away behind the horizon;

even out of view Kalsang could still feel its pull. As his altitude dropped he began to make out features. Thousands of islands stood as citadels facing the furies of a world-arcing tempest.

Kalsang, encased in his shell of illusion, plunged into the boiling sea. For a while he was buried in a blanket of green turbulence and the roar of water rushing against water. Then, through the churning murk, lights appeared. Gradually these grew sharper and the outline of a city became apparent as a collection of phosphorescent lights. As he drew nearer the devastation generated by the incredible tidal currents began to become noticeable, chunks of buildings, giant dislodged forests of seaweed, struggling fish some many times larger than whales, all manner of debris.

A high-pitched sound became discernible, a wailing. The volume built as Kalsang descended; a moaning like the screams of a million whales struggling against a million harpoons. The death-song of an entire world.

Impossible sadness flooded Kalsang's heart. He shook and squeezed his eyes shut against the waves of misery assaulting them. He opened them in time to encounter the terrified face of one of the beings rushing towards him, so close that Kalsang automatically reached out to catch the flailing hands. The curtain, through which he could not reach, was light years and centuries thick, but the being's guttural howl, as it flew by, was instantly translatable. "Help me! Save me!" Kalsang watched helplessly as the being floated away.

More aliens hurtled by, clutching at the water, at pieces of debris and at each other. A mother reaching out hopelessly to her children. A ball of beings embracing each other tightly, their eyes clamped shut, bracing against the inevitable. Another being, crushed between massive slabs, its life painfully squeezing out into the rushing sea. Kalsang strained to meet their eyes, to make some meaningful contact, to connect. More beings, a cloud of thousands screaming, terrified people being dragged to certain death.

Their cries were not the cries of strangers. Kalsang knew them. His lives and their lives were intimately interwoven. Together they had created a universe, had been each other's constant companions, had fought, had loved, and had ignored each other for countless lifetimes. The frantic, helpless people flying past, he recognized as his family, his own long-lost mothers. Time and again, in numberless previous lives, hadn't they nursed him, cleaned him, cared for him, painstakingly and patiently taught him, and cherished his life above their own? This is what he had been taught since he was a child monk, left by his tearful mother at the monastery, her compassionate hopes for his future only slightly overcoming her natural attachment to her son.

60

As he reflected on this, the distinction between these beings and his own lovely mother diminished, and a great sadness ballooned within his broken heart and overflowed in tears. Now they were suffering, drowning in agony, frightened and lost and in shock. They did not recognize him, but he recognized them. Their pain was the same as his pain, but they were many and so were many times more important, as he was only one.

In Kalsang's trained imagination, black blisters of smoke began to peel away from the multitude - their fear, their anguish, their frustration and anger, their grasping - all gathered into a great black ball and he breathed it in. The molasses smoke poured into his nostrils and sank within his breast, falling to the bottom of the breath. Waiting to receive it in in his core was his shadow, the collected remnants of lifetimes of delusion. Through the power of compassion, the darkness distilled into light and he breathed it back out to them.

The process repeated. Black smoke rushed in from the beings and white light returned to them. Kalsang tried to focus on individuals, to keep the process from becoming abstract. The child sobbing and hugging her knees, alone. Two lovers swimming desperately to catch the other's outstretched hand but being pulled away forever.

Kalsang longed to connect with their pain and take it away, but he was trying too hard and his efforts solidified into an impregnable wall between him and them. Even so, the echo of their terror lodged in his heart and grew until it overwhelmed him. This wasn't an exercise dreamt up in the sleepy safety of monastery or retreat. Those beings were falling into an endless abyss and, protected as he was, even he could not keep his composure.

The dark evil collapsing this world became his own monumental isolation. He was so far away from anyone he had ever loved and who had ever loved him, and it was a separation he was unlikely to escape. As the maelstrom overtook Kalsang he became lost in panic.

Crack.

His clenched teeth broke through a hard pebble lodged forgotten in a back molar.

"Amala."

Kalsang clung to those last fragments of hard cheese, as if his sanity depended upon it – rolling them between his tongue and the roof of his mouth. Back and forth, over and again, predictable, safe.

"So, you have finally found your Self, and in a piece of cheese?" teased a memory of the voice of his precious teacher, Lama Wangmo. The voice seemed so clear and yet no one was there.

How absurd, isn't it? The laugh began as a tight giggle and then his whole body began to shake uncontrollably.

When he recovered himself, Kalsang dove back with renewed purpose into the river of pain and confusion as it pulled both he and the alien beings towards their destruction. This time he sought no feeling of either separation or togetherness – everything was as it was, and that was enough.

This time as the dark smoke reached his heart it spontaneously ignited into a glow that flared up and then exploded throughout Kalsang's body, flinging his breath outwards, a supernova of bliss, its shock wave annihilating any suffering it encountered. As the flame overtook each being it sheltered them in a protective cocoon of peace. As warmth flowed into their hearts it filled them with solace, comfort, and courage.

Kalsang flew along with them, feeling their misery while dispelling it, carried along by the same irresistible tide. As the blackness on the horizon grew darker, the light released from Kalsang's heart exceeded it.

Eventually the neuroview shattered into fragments of static, only to reappear back in the aquarium spacecraft. The sad sentinel turned to Kalsang and looked at him directly with many eyes. In its whale-song language the alien announced a eulogy for its world. The tone conveyed an unmistakable warning. "If our loss is to have any meaning don't do as we have done."

Its task finished the alien slumped back.

A spiral of atmosphere and water leaped off the planet into the darkness and began the orbit down into the black hole. The planet faded brown and began to break into rubble.

The face of the being contorted in agony and his voice collapsed into a guttural sob. He was so utterly alone, except that he wasn't. Kalsang was with him. As the being's voice collapsed into silence Kalsang sang to fill the void.

Dear friend from a distant lost world
you who were my mother for limitless lifetimes
just as your kindness has now borne fruit
in my many opportunities for joy
just as your care has now borne fruit
in my freedoms and leisure so difficult to find

just as your striving has now borne fruit
in my persistence on the paths of the Victors
just as your friendship has now borne fruit
in the poise, which tames my restless mind

In just this way so too will I,
Kalsang Jampa,
solitary meditator with few realizations,
for you become
the sun warming your frozen heart
the open sky free of every obstacle
the wide river carrying you to the ocean of endless bliss
the firm gentle ground to hold up your peace

The signal carrying the message had run out, flowing through the maze of circuits and amplifiers like the last grains of sand in an hourglass. They focused in a parabolic antenna on top of the Terrapod and launched Earthward on a beam of laser light, instantaneously puncturing the thin atmosphere of Triton.

Looking back from the quickly changing vantage of the signal, in the first second a small pink world snapped suddenly into relief against the deep blue of Neptune. In another few seconds both worlds were swallowed by the ubiquitous emptiness of space as the signal began its long journey, via a relay of micro-satellites, to an uncertain reception by those at Mirtopik who controlled the receiver.

Meanwhile Kalsang sat, over and over again breathing in the agony of a world long dead and breathing hope out into the universe. Fullness pervaded his tiny hermitage. Electric offering lamps flickered before a simple altar, backlighting neurographic images of the Buddhas and meditating gurus. Cooling butter tea surrendered its steam into the Terrapod air. A neuroview screensaver of a three-dimensional mandala replaced the static of the completed transmission. Kalsang sat in meditation and wept. The beings he had encountered on the dying world sat silently in meditation around him. The spheres of butter tea on the floor began to congeal. The mandala continued to rotate. Neptune rose, and Neptune set in the skylight above. Kalsang's tears collected on his cheeks and evaporated in a steady cycle.

He sat for a long time - breathing in darkness, breathing out light. This was his true family, a universe of Dear Ones suffering purposelessly. He would not abandon them.

CHAPTER 5

Francesca

The Sun burns harshly on the broken walls of the Justice League of the United Sys of Gaia as our tale begins. Wind whistles through the wreckage. A slab of twisted metal panel creaks in response to movement pushing up from beneath. Fingers with ivory polished nails feel their way out along the jagged edge and melt into the steel as they clench down.

"Urrghh."

The metal turns to liquid pouring down around the form of a woman before seeping away into the ground beneath.

Transmuta staggers to her feet and surveys the wreckage.

A minute before they were all there with her, all the other Super Friends, enjoying another comfortable long day. Green Arrow was making them all espressos. Wonder Woman was knitting an invisible scarf. Superman had gone into the toilet and was staying there far too long. Aquaman was ordering pizza and forgetting the anchovies. Evil had been defeated so long ago everyone had almost forgotten about it, but they still liked to watch mnemes of the good old days when they had fought the good fight.

Now they were all dead.

It wasn't something they were coming back from. Body pieces were everywhere. They had all blasted out from the inside.

Why had she alone survived? It wasn't fair. There was no reason for her to be spared when all those she loved were taken.

Tears drip down, sizzling through the pavement.

Who had done this? Her fists steeled, ready to strike but there was only the wind and the sun and her.

The dark ball in her heart pulsed and she regarded it coldly as she always did, keeping it under control.

Then she knew.

The others had forgotten where evil truly lived and were unprepared for its sudden blast with their souls.

Transmuta hung her head in grief as she wandered away, trudging through the asphalt down the road, and leaving the wasteland of her love behind her.

* * * * * * * * * * * * * *

The hour before sunrise had been the least unbearable of the day. Bending before the dawn's promise of another pitiless assault by the rising sun, Francesca Xavier Salvador dropped another sapling down the planting tube into the parched soil, and brushed compost and straw into the hole around it with her foot. Pulling another length of microdrop irrigation tube from the spindle on her belt, she carefully encircled the fragile sprig of green, anchored a sun screen in place, and documented the planting with her neurovisor, which recorded the placement, size, and species of the tree. As it grew, surviving a thousand threats to its existence, the tree would continue to dribble ecos into her account.

"Salvador, that is the fifth Polymorpha Oak you've added in your row. It will shade out my whole stand. If you don't take it out the register supervisor will debit you."

And you are some idiot with no other purpose than to make a miserable day completely impossible? "Pull it out yourself, or do you need someone else to protect you while you do?"

The sweaty guy with more stomach than guts almost made a move to take her up on it but pouted instead. "You know, I could come back later and do it."

Francesca growled in response, something beyond language but more effective at expressing her complete disdain of such a wimpy threat. "And I could come back later too. You have to sleep, don't you?"

"Bitch."

The loser couldn't even risk an exclamation mark with that. Pathetic.

The sun began to burn over the Sierras, melting the landscape back into rippling mirage. Why did daylight always have to be so excruciating? Francesca only hoped that the drip feed from the microdrop would be enough to keep that tree alive, so its carbon could earn her ecos to give in thanks for food. Because, if she didn't she might be seen as ungrateful, which was a recipe for becoming even more hungry. Funny to think they used to grow food this far south in the Valley. If they still were able to maybe she could fill her stomach without feeling grateful to anyone. Funny to think that money didn't use to have memory.

The supervisor walked by and leered at Francesca, but from a safer distance this time. He'd learned first and second hand that you could look at fire from a distance, but that it could be painful to touch.

Another tree in the ground after a few shrubs. A mesquite whose thorns could penetrate the soles of anyone who might come to claim her nest eggs as firewood. Francesca documented the planting and waited for the calculated ecos earnings over the 40-year life of the bush to appear in her neuroview. She bent to pack the dirt and plant the microdropper, orienting it so it's funnel might extract the maximum condensation from the atmosphere to feed her plants until they had long enough roots to tap into the ever-retreating groundwater. Her shirt stunk from too many days with too little of a water ration to wash it or shower. The number of ecos from her plantings that finally manifested in her mind was depressingly low.

When the sun had risen too high to be workable, Francesca trudged back to her tin box and wiped the bird shit off the solar panels to push up her eco count, and nudge down the Hub upside down thermometer at the entry gate. Inside, under the flaccid swish of her fan, she relaxed in her hammock and fantasized about who she might sleep with next for his shower allocation. The trouble with that strategy was other girls were onto it, and so the guys who looked the best always stunk the worst. Fortunately, the guys were less discerning because Francesca was sure she wouldn't want to sleep with herself. She washed as much of the morning's grime off her body as she could with nanosorbs, but there were parts that she had wasted precious roof water getting to. All for the privilege of returning to stew in her own sweat until the fire in the sky sunk into the evening and she woke herself up for a dinner of beans and rice and green weeds from the roof garden. Same thing as yesterday and every year.

Almost nothing sucked more than being poor, except for idiots complaining about how good she had it. At least the entertainment was cheap. Francesca zoned out and let her mind float free in an ocean of hallucinations that projected from the collective minds of human animals on the neuronet. In seconds she was hurtling through the universe, overcoming evil in the defence of truth and justice amidst the ruins of the American Way. Comics. Francesca, more than anything, enjoyed inhabiting the oldies when people had better imaginations of what prosperity could look like. If people these days had as much as they had daily wasted before, they wouldn't know what to do with it. Of course, as the footage from the past revealed, it hadn't been enough to earn most people a smile.

Francesca assumed the role of Jenny Quantum, the too hopeful spirit of a pre-collapse 21st Century, from someplace called Singapore that had by the 22nd Century largely slipped beneath the rising waves. All the villain's plots seemed so quaint compared to what had already happened. Cities sinking below the oceans and others being emptied out as everything dried up. Whole countries of people on the move chasing whatever was left to live off while real villains, ones too bad to imagine, stole whatever was left. It wasn't until the Ecolution sorted that shit out, creating money from fixing the planet, that it all started to settle down into something people could live with. If you could call surviving off tree breaths and intercepting the stink off your own shit living. Even on the neuronet you couldn't ever get away. You couldn't eat the cake you didn't really have.

Francesca was halfway through saving a fake universe full of tragic entitlement when her efforts were interrupted by a message. She winced and left it for later because, having no real friends and being rejected by her family, it could only be some kind of hassle. When she did look sometime after midnight, it wasn't the kind of news she was expecting. It wasn't bad, and, in fact, it was so good she was sure it would be some kind of joke if anyone would give a shit enough about her life to mess with her. The truth was, no one did, and so she spent the next hour screaming in disbelief and drinking those last bottles of crappy home brew she had saved from some wedding.

The next morning Francesca did not wake early to head for the forest farms. Instead she slept longer than she could stand, opening her eyes every half hour only long enough to rethink the message and recheck its signatures to be sure it was real. And only when the heat became impossible to resist did she pull herself out of bed to face the crazy news.

She had a job! Not a community improvement project, not a Hub obligation, not a 'thank you for nothing', not some drip-feed from a failing planet, not a favor for a 'friend', not a Net business where you had to pay your clients for the privilege of serving them. A real job with a real Com; a job with a regular salary in ComScript you could use in a real Com store. Francesca wasn't sure if she actually knew anyone who had ever had one.

And not with just any Com - with Mirtopik, the best, the one promising everyone everything. Francesca remembered applying. It had been a dare to herself on one of the most awful days. Some link she saw on a comics site that she thought herself into before her sense of the futility of life could close it off. She'd filled it in as X-Woman 'Jean Grey', as a joke, and changed the name to her own at the last minute. Which made it even funnier that someone in human resources would believe that an applicant would have the power to read thoughts and bend reality with her mind. Maybe it was some other fan who enjoyed the joke. It didn't really matter. She, Francesca, a woman that life had tried to rub into nothing since she had come into it, had finally been handed something.

She had a job. An actual job.

Francesca realised with horror that her shower water was still contaminated and unusable. The nanosorbs would only take off the outer layer of grime, but not the smell. Hopefully they would have a shower she could use at Mirtopik, otherwise they might think twice. She ordered take out with delivery using a chunk of her savings - because - why not? And, when she opened the door to receive the pizza, a package she hadn't noticed on the way in was there too. Inside, her very very own superhero costume - a Mirtopik Comsec uniform and dropstick. She ripped off the packaging and pulled up the leotards and slid the shirt down over her lanky, smelly, figure. At least she wouldn't show up dressed like a beggar. Francesca sucked down the protein shake that had come with the pizza and yanked her black tangle of mane harshly into shape. Her sharp Latin eyebrows furrowed, and her angled features composed themselves into a disciplined ferocity that disguised their youth. She decided against lipstick. Everything on the outside was straight and clean as a razor no matter how cut up her insides could be. That was for her to know and no business of everyone else.

Francesca snarled at the mirror and admired her fangs, excited to get them stuck into the first new thing in her life. And then she resolved to stay up for her last night, freaking out while keeping her cool at the same time. Working it out. Crunching her abs and pumping out the push ups. Readying herself for anything.

When the alarm clock in her head rang to tell her the sun was mere hours from rising, Francesca's feet hit the floor so hard the mirror fell off the wall and smashed into a billion tiny fragments. She shook her head at the wreckage and stepped over it as she headed for the door. She wasn't coming back.

Francesca worked the bolt on the front door and found to her disgust that the thing was broken, again. Why did they always have to build the inexpensive units out of the cheapest shit? Didn't they know *los pobres* like her appreciated quality too?

Then she whiffed it, up there in the gutter, she didn't even have to look. Then she did because she couldn't stop herself. Ugh. The dangling putrid tail of the rat that had died last month up in her rainwater gutter. And that skunk of a landlord didn't have the shame to do anything about it even though it had defiled her rainwater tanks and had forced her to pay ecos for bottled water. And speaking of ecos, that rainwater tank had been leaking over her panels and the slime build-up was severely reducing whatever ecos she could claim from the electricity produced by the flat. The lousy shit owed her. She banged the door, so the asshole could notice her leaving.

"Hey," Sue Zims, the one neighbor Francesca actually liked, shouted down her, "do you know what time it is?"

It was only then that Francesca realised she was actually leaving for good and taking three months unpaid rent with her to replace her deposit plus what the scumbag owed her. Everything she had worth owning was in her backpack since her comics were in storage. So, what was the point of anger towards all the people in this place in which fate had stranded her for far too long?

Francesca felt almost guilty, slinking down the dirt track alley leading through the units and forest farms towards the SkyTran station, hoping to make a cleaner getaway. Maybe some people, maybe those born here or something like that, maybe they might feel some connection to this absolute hole of a place. But the rest, like herself, had been trapped by the tree planting project that offered a chance to generate ecos. Poor suckers. Too bad they all couldn't share her ticket to freedom.

After a few clicks of hiking through the trees, Francesca reached a transit node and queued in line at the base of stairs leading up to the SkyTran. Above her whizzed the traffic on magnetic guides, individual passenger gondolas and flyseats slowing to drop off and pick up passengers at the top of the stairwell, as well as freight containers and empty container claws.

Many in the line looked away at the sight of her uniform, even though she was only Comsec and had no authority here. Somehow anyone's cop was everyone's cop. That could be good news for her or bad depending on who was checking her out.

Like the bloodstained junkie eyes glaring at her from a few places back in the line. Some big white Rev head decked out in dreads, which just looked stupid, if anyone asked her - another freak looking for trouble and trying to stare her down like he was as big as he thought he was. He was high or crazy or both - she could tell by the way he kept blinking his eyes.

Francesca, alter ego to M'gann M'orzz, with her x-ray eyes, looked straight into this guy's internal organs and considered, which she would target if he got out of line.

She knew the type, the desperate stench of failed manhood looking for any angle of attack. She felt the usual anger, a wary snake sliding up her neck.

"Yo ComSec. You in the wrong Hub. Hey."

Francesca couldn't give a shit about this loser nuisance guy unless he came closer, so she breathed, clenched her fist, and let it go.

Especially because there were kids around, fussing about because the line was too long. They should have two lines, a special one for the families and the kids, like that one sharp girl in a red sweater tugging on her brother's hair and looking for her momma's reaction. God, she looked so much like Elena.

Francesca was overcome with the desire to reach forward and hold tight around the little girl, to wrap her cape of invisibility over her and never let another cruel eye fall upon her. Tears welled up and she pushed them right back down where they came from.

The freak maintained his position in line behind her going up the stairs and Francesca almost forgot about him. The little girl was now purposely plucking the back of her brother's jacket, almost but not quite causing him to fall back with every forward step. Her momma was focused on ordering her route through her neurovisor, intentionally oblivious to what was going on.

Francesca followed suit, focusing her mind on her account balance, which was, as usual, next to nothing, and transferring a significant proportion to the SkyTran ticket for her visualised route. She was almost about to ask the family if they wanted to share a gondola, if they were going in the same direction, but that was so completely unlikely, so she didn't. As she moved into the flyseat queue and the family into the gondola queue her peripheral vision picked up the shuffling freak move in between them.

Pop. Pop.

Que pinga? The asshole, closer to her now, was obnoxiously blowing gum bubbles. Pop. Pop. He stunk like a toilet, like he was high on toilet bowl cleaner or something, and he began to giggle in a dangerous way. He was setting off all sorts of total psycho alarm bells.

Pop. Pop.

Francesca could forgive him for being a psycho because that was just something dick cheeses like him couldn't help, but stupid irritating habits like that were just cause for murder.

POP.

Then it happened. The little girl with the red sweater backed right into him in a reaction to her mother wheeling around to scold her.

The freak rounded on the girl.

"Watch who you are touching," he screamed down into the little girl's face.

Her mother was in shock, stepping in between the freak and her son, like her daughter wasn't in the most direct danger. It wasn't a decision the poor woman made, just a natural impulse, but she'd never forgive herself. And that was the thing that set Francesca off.

What happened next was just automatic. Francesca's skin hardened into cold stone. "Yo," she shouted.

As her flyseat started to move down the ramp towards her Francesca prowled straight into the freak with an almost provocative gait and, while he was momentarily disarmed by the unexpected motion, she flicked her dropstick neat up under his nuts.

"You want 20,000 volts?" she asked while staring dead eyes up into his glazed ones.

"No." The freak surprised her by having some sanity left that she didn't expect, and this stopped her from killing him, which was what was maybe going to happen in the first place. The snake in her neck coiled back and her mind went all cool and razor sharp like it always did when it needed to.

A flash of red laser light came from her neurovisor and scanned his. As expected, the freak's SkyTran ticket mneme was sitting there for anyone to rip off his visor. People always stored things that they weren't going to keep, like tickets and receipts, right up front without security. She activated the app that copied the ticket mneme to her neurovisor and deleted his out of his brain.

"What? Ah."

Zap. Francesca hit the freak with just enough charge from her drop stick, enough to hunch him up like an armadillo, hopefully enough to keep him from ever adding his lousy jerk junk to the gene pool and shoved him into her flyseat as it rolled past. She mentally changed the route to take him to ghost town El Centro and since she had locked the ticket he wouldn't be able to change it.

The little girl was bawling. Although Francesca wanted more than anything to comfort her and her family, to share a little moment of love and appreciation to take with her on this lonely journey, she instead did what she always did. She ran.

Francesca jumped on the freak's abandoned flyseat and changed the route on his ticket she had stolen to take her to LA, to Mirtopik, and far away from here. As her flyseat paused before jumping from the platform, Francesca stole a last glance at the girl in the red sweater, rubbing her eyes as they followed her rescuer. They made eye contact for a moment until Francesca flinched. *I'm leaving you again.*

And with a swish she was off and flying like nothing had ever happened. Like a switch in her mind somehow turned the whole thing into a nothing. Why was it, Francesca wondered, that when crazy moments like this were over they became instantly unreal, like she had just been some kind of neurovid actress playing a scene or something?

As Francesca flew out from her station on what was basically a supercharged ski lift, she checked out the damage on her account. Buying that moron's ticket had put quite a dent in her already dismal savings. Damn. She should have just sent him around the block, but he'd pissed her off that bad.

As her flyseat elevated up onto a high guide for a long run Francesca's head started to spin and she could feel the sadness overcome her. The encampments along the SkyTran line below her began to blur and spill into each other as agonies of memory echoed up from below and rebounded in her heart.

I'm sorry, so sorry.

Francesca was still sobbing as she glided West along the 10 through the mountains towards LA. Many hours later a depleted mad woman stumbled down the stairs of a SkyTran node at the address of the recruitment centre. The Mirtopik Needle down the street pierced the clouds, cutting such a sharp contrast with the beaten down city spreading out to the horizon in all directions as to seem almost invisible in its impossibility. It took balls to make a building like that in this day and age. The materials they built it with, they said they would one day make an elevator into orbit with that stuff. That was August Bridges, the only guy with any plan left beyond trying to hang on.

And she couldn't believe all the good-looking people. Everyone dressed in the latest styles, which for Francesca would mean anything not endlessly recycled. The colors. It was late afternoon and they looked so fresh, having spent the day in actual air conditioning. Imagine the expense. The only thing more out of place than this tower into heaven, but invisible for completely different reasons, was a muddy, smelly, sun-baked creature from the tree farms. No one seemed to look at her - as if she could not possibly exist looking this bad. The smell, they couldn't ignore that, so they were pretending something nasty was floating from out of sight in on the wind.

Taking possession of as much dignity as she felt she could allow herself, giving the minimum indication of shame required for people not see her as also delusional, Francesca made her way through the crowds, which parted before her.

The centre was closed. According to the meme announcing her employment it was an hour before the closing time. Francesca pounded on the plexi-glass, but the people inside obviously felt they were happier with some barrier between them and her.

"Can I invite you to dine with me?"

Francesca was about to complain that what she deeply desired was for this person mocking her, among all the assholes on Earth, to drop dead first. But instead she turned and forgot everything because the asshole was one of the best-looking assholes she had ever met.

"Dine?" It was the best she could manage on short notice.

"Yeah."

There was a pause during which Francesca imagined the guy without clothing.

"I would offer you some money, but I don't want to contribute to any bad habit."

"What?" It took a second to realise the depth of the unintended insult.

"Hey. Don't worry about it. You looked like you needed some help."

"Help? You want to help me? How about this. The only thing between me and the rest of my life is this door. If you can open it, we can both pretend we never met."

"You're ComSec?"

"In from the field."

"No me digas. Ok, I've got the key."

The guy's name was Raoul. He was ComSec, a recruit trainer. It took some time before Francesca could look at him without wincing, and she thanked all the Saints and Orishas that he never was assigned her instructor. It was bad enough that passing him in the corridors made her horny as Hell. Ordinarily she would have jumped him. The biologic in any guy's head would never say no to that, but Raoul never seemed to have anything going on that way, enough so that Francesca decided with despair that he had to be gay. Since the humiliation of being turned down, on top of the embarrassment of their meeting, might be too much to bear, she stayed her distance. Instead he knotted up in her brain as an obsession.

The days in training, the realisation of everything Francesca could have imagined for herself, was interrupted by this excruciatingly repetitive mental dysfunction. Still, she did better than anyone else, which wasn't necessarily saying anything. Usually she tried to not draw attention to herself, but probably this time she was trying to. She could have slept with some other guys to get him out of her head, but the few times she did it felt weirdly like cheating.

So, from then on, during the whole time in training, the only regular conversation she let herself have with anyone went like this.

"When you gonna pay the rent?"

Every day the same response, "When you gonna deal with the rat?"

After a month her landlord stopped calling, and she actually missed it.

And then it was over. Some scrawny pimple face came in and called her, and Francesca followed him. The dude took her to another guy who had her wait to meet some other woman and then finally she was assigned to a job, Comms Monitoring, the one she'd decided that she needed to get for no reason other than that she decided to get it. Most of her life was like that, just following her intuition to wherever it would take her. Having purposely over and under performed in the right spots to get the placement, Francesca was not surprised when she did. It sounded good for her, stamping out Hax from the networks and snooping in on things she wasn't supposed to. That and the assignment was out of the way in case she went nuts again. She hadn't thought this through before, but it just worked out to be good that way. Francesca was always discovering after the fact why she'd ended up somewhere. Sometimes it was good and sometimes messed up, but she tended to move on without worrying why, which was the only thing that made any sense when you thought about it. Why bother breathing if you wanted to get right down to it?

After a few months moving from gig to gig she ended up plugged in at the Deep Space network, which was okay even if a bit closed in and poorly lit and it was dead end nothing from a security standpoint. She was surrounded by nerds, whose pre-pube fascinations with far away long-ago lights in the sky she did not share. They were nice enough.

What Francesca didn't let them in on were her comics, because geeks would be into them like a horde of pigs. The job was perfect for piling through her daily delivery of custom prints. She used to only be able to not pulp a few of the best ones, but on salary with nothing and no one to spend it on she thought she might focus on collecting. Most people wouldn't understand actually reading when you could just storyline your body through the neuroview, but that had always felt limiting to her imagination.

Francesca slurped on a cup of java and cracked into a new indy character, Ante Laksmi, insurance actuary by day and super-heroine when the numbers added up. Her power was to know the actual risk of anything as opposed to something worse happening. Her baseline seemed to be 1 and 30,000 because that was the number of days a person could live, which were also the days she could die of any cause. So, she wouldn't jump in a car, but she didn't mind walking into dark alleys. She wouldn't carry her own gun, but she wasn't afraid of lightning or swimming with sharks.

Francesca wondered what the risk was with freezing people in her imagination and carrying them around in her head. Elena, this guy Raoul, others she had not invited in, but which could never take the hint and leave. Was the chance that this would kill her greater than or less than 1 in 30,000? On any given day.

After a few weeks Francesca had read as much as she could while justifying it as being work and found herself roaming around the cubicles just to keep her blood flowing. It didn't make a difference since most of the security monitoring was done through her neurovisor and basically the same nothing was happening today as happened yesterday.

"You're new here?"

A geek in a rumpled tee-shirt with crusty unwashed hair and Silver Surfer custom cover on his neurovisor interrupted her as she was checking the encryption on staff mnemes. She would have ignored him, but she realised, since she was standing in his territory right next to his desk, that it would be more than ordinarily rude for her to do so. Also, the Silver Surfer cover was cool because even people who read comics mostly wouldn't know stuff that old. She wasn't a geek, so she didn't mention it.

"Comes."

"Yeah, I guessed that from the uniform and the stick. What's your name?"

"Francesca."

"I'm Wolf." Francesca would have ordinarily been satisfied with that level of information, but she was bored out of her brain, so she decided to indulge him.

"Hi Wolf," she decided to avoid any of the blah blah blah stuff and get straight to the point, "why do they want such a high level of security on you guys? I mean there are blocks and traces on all of your neurovisor feeds and encryption extending even into the mnemes in your brains."

"They do?"

"Yeah. You wouldn't see this much security on clandestine military units, but it's not like anyone even tries to get in. I haven't had any Hax since I got here, and the information is just a bunch of stuff on stars and planets. Everything is so nailed down."

Wolf shrugged and answered with a mouth full of donut. "Must be the IP."

"What's up with that?"

"IP. Intellectual Property. Don't you know this room is the whole reason Mirtopik Com exists?"

"Really?" The job suddenly became hugely more interesting.

"Yeah. This is the place where all the feeds on the aliens come through. We maintain the network. If anything comes through with high tech info Mirtopik will want to know about it."

"Has anything like that ever happened? From what I heard most of the stuff is pretty general 'Here We Are, We Come in Peace' stuff. Everybody says Mirtopik has hardly made a dime out of any of it."

"Yeah, that's pretty much true."

"Who the hell would want to steal a bunch of useless alien chitter chatter?" Her sudden interest in the job was just as rapidly disappearing.

"I dunno. You want to see for yourself?" Wolf synched their neurovisors and directed her to a directory of mnemes. "They are all there."

"What's all that there?"

"The traffic to and from the Triton array. Everything we ever picked up or sent out. Check one out."

Francesca focused on a mneme and opened it. Instead of any alien freaky stuff, she heard instead a well-played rendition of a classic Cuban jazz song that they used to play on the streets back home. Her hips began to sway with it. These aliens knew how to play.

"What are you doing?"

"I think you're showing me the wrong place. Must be your music directory or something. Not bad taste though."

"No, you are... Ah, you must have opened a C30."

"A what?"

"C30. He's a clone who works for Bridges. He comes around a lot, about as close as we ever get to the boss. Nice guy, not like you'd expect, you know? He likes to play music, he sends his material down the wire and broadcasts through the Triton array, says he's sending the vibe out to the stars apparently."

"He's allowed to do that stuff? I thought there was some restriction of telling the little green guys about us instead of the other way around."

Wolf blinked his eyes. "Well yeah, technically, except we put out a lot more at higher power just through regular radio traffic. Anything from Triton would have trouble showing up against the noise."

"Really. But it's still illegal?"

"I suppose so, maybe. Anyway, the big guy lets him do it so who am I to complain?"

Francesca walked to her office with a new something to think about. The alien stuff didn't interest her that much. Like many people she didn't see the point. There were mouths to feed and cities being drowned by rising seas. Who the hell cared what was being said on the other side of the galaxy? It was all pretty indulgent as far as she was concerned, but the geek had given her a mystery to ponder. Who was this guy C30 and why did he get away with this? And why was a guy as high up the food chain as August Bridges even interested?

She found a bunch of his stuff - he was sending out almost every day. Pretty eclectic mix but with enough repetition that was suspicious in itself. Why send the same song out across the universe more than once? No more Cuban tracks either, which sealed the deal. What were the chances she's picked just the one that had connected to her? Signs like that were meant to be followed.

She put a burrito in the microwave and laid back to enjoy the first track she'd tripped over and flip open today's funny pages. The track turned out to be surprisingly long, a montage tribute to her childhood. Those songs took her back across the Caribbean to plastic strewn beaches and sprawling lantanas and tiny birds the size of bees. It reminded her of the good stuff that, together with all the dark, had helped make her what she was.

In her office, closed off from the world, Francesca danced.

CHAPTER 6

Calvin30

The mathematics of our existence is trivial. First principles, collections of maxims, a few rules of thumb, and the wide world all the same. All there is to it. When the million trillion things overflow our spongy brains, draw a line around them and call it done. Keep it simple stupid. Cows can round to perfect spheres, latitudes lurk with gnomes beneath the mushrooms, notes stand petrified on the scale afraid to swing, and two dollars and three make five of anything. Fairy tales for children. Here's a good one.

Once upon a time, it doesn't much matter when, some naked apes begat and begat and with some magic words tried to remake the world as they saw it. The place was soon full to overflowing with all manner of contrivances and associated packaging, imaginary money, and inadequate parking. All the animals, two by two and painted with the same spots, lined up straight to make it easier for the naked apes to eat them. Forests and fields stood the same height in tidy square plots free from pesky wild things, which might catch in the blades. Seasons, continents, any old time of day, all just a naked ape finger walk away. Even the magic words seemed to settle down into predictable formulae - steady like a pulse before a heart attack.

One day the naked apes, not content with their success in reducing the whole of their planet to standardized and dysfunctional pieces, turned their attention on themselves. Soon they worked out a way to reproduce themselves as exact copies. Now, it was hoped, not only would the world be the same as they'd known all along, but there'd be no new faces to tell them any different.

The naked apes tried to live happily ever after but, like all good fairy tales, this one ends badly.

* * * * * * * * * * * * *

There can be no surprises for someone with a thousand eyes.

Hiding anywhere, on a plant, on a fly, in your mind, someone is watching always. In this case, from the vantage of a flat white circle of paint identical in shade to that surrounding, a million retinal molecular chips transmitting a bug-sight prism view down onto a desk so nondescript that it could belong to anyone. Projected into his mind's eye through his neurovisor, Calvin30 spied on a Plain Man whom he, painfully, despised.

The Plain Man grimaced distastefully at the late time. He squeezed a sheet of paper from his desk up into a tight ball and tossed it into a waste bin where it joined some thirty of its fellows. A tremor of agitation was absorbed by the suspension of a chair that was slightly too big for its occupant.

The Plain Man stared along the unadorned walls of his office, where the shadows had long ago bled out to tint every surface the same shade of monotony. His thin brown fingers drummed an agitated tempo on the peeling veneer of his second-hand executive desk. The moron muttered.

"Ah, w-where the hell is C30? The little bastard thinks he can fool me, does he? Ah shit. Why do I have to put up with this? Who does he think he is? Does he think I am going to take the fall on this? Ha. I've got him. I've got him this time. Uppity recopy. Ah, where the hell is he?"

The Plain Man vigorously scratched the back of his neck leaving long welts from his shoulder to his ears. The pain resulting from this habitual action seemed to provide some relief to his anxiety and he dug his fingernails in with greater ferocity on each pass.

Then, with renewed determination, the Plain Man focused his attention into his neurovisor. "Bonita," he yelled into the over-conditioned air of his office, "Bonita."

There was no response.

"Damn thing." He tore away his neurovisor, breaking blood vessels and adding another layer of bruising to his forehead. "Ouch."

The Plain Man regarded the wiggling tendrils of his visor with distaste as he twisted the stalks of the eye tracking axion back into place. A sparkle of laser light indicated that the device was once again operational, and the neurovisor roots again scrambled about looking for undamaged micro pores in the Plain Man's skull. A succession of complicated contortions, accompanied by copious profanities, occurred as the Plain Man wrestled with the angry squid copulating his forehead. He struggled to gain the right angle to counteract by gravity the damage done to his machine, draping his corpulent carcass crossways across his desk and hanging his head down over the edge. From the bird's eye view the scene unfolded like a pantomime of shame.

Then, through triggering a cerebral toggle the Plain Man's neurovisor allowed Calvin30 to dig beneath skin deep and take a more intimate peek into his quarries state of mind. With his synaptic connections finally renewed, the Plain Man composed himself, unaware that his neuroview now had room for two. A middle-aged, harsh faced woman with saffron and green dyed hair appeared floating in the view field.

"Bonita, where the hell is C30? He's over two hours late," panted the Plain Man.

"How many times C16? I told you I don't know already." Bonita groaned wearily at the balding, acne-scarred, most recent head to materialize in the space in front of her desk, hovering with half a dozen others like a school of guppies. Calvin30 had hacked her neuroview as well, so he could look back at his brother through her eyes. The new perspective did not improve the view.

"I'll tell you when he shows up. Why are you always upside down?"

"Nothing. Nothing." The upside-down head flushed as it struggled to right itself before abruptly disappearing.

"Whatever jerks your chain."

Calvin30's Bonita view switched to again looking down from the ceiling as the Plain Man clumsily pulled the neurovisor out of his head again.

"Sons of a b-b-b-bitch. How they expect me to get any work done with substandard g-g-garbage like this?"

"What a drip," Calvin30 quipped, as the neurotically challenged object of his contempt hurled the neurovisor on the floor and stomped on it causing the center to crack.

Staring at the crumpled neurovisor for some minutes, the Plain Man finally bent down nervously to scoop it up as if it were a damaged baby bird.

"Oh, for P-P-Pete's. They said they won't give me another one." Stooping, the Plain Man pulled open his desk drawer and took out some tape, which he wrapped, in a thick wad, round the broken bridge. Draping the jury-rigged result back over his forehead, he threw himself into his chair and turned his back on the universe.

"So good to see you are getting up and about bro," Calvin30 offered from the floor by the door and in the flesh.

C16 spun about, his heels failing to stop his spin until his eyes had just passed by Calvin30's line of sight. He sprang up to face a face, which was, thankfully, a properly attired and so much better-looking version of himself.

C16 was piled into a threadbare suit and loosely knotted tie; not just out of fashion, but beyond any notion or awareness of style. Contrast that with Calvin30's polished man-in-green ensemble, a clean and calculated custom cut business kurta plucked from out in front of the latest trend. Here stood a man of substance sporting authentic leather jutti and immaculate makeup.

Everything else was depressingly identical, subtracting some minor indignities of age, both too thin to be imposing, soft light brown skin and branded with matching birthmarks on their prematurely balding scalps. His brother and he looked at each other with the same brown eyes outlined by full, thick eyebrows meeting at the top of distinctly pointed noses. Both had rather long fingers for the size of their hands.

But the differences, though subtle, were immense. C16's face was screwed up with a constipated countenance, his skin beset by outbreaks of infected boils. Other than these unpleasing aspects he would be utterly unnoticeable. By contrast, there was nothing ordinary about Calvin30. Each morning in the mirror he appeared positively beatific with a broad, flowing grin that bestowed upon his otherwise humdrum face an odd yet compelling charisma, there for all to please.

"Disturbed about you bro. Idle at a desk all-day. Harsh for the heart, hard on the haemorrhoids." Calvin30, man of many names and mastered by none held out a hand to his brother, who sniffed at it like it was rotten fish.

"I-I've . . . you've got a hell of a lot m-m-more to worry about. You. Any f-f-fregging nano ComSec is going to be in here ripping the cubes out of our neuroservers."

Calvin30 yawned while his brother from no mother droned away.

"Bro. No need to profane in vain," Calvin30 stretched, wandered to the center of the room, spread his hands comfortably on the back of his brother's chair. He looked opaquely into C16's eyes, which flinched away.

"Perhaps organize some plastic surgery, some triage on your loused-up visage of ours."

Words swung confidently off an underlying cadence.

"See your acne's back on the attack. Too much fuss must be pushing out the pus. You - need - to - re-lax."

"I g-g-give you ten. Ten s-seconds to explain ex-exactly why I. Why I sh-shouldn't report you to ComSec im-im-immediately. Who authorized the alteration of mneme ET190012? See, I-I know, I got you on th-this."

Calvin30 smiled as his brother's gaze burned holes in the wall somewhere to the left of him.

"How close did you nose that neuroseal bro? As a law you should go slow when leaping to the letter, because the number looks a little low to me. Whoever screened that mneme was a sweet sixteen. Who should that be?"

Calvin30 walked to the window. Surveyed the scene. Paused for the insinuation to sink in.

"Wouldn't twirly squirrel about it my twin." He caught himself yawning again. "Space is a long place for things to go wrong. Tell them it's a neurolink glitch at the Saturn transponder you tried to fix. Sell them that song or drop the bad notes and just carry on."

In his mind Calvin30 composed a bass line around the rhythm of his brother's grinding teeth. Here was something for the nosy shrew to chew on. Fool goes looking for a new clue, so what does he find? Finds he don't even own his own brain signature. Stop the presses for the non-headline. What's a clone without his ID? Same inside as outside, just a no one, no one at all. Calvin30 enjoyed the moan as the red in his brother's face bled into the monotone blend of the carpet.

"Got to mind what might cling to your behind bro or consign yourself to wiping it down. Either way re-lax. Everything is copacetic. Documented. We never received the original. Got it?"

"The or-original? What are you saying?"

"We never received the original," Calvin30 clicked his fingers like a hypnotist, "the message spliced when we received it. From Saturn. This is not your-or-my problem."

"Bull-Bullshit," C16 protested feebly, "I don't believe a goddamn word that comes out of y-your twisted little m-mouth."

"Believe what you conceive. Quantum-encrypted. Check the source brother. How could I have anything to do with it?"

"Faked," C16 cracked his knuckles, leaned forward, sucked his breath, clutched at straws, put on a brave face, and a stiff quivering upper lip.

"Peruse the codes if you've no better row to hoe. Gotta go. Loathe you later, brother."

Calvin30 flicked a manila envelope to an off-guard C16 who fumbled the parcel to the floor. He stood there like a stunned pigeon staring at its reflection it just hit. Let the impudent drip take on August Bridges if he dared - who else could switch the signal out on Saturn? It was almost lamentable that C16 lacked the balls.

The door to his sorry brother's office swung away and Calvin30 strode assuredly forward down the corridor. That grimace on C16's face had undoubtedly made his day. Unhooking his 'pipe' off its hoop, lipping the reeds, he blew a few licks of a luscious Antoinella Marsalis number, a syncretic meditation on 21st Century jazz standards. Pulsing lyrics darted gaily down the bureaucratic corridors, luring out both furtive smiles and Gaelic salutes. Calvin30 held his instrument out to venerate it. SlySynth 88, electronics hand-tuned, smooth fat tenor, a true classic. He'd traded a battered Altoharp pocket sax for it, with some techno who was a collector. That old Altoharp didn't play like this baby though, even after Calvin30 had the all the necessary extras installed.

And why not celebrate when friendly fate designates a humble clone to play the solo break for the whole solar system. Buried beneath the deep note in that double bar polyphonic measure his buffoon brother had uncovered was the ET key that would set him free. Into only his waiting palm the aliens had passed over such a spectacular aria of promise and ill omen. The specifics of that message were more sublime than even he, Calvin30, could possibly have imagined.

He paused at Bonita's office and seduced her with a serenade. She frog-lip smiled. Eighty-seven brothers and just one with style. Go figure.

Life, in the first round, was a downer. Being a clone, owned by the Com, was like being a dog. Throw you a bone you jump how high. Sure, word was clones had rights now. In days of yore, Coms owned every neuron in your noggin. This was the reason for your season. Intellectual property control. A once off's wits and soul had wings, but a clone's had to stay fixed. Nowadays a clone can walk straight out that door. Don't matter. People have expectations and it's too hard to be anonymous when there are so many copies of your face floating around the place.

You could change the face, get a total plasto, but what was the point? Fact was a clone's genes were gummed in the machine. They'd engineered you to feel filial *obliges* with some sort of kiss-ass allele, for the Coms had made more than the man. They made the family. They made the world. Then the biological problematical - all clones knew their Coms to be the only possible means of reproducing. The Com's success was the clone's success. Not *vice versa* because a clone, like a lone termite, was entirely dispensable to his nest. They'd taught you that all your life and they never let you forget it - most of all the other clones.

Panarchists too, just like all good racists. If they didn't want someone to kick around, then they wanted someone to look down on. Take the whole Clone Rights Campaign. Was it to liberate the clone, or to litigate his elimination? Words like unnatural, aberration, unhuman, perversion. Were they talking about your status or your existence? Wasn't everybody happy now? Clones were "free", and Coms stopped making them. Hypocrites could have their hate and eat it too.

Life sucked so hold the presses. So why not focus on a locus more fun? Take advantage of the pleasure in the treasure in your tragedy? Living as a clone could be a groove if you knew how to move with it. The Essence of the context, the key, the big light bulb in the sky, came one dreary grey morn, insides wrapped into a whorl, wishing to hell that anyone might notice. Slaving endless hours in Exec Services, fighting for the tossed crumbs, chanting the same dumb mantras as the other grey suited dwarves jockeying up and down the java powered pyramid, as if dissipating into cramped ambition was the subway to success. Desperately desiring distinction, owning something that would not be only a post-dated edition of someone else.

Then it dawned on Calvin30 that one fine day - he felt this way. So did everyone else. Clones and Originals and their dogs and their fleas - all blessed creatures needed someone to be.

Nothing had since been the same.

Everyone, Calvin30 surmised, every last wise guy one of Gaia's own, were nothing more than mere marionettes twirled about on strings of fear of losing what a clone, by birth, by being, never possessed in the first place. Realness bestowed itself upon Calvin30's Pinnochionic self in a blessed flash of satori. "There are no strings on me."

Calvin30 began to cultivate buddies. His level in the Com pond lifted effortlessly upward. His upper hand - a clone is not an opponent. Like some wise cracking African American manservant in a memory lane movie. Like those boundlessly cool oppressed past captains of hip hop, bee bop, and swing. Like only the most splendid of niggers, black then like clone now, dancing on the bones of our presumed masters. We entertain you while you constrain us, but jesters will get their just desserts.

People now came to Calvin30, lapping at his font of fresh confidence like thirsty dogs.

"For a clone," the Originals shop-gossiped, "that C30 is hunky dory. Yuck yuck yuck." Not grovelling, grotesque, jittery, skulking, shifty or shabby like his ilk - a decent up-to-code sort of Joe. "You almost wouldn't guess he was one of, you know, Them."

Which he, unequivocally, wasn't.

In this way Calvin30, the despised, metamorphosed into associate of foremost resort, savage noble, and counsel to the harried workers and contractors of Mirtopik. They in turn converted to begin to trust and depend upon him.

Which made them easy targets.

> *Calvin30, trusty true,*
> *He gonna walk those miles in your shoes,*
> *top that mountain, wind and climb*
> *Look out, about, feel so fine in the sunshine*
> *Fly bird, fly, flap sap, sing,*
> *Marvel that world beneath your wing,*
> *Rush the sun, then splat, fall flat*
> *Down to waiting windows, power lines, hungry cats,*
> *Spin down in a whirl, sad slow swirl,*
> *Flag unfurled, come undone uncurled, meet boy lose girl,*
> *down down*
> *with those big bad world,*
> *bad big bad world*
> *Blues.*

That was but one of the tunes Calvin30 played people on. Chords that just kept progressing round back into themselves. The dependable melody of free fall, which, if people were to be their honest selves was the fondest song they'd ever sing.

Take admiring Bonita. She was older now, a ripe sacrifice for the God of Small Comforts, swelling fat with sweet loneliness. Despicable in every diminutive way. Yet there was greatness in her. Desperation so deep she'd take come-ons from a clone; a potential for degradation beyond her mildest dreams.

Calvin30 posted romantic emails in idle moments that hinted at his identity in the blanks she filled in. Soon, one bad day settled in a long list of them, the emails might stop. Maybe become abusive towards the obtuse boob. Or, if Calvin30 were bored that week, he'd dip into some Mirtopik account and hire someone to stalk her. All up to the whims of minor muses. Today she was feeling pretty good. Smiles come before tears. Stopping for the shoe to drop.

"How's your idiot brother doing?" she asked, hopefully conspiratorial.

"His last expression?" Calvin30 gave his impression, eliciting a jelly full belly laugh from the love-struck cow.

"Tee hee. You're so funny. Hey, I've got a call for you from Luna City. Sounds important."

"The Man on the Moon as always *ataxia in perpetuum*, no down time for the wicked." He awarded her with a wink.

Hee haw.

"Don't I know it. Anyway, the woman told me to make sure you called right away. You're not starting something on the side, are you?" There was a more than a little interest in what his response would be.

"Ah, no, my paramour. You know there'll never be another you." So, fortunately, true.

As Calvin30 wandered away towards something new, an elevator door opened to spit out a tousled youth bedecked with a bicycle helmet. Intently chewing betel nut, the boy browsed the flow of mnemes in his neurovisor. Calvin30 made way with a flourish allowing the courier to elbow through. The genuflection captured the boy's attention.

"Hey, yo a clone isn't yo?" The courier poked rudely at Calvin30's torso. "I know cause I seen some of yo series last time here. Freaked I out. All the same yo guys, like quadzooplets."

"Alive to be at your service."

The bozo shifted the tuft of betel in his mouth and flashed a pink stained smile. "Sure. Yo know dis fat ass moc sits down the hall there? Yo take this stuff to her. Yo know always thought yo dudes is straight down, made for the work, right?"

Calvin30 swivelled dutifully to point out Bonita's unoccupied office. She had vanished, along with most everyone else on the floor, off to a staff meeting with free pizza. Timing was everything.

"Here," the boy thrust a handful of neurocubes onto Calvin30. "Give 'em to the old moc when she get back. I'm late." Thanks. Boy. Now, did the presumption of young massa upset Calvin30? Not one bit. After all, to be a clone was to be of service. And one couldn't fault a puppet for his strings.

Now Calvin30 would give those strings a pling. Quick call to front desk security on the neurovid. "Hola, Mister Ray. C30 on the phone. Yeah, that's right, me. Hey, is a flycycle parked illegally near the base level elevator doors? There is? Cause I think I just saw the owner coming down the lift."

See you later elevator. Calvin30 kept the neurovid channel open to watch the security man no longer watching the monitor mnemes as they hovered after him, flapping like bats. Ignoring them as he followed the boredom easing purpose of pursuing the bad guy.

One eye on the ComSec officer who wasn't watching him, Calvin30 swung off to pass out his largess. A minute later he returned. Empty handed. Gifts delivered to all God's children.

> *New Alan's promo to old Jorge's desktop.*
> *Promises betrayed might trigger a work stop.*
> *Unpleasant surprise, hapless happenings*
> *Old Jorge had applied for that same opening.*

> *Top rush job to do now under in-box overflowing*
> *When Joe never finds it his boss will be glowering*
> *Vaguely worded memos on the top of the bin*
> *And Urgent work slid further deep down within*

> *Gossip office Noel gets one breathy letter.*
> *Married Angela to Kent one-man-better.*
> *A manager doling out great over-time.*
> *With sighing and kisses and bottles of wine.*

Ho hum dee dum do dee dee.

A meander of meaningless maleficent monkey wrenching. Don't mean a thing if you ain't got no swing. Calvin30 was not some cat who would drop notes out of place. The direction of this section of Mirtopik, Business Development Integration, the Beady Eye, was in the middle of a rapacious ingestion of a lesser section, Intelligence Information Assessment. IIA was the Com's eye on the ball, auditing information flows from the Syns that spied on Mirtopik's competitors and clients. BDI was originally the public relations branch. Through means smooth and nefarious, Calvin30 had encouraged the courage of a nervous BDI boss to grab the horns by the bull and steer Mirtopik up its own ass. To stop the leaks of "sensitive" information at source by keeping the awful truth out of the Com entirely. The takeover had become a perfectly proactive bureaucratic prophylactic for reality. And to properly mushroom the ensuing information vacuum, a powder keg of office politics needed a spark to start the fuse. And the scratch of today's mail mismatch might help light it off.

Calvin30 checked the wall clock in the elevator. Still set 15 minutes behind so those running late this morning had been just that fashionably extra bit late. The devil was in the details. Calvin30 set it back 15 minutes forward.

Then he switched on his neurovisor to examine his mnemes. The foremost in red, fear and dread, came from August Bridges, the Man with the only Plan. Calvin30 listened through them, gratified by the tense tones and tempered tantrums. To mess with the most powerful man in the solar system with all the impunity of his obscurity - wasn't that just the ultimate thrill?

The AGM was advancing, and the Captain was under heat to greet his hatchet man. That August would fly right, Calvin30 was without doubt. August always straightened up under stress. It would be nice to be a fly upon the wall, but no need for that at all. Situation uncritical and under control. Setting the stage, though, had pushed out Calvin30's frontiers by far. Foiling an assassination was many times double the trouble of oiling the gears to get it rolling. The hardest part had been getting the equations to balance his loyalties to all sides without remainder.

Calvin30 left a missive for August via their unusually confidential neurolink.

"August, Boss. As befits the late innings my comments are minimal. I'm close to pinning down the plot to have you shot. Since you're swimming into the AGM, I'll just consign what I find to my man on the inside, exercising our usual discretion, of course. By the way, a small situation might require rectification. Clone in my series, 16, caught his hands on a cookie from the wrong jar. Meaning he took a look at your communion biscuits, not the ones meant for the starving masses."

With others Calvin30 could gain from their pain, but C16 was just a dead loss. It was hard to appreciate the pathos of those fated by birth to be hated. Such a shame, Calvin30 felt, to waste more than a half thought on such a half-wit, but C16 had been a pain one time too many. Jealously sniffing and zealously desperate in his particularly pathetic way to upset the upstart, and for all his disingenuous efforts he had finally managed to catch a scent. The fool had tripped across one of Calvin30's clandestine connections that allowed him first and August thereafter, to check out the E.T. phone zone.

This was the "cookie" C16 had found his fingers lingering on - a time-lapsed pre-capture of the Neptune array intersteller in-tray. Those broadcasts were then rebounded out to space from where, a week later, they bounced back to

Earth through the official channels. Last week's mind-blowing message had, of long-awaited necessity, been for Calvin30's eyes-only. The magnitude of the earthquake it would trigger was boundless and the time to react too short, thus the crude hack job that C16 had uncovered.

"No emerging urgency Boss. No smoking guns to ruin our fun just some loose ends to tie up. Scared the smile off the sticky beak, but between late and never we may need to formulate a more surgical solution."

The elevator opened and Calvin30 popped down to the taxi stop. Those that passed him on his way included members of several clone series including Calvin. None, Calvin30 noted, walked or talked with birds of their own feather. Either they tried to brown their nose with some of God's Only, or they walked alone and forsaken, muttering away to themselves under hypnosis by their neurosis. The disdain towards them evident in the faces of the Originals mirrored the hole those clones had dug in their own souls.

Calvin30 puffed out his strut. He alone had not disgraced the race. Big Daddy C0 would be so proud.

Calvin Zero came from New York, a typical mixed breed bite from the Big Apple. By all reports Calvin30 had found around, C0 was a sharp-tongued, abrasive asshole. They kept cloning him a hundred years past his due date because his replicates were generally obsequious, over achieving brown-nosers. The old Alpha would be chucking in his grave if he saw the spineless marionettes the clone mills had churned out of his genes. C0 had met his maker long before Calvin30 was pipetted out of his wet dreams, but Calvin30 felt some satisfaction in inferring that the original version of the Calvin line had constructed some strategy to maintain self-respect. The odds for doing so were obviously 87 to two against.

Calvin30 yawned and hopped down the escalator to a landing overlooking a fifty-five-floor drop. It was a pleasant day, a light sea breeze shivering the gray green eucalyptus in the platform park, brown squirrels chasing one another down and up branches. A harsh winter sun infiltrating the thin cloud filter - another hot January day. Calvin30 waved a cab down from the rank. While waiting he switched his pipe to trumpet mode and toyed with a Chet Baker tune. He braced his breath against the blast of air from the jump jets as a driver-less volantor lowered from the sky to land on the landing. Calvin30 climbed inside. "Account Type: Local, Net, or Com?" a female voice droned in his mind.

"Mirtopik ComCred 230A75X," he thought back.

"Thank you for choosing Hsing Wen Net, please choose your destination," directed the digital driver as a map of the city beamed down through Calvin30's neurovisor. His thoughts pointed out a compound of buildings in the middle left.

"You have chosen the University of the Sovereign City of Los Angeles, is this correct?"

"You better you bet."

"Please rephrase."

"All right. Yes."

"Please select a building," the neuroview drove through a three-dimensional view of several building entrances. "Stop on the dot."

"You have chosen the Lovelock Institute of Extraterrestrial Studies, is this correct?"

"Oh Yes."

"Calculating least time pathway. Your Com charge exchange rate to *ecos* is 58 ComScript at current trading."

Calvin30 leaned back in his chair in the air. Set his seat's auto massage to attack the knots in his back, as the volantor launched off the landing pad into the uncrowded sky lanes. Down below spaghetti lines of crowded bicycle paths and criss-crossed SkyTran lines weaved over suburbs and dipped under nature corridors planted atop the old freeways. Fields in those forests were used for emergency safe landings until a driver changing a turboprop had been eaten by a bear sometime last year. Question for the court: "Was the bear still representing the State of California when he crunched said driver for lunch?"

Calvin30 surveyed the scene down the plain to East LA where the shining shimmer of cheap solar roofing tiles and aluminum rainwater tanks reflected the sun back into the clouds. Cloned homes, self-similar and self-contained, feeding the Grid to pay the mortgage. Up front, where he was flying, was Uptown, growing ever greener as it spilled into the brown hills. In better days, as LA surfed down the Second Wave and helium-3 was cheaper, terradomes of the rich and famous had shown off their wealth with garish climate conditioning. The world might be going to hell, but it's heaven by our pool.

But since the cost of giving the finger to Gaia kept going up, Uptown domes had flipped inside out with planted tree roofs mingling property lines with trespassing canopy, swapping with the terrapod buildings bound to their roots, photons and carbon for nutrient-rich nano-loot sucked from the vegan soy latte veins of those who lived inside. The houses lorded it over the lower class down Valley where desalinization ditches switched back and forth betwixt the pod homes and the public parks.

The thing was, bling was still king in LA. The obvious split between the whipped and the rich, so key to fuelling discontent, was still laid out here like nowhere else.

Calvin30 fidgeted in his seat, impatient to reach his destination. These new automated cruisers bored him. He missed his chats with real taxi drivers. They always lived worldviews dedicated to the most fascinating conspiracy theories, which were so much fun to encourage. Sadly the confederated cab Nets now only took ecos or Hub locals, either that or the discount they put on Comscript would draw unwanted attention from the auditors. And this was LA, first center of the Second Wave, the Golden Abode. Oh, the times they were a-changing.

The cruiser climbed down to the curb. "Thank you for choosing Hsing Wen Net. We look forward to driving for you again soon."

Calvin30 moved out and the cab hurtled off down the drive, missing the mops of a group of undergrads by an exact, mindfully micro risk margin.

He ascended some stairs into an unimpressive concrete square that must have been at least a century past tense. The walls were clean, but the scent of mildew was omnipresent. Along the walls were holoframes brimming with maps and images of other stars and planets magnified from the miniscule into magnificence. People were seeing into the heavens these days the way Calvin30 saw into people - with great detail but you couldn't go there.

He wound his way into a maze of hallways threaded with fiber cable conduits and stopped before a set of white doors with an environmental hazard sign painted on them. He pushed an old-fashioned intercom button. A grandfatherly English man wearing a gray, threadbare cardigan opened the doors, "oh Dr. Twelve, it's good you've finally made it. Please do step in."

"Dr. Keith Myren. My pleasure in perpetuum." Calvin30 had bumped across the good doctor at a Dublin astronomical symposium, which he had infiltrated under cover as one of his brothers, a non-descript section manager from Mirtopik astromechanics.

"Come, come this way, I'm excited to show you something."

Calvin30 followed him to the back of a large room stacked with boxes, filing cabinets, and white boards until they stopped at an ancient style computer console on a desk piled with yellowed papers. No one had thought to give the coffee cups a rinse for a geologic era. Faded doodles, obscure notes, abstruse comic strips, and calendars of years past littered the walls. To stand closer to the good doctor, Calvin found it necessary to reposition three freestanding whiteboards filled with scientific graffiti. Myren blithely tapped away on a centuries old computer console, navigating a long succession of directory webs before reaching his destination. Calvin30 took note of the pass code over the old man's shoulder. No neural imprints or other impediments would interfere with his return.

"I have just found the sort of thing that you suggested to me the other day. As you know we have been working at converting the Oort telescope array to include gravimetric readings. Of course, you know, this was all your idea. I forget. Oh yes, here it is on the screen. This is Scorpio 18. A rather uninteresting star at first glance, G class, like our sun really, fairly typical. Except when we look closer." After an awkwardly long period of staring intently at a spinning hourglass, the screen painstakingly zoomed to a new focus.

"Oh, bother this software - I refuse to upgrade. It seems to me that the Nets and the Coms between the two of them are never going to produce a stable platform. Okay there, in close proximity to the star, just at the pointer."

It was not at all clear what, in the blurry blob, was the big deal.

"There, you see? Two concentric rings perhaps asteroid fields, except they seem to be attracted to some massive objects resting within their respective orbits. The gravimetric sensors and x-ray emissions confirm your prediction. There is no other conclusion possible. What we have here are two small black holes in close orbit about this star. Truly amazing isn't it, I've never seen anything quite like this. How did you ever suspect it? Let's take a grand tour, shall we? I've generated a neurosim from the astronomical readings and from your theoreticals. Here, have a seat so you won't lose balance."

As the neurosim loaded Calvin30 saw the floor drop soundlessly below his feet as he floated through the ceiling and above a quickly vanishing campus, countryside, continent, planet, and solar system. Light started to stretch apart, blue ahead and red behind until a sudden splash of soft blue permeated the whole view.

"Cerenkov light," giggled Myren admiringly. "Those programmers think of everything."

Behind them the red became encircled in in rings of the blue, an odd contrast of color like the spectrum had swallowed itself.

"It's impossible of course," chortled Myren. You can't go faster than light in a vacuum, but in water you can, and it gives off this kind of sonic boom composed of blue light. Very good imagination the chaps who designed this transition."

Soon the light rings began to contract back over them, tightening until they vanished into the blue, and then their view resolved into discernible things. As they zoomed in on their objective, Calvin30 shivered from deja vu. The black maw chewing up the stars and jawing down a planet. The multi-headed screams as the multitudes were consumed. Too sentient to dismiss, but too long ago and far away to fuss much over.

As they flew closer in their spaceship of thought it became clear that, instead of one hole in space, there were two.

"Amazing, simply impossible for there to be a pair like this," pondered the Professor in wonder.

The room faded back into view as the neurosim finished.

"Now how did you guess it was there?" asked Myren bending over the edge of his desk.

"Here," Calvin30 shoved over sheaves of paper covered with mathematical formulae and incomprehensible diagrams interpreted by anonymous Syns from bits of the aliens' feed. He was hoping Myren would give him the vital confirmation.

"Let me see," Myren tapped at the computer to bring up some reference files. "Yes, yes, ah hum. And this here is the cosmological constant? A very unusual notation."

Calvin nodded knowingly at the indicated squiggle and watched as the professor read and returned to the keyboard to bring up further references.

"Quite an amazing hypothesis. Yes, the mathematics checks out. Yes. Yes. Congratulations, I'm afraid that you've managed to describe here a physical process that is entirely impossible."

"How so?"

"How so?" Myren crinkled his nose and squinted back at Calvin30. "Oh, I see you are being modest. Quite right. If this were true it would be amazing. Here," he indicated a row amidst the arcane mathematical script that

Calvin30 had handed him, "you've reconciled generating a stable region of negative energy with the Second Law of Thermodynamics. I mean, this statement here, it effectively allows you to twist space-time back on itself, but only for a while, eh? Buy now, pay later. Fascinating stuff. Of course, interesting mathematics is just a starting point. It would be necessary to check its consistency with the Physics, to create experiments to validate it. I myself am, of course, highly sceptical that it would work but the elegance of it, it is so revolutionary that you would think it had been developed by some advanced extra-terrestrial civilisation. That is what you Mirtopik chaps are all about, isn't it?" Myren scanned Calvin30 with a conspiratorial glance.

Calvin30 noted the indicated sections and repossessed the sheets.

"On that, my dear colleague, I cannot comment."

"Good God, do you think that the bizarre configurations of these debris fields might be due to the decay of some kind of locally coupled singularity. One that might have been purposely generated? Fascinating, but how is this observation connected to theory? Besides the atypical patterns of debris, Scorpio 18 is a typical class G star, one much like our own in fact. As you suggest, I see nothing that would draw my attention to it as a test case for such a revolutionary physical theory. Instead I would have thought that you would be studying high energy field dynamics around quasars or looking at black hole event horizons."

"We can't really reveal our antecedents on this just yet, what with resources so competitive these days. Doubtless you follow." Myren acquiesced and grimaced sympathetically. "Yes. Competition for Com funds has become exceedingly aggressive of late - not like the halcyon days of the Second Wave."

Calvin30 reassured his friend. "My lineup is still polishing off the speculative edges, but I promise you that the final effort will be a collaborative submission. We'll develop the physical thesis and you'll furnish the empirical verification. Perchance by March - to Astrophysiks. I guarantee that this will be a landmark treatise but can't reveal more for discernable reasons."

Myren returned Calvin30 a conspiratorial smile. "Of course, I've already begun my draft from our earlier conversations, but I'll need some details."

"You are the sole person in your patch with secure access to the Oort Array, aren't you?" Calvin30 merrily interrogated Dr. Myren's eyes. "We don't need the street to compete in our beat."

"Oh no. Only myself on this one. No one else."

"And you are not connected with the Nets?"

"Oh no, perish the thought. We are a Com funded institution. I mean, this is LA after all."

Calvin30 pondered the Doctor's response while his thoughts composed around a possible plot. In due time, he might need his friend to rescind this loyalty. A disputable old nut shaking the tree for the Opposition could be useful, as Myren was a scientist and society was accustomed to ignoring them.

"Well then, we do have our season. For these reasons, can you restrict access to those feeds?"

"You can count on me Dr. Twelve. Pray do not keep us in the dark for too long."

"I'll be contacting you post haste, just keep people pointed away from that patch in the sky, and not a peep to the public, especially your pupils."

"Oh no, perish the thought."

Calvin30 observed with pleasure the glow building in Myren's eyes. The old fish had sucked down the sinker and the bait, slowly sipping tea while the hook set in his jowls.

Dr. Keith escorted his mysterious, newest best friend to the door. "A Nobel Prize, I am sure of it. We must move this fellow along before it is too late."

Outside, Calvin30's mind revolved while he waited for the cab to drop in. Such an ecstatic buzz it was to zoom in on the cosmic residue of the aliens' denouement. For a moment Calvin30 ruminated on the deranged game he was contemplating. Across all days of yore and the ordinary course of human avarice, it wouldn't take a prophet to forebode that, given the choice, the aliens' warning would be ignored. Even with clues from his dear PhD to boost the alarms, most would choose glory in their own time over some chance of future horror. Look what they'd done already, turning up the Earth's thermostat past tolerable for the smallest of instant comforts. Why wouldn't the desolations of strange races far away in cosmic spaces only happen in such places? Far be it for a common clone to interpose before such a probable garden path.

For a moment he considered leaving well enough alone, but then, in Calvin30's augmented mind, August buzzed another frantic memo to his clone. Suddenly the time horizon unclouded. The question was control, and to be the sole holder of this whole truth was like winning the lottery. It would be arrogant for such a lowly clone as he to throw away to swine such glorious pearls so carefully sown. No, he would confer them sparingly, one by one, and along the way he'd have his fun. Resolving a scheme, Calvin30 framed which scenes to critically omit when he transmitted the bits back to Saturn during the night shift. Then he neuro-chatted up some Hax crowd to evaporate the professor's data cloud.

The cab sat, meter running, while Calvin30 stood on the curb-side absorbed in thought. He felt the sea breeze on his face and looked up out over Santa Monica as the clouds parted to reveal the half-built needle of the Mirtopik Com building piercing the skyline. In the original marketing, the building was meant to demonstrate technologies that would one day build an elevator into orbit, but the money had run-out mid-construction. People had moved in anyway once it became apparent that it needn't be completed. Many of the offices were rented by the Nets and other sworn enemies of Mirtopik.

Amidst a sea of such unfinishable ambitions it was the best part of humanity to settle on compromise. Only proper and decent to take things halfway, to a comfortable mediocrity. Halfway between this and that, between stasis and chaos, between heaven and hell, between the Earth and Moon and Stars. Maybe, if the universe can't pick us out, it won't destroy us. The real reason 'once-offs' hated clones, Calvin30 surmised, was because they were secretly jealous. When the Big Sky Guy decides to let fly with the thunderbolts, with clones there's always a good chance He'll pick the wrong one.

So, given that halfway was where people liked to take things, where do they end up? After all, halfway between something and somewhere was usually nothing and nowhere. A simple choice, like worm holes with unlimited promise, but with ultimate consequences. Where would people find the halfway in that?

The cab's horn attracted his attention and Calvin30 climbed inside, but his eyes stayed with the incomplete peak of the Mirtopik building. He smiled smugly as he wetted the reed in his pipe. Take one fuzzy blur of an interstellar grave, add one magnificent age-old dream of manifest destiny, and divide the difference. That was the standard recipe. Very, very few people knew how to go halfway properly. John Coltrane for one, that mystic prophet of 20th Century jazz, ground zero of Calvin30's musical heroes.

Paranoid brothers who break out in rashes
Flaky professors with neurodrive crashes
Such simple joys in the gifts that I bring
These are a few of my favorite things.

Start with an improvisation ringed around a familiar melody. Calvin30 began to blow. Halfway between the two, if you knew where to find it, was a Love Supreme.

UP FROM THE ROOTS

‘As he was sitting there, Ven. Ananda said to the Blessed One, "This is half of the holy life, lord: admirable friendship, admirable companionship, admirable camaraderie.
"Don't say that, Ananda. Don't say that. Admirable friendship, admirable companionship, admirable camaraderie is actually the whole of the holy life. "

~Shakyamuni Buddha, Upaddha Sutta

CHAPTER 7

Francesca

Francesca pulled her hand out from the front of her pants and reached for her cup of cold instant coffee and gulped and gagged herself awake. There was no accounting for taste with this nasty stuff. The volume of the weirdo clone's music she'd recorded from the Deep Space network jumped up in her neurovisor in concert with the abrupt rush of awareness. She hummed along as she headed to the bathroom to wash up.

She'd been listening to the music aimed at the stars all through her night shift, which blended with her day shift. Basically, Francesca mostly slept in her office because it was the only place that felt like hers since for ages. The music wasn't bad really, and her musical education, in common with all kids growing up on the streets in Cuba, was coming back to her, which she liked. This guy was inspired, which made her reconsider a prejudice or two she had about clones. The only thing about the recording that bugged her was the static, like something was running in the background. It was a shame this guy didn't record direct through the audio feed on his instrument instead of recording from a remote mike, especially if this was going to be travelling through the galaxies for the next billion years. Actually, it was annoying because sometimes it sounded like a digital squeal, like the guy had feedback going on. With music this good, why was the recording so lousy? Sometimes it got so bad she'd catch herself actually jamming to the background stuff and not the song.

"Hi Wolf," Francesca called as she passed on her way back to her office. The new blonde bitch warming him up gave her the Evil Eye like she was saying no go on Wolfy's wormy frame. Francesca crossed herself just to be safe. Even as white knuckle as things had got in that department, Wolf's measly ass would have a hard time making it onto the menu. Francesca returned with a cold, flat, *who-the-shit-are-you-do-I-care?* look and kept walking.

"Hey, Francesca," Wolf came down the corridor after her, which must have pissed the blonde chick off. "Francesca, can you do me a favor?"

"Sure."

"Look. I need to review the feeds from Deep Space and we are short staffed. I was wondering."

"I'm pretty busy." She wasn't really. Francesca was more bored out of her mind than she'd been in forever, but you had to say that, or people would start asking why you were there.

"Well, yeah, I know. It's such a thing, but I'm really in a bind."

"Okay." Because she was such a great zero hero.

"Okay? What? Really?"

"Sure. Don't make a habit of it though. Boss wants me on the ball - not doing too much other stuff." It was bullshit. No one had talked to her in the last month.

"Oh terrific, this is really, really great."

Francesca smiled at her cup-flowing-over generosity. "It's cool."

Wolf linked his neurovisor with hers and bumped over some mnemes with instructions and pass codes. "Basically, what you need to do is," *blah, blah, blah.* Francesca picked up on the job pretty quickly, just open the mnemes and look them over, highlight the clear bits and run pattern recognition software to tease stuff out of the garbage bits.

"So, this is what, alien stuff?" Actually, that part seemed interesting.

"Sure, some of it is. Most is just standard diagnostics and astronomical observations though. It is pretty rare to pick up ET. We've only seen a handful, but they're in there."

Francesca walked back to her lair and shot a few more wadded paper baskets in the trash-can before starting in on the new job. It was, if possible, more boring than scanning for Hax attacks that never seemed to happen. She slipped her hand down her pants again to give the itch a scratch and pulled it out in alarm. Who was she going to imagine herself with anyway? The talking head of August Bridges as always blabbing away on the staff video monitor? A bit boring because everyone had had him already. And there wasn't any good local material, the staff in this section was way too nerdy. And besides, hadn't she'd told herself she had to get a grip. The only direction this led to was cheap and nasty, but despite herself she grabbed a towel out of her locker and signed out to go to the ComSec gym.

An hour later she was doing something physically hot with some mentally vacant dude who was sprawled out under her on a storeroom table somewhere.

The idiot had the audacity to want to shower with her afterwards before she had to tell him to get out of her space. It was the predictability, after the initial rush, which wore her down. She knew the shrink-wrap around it, a way to reclaim power because of what happened to her when she was a kid. It was more impersonal than that really, she just wanted something that wasn't pathetic like that guy. It was hope really, giving humanity the benefit of the doubt. If basically she wasn't an optimist, why would she keep getting let down by the sorry state of people? You let them in and they mostly couldn't even stay hard let alone stay clear.

Francesca towelled off, dressed, and headed back to the lift. Great and lousy always seemed to come together at the same package like two sides of the same coin. The lift opened to a strange looking man who seemed puzzlingly familiar, as though she had run into him many times but was also seeing him for the first time. There was a strange vibe coming off him, as much as he tried to cover it by making out like he hadn't a care in the world, which of course couldn't be true because everyone did.

"I know you. You're the new face in Deep Space."

Friendly guy. Francesca knew all about friendly guys. She played it cool.

"That's me."

"I see. Wolfie's saying you like my playing."

The clone. That's why he seemed so familiar. Francesca mentally ran through the faces she'd seen since arriving in Mirtopik and concluded that she'd definitely run across his brothers, spread across a range of ages. Weird stuff.

"Yeah. You're good." Her intuition told her to play the dumb Comsec lugnut role here. "Some of it reminds me of the stuff where I grew up."

"Oh yes, Latino jazz is unsurpassed. I am happy to pass on more of my pieces. It is a pleasure to perform for those who who appreciate *el primo*."

This guy had a strange way of talking. It reminded her of Green Eggs and Ham, that crazy book she used to read to Elena. Like a cloud passing behind another cloud her mood darkened.

"Uh. Thanks," she muttered, "I'd like that."

"Consider it my pleasure." The clone pulled the instrument hanging on his neck strap and started to play various riffs as mnemes started to stack up in Francesca's public neuroview directory. "I've indexed my songs by notes not words, from my end it cuts in thirds how long it takes to float tracks to my friends."

End friend song long fox in a box on a train in the rain. This joker was on top of some game, and Francesca was definitely going to screen those files for Hax and hooks before she listened to them.

"That's cool," she smiled approvingly.

She swore the clone's eyes sparkled. Francesca felt drawn in despite herself.

"Let me know if you think anything syncs. I'll transmit through some more."

"Thanks. What's your name?"

The clone paused for a moment and his brow furrowed, a chink in his charm.

"Calvin30. C30 to my friends."

"Thanks Calvin."

The clone got off the lift a few floors down. Francesca's mind went into overdrive. She had a gut feel that meeting hadn't happened by accident, there was a heavy pull around the guy and she was going to be careful about getting sucked in. As strong as the impulse was to google his details through the ComSec system, she had a feeling he would be on to her game the minute she did. Francesca found an observation lounge with a forever view and laid back on the couch to check out the files. Satisfied that they were clean of viruses, she opened one to listen to. Right on target it hit her most raw nerve.

It was long ago in a shitty little apartment with dirty windows in Havana. Drunk men being un-gainfully employed with music shifted in and out of the rented storage containers across the street. They were playing the same song back then that Francesca was listening to now in her neuroview. They kept breaking and starting over because they were too wasted to get it right. They were pathetic and more dangerous because of that. Francesca ignored them and concentrated on drawing pictures with her niece, trying to out monster the monsters. They were bringing amazing super-heroines into being. Laser beam nails, and fairy wings, and jaguar spots that looked stylishly bad-ass.

A late afternoon rain flurry rattled the tin roof. Elena looked adoringly up at her with those big soulful brown eyes, "What super powers do you have Tia?"

"Me? I am invincible. Nothing can stop me," Francesca had bragged, in a way that was soon shown to be hollow. They ran amok around the apartment. Francesca deliberately took the full brunt of whatever missiles Elena could hurl at her. As Francesca fell back laughing on a lounge, Elena hurled herself head first into her midsection and winded her.

"Tia, are you okay?"

Francesca recovered and rose to her full adolescent stature. "Huh that? What do you expect from being hit by a meteor? But it hasn't stopped me."

The rain stopped and, along with it, the music. Francesca only noticed as the sound of drunken voices came bumbling up to the landing outside the door. That meant Hector was coming back. Francesca hated that guy, her sister's new husband. When her sister was away, like tonight, he was always sleazing, touching her ass or coming up behind her and sliding his hand under her shirt and making some lame joke about how her melons were ripening.

"Jesus. You're drunk." was a complaint that was safe but never diffused anything, and only excused the creepy behavior. Her sister was so desperate around the asshole; he had her so wrapped around his greedy fingers that she couldn't say a word. In fact, the bitch got jealous, as if it was Francesca, at fifteen, who was some kind of temptress coming onto that detestable bastard. And Momma, where was she? Who was she? Who the hell knew that? Even when she was at home laid up in her bed and not whoring around the town looking for some white knight that always turned into some kind of dark abscess on what was left of their family. For sure she had had to deal with worse than Hector over the years, a lot of guys had beat the crap out Momma and her sister and her as the result of one drunken tantrum or another. What a bunch of crybabies.

The door slammed open and Elena grabbed her hand so tight at that moment that she thought it would squeeze off. By the time Francesca looked down to comfort Elena, the tables had turned.

Elena looked up at her with wide steady eyes. "I'm not afraid. You can stop them Tia. Nothing can stop you."

"Yeah, don't worry querida. We'll be all right."

Elena smiled conspiratorially back at her. "I know." But Francesca didn't know anything.

"Hey Hector. There's that sly little puta with the ripe pechonas. Mind if I break her in man?"

Francesca froze. Hector she could probably handle, but two men?

"There ain't nothing to break-in, not in this town. I don't mind amigo. Don't leave no marks though. The little one's a biter, you got to watch for that."

Shit. The offhand way Hector had said it, even through the separation of many years, still made Francesca's blood cool.

The stranger, now a faded blur of menace in her memory, stumbled towards them. He was big.

"Get him Tia," screamed Elena, daring the stranger to bring it on.

Francesca tentatively stepped forward, guarding her niece.

"A fighter eh?" smirked the stranger, the stench of rum he brought in on him was the only part of him that had stayed with her. One swing and Francesca was flying. He towered over her, laughing, as he fumbled with the buckle on his belt.

"Hey Man. I said no marks," shouted Hector. The man's attention wandered behind him.

"Say she fell down."

It was an opening and Francesca went through it. She kicked the stranger with everything she had and, unbalanced with his pants part down, he fell.

"Hey. Fucking bitch."

Francesca pushed past Hector knocking his drunk ass over and ran to the landing and her freedom and her eternal imprisonment.

"Tia! Tia!" Elena shouted desperately. "Come back. Come back. Finish them."

And that was it. Just a few things happening for some stupid short moments and then you couldn't go back. She *was* coming back - she'd promised. She'd come back, as soon as she found someone who cared. She'd come back. She'd been coming back to these moments for seventeen years and the shame burned unbearably in her soul each time. Francesca had been only a teenager then, but she could look for all the excuses she liked, and it didn't change the fact that she had still gone, leaving Elena to God knows what fate, and hadn't done shit for her since.

How old would Elena be now, mid 20s or something? No, she would always be nine, looking up to her Tia without fear, waiting for her to finish them off, defender of the goddamn stinking universe. What a pathetically useless superhero she was.

Francesca flipped off the music and squeezed her head, hoping it would just pop off. The hole in her heart grew ten thousand times, so big she fell straight into it and wished she'd never crawl out. And she laid like that sprawled out on the couch sobbing and feeling sorry for herself listening to that painful music. And then the music stopped, and some idiot came into the lounge and looked at her with equal measures of pity, bemusement, and discomfort until Francesca hauled her ass up out of it.

Propping herself against a wall Francesca stood up on her quivering legs and began an impossible walk to the door. With each step forward, she recovered some power. Smoothing her uniform, she reconstructed herself. The hole in her heart stayed put, but her body walked on away from it. Why was it one event in a life could become the center of the whole thing? Like you could run as fast as you wanted, but you'd still be orbiting it from the same distance and hadn't really gotten anywhere at all?

As Francesca headed to the mess for dinner she turned her mind to more recent problems. Like what that criminal clone was up to - that's what she wanted to know. Something began to bug her, something little and hardly noticeable, which was the sort of thing that always turned out to be at the middle of everything. Something too small for most people to notice, when they weren't paying attention, but there it was, bugging the shit out of her, and she didn't know what it was.

She bought her soup and sat down by a window to slurp it. The rain was coming down hard, one of those freak storms that made the whole Needle sway. It made the city below, its buildings outlined by low watt LEDs to keep a skyline going at night, roll. They flickered in and out from under a bank of quickly moving clouds, looking like broken moonlight on a choppy sea.

"Hey there." Mister Freak from her afternoon delight waved at her from the doorway.

Francesca flipped on the music to better ignore him and started going through the Deep Space files. To the guy's credit he caught the bitch vibe and went to sit with his friends. Maybe she'd give him a chance again, probably not. See ya.

Gracias a Dios the track she was listening to was not Latin. Another slurp on her mug and then it came all in one flash. She almost dropped her mug into her lap. This kind of stuff happened to her like that. First some feeling, like an itch she couldn't quite scratch, and then, bang, the whole enchilada.

This was the thing. The sound quality on this new stuff from the clone was flawless, just perfect, no ticks or squawks or tweets. Nothing except the music. Why would the clone serve up his best stuff to a perfect stranger and send out shit to the universe? Would aliens decline to come invade this pathetic planet because the sound quality was questionable? It didn't make sense at all. And the reason why?

Francesca cracked open the Deep Space files and opened them on the audio player, volume low. And there it was, the crap. She listened to music sent to the stars and flicked back to other Deep Space files listening to them not watching them. The crap again. That same crap. When the clone was sending the music out, he was getting things back. So, this is why the higher-ups didn't mind. The music wasn't serenading any potential Sleestack army from Alpha Centauri. It wasn't going anywhere. It was going up so they could get the stuff coming back down before anyone else saw it.

Francesca started going over the files, checking the signatures, and listening. And there it was, a few weeks or maybe a month later after the music went out the 'official' file with the exact same pattern of crackle and pop would come in.

Her soup sat there going cold. When she finally reached for it, she noticed someone familiar watching her through the marbled glass as he walked calmly past in the hallway outside the cafe without breaking his stride. As if he had only casually glanced her way, but just intently enough that she had felt it on the back of her neck. Was it her mind playing tricks, another clone in his series perhaps? How many clones wore a musical instrument around their neck as they padded about? Did he want to send her a message, that he had caught her catching him in the act? Francesca had no idea and the thing was, in anyway that would make a difference to her besides the welcome distraction of solving a puzzle, she wasn't sure she cared.

CHAPTER 8

Kalsang

Kalsang was exhausted. He was eating only intermittently, with no sense of daily interval. No more calls had come in to interrupt him, not even system checks from the engineers on Earth, which was unusual. The overwhelming feelings of compassion he felt for these strange beings only grew steadier. Like this, from moment to moment, they seemed lovelier and closer. But these beings had been dead so long. Their world maybe didn't exist already when his grandparents were born, or possibly before. Even to talk to Aurora back on Mars, it took many hours for their messages to travel back and forth. How much further away had the alien's world been?

Maybe it was the powerful circumstance through which they first came into his mind that had given them such clarity. Even when he relaxed a bit. Even in his dreams. They were such an intense vision that he caught himself talking to them, reassuring them so they wouldn't find their sudden transport into these strange cramped quarters too disturbing. They had strange names.

"Not to worry dGhani. Your Anila is right there, isn't it?" Kalsang imagined himself pinching the cheeks of a young one whose second face was only starting to bud. dGhani's first face glanced up and sniffed, almost smiling.

"Ah good. See, right there. Yes, you see?"

Of course, no matter how he consoled them, they would revert subtly, and the horrified stare they had held in their eyes when he first saw them would return. Then, sometimes, he would cry a little for each of them.

It wasn't so much a deluded mental factor, Kalsang felt sure that his precious teacher, Lama Wangmo, had intervened to catch him from going down that path. The beings were just there in a very substantial way that was very easy to visualise. Like the path up to the gompa at Lhopa Khantsen where he had spent his days as a young monk. Very comfortable, but not too attached, because he had moved away from there so long ago and was excited to leave for more training. So not deluded, but odd.

"Are you taking us home Melded One?"

The request came in that eerie whalesong voice, but somehow Kalsang could understand what the girl meant.

"Home is always here, isn't it? Small room, big universe," he widened his hands apart for effect. "Always here," Kalsang pointed at his heart.

The being, dSong, was that her name? She smiled sadly but didn't seem convinced. Kalsang felt reproach there, at how little it seemed he had to offer when so great had been her loss. There was a fine line between wisdom and platitude, and he feared he had crossed it.

"I don't know if I can, but I will try."

dSong returned his smile with a faith Kalsang felt he hadn't earned.

"I will try."

At that she faded back into the huddle of aliens, despite Kalsang struggling to hold on to her appearance. He had lost her again. It was a strange thought. Wasn't this the first time they had met?

The aliens, as a group, remained though, steady in his mind's eye, and Kalsang enjoyed giving the light out to them, making them clearer and clearer. It was amazing really, how a people so long erased had come back to life in him. He felt so responsible for them.

And then, after some time, his focus began to dim, and a subtle dullness began to permeate his concentration. The mind lost its lustre and refused to sharpen despite strenuous effort. Finally, he found himself struggling to stay awake whenever he sat down on his meditation cushion. There was nothing to do in such cases but to let things go for a while.

Kalsang brought to mind the mneme Aurora had sent just before the aliens had come. She was so upset. No one is listening Kalsang. No one is listening. A whole world of unique life, billions of years in the making, the only other lifeforms we can actually touch. Our own sisters in our own solar system, and we are going to destroy them before we even know them.

What to say? Aurora floated in his mind next to d'Song and they seemed to be asking the same question. Why was there so much pain? So much ignorance? Destroying the tiny beings on Mars seemed trivial beside the horrific loss d'Song's people had suffered, but the cause was the same. From the technological diagrams, which opened the aliens' mneme, the destruction of their world was something they themselves must have created. They wouldn't have known what they were losing when they set it up.

"I understand Aurora, it is so sad, but never give up. Never give up. Do what you have to do. It is the only way isn't it? Like that. And I am always with you."

Kalsang sent the message, which was inadequate but all he could do. What to do? For a moment Kalsang was paralysed with anxiety. What could a small monk so far away do for anybody? Was he just taking some vacation out here when he was needed elsewhere? There were a thousand arguments both ways, but what worried him most was that up until now his decisions to travel so far away had seemed too comfortable, as if he had made them before. Did he have some karmic habit of running away?

It was too much to hold in the mind, which Kalsang decided he needed to stabilize now. Something other than thought. He needed exercise. Kalsang tried to practice prostration. Again and again his hands onto his crown, forehead, throat, and heart before he carefully lowered himself downward to a prone position before the altar and slowly stood back up again. It took such concentration in the low gravity to avoid shooting forward into the wall and bouncing about the cabin. Standing up while keeping his balance was very tricky. After stumbling like a drunken monkey for too long he gave up and sat down.

Kalsang checked his texts. One by Sogyal Rinpoche, a great 21st Century Master, recommended going for a walk. Kalsang carefully wrapped up his book and placed it back on the altar. He looked out the portal across the dim glow of the pink snow-scape of an entirely alien world and grimaced. It occurred to him that he had never actually been outside. Not just him, no human being had. Such a mysterious unexplored world waiting out there. Why had he not once contemplated going outside?

In a cabinet in the docking station was stashed a canister, which contained an emergency space suit. Kalsang opened it up, stretched it out along the cabin floor, and inspected it. The internal diagnostic computer gave an all clear on the suit's integrity. The suit was in two parts and joined on a metal ring at the waist. Kalsang pulled on the suit and fastened the top to the bottom. He attached the gloves and boots and, after inspecting the seals, donned the helmet. When all equipment had been checked over and was positioned correctly, he ordered the evacuation of air from the lock and the door opened out onto the brave new world.

Kalsang stood in the angled doorway, looking out as, for the first time his hermitage moon was liberated from the small, immobile lenses of the cabin portals. Before him was a silently vibrant world awaiting investigation.

One small step for a monk.

Kalsang stepped out of the capsule.

Once on the surface his little outing quickly became intoxicating. What a wonderful place. He skipped around, kicking the snow up into wispy puffs that never seemed to settle.

Wow.

He bounced around in wobbly dance losing his balance often. Out of sheer joy he bounced randomly into the low sky. This was more fun.

"He, he, he."

He rolled on the ground creating a flurry of the strange talcum powder snow that for a short time obscured his vision, confusing him.

Oh no, he had better be careful.

He propped himself into a seating position, panting, and waited for the hazy smoke of snow to settle.

As his view returned he was overwhelmed by it.

Outlining the horizon were the surprisingly high walls of the impact crater within which his Terrapod rested. The floor of the crater was crisscrossed with smoky pink snow berms, unusually symmetrical as they built up over the eons from the pathways of snow ejected from the bizarre black geysers that covered this part of Triton. Other parts of the crater floor were perfectly polished lenses of nitrogen ice where the internal heat of the moon, generated by tidal friction with Neptune, had slowly, at sometime in the remote past, thawed the surface. The geyser contrails traced parallel black lines across the low sky. The ominous indigo mass of Neptune slowly rolled across the background of night. Amazing.

The aliens had followed him out and were enjoying his fun. They swam about him, their tentacles whirling round in a graceful dance, their skin radiating a pink glow matched to the surrounding that made them appear to dissolve into and out of view.

The small ones, especially, jumping at the chance to play like little monkeys. d'Song and d'Gnnr chased the others trying to tag them, squealing in high-pitched voices that sounded like dolphin chatter.

"Ha ah ah."

It was good to see them all having a good time.

They made a short hike over to a patch of ice, polished so smooth that when he bent over he could see his own face reflected back, or rather his toothy grin lit up by the lights in the helmet.

He had not aged as much as he thought he might have, but he did look less baby-faced and more serious.

"Oh, how handsome. Hmmm." That's what Amala used to say to him. His fingers attempted to snap within their padded gloves.

"Temporary."

He noted with minor alarm the length of time he had been out and hopped back towards the shining lights of the Terrapod. He stood by the side, taking one last look around, and began to climb up the gantry.

Two of his right hands reached for the railing to pull him up the last step but missed. They passed right through.

How had that happened?

Kalsang slipped on the ladder, and slowly tumbled feet over head down to the ground. He bounced several times in slow motion before coming to a rest. Methane and nitrogen snow exploded from the surface in great glittery puffs with each impact and additional disturbances caused by the flying monk's flailing arms. He lay where he fell for some time, giggling uncontrollably.

When Kalsang finally recovered himself and tried to sit up he found that he couldn't. His suit was over pressurised, blown up like a great balloon. Movement was impossible.

As he struggled his situation seemed more and more impossible. There was no one who could help him and the thought that he would freeze alone here became more and more solid. The ice of fear was already beginning to grow in his heart. Panic seized Kalsang's mind, until he remembered to let it in and not hold it out. The way Mila had conquered his demons. Invite them in.

What a way to die, he thought at that moment, remembering how giddy from the novelty of his adventure he had been only a short time before, completely hilarious. Kalsang chuckled and this helped to calm his nerves.

What a way to die. A frozen monk blimp slowly collecting snow dust until he was completely covered over, a nice little hill of pink. Cold hell karma left over from flicking some flea out in the cold? Because he was a famous monk, maybe they would write about his death, so dignified.

"There once was this Khenpo from Drugu who did that, and his space suit puffed up and he froze into the surface of the furthest moon." Such a lesson for the young monks about fleas.

The aliens shuffled around him looking concerned, but they couldn't help anyone.

"He, he, he. And then," Kalsang told them, "when they come looking for me, if they bother, all they find is an open door and no Kalsang, no tracks, just a little pink pile. You will have to tell them where to find me."

He could feel the aliens' concern for him, their worry for his well-being in each of their many eyes.

They sang to him in that strange whale song and he found it comforting.

After he blinked the tears from his eyes, Kalsang looked around for a way out of his predicament. His neurovisor was knocked to the side of head and wouldn't refocus no matter how hard he twisted his neck. His wrist-pad might have a pressure regulator on it, but he could barely move his arms to his sides, let alone across his body. He marshalled a concentrated effort, kicking from one side to the other like an inverted turtle. No luck. Amazing how the distance from one hand to the other could have such a dramatic problem, while flying for light-hours had seemed so ho hum.

What to do?

Panic. Come on in. Have a comfortable seat and bring your laser beam focus with you.

The suit sensor secondary output on the rim of Kalsang's helmet indicated that he still had plenty of oxygen. There was time for the solution to his quandary that might be floating around in the back of his mind to come to him. But of course, this might truly be the end of his life. Karma of this lifespan couldn't be added to.

Thinking this way triggered a wave of nostalgia. Death as a meditation topic was certainly more abstract than death as an experience. What would he miss? Tibet? His family? His monastery? The aliens? Although Kalsang had fond memories these aspects of his life in one way or another seemed remote, as if they had happened to someone else. It would be sad to say goodbye, but these people and situations had all changed since he had last experienced them, and a new rebirth would reunite him with family and friends lost long ago. No, his sadness seemed to orbit about this single point; that would not have a chance to complete his guru's instructions.

Kalsang found his mind travelling out across space to another time. A song floated to his lips.

Wisdom and compassion must flow
between one heart and another.
Listening, contemplating, and meditating are the means.
The kindness of the guru is the essence.

"Please, oh my Lama, protect me from fears!"

And, to calm himself, Kalsang turned his mind to her life story and the special qualities she possessed.

Lama Tsultrim Wangmo was exceptional as a guru in almost every way. One could begin with her gender. She was a woman who became one of the most highly regarded Lamas within the male dominated Tibetan monastic system. The Dalai Lama had recognised her as the latest incarnation in a long line of Tulkus reaching back to the bodhisattva Langri Tangpa, and she was also said to be an embodiment of Green Tara, the Female Bodhisattva of active compassion. However, Lama Wangmo was no Golden Child. She had earned her credentials the hard way.

She was originally named Zhang Li An. Her mother was Tibetan and her father Chinese, a professor of Astronautics at the prestigious Shanghai University. She was inseparable from her father and followed on his coat tails to begin a prestigious career as an astrophysicist with her doctoral thesis on the effect of gravitational lensing on extraterrestrial radio transmissions. Then the accident happened. Her parents, on the way to her dissertation, lying dead amongst the twisted wreckage at the base of a collapsed bridge.

Beyond consolation, Li An left the city for a while to visit the relatives she had never known - her mother's family in Tibet. There was a scandal. Li An's mother had followed her husband to the city. There urban snobbishness towards all things rural, and persistent Han chauvinism towards those of alternative ethnicity, conspired to embarrass Li An's ambitious father. In deference to her husband's sensitivities, Li An's mother had buried her past. The decision became a source of secret shame, for to deny one's ancestors showed great disrespect in both Chinese and Tibetan cultures.

Li An, while cleaning the apartment, had found the shoe box of unsent letters. Please forgive me my beautiful mother.

Kalsang imagined Li An driving her jeep apprehensively through a large herd of sheep and up on a group of yak hair tents, worrying about the impending reunion. She had told Kalsang all about this. Her mind was alive with apprehensions and questions. The Chinese had been the unwelcome oppressor wasn't it? At least that's what Li An remembered from her more contemporary high school texts. Other undigested facts bubbled randomly to the surface. She had driven for days through the vast Tibetan Systems, regions within historical Tibet under Tibetan self-rule through limited sovereignty arrangements with One China Many Sys. Theoretically, as a recognized System among the Many Sys of One China, the Tibetans had formed their own Gov and had control of most internal affairs generally without outside interference. They could manage their natural resources and had veto power over immigration policies and a host of other carefully delineated powers. They had no control over foreign policy and had to conduct their economic relationships through One China according to the rather lopsided National Framework. And of course, there were many eminent Lamas she had seen on the Web performing mysterious ceremonies, lending moral credibility to public appearances by political nominees and supporting the 'renewal' of public figures who had fled to the monasteries following some scandal. She had occasionally enjoyed the broadcasts by Tibetan Buddhist monk-scholars of warm-hearted, though often erudite, religious teachings.

But her single pointed focus on her academic career and in gaining the approval of her father had been all consuming, and she had neglected to inform herself properly about her Tibetan heritage. Now, of course, she regretted this.

How her parents had met was still not entirely clear to her. And, on top of it, her father had stolen her mother away from her family, never to return. Perhaps they would be bitter? Li An braced herself for rejection. Instead she was greeted with an ocean of tears, white scarves, and warm embraces. She had come home at last.

A year or two later, when the Warming pushed the climate past another tipping point, a China on the brink had nearly fallen over. The best attempts at modern agriculture sequentially failed and the political situation fragmented. All of humanity was joined in a global anguish that, fifty years later, was yet to fully stabilise. The last Great Famine. During those amazing years, Kalsang's guru displayed extraordinary generosity by sharing everything and caring for anyone who took refuge in their village, Tibetans and Chinese alike. Night and day Li An had driven herself to exhaustion working to help others. She had once voluntarily gone without food for a month, quietly giving her own food to those more vulnerable, or frailer of mind. But, despite her efforts, many died and in a daze of despair and starvation she had wandered into the hills to die.

She had collapsed by the fire of the great Dilgo Jangchub Rinpoche, one of the greatest solitary meditators in Tibet. Kalsang smiled at the memories his name invoked. Jangchub Rinpoche was Kalsang's teacher as well. A quiet old man always dressed in a tatter of patches from discarded monks' robes. His words were few, but his instructions were profound. Kalsang felt that a few comments, delivered with the usual dry humour, from this great master conveyed more realisations than a year debating the most esoteric subjects with the best scholars of Ganden.

The proof behind this sentiment had been demonstrated when, after the famine, Li An had descended from the hills as Lobsang Wangchuk and entered Ganden Monastery, the foremost centre of the Tibetan Buddhist revival through the first half of the 21st century. Women were not even permitted to stay on the monastery grounds after dark. However, with her guru's mystic blessings, she effectively disguised her gender beneath monks' robes and was granted admission. For ten years she studied the great classics while concealing her identity. She was a brilliant student, and at the end of this time she attained the grade of Geshe Lharampa, the highest of monastic degrees, with a rank of equal first within the monastery.

Then, at the end of her examinations, His Holiness the Dalai Lama had stridden calmly up to her. "I have only one final question for the venerable Geshe. Answer this correctly and you are indisputably the best that Ganden has produced in a hundred years." All the monks had leaned forward with great anticipation. Kalsang had been there, a young boy of nine, huddled together with his classmates. What profound question was His Holiness about to put to this magnificent scholar?

"Are you a man or are you a woman?"

The great Geshe, eyes filling with tears, quietly turned and walked out of the monastery, back towards the hills from whence he had mysteriously come. As His Holiness turned to walk away Kalsang saw the old man smile and overheard the hushed remark, "how wonderful, most excellent."

Kalsang did not discover the full truth until years later when, possessed by an intense fervor, he had gone in search of the elusive scholar. Following a confusing trail of clues and rumor he had finally located the hermitage. Instead of the great Geshe, eyes full of fire and insight, he had found only a gray haired woman tending a fire. Kalsang smiled, remembering how with great pride he had marched into the campsite and declared that he was looking for his guru, the great Geshe Wangchuk.

"Perhaps you had better take a seat. Then, after a while, maybe you will be able to see the Geshe." For a week Kalsang had sat outside, bundled against the cold wind while the old woman periodically disappeared into a cave, apparently conferring with the great meditator for long hours at a time. Finally, full of impatience and impetuosity Kalsang had stood up and confronted the woman. "Look Anila, I have traveled a long way and with due respect I will not be put off any longer. I am going to ask the Geshe to be my teacher now." He then strode confidently into an empty cave.

When he emerged from the cave his puzzled expression caused the old woman to double over in laughter. His face became red with anger. Wiping the tears from her eyes she had given him a very strange look, as if she were a long lost relative of his who had not seen him in many years.

"Okay," she said, "I accept you as my student."

CHAPTER 9

August

Conversations among the assembled Directors dropped off as August's hair preceded him into the room. The divine desolation of the moonscape visible through the teardrop shaped windows of the Apollo room seemed to suck the last voices out into the surrounding vacuum. The silence that replaced them was a proper fanfare for the arrival of a god. August replied with a smile, giving his leave for the universe to continue.

Gudanko's hands twitched as he adjusted the collar on his kurta, perhaps giving away some effect of the absence of breakfast on his hypoglycaemia. Perhaps not. "I see that you have arrived. At last. We have been waiting."

Vladimir Gudanko's impeccably tailored presence dominated the far end of the room. He was the CEO of Energia Nova, a Com that had recently purchased a large interest, although not controlling, in Mirtopik. From a purely commercial angle, it was a good match. Energia Nova was the dominant space transport business. Mirtopik was the major conglomerate monopolizing the lunar Helium-3 supply, and thus controlling the fusion energy industry that had was the main power source of the expansion into space. From the perspective of the clashing personalities of the two companies' leaders, it was a disaster.

Gudanko smiled at August, or as close to a smile as the Ukrainian could approximate. August smiled back. How he loathed the man. Gudanko had been a complete pain-in-the-ass since he had come onto the Board, mounting a single-minded campaign against August's vision. What galled August the most was that Gudanko was just a numbers guy, but a relentless one. Nothing mattered more to him than the steady accumulation of the indicators of power.

Gudanko's strategic vision never rose beyond assuming control and the chief tactic he used was to bludgeon his opposition with the bottom line. August refused to see him as a worthy opponent. Now, however, the dismissiveness that he usually directed towards Gudanko was replaced by a cautious reappraisal of the man most likely to want him dead. Of course, Gudanko wouldn't act against him directly. That would require passion.

Gudanko scanned the room with opaque blue eyes. Was he counting out his alliances or confirming the locations of the bathrooms and emergency exits should the need for either arise. It might be all the same with him. The wearying predictability of his movements convinced August that Gudanko could be discounted as an assassin. It would be too inconvenient to his schedule.

Dmitri smiled wryly from across the room, quietly reflecting August's contempt for Gudanko's insipid manner. Thankfully though, Dmitri refrained from crossing the room as was customary for him, to exchange hugs and kisses. The action would have triggered a line-up of supplicants that would have left August exposed to a potential transfer of fatal nanodroids.

August quickly assessed the twenty odd women and men gathered in the room, all uncomfortable in adapting their balance to the lower gravity. Besides Dmitri, none had bothered to visit Mirtopik's principal asset, their He-3 mines on the moon, no doubt due to Gudanko's complaints about cost. That he had allowed the expense for this meeting sent a clear message. They were coming here as one last homage before they finished him off.

His killer would likely be a woman. August didn't know why this would be, but today he trusted his instincts. Miranda Nirai perhaps, the leader of thus far feeble successes by the panarchists to insert their influence into the Mirtopik Board. That would be unlikely given that a mainstream panarchist would not want to touch off a war. Her protégé, Siobhan Maclean, more radical but perhaps too obvious. Helen Rodriguez, from the Los Angeles office where Calvin30 had identified the threat, ambitious and unyielding, Dmitri often complained to August about her. She was tense, incessantly picking at the static cling of her sari, but perhaps no more so than usual. Her face was subtly pinched in a way that August felt mirrored his own internal anxiety. She was waiting for something, watching everything closely. Perhaps she was his assassin. Perhaps not. August reminded himself to restrain his impulse to race to a conclusion. Looking for a specific killer might blind him to an attack coming from an unexpected corner. Right now, his back was the main thing that warranted watching.

August returned his attention to the issues of the moment, such as the absence of breakfast. It cut against the grain for August to withhold generosity, especially to esteemed guests who had travelled so far and, more to the point, who would today decide his fate. Still, the food had to be scanned and, besides, it fit with his strategy to keep Gudanko off balance with an empty stomach. He had noticed that Gudanko's state of mind was invariably linked to his metabolism. It was his only weak link. Seeing his enemy suffer, or imagining it happening beneath the unperturbed surface, was just an added bonus.

"Welcome my friends, I trust your flight up went well."

Judging from the dishevelled and exhausted appearance of some of the board members, the flight had gone about as well as could be hoped for. First there was the crushing acceleration required, even with a top of the range space plane, to escape the Earth's gravity. Then there were the myriad discomforts of zero gravity that remained uncomfortable even for someone like August who was acclimatized. The travel time was nearly a day and a half, even when one didn't include the stopover at one of the orbital space stations waiting to transfer to a lunar ferry.

The wonder on most of their faces, however, reminded August that such hardships were scarcely noticed by those experiencing the moon for the first time. Today they lived an experience shared with only an elite fraction of their fellow Earthlings. And to arrive here with all the fanfare of power was an experience of raw orgasm. Celestial overlords, from their heavenly palace, looking down on the farcical insignificance of the mother planet. All of them, perhaps even someone as bloodless as Gudanko, were in awe of their accomplishment.

And August was glad that they had come. Today could very well be his final battle and he was happy for the advantage of fighting it on his home turf.

"Where is the food?" August exclaimed in staged horror.

"I was going to ask the same thing," Gudanko commented dryly.

"One moment, apologies my friends," August made a show out of dressing down Linda while almost-but-not-quite out of hearing range. She did an admirable job of playing along, exiting the room on the verge tears. August resolved to add a healthy bonus to her paycheck this month.

"My sincere apologies. Evidently there are some technical difficulties in the kitchen holding things up. It may be a few minutes."

"There seem to be some difficulties in your organisation, as might be expected." The usual dig from the chronically pedantic.

August grimaced but continued graciously, "I'm worried that our general business might run into the AGM schedule. Should we start now so that we don't leave the shareholders waiting?"

After these usual housekeeping discussions were finished, a tea trolley was finally wheeled out and the shareholders left their chairs to commence the real business of the day. Touching base, inquiring as to the well-being of the others' spouses and children, commiserating over failed business dealings, marriages and divorces, exchanging bets on the next Lunar Formula 1, and extending invitations to lunch, to dinner, to spend time at each-others' vacation homes. Groups formed and broke away from the main table.

Gudanko stood by the tea trolley refilling his plate and sipping his tea and scalding his mouth when August unexpectedly patted him on the back.

"How are you going old boy? The food certainly took long enough, eh? I'm famished." August sipped the triple scanned cup of tea that Linda had provided him.

Gudanko responded with perfunctory cordiality as August picked up a cake from a full platter, winking cheerfully into the Ukrainian's stalwart gaze. "How's young Julius these days? Still popular with the girls I hear? Such a scoundrel." He gave Gudanko a nudge.

August imagined that Gudanko returned a scowl, which of course he didn't. Before taking another sip of tea, Gudanko paused to run his tongue over the scalded flesh on the top of his mouth. Gudanko, a conservative captain of industry, was known to be acutely embarrassed by his son's scandalous exploits, which were constantly appearing in the neurobloids. Again, the man gave away nothing.

Dmitri and several more astute board members cocked their heads to watch. August was clearly throwing down a gauntlet, even if Gudanko didn't deign to notice.

"I hear that you aren't too keen on some of our little projects up here? We'll just have to give you a bit of an education," August prodded, a bit louder.

More heads turned.

"I think I've had all the education I need," responded Gudanko stiffly, giving away the minimum exasperation for August to work with.

"I'm sure you have. A great deal of education apparently, in engineering. Tell me, did they provide any technical training on achieving greatness?"

Gudanko's face flushed mildly. He regarded August as if he were casually evaluating alternate options for pest control. The attention of the room compelled him to respond.

"The same as with any other thing. Step by step from steady foundations."

August shook his head disapprovingly. "Step by step to the stars my friend? I would think the only way is to fly."

August collected another cake and walked away to rejoin a group of senior executives and Board members. Occasionally August would glance through the crowd at the ghostly neurovisor images of the shareholders signing in for the Annual General Meeting. One by one they appeared, sitting in the same room in chairs that weren't physically there. Although the shareholders could see one another, they couldn't see the Directors chatting and eating cake and walking through them. A shiver passed through August - a momentary flashback to his dream and his inexplicable Moon-walk escapade and a reminder that, depending on the outcome today, tomorrow he could become just as insubstantial.

Soon the neuroview version of the room was filled to capacity with shareholders and the Directors made their way to their seats to log on to the session so that they too became visible in the world of ghosts. August surveyed the audience before making his own entrance.

Representatives of nearly every nationality on the Earth were present. This was one of the truly undeniable advantages of the free Coms. The panarchists, although they collaborated around the planetary environmental cycles and in the ecoversion of Com rivals, were invariably composed of one ethnic or religious group or another, and they defended their tribal identities fiercely. It was the grand paradox of the times that the self-proclaimed defenders of the planet possessed no shared global culture.

August knew, of course, that this was a superficial assessment. The gathering of shareholders was far from a utopian harmony of difference. It was a seething battleground. For a start, many in the audience were battling for the other side. Hub investors and holdings by ecoverted Coms made up a significant proportion of the shareholders. The only thing holding them in check was the fact that they hated Gudanko even more than they hated him. Gudanko had won his shares by taking advantage of the Last Famine in Russia through becoming the buyer of last resort and through a long list of other efficiently executed immoralities. August may have been a turncoat, some might gladly kill him if they had the chance, but for the moment he was the lesser of two evils. By remaining flexible to the demands of the Rev campaigns and generally maintaining the terms of the Peace, he had avoided a head-on confrontation. For the time being the panarchists had been content to pick away at periphery holdings, like BilongMeCom.

Another bloc was the big industrials, which for the most part was Energia Nova, their subsidiaries, and alliance partners. This was where the main threat to his leadership lay. The players not in these two blocs were an odd assortment of free investors and space enthusiasts. This was where the balance of power lay, and it was to this group that August planned, as usual, to make his pitch.

August made himself visible to the assembled neurocast participants and ascended to the pulpit with an exaggerated moonwalk bound. "My friends," his voice cut through the murmured conversations of the audience.

"I welcome you to the Moon, and beyond. Together we have travelled a long and winding road to reach our position today. There have been many challenges along the way, but we will prevail! This year has been the most dramatic in the modern resurgence of humanity in Space. In this year alone, we have nearly doubled the number of known extra-terrestrials. Doubled the number. Think about that. Ten years ago, when our team assumed leadership, Mirtopik Com was in disarray. Our critics were sounding the death knell for free capital. The Second Wave had imploded. The era of human exploitation of Space seemed set to end."

"What's changed?" a dissident voice, a plant, interrupted from the neuroview gallery.

August responded on cue. "Well, my friend, what has changed is everything. Everything changed dramatically with the arrival of a simple radio beacon from a distant world. Hope came that day, hope that humanity would at last find our way into the stars, with the awareness that our efforts at space travel here were being repeated a thousand times over throughout the universe, with other species likely to be significantly further down the road than we were. Mirtopik is the only Com to take the initiative in intercepting these communications from these advanced civilizations, and now it is only a matter of time before the technology for space travel is delivered to us. This will allow humanity to relieve our pressure on our precious Earth and the crippling pressure of the ecological constraints of a single planet. We will develop Mars, the solar system, and eventually the universe."

Disgruntled voices issued, not only from the neuroview gallery, but from the Board.

"With our new Neptune Orbital Listening Array, NOLA, we have opened new doors, we are already unlocking the secrets of a continually expanding future for humankind. And YOU are a part of this. The meek may inherit the Earth, but the bold will inherit the Universe."

August continued when he should have stopped, riding the wave of his own megalomania into the brilliant future waiting before him. As the wave crested he returned to an audience that he had, by now, left behind. Scattered applause greeted his return.

"Well, don't take my word for it," August declared, "Let's see the latest."

This statement was a tradition, repeated in every AGM since August assumed the helm. He felt it was good to expose the shareholders to the thrill of new discovery in the making. Many shareholders held interests in Mirtopik Com just for the excitement of these yearly unveilings of new worlds and exotic beings.

The mneme was announced by the same man each year, a bald headed and monotonous official in a white coat who was supposedly the head of the Division of Extra-terrestrial Signals but was in fact an actor hired to play the part. August understood the power of the cult of the familiar.

"Today we bring you mneme 200105, a new download from NOLA. This one is from Hercules Gamma, a television transmission and documentary of ritual behavior - incidental broadcast - 2 hours length. ET preliminary classification to saurian xenotype with fungi dominate ecosystem."

As the mneme began to play they found themselves within a primordial mist, parting here and there to reveal a tangled jungle composed of an incredible diversity of what were apparently gigantic mushrooms. A group of furry lizard beings covered in ornate body paint and wearing fantastical, top-heavy hats shaped like satellite dishes, wound their way carefully along an overgrown trail. They had long, jointed fingers that seemed more like tentacles as they bent in more than one direction to grasp things. When they stood still in any spot, the color of their unpainted skin seemed to change to match their surroundings.

The leader of the group held out his hands, halting the progress of the group and silencing any residual conversation among the shareholders. The mushrooms began to sway and then to shake violently as a herd of gigantic animals, snapped and crashed a path through them and into view. The parabolic disk-shaped head racks of the herd animals matched the shape of the over-sized hats worn by the lizard beings. The eyes of the herd animals, mere pinpricks, were positioned to the side of large hollows in the head crests so that their field of view would be severely restricted. Even so the great beasts seemed to have no trouble seeing where they were going, and precisely targeted the surrounding vegetation with their prehensile lips.

"It is suspected that ultrasonic, or perhaps even electromagnetic, echo-navigation signals are employed by the quadrupeds," the presenter explained.

As the column passed, lizard beings crept out of the brush and excitedly examined every aspect of the animals' passage: droppings, tracks, and browse. They took samples and measurements with technically complex instruments.

"Perhaps they are scientists?" someone called out.

"Or hunters," interjected another voice.

As the audience speculated, August faded from neuroview and carefully examined the conference room. The Directors were absorbed in the presentation, their heads bent at odd angles and their attention blinded to his return. Only Helen Rodriguez's head turned, looking away from him as he looked at her. She might as well wear a sign, August thought. Through his thoughts, August checked in with ComSec regarding the status of nanoweapon scan of the room.

"Nothing's registered sir."

"The second anything turns up."

"We'll let you know right away sir."

Calvin30's neurolink was still set to voice mail, the little shit.

Their study and collections finished, the lizard beings froze in place long enough for some of the audience to call for resetting the neuro-projector. Then, slowly, the lizard beings' bodies began to contort, and slowly swell, to approximate the shape of the herd animals. Skin colors changed to their same dun hue. They dropped on all fours and shuffled about, mimicking the ponderous gait. As a group, they gathered to vomit into the manure piles and then began to chew their carefully collected samples of browse. When the samples had been devoured, the eyes of the lizard beings narrowed and slid along a ridge on their heads, so they were now facing to the side instead of in front. Then, as functionally blinded as those they were miming, the lizard beings lumbered away following the path of trampled jungle.

The demonstration faded away.

Gudanko's soft voice interrupted August before he launched his wrap up. This was the moment the accountant chose to start the battle.

"ET is not a return. It is a speculation that will never pay out. How long has humanity been playing this game? Almost 150 years. 150 years and only a handful of broadcasts from the entire galaxy. And we have scanned a good proportion of what is within listening range. We have had to go to the edge of our solar system to build telescopes sensitive enough to pick up whatever remaining whispers are detectable. Another 50 years and there will be nothing left to listen to. This is a scientific enterprise, a brilliant and extraordinarily expensive one, but it is not a business model."

And then he sat back down. August fumed at the impertinence of the interruption, but he was prepared for it. He was not prepared for what happened next.

"I believe our panarchist colleagues have something to add," Gudanko threw in just as August opened his mouth to respond. As Siobhan Maclean rose to Gudanko's introduction, August smoothed his hair to calm his nerves. The panarchists and Gudanko now in alliance? Impossible.

Maclean intently stood up. Her randomly chopped back red hair and severe, homespun khadi salwaar kameez disciplined her Gaelic good looks into a fierce ensemble. August had invited her onto the Board with the aim of keeping Gudanko in check.

"Thank you, Vlad," Maclean's smile was pinched; collaborating with her sworn enemy must not come easily, "Thank you August."

"We realise it is not on the agenda, but we have recently come into possession of an extraordinary mneme from the Mars One station that has direct bearing to the current Mirtopik Com strategic vision, which you have laid out so well August, with your permission."

"Well. I, well."

At that moment the collective gaze of the Board and shareholders started to shift. Although their eyes were all on August, the focus began to soften, as Anya's eyes had as they had moved through him. Could they see how illusory his ruse was, how it was nothing but a dream? Panic rose through his body; a feeling August could not ignore this time. He was losing it.

"Continue on," Gudanko directed, calmly registering his opponents fear.

"Right," Maclean cleared her throat. "As August has shared with us, the current plan for use of any space travel tech the aliens might provide will be the industrialisation of Mars. However, we believe that doing so may contravene the Covenant on Ecological Rights."

"Ecological Rights?" August scoffed despite his efforts at self-control. "Ecological Rights don't apply in Space. That is a basic principle of the Peace. This is a Com matter."

"Well, the Peace puts the border of Space at the furthest extent of the ecosphere. However, there appears to be a real possibility that an indigenous ecosphere exists on Mars, as outlined quite passionately by one of the key specialists in this area currently on the planet. Please gauge for yourself."

The mneme opened in the AGM neuroview, starring a woman who August recognised. She was less pretty now than she had when they had met.

"...what people don't understand is that all the ingredients are still there. Water, heat, chemical food. And the microfossil evidence that they have been here before. We know all this. How can we turn our back on what might be our only sister world in our solar system's story of Life? They are right here Kalsang. Right under our noses, and it is all too inconvenient to look for them. Because, if we did, we would find them, we would find them, and we would know that our own microbes, so much more advanced, would take over their planet in a geological instant. So, they don't want to know that. It ruins all their plans because coming here on the scale they want to simply won't work. Or they would have to admit to the world, which we all know to be true, that they simply don't care. Look at the state of the Earth. We wrecked it. So, we all know where that attitude takes us. People live it every day."

"People live it every day," Maclean repeated. "We do. And this is the reason this whole adventure in Space is flawed. We must learn to live within limits."

Gudanko cut off Maclean's impending anti-Com diatribe. "What our panarchist colleague means is that, even IF we get the technology from the aliens, we might not be able to develop Mars, and if not Mars, where do we go? Where? So, you see, August, not only is this a pipedream, but it is an ill-considered one from the beginning."

The Board and neuroview gallery erupted. Familiar battle lines were redrawn with a single focus - change at the top.

August could only stand, his mind separated from the world around him, while they argued over his fate. There was nothing he could do to re-engage. His fate was overtaking him, and his mind was trying to creep away. He had to do something, but all he could was watch. Then part of him noticed that their gaze had come back to him and that they were waiting.

August decided to wait with them, which was what saved him. The room and neuroview became uncomfortably quiet while the tension grew. They began to fidget. Then, his clarity returning as their attention on him tightened, August spoke.

"Thank you, Siobhan. Very interesting, but nothing new. Aurora, I mean Dr. Davidson and I," August was grateful that he never forgot a name behind an attractive face.

"The two of us started this conversation years ago. In fact, if you look, her research is funded from my priority projects for particularly these reasons. We have been working on this problem together over that time. You know what we have found, after years of dedicated investigations? Nothing. There is nothing to suggest that indigenous life still exists on Mars, but that, contrary to Dr. Davidson's passionate plea, it went extinct billions of years ago. However, I have a complaint."

August gripped his hair to highlight his distress. What he had to say next was brilliant, even by his own standards.

"This is obviously a personal communication of Dr Davidson's that someone has intercepted. Why else would she address us as 'Kalsang', a friend of hers? This is intolerable. I take the invasion of my staff's privacy personally. This is especially so since it has been documented that Aurora, having spent many years so far from Earth, is suffering from the inevitable psychological consequences of a prolonged mission. You are all aware of the state of mind this will produce. This is not an official scientific report, which has been subject to peer review. This is a cry for help from someone, a friend, who is suffering profoundly. For this I would like an apology."

He could see by the way that MacClean shifted in her seat that she hadn't anticipated this counter attack.

"Where did you get this?" August pressed his advantage.

"It is from a reliable source."

"Was this reliable source Dr. Davidson?"

"I, we cannot say."

"We? You mean you cannot betray a Rev operative working within Mirtopik Com. We? Really Siobhan, where does this stop? As a Director, do you have any responsibility at all to Com investors? Did you not join the board as a partner? Are those not the terms of the Peace?" August looked pointedly at Gudanko who smiled placidly.

"August, I share your concerns, but does it make any difference? It is the responsibility of the Board to consider risk, something it has not been in the habit of doing for some time. That is why I chose to allow this demonstration of a mneme that is already viral in the public domain, something you should already know. Lack of evidence is not evidence of absence. Whatever the merits, the development of Mars will not occur without resistance and this simply highlights that the game we are playing has no clear return."

"Does it matter Vlad?" August pivoted, "True, we have no clear return. We have a massive sunk investment with hardly a percent back - a complete loss by any definition. We can't expect to recoup that kind of outlay by selling neurovision rights to alien transmissions for heaven's sake."

The room fell silent. MacLean, confused mid pounce, stalled in an awkward half crouch. "August, what are you saying? That ET *isn't* the big picture? You can't back pedal so easily.»

August smiled magnanimously. Maclean diplomatically grimaced in return.

"No Siobhan. Making money is the big picture. We are a Com. We make money. That's it. End of story. Isn't that what your Revs are always telling people?"

Gudanko actually stood. "Then it is over August. Respectfully you have not delivered what you promised. As I have been arguing it is time to pull the plug and return to a more stable approach."

"That may not be a good idea my friend because if this investment is abandoned, then an awful lot of us," August scanned the room, making eye contact with each potential ally, on the Board and among the shareholders, "have made some very bad business decisions. Truly spectacularly bad decisions. The cost, just to build NOLA is what, say fifty times the annual gross profit of Mirtopik Com? Pretty catastrophic, even for a Com this size."

August paused to assess the dangerous boil of confusion in the room. His hair stood at attention in every conceivable angle as August waited for the right moment, until the audience's heads begin to turn back for an answer.

"What is left for us? Eco-isolated manufacturing on the Moon - a good idea – but not enough to keep us in any major position of influence. Non-toxic substitutes exist for most things we can make up here. What is left for us? What can we sell? What is our business?"

"Space, my friends, space, that's it, freedom, that's all."

"Look."

Gudanko raised his voice. It was unbelievable. August would have taken pleasure in the accomplishment of finally provoking his enemy, had there not been so much at stake.

"Look." Gudanko took a deep breath and levelled. "It's simple, it always has been. We have monopoly power in Space. We dictate the terms to our suppliers. This is not about freedom. It is about making hard choices. It is about extending our control and punishing our competitors."

"Vlad," August cut Gudanko off fiercely, "we lost that war." August allowed a silent consent to fill the hole he had punched in his rival's muted bluster. "We did. Nobody here would dispute that. We lost. We lost the war and now we're losing the Peace. The panarchists have won because they are right. We are dinosaurs really, still walking around in our bones. Look, maybe we have scraps of Russia, Kiev, LA, New York, Singapore, Shanghai, Berlin, London and this small dot on the Moon - that's all - the free Com holdouts. That's a very small piece of the pie. Even the Govs don't take us that seriously anymore."

Maclean was smiling despite herself. Gudanko was trembling with suppressed agitation. The neuroview hummed with argument. August waited until their attention returned to him, as he compiled his closing argument.

"My friends, only Mirtopik Com represents frontiers still open. No other Com, no other institution, upholds the age-old dream, and I believe genuine promise, of a human future in Space. This alone accounts for the continuing stability in our stock value. Turning our backs on the Mirtopik dream will have further reaching ramifications than the viability of this Com. Markets are creatures of perception. They thrive on optimism. An admission of failure here will therefore impact every other conceivable investment. And the consequences will be even more dire for long term Gaian restoration." August noted the number of faces in the neuroview that turned in response. The panarchist presence was roughly what Calvin30 had reported.

"What is the Peace my friends? I submit that it is our name for the balance of progress and necessity. Of necessity we carefully manage our footprint on the Earth. But the constraints of necessity, the daily million compromises, are endured only because of the promise of Freedom. Take away this promise and there is no saying what the consequences will be."

"Doesn't this contradict what you said earlier about making money?" interjected MacLean.

"No, Siobhan. That is a good question. I stand by what I said. Our purpose is to make money, or rather to realize the potential of Capital. And what is

Capital my friends but the promise of Freedom? So, I implore you, each of you, to carefully consider the nature of profit and loss when you decide today on the future of Mirtopik Com."

No one spoke. Gudanko rocked intently in his chair.

"Oh," August added, "and a few words about the continuing productive partnership between Mirtopik and Energia Nova. The long-term opportunities coming from ET are supported by the steady advances in faster, better spacecraft provided by Energia Nova. Because of this effective collaboration over the past decade, the costs of ET are mainly fixed other than operational on-costs and the pittance we pay the monasteries each year for our cheerful monks to keep doing their thing out at the Listening Arrays."

No one advanced another question, perhaps out of fear that August would continue speaking to the truth of Mirtopik's financial vulnerability. August ducked down to sit with the rest of the Directors on the neuroview stage.

August, his performance finished, distractedly watched the conclusion of the meeting of ghosts, his neurovisor focused more on the perilous reality of the Apollo Room around him. August's allies on the Board were, for the most part, re-elected and the resolution for his dismissal failed. Even Gudanko seemed resigned to his loss. The shareholders, in general, made it known they weren't happy but, in the, end the Board reaffirmed their commitment to stay the course. August rose to acknowledge the vote of confidence in his leadership. It was a bad way to win by rubbing people's noses in their own desperation. Chances were this would be his last victory. But it was still a win. He still had what it took. His hair nodded presidentially to the slowly dissolving audience.

An arm brushed against his. August's attention winked back to the room. It was the moment he had feared, Helen Rodriguez squeezing in between him and Dmitri, in complete breach of protocol, as the Board stood to thank the shareholders.

"What are you doing?" August hissed at his attacker.

"Sir. I."

"Get away from me!" August vanished out of the neuroview and strode quickly toward the causeway that suspended the Apollo Room above the main Luna City complex. He still had time, he reasoned. The nanoids would take time to get through his skin. They may have a timer, something to create a natural appearing physiological breakdown over time that would be difficult to link to an attack. He hoped. They hadn't given Illya that same consideration.

The causeway was covered with a curved transparent roof, visible only where sections joined on the steeply angled descent. The architecture infused a feeling of space flight into each hugely elongated step as August fled for his life. A shrill voice, at first ignored, pursued him down the corridor.

"It's the panels!" shouted Helen Rodriguez as she ran after him. "He's put something on the causeway panels. For God's sake, just stop."

The honest concern in the voice brought August to a tentative halt. As he turned, a sharp hiss of escaping gas brought his attention back to the base of the causeway.

"Hurry August. Run."

August spun and began to beat his way back up the ramp. The hissing sound became a crack and then a roar, as time dilated and a frantic wind gnawed at his progress. Helen stood bravely in the doorway, temporarily delaying the airlock from snapping shut until the computer resolved the equation that balanced the risk to the life of one person against the risk to many. August's breath was sucked from his lungs and they shrivelled around his heart and heaviness clutched at his heels. The skin on his face began to freeze. His feet went suddenly numb and this affected his balance. He tripped forward into the blue skinned arms of his savioress as they fell backward into sudden safety behind the slamming doors of the airlock.

In the weeks that followed, August's mind obsessed over the images that followed this narrow escape. The approach by Dmitri to resuscitate a semi-conscious Helen, and her sudden, terrified retreat from his approach. The accusation. The security camera neuroscript downloaded from the moment of August's exit, from her unidentified source. The mneme showing a circumspect Dmitri puffing on the clear panel at the base of the causeway and rubbing it with his handkerchief as if remove some blemish from the view. The results of the ComSec analysis, a fragment of panel covered with the residue of a powerful nanoidic acid remotely activated by radio frequencies. Dmitri, his comrade and friend, the one person to stand by him through everything, crying out at him as the ComSec officers hustled him away.

August rolled over in bed and ran his finger down Linda's naked back. She turned too quickly and smiled eagerly. She would have to go. A wave of nausea rose rapidly from the pit of his stomach. A minute later he was hunched over the toilet, throwing up, his body shivering in complete revolt to his will.

"You okay, Sir?"

Sir? August wondered why he kept repeating this mistake. After his near brush with death, a strong sexual attraction had manifested toward the woman who would have given her life for his. Helen was a strongly built woman and, like August, determined and self-possessed. He visited her several times in the medical unit, and laughed at her jokes, before she had shuttled out with the others. The delicate web of political alliances at Mirtopik effectively cocooned him from making an approach.

So, he had ended up in bed with Linda. Power made some things far too easy. Now he felt more isolated than usual.

"I'm fine Linda. I need to be alone now, okay."

August heard the door slide shut as he cleaned his face. ComSec would have her on the next shuttle Earthward and out of his life. His mind turned back to Dmitri.

"Why?" August had asked.

The memory that most disturbed August's mind, Dmitri's tired voice repeating in his conscience, "I looked back August, and I couldn't look forward anymore. I tried to save you man, to change your mind. But you didn't listen - you didn't leave us any other choice, did you? Stubborn ass just like always."

What in hell was that supposed to mean? What had happened to turn his most trusted ally into his enemy?

Look back? Look back when it was all he could do to keep the future clear in front of him? Look back when the promise of tomorrow was so grand and so near to his grasp? Look back? For what? Looking back only ended with Illya. Dmitri and the great man had never been close anyway. And that sad tale explained nothing.

It was Illya who had introduced August to his mother's country, the beautiful and tragically scarred Urals. The effects of the insidious stain of radioactivity on the land had left its mark on the brave Cossack men and women and their children. Yet, despite the tragedy that defiled their generations, they maintained an admirable if unsustainable, in some ways perversely fatalistic, idealism. Illya, had shown them how to harness their own power - how to believe in themselves rather than drown in self-sacrifice. August had brought to the table his American entrepreneurial flare and sense of the possible. With his ambition and Illya's leadership they had built MirtopikNet into a great economic force, linking thousands of Hubs across Russia into an efficient and mutually beneficial Net with the great industrial ecologies of Europe, Central Asia, China, and Japan.

It was there, in Tokyo, that August had seen his chance. The Nets had locked down the markets and were on the ascendancy, the old world-order in disarray. The great Japanese Coms had spent their wealth on the Moon, but the return no longer justified the risk. They needed customers for their new clean helium-3 fusion energy, but their developments threatened the economic exclusivity of the Nets.

Illya had not seen the opportunity to take the stars. Illya had died, not because August had killed him, but because the fool had gone to the Revs. Mirtopik's new investors had ignored August and had dealt with the problem in their customary fashion.

The memory of the day still haunted him.

Illya Mikkalovich did not fit in as he ducked into the cafe at Narita. His two meters tall lanky frame and great promontory of a beard - he was even more of a giant when walking amongst the Lilliputian Japanese. His growled complaint regarding the awkwardly small seats set the table vibrating.

This was the first time August had seen him in over a year since the fateful vote that gave birth to Mirtopik Com. Illya did not waste time on pleasantries.

"What do you want August?"

"I want for you to stay alive."

"Oh August, my son," August winced. Genuine love still lingered somewhere behind the man's hard eyes. "you want me to stay alive. I am very touched. Such a kind sentiment. How do you propose that I do this, staying alive? With my honor intact?"

"Look Illya, we don't want a war. These people are very predictable, you taught me that."

"Yes, this is right, only I thought that you were not. Although to give you credit, I didn't predict this."

"Look, you're not going to accomplish anything with a direct confrontation."

"August, it is our souls I am fighting for."

"Illya, just back off for a while, I'm asking you as a friend."

"And I'm asking you as friend," the sarcasm was thick in Illya's voice. "What do you want? To have people who share no love waiting on you like dogs,

as eager to eat what you toss them as to gnaw your bones when you fall. It is lonely at the top Augustus Mishen'ka, very, very lonely." Illya drained his glass of sake, poured another from the pitcher and drained it again, keeping August pinned down with his furious gaze. "What do you need August?"

"Illya, they'll kill you."

The table groaned as the giant pulled himself from his seat to tower above him.

"If they do, it won't be on my conscience."

He slammed the empty glass on the table and walked out. One waiter looked to another who looked at someone out of sight and behind a corner. August stood to follow Illya only to watch the great man crumple in the doorway. An autopsy pronounced the cause of death as an aneurysm, the spontaneous rupture of a weak blood vessel in the brain. Natural causes. August knew better. There were ways men had invented for killing men that left no mark. As Illya fell, his eyes fastened on August's. Their tears reflected in each other's.

Dmitri was full of crap. All looking back brought was pain, not insight. Something else was at work here, some gradual realignment of the political heavens that had gone unnoticed during his exile. Some monster that had grown up behind his back while he had been preoccupied with surviving the AGM. Something that Calvin30 should have told him about.

Where the hell was that little pissant?

CHAPTER 10

Calvin30

It came as no surprise that news of August Bridges' demise had been extravagantly exaggerated. Calvin30 felt almost guilty to have sat on the inside track when he could have had August's back, but every season had its reasons and he had his. With the plot foiled his attentions could return to lesser mortals - such as that chick from ComSec checking his tracks. Why had he handed her a key to a lock she wasn't even trying to crack?

Certainly, Calvin30 hadn't anticipated someone sniffing so close to the core. It was an unanticipated intrusion, but then a quick sounding of the sniffer suggested that she'd stop if the scent she was sensing led too close to the top. So, he'd fronted up to her with nothing to hide, a warning disguised as a friendly aside. It bugged him for this to be so out of the bag, but the risk in these things was also the rush.

And it was not regrettable that someone must pay for unsettling his day. Calvin30 padded back to the Mirtopik Needle to check on a certain wolf pup he kept as a pet. On his way he peaked down from the ceiling paint to see how the pest was persevering through his punishment.

Calvin30 spied a Wolfie who had survived on powdered donuts, squeeze cheese, and jolt java for several weeks. His body oil saturated tee-shirt was molded to the shape of his cheap office chair. His defiant mohawk lay limp and defeated across his forehead. His hands twitched while his eyes flicked following the invisible screed in his neuroview. A temple massage unit designed to prevent vision tunnel syndrome gummed away ineffectually, as the rotary mechanisms became ever looser in their housings.

Good to see that the naughty Wolfgang was still in the Hell he'd brought on himself by giving that jezebel those secret transmissions. A tremor rode up the back of his twitching. Oh Wolfie. Not the shakes again? Two months in rehab to beat them last time - java withdrawal could be such a wild ride.

Calvin30 walked in, as if on cue, with a tray of steaming java for the program crew. Wolfie nearly jumped out of his seat in gratitude. In one second more would his head have exploded? And soon as the last drop passed his lips, that's when the regret began. What of his son, his wife? He really needed to cut this shit for good – but when the job was over, and he had back his life.

Wolfie cast an appreciative smile to his rescuer. That C30 was one hell of a nice guy, Wolfie's eyes all but sighed. Not like the others of his kind.

"Hey Wolf, what lifts?"

"Not my ass for one C30, damn it's sore. Thanks for the java man."

"They work you guys too hard, I'm concerned about your health, nobody seems to listen to me anymore. Oh, here you are Christine. I didn't bring donuts this time; you kids need something more nutritious, so I brought some fruit. Have an apple."

"Thanks, C30."

Thanks, C30. The comment touched Calvin30 so much. Thanks, C30. That's what they say in that patronizing way, while he was the friend who stuck by them to the bitter end. August was different. So genteel using the full clone appellate of Calvin30. No need to discredit those who were not a threat. A terribly bad underestimate for the big man to make.

Such sublime dysfunction it was where those above, as befits their presumption, prejudge those beneath, who in turn preserve upper-class ignorance by obscuring the truth. In this information vacuum Calvin30 bloomed.

Calvin30 smiled beatifically at his young acolytes. A friend who is freed is a friend indeed.

The current kerfuffle, a complete overhaul of the Deep Space Network, was an idea whose time had come from a chummy confabulation over a hot rum with the once unflappable Ralph Kingsbury, Deep Space Director. Calvin30 had bolstered Ralph through a deplorable divorce whilst diverting payments to his wife's lawyer from another body's bank account.

Calvin30 grinned for Wolfie. His expression was a perverse balance of wizened subservience and benign informality.

"No problemo Wolf. Gotta prop the people who perform. They should pay you more though."

"Tell me about it."

"How're Monica and the little tyke surviving all this?"

Wolfgang looked up at his friend, tears welling in the corner of his eyes, "I'm worried C30."

Calvin30 nodded sympathetically whilst noting the java shakes approvingly.

"Don't worry Wolf. Monica's not a fly by night sort of girl. She'll stick by you. She reminds me of, you know Angie? You know the one. Roger, from Stellar Navigation's first wife. Angela, that's it. Oh shit Wolf. Hey, I didn't mean anything by that. I'm such an idiot."

"It's all right C30," Wolfie reassured him nervously, "Chris and me we are going to get through this one."

Pretty Christine smiled, which made Calvin30 smile at her. Her psychological profile, her history of obsessive and self-destructive relationships with married co-workers, was hand-picked forbidden fruit - a present for his friend Wolf. Calvin30 wondered if her qualifications would rise to the occasion.

To be honest, the situation didn't interest him one way or the other. Calvin30 yawned. What previously might seem a fun scene was becoming tedious and routine. He really couldn't give a rat's ass whether Wolfie's marriage busted, or whether Christine would fall on her back off the wagon. There was no purpose in this proposition. This was still finger painting with the same old shit while he should be immersed in the process of producing his masterpiece.

"You know, I could care less about all this crap."

Wolfie and Christine looked at him quizzically. Calvin30 scowled and brusquely left the room.

As he stalked off he overheard Wolf shrug, "I wonder what's bugging him?"

"I dunno, want another apple?"

A few hours later, riding the whisper train line gliding out to sea, Calvin30 watched LA become a line on the horizon. The SpaceX terminal would arrive in an hour, so he let his mind linger on the notes resonating in his brain as his pipe responded to his fingering.

If the time had come for him to be his destiny then it was time to give up these childish things. Calvin30 deleted the recorded mnemes of Christine's psychiatric sessions, setting her free.

"Self ACT-U-AL-I-SATION"

It was all there in those files, the ghosts in everyone's machines, and the cipher to Calvin30's success.

"Self ACT-U-AL-I-SATION"

And so, it all began.

Flipping into the past he found his own file and flicked it up on his neuroview.

There he sat, new-born and gleaming, delivered.

"Self ACT-U-AL-I-SATION."

"What does that mean to you?" It was the voice of her. Even after years had erased the woman, her voice still stirred something. Helen Van Driel.

Looking out of her eyes he could only glimpse bits of the whole world she had presented in their sessions. That ruby birthmark dripping down her confidently fat arms. The conspiratorial friendship offered through her laughing smoker's cough. After the Clones were freed, the Com had assigned her to help him try to fly. It was mostly wasted effort since the rest of the clones had clung terrified to the nest.

But not C30.

A lithe twenty something, same age as C70 now, studied her question.

This was the opening scene.

"It's upside down."

"What is?"

"Maslow is."

"We were talking about Maslow and his pyramid of needs. Did that mean something to you? What do you mean by saying that it's upside down?" Cough.

The boy frowned.

"Maslow says that needs come first. We need food love and everything to be, to be self-actualised."

"And why isn't that true? Everyone needs love."

"Who loves clones?"

"I see." Cough. "How is your music going?"

The music. His salvation. At that age he could hardly blow a scale, but even then he had known it was the Truth that would set him free.

"Jazz. Jazz, that's what I'm trying to say."

"Say what?" cough laugh, "you are losing me Calvin."

And so he had, but he had found himself.

"Maslow's pyramid is upside down. Who loves someone who isn't, self act-u-al-ised? You see? That's where it comes from. It's when you forget, when you forget everyone leaves, puts you outside, swipes your food, dries you up."

He watched her arms cross.

"So, where does Self Actualisation come from?" Always canny was his Helen.

"The top of the pyramid, it's a tip. Out of thin air. From Nothing."

"Oh, Calvin. I'm not so sure."

"No one is."

He remembered when that line had first hit him, listening earlier that day to Coltrane, washout junkie, black in a time when those three things together meant nothing but nigger. Who was going to love that man? Where were the satisfied needs playing a Love Supreme? The purest improv ever to pour from a man's lips sprang straight from the empty in his soul.

A buzzer buzzed, and Calvin30, riding Helen's perspective hobbled past the boy to check with the receptionist.

He remembered how, after she left, he had spied in her diary on her desk, "Password: Exc3Lc10r."

And that was how he had come to carry a copy of Christine's confidentials. Hers and those of many more. In them he had uncovered that it was not only clones who felt alone in their skins.

"Exc3Lc10r." The key to sailing on an open sea of sorrows.

"Self ACT-U-AL-I-SATION."

The ocean blurred by and the sky never seemed so wide. Today. The Nothing in his heart and the Nothing beyond - all spanned by the grand arc of his plan. It was the closest he had ever felt to God inside himself.

"Just give me that old time religion."

Gospel hymns of Mingus had been rejoicing in Calvin30's pipe since he woke this morning. He patched into an on-line jam group that grooved on that stuff and joined in once he got the Spirit right. The organist had a light touch that reminded him of Shirley Scott.

Brother Calvin30 the Obscure, whose Papa was a holy rolling clone, could fe-eel the power of the Lord. Alleluia.

"Dong. Arriving at LA SpaceX. We hope you enjoyed your ride and we look forward to traveling with you again."

Calvin30 turned the tenor part over to the next guy in line, and the leader God-Blessed him for his time.

"Got some soul in ya brother Calvin."

And also in you.

Calvin bowed down the carriage to the mostly deserted train, earning a few quizzical glances. Then the train parked, and he walked out to wait in the gantry with a handful of select souls and assorted freight, soon to be launched into Earth orbit.

His news was too huge to be delivered by neuroview. Calvin30 needed to feel the notes as they were placed, face to face, with August. Playing the great man like this couldn't be done from a distance.

Their rocket softly lifted off underneath the dirigible that would take it on the first stage to the stratosphere, costing less Ecos to launch that way.

Calvin30 watched as the Moon grew bright on the edge of night. Rockets flared and soon they transited at the Mirtopik International Space Station to the waiting Luna Shuttle. Passing the departure lounge he inconspicuously espied the returning Directors smiles and scowls. Gudanko was all frowns.

Soon they were onward to the Moon, and Calvin30 watched the blue Earth shrinking to fit within the observation deck rearward frame. As he rose, he composed, blending Mingus with King. *Ladies and gentlemen, I have your Dream.*

The Dream was the theme, for it was August and his Dream that would set them all free. Or maybe not. Did it make any difference? The striving was gratifying, not the arriving.

As they flew round the Dark Side and the Blue planet dropped from view, Calvin30 renewed his ruminations on the Grand Man.

He remembered when August took over back in the Twenties. Before then things had been far less fascinating. ApolloCom, as it was then called, was a drunken and decrepit blob that had vomited itself into the solar system on a Second Wave binge, busy selling off its bits as it imploded. With impressionable eyes, a fledgling Calvin30 watched the Com bosses drop from their top windows like a falling flock. And then, August Bridges had arrived all white horse and sun rise.

The Nets, needing the Coms' Moon energy to boost their efforts to stabilise the climate, rode to the rescue. August Bridges, their prodigal son and Steward of MirtopikNet, led the charge.

Calvin30 had harvested fields of irrational dreams while the greatest corporate restructure in human history commenced and MirtopikNet choked and gagged and irretrievably transformed trying to assimilate a creature of a fundamentally different chemistry.

Upwelling ripples from August's dramatic splash nourished a rich ecology of narcissism upon which Calvin30 had learned to feast. The nearer to August one got the more dramatic was the effect. And the possibilities in August himself were awesomely endless. And August, sensing possibilities that lesser mortals had missed, summarily summoned Calvin30 to his side.

Today would be the blessed consummation of that marriage. The landing module puffed softly down onto the regolith and Calvin30 in his space suit hopped down. As he sauntered towards the airlock he passed a mechanic bent over the engine of a Moon buggy.

"Where do you think you are going?" growled a voice in Calvin30's head.

It was August.

Calvin30 pivoted on the spot to face him.

"Hi, Boss."

"I couldn't find you."

"It's not easy to do. We all look alike you see."

August shrugged, stalked to the buggy, and stepped in. Ever dutiful, Calvin30 dropped in beside him. The buggy wheels spun and suddenly gripped, and they jerked out into the dark, quickly leaving the lonely few tubes called Luna City behind. Ahead loomed the abrupt walls of Plato Crator and soon they were zooming under the tunnel leading through them.

"How grand," he proclaimed as they passed the point of listening-in range. "Mind if I play. Some new riffs to share. Fine tunes for a private ride out on the dunes."

August considered him carefully.

"The same ones you have been serenading the stars with?"

"The very same."

The dark in August's frown flickered towards off.

"Well good. I always enjoy listening to what you've learned from the latest muse."

"No mere ditty this Boss, the Universe has given us our Magnum Opus"

"Really?" Calvin30 could hear a smile start to crack, "then we should have a long ride."

As they sped across the grey dunes, they communed the moments in silence while churning a great plume of dust behind them. The half-Earth hung high in the South.

August, winner of three spins in the Luna Formula One, deftly steered around ejecta as they emerged through the high cliffs of the Plato Rim, then shot across an open Ocean of Rains towards the imposing Alpes Montes.

They rode for half the day without much to say. Calvin30 laid back and played an ostinato to the night sliding across the Earth, from New York to LA. They drove past huge Hoppers with their trove of Helium-3 ore heading North from the shores of the Sea of Tranquillity. He waited for August to end the zen of their drive, which he finally did when the Plato Rim sunk safely out of view.

"Dmitri. Did you know?"

Sigh. Start wide to maximize unease. "Anyone from your early days ought to be thought to harbor misgivings."

"But Dmitri. Dmitri. I could always rely on him. The man was one of my best friends."

"A perilous occupation in this minion's opinion."

"Don't mess with me. Did you know?"

"Know? No. Suspected? Yes."

"And you didn't tell me. I could have died."

"Doubting your friend, would you have stayed sharp, or would you have been dulled by the dark?"

"No. I had no idea. My eyes were everywhere but on him. The last person I would have thought." The duplicity had sliced deep and August seemed suddenly sad.

More pain more gain.

"Not so Boss. Your eyes were on the prize while other eyes were on him."

August's face relaxed.

"Helen?"

"Can any man watch for attacks from behind his own back?"

"But without Dmitri?"

"Without Dmitri. Would you have been so strong on the stand without him, your ally, standing by your side?"

August stopped accelerating. The Montes Alpes, framed against a deep absence of sky, shot up starkly before them.

"No."

The Earth set behind the peaks as the silence seeped in.

"As your humble servant, I am satisfied that you survived. And well it seems."

"Yes." The conclusion was incontestable, but Calvin30 could see in August's eyes how much that understanding cost.

Ka-ching. As a soul dies an Angel somewhere earns his wings.

August cruised on, lancing into torturous terrain flanking the Alpes. August did not decelerate as he plunged the buggy, twisting and bouncing, through the broken country. Calvin30 dug his digits into his seat, wondering whether he'd awakened some death wish whirling Dervish.

Then the peaks leapt aside as they fell into a steep canyon, where a six-mile wide finger had swiped through the surrounding ranges.

"Vallis Alpes, one of the few visible fault lines on the moon." announced August, breaking the silence.

"Spectacular." Because it was.

At that, August banked the buggy towards the valley wall and propelled them into it. Calvin30 braced for a crash when the mountain slid open and the brakes slammed on only after they were inside. The floodlights on the buggy illumined a gray tunnel plunging before them into the lunar crust. Still fairly freaked, Calvin30 the meek followed August as he left the buggy and walked into a waiting airlock on a small container office.

"Welcome" exhorted August, popping open his visor to reveal a wide grin, "to my Bat cave. It's an abandoned adit tunnel for one of our tantalum mines. Care for a cup of tea?"

"I need to wash out my suit backside first."

August laughed. His mood had modified.

They ascended a stairway, which ended in a small kitchenette. August tipped a thermos into two tea mugs and motioned for Calvin30 to take one.

He glared as Calvin30 squelched a grin and looked away. Having asserted his authority August smiled and his eyes widened greedily.

"Wormhole?"

"Yes," Calvin30 looked up again, grinning.

August was quiet for a moment. "I see. From where?"

"Scorpio 18."

"How close is that?"

"Near to here, around 45 light years."

"How did they do it? Do you know?"

"The mneme had full specs. It's all been clipped."

August brandished his victorious fist, stretched back on his stool and whistled. "No shit. Well, we did it."

"There's a catch." The best lies were grayer shades of true.

August frowned.

"Apparently, the wormhole has certain inherent instabilities that have the potential to be somewhat, um, dangerous."

"What are we talking here?"

"Don't locate it too close anything we care about. For instance, the Earth. Safer to stash it in Space." Tell the whole truth and nothing but.

"That bad?" August's hair drooped.

"The Gods of odds are with us. Large magnitude instabilities have only a minute probability of occurrence. Mankind has played chicken against much better chances of utter destruction. Hey, it's not my racket to manage the risk. I'm just the messenger."

At that he reached over and plopped the mneme cube in August's offered hand. "I thought I'd best deliver this in person."

"Good idea." August rolled the precious crystal in his fingers.

They returned to the buggy and backed out of the mine shaft. Time stopped as Calvin30 watched sagacious thoughts wrestle for August's soul.

The Brother was taking the slow way home, stretching their trip closer than comfort to the empty on the oxygen gauge.

But Calvin30, did he try to steer?

No sir.

Did he deem to intervene?

No way.

Did he preach a plan or beseech the man?

Nuh uh.

Was he moo-ooved by the Spirit to spare the Sphere, even if only to protect his own neck.

He didn't, man.

No, he didn't. And why? Why you ask? I'll tell ya.

Praise the Lord.

That's right. You heard the man. Praise the Lord. Because if ever there was a circumstance for HIM to manifest HIS Holy testament. To hold HIM to that rainbow vow told to Noah on the shore of The Promised Land. If HE was troth to the Love of the Lamb and was ever going to de-liver. That time was now.

Now.

Say it.

Now.

Sing it Sister.

And she sang it, sang it sweet and sang it low, down that long, dry, dusty road home. To the Promised Land?

That's the One.

After they arrived back at Luna City, loitering before the airlock, August looked deeply into the eyes of night to address the stars, his Masters, and with a voice hovering as close to contrition as modesty insisted, declared his intentions.

"We can't let the Directors decide on this. It must be fait' accompli or they will steal it from me."

And with that the Divine Creator drove HIS alpha up HIS omega and disappeared into Nothing.

Into the pointy end Of the Pyramid.

Back to where everything began.

Self ACT-U-AL-I-SATION.

CHAPTER 11

Aurora

Aurora woke early. The rest of her mates were tucked into their swags. As she unzipped the sound damping buckeygel sheet at the end of her tube she could hear Terry snoring below her. She climbed out and ducked into the main cabin and made herself a cup of tea. Denali activated and wandered over to nuzzle her legs. She carried her steaming mug into the forward observation module to watch the sunrise. Xiao Li was already there, as usual. Aurora sat down quietly beside her, and Denali collapsed on the floor with a grunt.

"Morning Shel."

"Hi Ror. How did you sleep?"

"Well enough. Nice sunrise."

"God blessing us with Her glory once again," Xiao Li replied matter-of-factly. Xiao Li carried her Christianity well. She wasn't a Bible basher. For her, religion was simply a logical consequence of living, as natural as breathing. Whenever she wondered how the others carried on without it she seemed more curious than judgmental.

"It is lovely." They sat together, quietly admiring the red and white vertical streaks of Elysium Chasma beginning its daily scintillations beneath the brightening orange sky.

"Can I get you a cuppa?"

"Thanks, Aurora."

"White and none, right?"

Xiao Li nodded.

Aurora returned with her milky coffee and some sweet biscuits. She was grateful to her friend just for being. She wasn't sure of what to make of the twists and turns in her mind from yesterday but put them down to exhaustion. It seemed far away from the clean taste of the tea and the warmth sitting in both her hand and her soul.

She meditated on the morning before them, content with each moment spent with her friend.

"Shell, what do make of all of this? I mean, I know you believe that this is all part of the plan by the Big Guy upstairs. What do you figure is up with us being here?"

"Oh, I don't know Aurora, the Great Mysteries and all that. I don't know that God runs things on the same level that we are familiar with. My best guess is that He just makes things possible - what we choose to make of the choices She gives us is up to us."

They sat quietly awhile longer, sipping and chewing. The rising sun slowly spread its tentacles across the firmament. God's morning exercise routine. Soon the main cabin behind them began to fill with rustling noises as the others began to stir, run showers, and cook breakfast.

"Shell, do you think that there is any chance we'll find life on Mars?"

"Well, Aurora, the Good Lord has a lot of tricks up her sleeve and this would be a great waste of space if not."

Xiao Li's typically Chinese habit of switching pronouns mid-sentence had an interesting theological effect whenever she talked about the Almighty.

"I don't know Shell. The Good Lord seems to me to be much more liberal with space than with life."

"Well, we're here aren't we?"

"Yes, I suppose that's true." A worry began to niggle at her. "But we can't really live here. I mean, these tubes and our suits are little pieces of Earth rocketed over here and we are just along for the ride. We can't really be a part of all of this." Aurora gestured towards the view outside.

"Can a nanobe or bacterium enjoy the sunrise Aurora? We are products of the same Creation as Mars, why shouldn't we belong here?"

"Because we can't stay." Aurora wiped away an involuntary tear. The unexpected emotionality took her aback.

"You want to stay?"

"Well, probably in the long run not as romantic as it seems now."

"Here, have a tissue."

"Ta," Aurora wiped her nose. "it's just that it would be some consolation knowing that this world is not completely barren. That some living thing will still belong here when we leave. Do you know what I mean?"

Xiao Li regarded her friend with concern. "Yes Aurora, I think I do."

The sun rose higher, the carbon dioxide frost fading from the dunes as the temperature outside increased from hellish to merely a deep freeze.

Xiao Li's face appeared to moisten, as if they were chatting during a wet Winter's day back home and not on a planet which was drier than any desert in Australia. The change activated Aurora's suppressed thirst. Her friend was beautiful, glistening. Xiao Li's features softened, like an Impressionist's painting, and seemed to flow into the air, which was now water. Her hair appeared to swim, independent of gravity, like prehensile tendrils with a will of its own. Her face seemed to split into many faces, bobbing in invisible currents.

"Aurora?"

The concern in the voice focused Aurora's attention on Xiao Li's worried frown and her friend's head merged back together.

"Aurora? Are you okay?"

"Yeah. Yeah Shel. Just. Nothing really."

"Let me know if those ones come around again."

Aurora was taken aback by the comment. How much did Xiao Li know?

"Let's get back with the others Shel." Aurora's face flushed as she changed the subject.

When they returned to the canteen Terry and Phillipa were stuck into each other again. Phillipa was in full form, fresh from an early morning on the Neuronet where she had been organising and reorganising funding and alliances, issuing carefully worded press mnemes, and corresponding with the Yanks about something. Terry was annoyed with Phillipa for taking unilateral action on issues that had not properly been discussed amongst the group. The rest of the crew was enjoying the spectacle of Terry getting well and truly up Phillipa's nose.

Lately, Aurora was finding it difficult to sit through these arguments. She had never felt particularly comfortable contributing to them in any case because the others seemed to be encouraged by her joining in. Her apparent, possibly short term, immunity to Outlanders somehow translated into a responsibility for setting the example, which was a responsibility that she would prefer to do without. She excused herself, glancing guiltily over her shoulder at Xiao Li. What had gone on there?

Aurora climbed back up on her bunk and flicked on her neurovisor to check her e-mail. At the top of her mneme queue were the three constant letters in her wandering, interplanetary existence, 'MUM'. Aurora cracked open the mneme and invited her mother's thoughts into her mind. And was predictably disappointed. Like all her mother's communications it was all a bit too clean, with words carefully selected to strip away any subtext that might betray what she left unsaid. Not that what she shared was untrue, and the sentiments were lovely, exactly what a lonely but proud daughter on the other side of the solar system would want to hear. What annoyed Aurora was that all her dealings she had with her mother were like that. Too sanitised.

There was plenty that might never be said. Aurora still following in Dad's footsteps, and even after he had stopped for good? How did it feel that Aurora had chosen him over her? But Mum liked clarity and wrapped up loose ends. The clear lines in Aurora's mind that made her into a half decent scientist - those came from Mum.

Why on Earth had she married Dad? Why, at thirty-six, did this still matter? A habitual flick of attention brought a mneme board into Aurora's neuroview and she began her response.

Dear Mum. Full stop.

That was all Aurora could manage. And then her words flowed away with unseen currents into an endless sea.

She switched off her neurovisor and lay back.

This was crazy. Why was she keeping this to herself? She need to tell someone about this now, but then she forgot to.

The next day day she decided to take Julia on a short field outing, bundling her up in the sled in a thick swag and bungees pulled tight. She argued that the cramped confines of the station were making Julia's condition worse. Phillipa had disapproved, but Aurora was in no mood to compromise. Chandra had backed her up provided safety protocols were followed to the letter.

"Great. The two people who should be on observation going on an outing. Am I the only one who sees this?" griped Phillipa.

The woman could get stuffed. Still, in the part of her mind that mattered, the guilt stuck. Anyway, it was ridiculous to get wound up about it. Aurora still passed all the standard tests as well as she ever had.

151

"Don't worry Julia. I'll keep an eye on everything for us."

"Wheee," enthused Julia softly.

Denali had dragged them out for a grand view south along the Chasma. As they went, Aurora shared Wheatbelt Wallaby stories with her friend, and they seemed to brighten Julia's spirits. She filled in her creation myth, the story of the sisters and the brothers and the lecherous Mars, with new embellishments.

"So Ror," There was a long pause as Julia recovered herself. "The planet - the planet just needs to get – to get laid."

Aurora snorted. Jules was still a funny bitch. "True? I think you are onto something. The poor horny old guy. Tell that to the terraformers."

Wheatbelt Wallaby and Blue Bilby followed dry skin shed by the Waugal, the Rainbow Serpent, who had long ago left the land following the water and now coils up under the polar ice with nowhere else to go. Maybe Blue Bilby is lucky, Wheatbelt Wallaby tells her, because snakes will eat little bilby bunnies. Blue Bilby points ahead, far down the skin, where it kinks over itself and then grows fat further on. The Waugal, Wheatbelt Wallaby explained, had eaten too many bilbies and numbats and was digesting them when he happened to slither through holes in the skull of Ginga, the salty croc, where he had been stranded by the retreating tide that never came back. There was nothing else for the Waugal to do but back out, and the skin slithered out off was left on both sides as this dry valley. That bit you can walk across where the skin breaks in two, that's what's left of Ginga, his eye socket bone. Hyblaeus Chasma to the west of it is the shape made by the weight of his bony head.

Julia didn't respond, and a quick check confirmed she had fallen asleep.

Dad should see this, Aurora thought happily. He'd love stomping around out here and the Dreamings he would have strewn about might just be strong enough to bring the Waugal back. It was fifteen years now she'd been exploring on her own. After Mum left him, to free him to his own devices and to move in with Joe, Dad had just pitched down stakes at the end of the same road in a bush block and began to wait for something that never happened.

When Aurora moved in with him, usually subtly and sometimes not, trying to get him back out walk-about, Dad had just shrugged. Sometimes he humoured her, but they never went far.

"No purpose left in it," he'd say.

"You can't go out without a fight with Mum. That's crazy. You don't have to do that anymore. You can go anytime you like."

"It's how I knew she loved me Darl, no point to it now."

That comment still pissed Aurora off.

"What about me Dad? What about Wheatbelt Wallaby?"

And then he'd shrug, and they'd go somewhere, usually to visit a mate and have a bush tucker barby and talk about the old days.

So, she'd left him puttering around his shed as he did most days, never more than a few stone's throws from Mum and her new husband, but almost never stopping by. Aurora had left and borrowed his spirit for the long journey as he apparently had one to spare. She was in Antarctica when the cancer came, and part of her was glad she hadn't made it back in time to see him give in to that too. Mum had been there to help daily, so it might have felt crowded. The other part of her felt like crap.

"What do you think Dad?"

"Not bad Darl, not bad at all," answered Waijungari.

Aurora studied the thin ridge at the confluence of the Chasma. It was just the right size to walk across, and too small for the Djambi rover to follow. A straight-line East was the center of the world of Elysium, the great Goanna Man himself. He called out to her heart, serenading her.

"I'll be soon on my way," Wheatbelt Wallaby sang back.

"Who are you – who are you talking to Ror?" whispered Julia.

"Nobody."

As they returned to the station Julia woke in a panic. "Rory, do you know who I am? Do you know who I am? Everything keeps disappearing in turns. I don't know what's left any more. Is it all like this? Are we just a crazy quilt patched together in our minds? When we die. When I die. Ror? Will anything be left?"

The answers drained away from Aurora's heart, like water into sand. Any reassurance she tried to offer just masked over the mirror Julia was holding up to her own face and she felt like a hypocrite.

As Aurora carried her friend in through the station airlock, Julia died. The finality of Julia's death, unexpected and sudden, was shattering. The worst of it was the unbidden feelings of relief; that she was off the hook from this claustrophobic responsibility. More terrible still was Aurora's anxiety that attention would now shifted to her own state of mind. That she wasn't being as clever as she thought in disguising her strange watery spells. Chandra was watching her every move now. Phillipa's hostility toward her seemed more overt, as if it were Aurora's fault the Julia had passed away on her watch. The woman kept twitching to say something but was biding her time until it would not be unseemly to say it. And what was truly unbearable is that any of this mattered. Julia, beautiful Julia. Gone.

Phillipa delivered a somewhat inappropriate eulogy. "And if any of you need to share your grief or talk things through, my door is always open." She seemed disappointed at the silence which followed.

Aurora had sprinted out to the utility shed after the funeral was over. She had to be by herself. Before the hour was out the door behind her opened and Phillipa slid in. Aurora pretended to not notice.

"I suppose you think you are awfully smart."

Aurora put down the rock core she was examining and waited for the inevitable accusation she had been covering up her Outlanders. How was she going to respond?

"Smart? How do you mean?"

"That little trick of yours at the AGM. Going over my head. As far as you could go really, I shouldn't have thought you had it in you."

"Excuse me?"

"Well, I'm sorry to inform you that it hasn't worked out as you intended."

"I'm sorry Pip but I really have no idea."

"Really. Nothing about this."

A light flashed in Aurora's peripheral vision announcing the arrival of the mneme Phillipa had sent her. Aurora closed her eyes to view it. Her hands gripped the workbench as she watched in disbelief.

It was an invasion; August Bridges had that right. That someone would go into her personal mnemes and throw one out there like that - it felt like having her skin ripped off while everyone watched. The only thing that kept her from losing the plot was her anger. That smarmy bastard implying that they were mates. Twisting her words around so they meant the opposite. Suggesting that she was off her nut. Aurora could count on one finger the people she'd come to hate, and August Bridges was earning that honor right now. And to think she'd ever found that asshole attractive.

Phillipa was waiting.

"Phillipa, would I have done that to myself?"

"No. I think you were caught out."

"What?"

"It has been a long time since you were on-board with our primary mission. You've always been pushing the boundaries to make a name for yourself."

"A name?"

"Well this time you've obviously gone too far. I'm putting my foot down."

"Pip. My name has nothing to do with it. This is our only chance to find Martian life. If we don't now, they'll wipe it out before we even know if it exists."

"Well, you may be right Aurora. 'We' will have to consider that, but that decision, that effort, won't involve you."

"Who else? It will take years to get anyone up to speed. Elysium Mons is on our doorstep."

Phillipa shook her head. "And I am going to put a risky mission like that in the hands of someone obviously suffering advanced stages of Outlanders?"

Aurora said nothing.

"You don't deny it. And to think it took August Bridges to point it out. I will tell you this isn't a good look for me as Chief Scientific Officer."

"Phillipa. How many notes has Chandra put against me?"

"You are looking to your friends to cover for you? Without you as cover they'd have to stop pushing their own pet projects and actually listen to me."

"It doesn't work that way."

"You don't think so? Do you think I achieved my position through naiveté regarding group politics? Everyone looks up to you as the one who has logged the most mission hours without distress, and this justifies them pushing their limits."

The accusation was over the top.

"That's not true. I've never been a stirrer."

"No. You are worse than that."

"What do you mean? I keep my head down. I concentrate on my work."

"You don't even realise, do you?"

"Realise what?"

"That you are their leader."

"Bullshit."

"Doubt as you may. The rest all hang on your every word. You set the example. I will not let that example be one which compromises safety. You will be leaving with the supply ship that was meant to take Julia."

The walls of the room began to diverge from the space they contained. Aurora tried to ignore them and find some way to respond to this impossible situation, but the feeling of disconnect was pervasive. Everything in the shed, including Phillipa and herself, seemed, for the moment, to dissolve into liquid. It felt strangely good, as if she could merge into an invisible ocean and perfect anonymity.

Wheatbelt Wallaby intervened suddenly, singing the water away. The walls and the world beyond solidified.

Phillipa watched her closely; and Aurora was annoyed at herself for giving herself away so obviously.

"Well then, since apparently I don't have a say in any of this, I'll go pack."

Aurora strode out of the shed, relieved when she arrived at the bunk station. A whirlwind of thought dispelled the burden of thinking unduly about her little spells or the fact that Phillipa might possibly be right. Could she be right? When she reached her bunk tube she gave the wall a frustrated kick. Screw her. Pack up and ship out then. Pass the buck on saving Martian life to someone else. Who else? Who else?

August Bridges, what a shit. It's good to see how concerned he was with doing the right thing. She could see his true colours now. This wasn't just a decision that Pip would have made by herself. She always played it safe with higher ups. No, that mneme would have put the wind-up August Bridges and, in response, he was shutting everything down. It would be personal too. He'd put the nail in by pronouncing that life did not, in fact, exist on Mars. And then he'd hung it all on Aurora, on her supposed irrationality, and then turned her convenient removal into a safety concern. He was the devil incarnate.

As the edge came off her anger Aurora began to grieve. How long would it be before anyone followed up on her work with priorities being redirected? A hundred years? Who knew really? And in that time, they probably could develop the kind of economical space flight August was after, and then it really would be the end of any indigenous life on this planet.

The weight of responsibility from this line of thinking became overwhelming for Aurora. Wasn't she getting a little ahead of herself? How could one person be that important? If that was the way things were going to turn out, who was she to get in the way? Then again, who was she not to get in the way?

Better to do anything rather than sit around. Packing was easy. All she had to take with her were the few carefully weighed possessions she had brought with her. In fact, most of these could be left behind. And then there was nothing to do. Terry came in to commiserate and, in turns, so did the others.

Aurora didn't feel like talking because talking felt like giving something away. The others finally gave up trying to milk some resistance from her and left her to her own devices. Which was fine with her.

She flipped down her neurovisor and began to review her findings, flying over her samples examining the wealth of information they contained. An entire fossilised microbiota. Why was she making such a big deal out of this? Any university department in the world would be happy to have her.

She could take her place standing on the broad shoulders of the pantheon of giants in her field. Sagan, Runnegar, Hoffman and Grey, Pella, Swedell, Shakya, Rieselbach, Yu – the heroes in her love affair with the astro-paleontological world, whose names appeared as citations to nearly every observation she made. It was not a bad fate. There was enough in these samples for lifetimes of papers. A lifetime of looking back.

Other names joined the timeline. The irregular men in her life who could never keep up with where she was going. All those names between Mum in the beginning and Dad on the other side were just points in the line that extrapolated to Mars. She had climbed that line with passion and now that she had gone as far as she could. What exactly was there to return to?

Aurora scrutinised the specimens as they scrolled past her view - microscopic blemishes that the untrained eye would mistake for crystals or layers of sand. Details, details, details. Life was in these details. Or rather within them was the skeleton of life.

Wheatbelt Wallaby waved her paw and her power shook through the ages. The small dots began to agitate and then stretched after their long sleep. The power of Life grew in them, an essence powerful enough, even at small scales, to create atmospheres and precipitate mountains, tenacious enough to survive trips to Earth on the backs of meteorites, to ossify for centuries and then to carry on as if nothing had happened. The small Dreamtime animalcules all cheered her for awakening into her Dreaming, for singing them back into existence.

Was there any question that Life was still out there somewhere on Mars? She imagined for a moment August Bridges' smirk that had sent her off to this whole adventure. Pointing out an impossible responsibility to her and then pulling the rug out from under her at the same time - the cruelty in that was unbelievable. How she loathed that man. Imagine his surprise when she came back from the field with actual samples.

Aurora brought up a neuroview map of Mars and began to scroll over it. On the scale of the map the journey did not look all that long. Weren't they already on the foothills of Elysium Mons? The only real barrier was walking across the rock bridge she had pondered when out with Julia. The journey would be uphill, but the topography was still accessible by sand sled. She and Denali could make it in a month, at most, with stops for drilling, and sampling the still-liquid groundwater. She had argued the case to anyone who cared to listen. For years, the plan, all the particulars, the lines on the map were all fixed in her head. All she needed was the Djambi and a few crew. Terry and Xiao Li had been chomping at the bit to go with her. What was the big deal?

Aurora was bitter as she contemplated her impending exit from the world she had grown to love. A world calling urgently for her to defend its heart. She had neglected to answer the call because of the dull anxieties of accountants, lawyers, and bureaucrats millions of miles away.

Who was to blame for that? She would go to her grave with an unbearable weight on her soul when it would be so easy just go now.

Go now. Risk everything, her safety, credibility, and career, all for one shot at the Truth. To be honest all she had were crazy ideas to go on. And yet it seemed as if the decision had been made for her. Aurora reviewed the mental checklist accompanying her plan. What she had to do was quite straightforward. She had a plan, and the plan successfully masked the whole box and dice of the insanity involved. She would complete the longest unassisted extra-terrestrial expedition in history. That was the plan.

Well, at the very least, Aurora reasoned, she could always chicken out halfway, pick up a few more samples, and miss a claustrophobic flight home in the process.

People would be sick with worry. They'd all think she'd gone Outers. Phillipa would go off her nut, Aurora thought with a grin. They would come after her.

It would compromise the safety of the group. She could be sued, labelled a loose cannon in her profession. And, if she was being honest with herself, Aurora didn't know how far she could get with a sled full of supplies and sampling gear.

It was a bad idea. Dangerous, unauthorised, with an uncertain return, but at least it was a plan, which was better than the alternative. The plan gestated into action. She could always stay out the day and come back in time for the shuttle, take the slap on the wrist, make a point.

For the plan to work she would have to escape undetected and she would need rest for the journey. She forced herself into a fitful sleep. Xiao Li and the others passed by her bunk from time to time to ask if she wanted to eat but she politely declined, feigning an illness.

At midnight Aurora awoke groggily to the whispered beeping of her neurovisor alarm. After a quick graze in the kitchen she pulled on her body stocking, zipped on her squeeze suit and helmet and, with Denali at her side, slipped out of the station and headed for the utility shed.

Unlike back on Earth, on Mars there was always time for thought. There was work to be done, but activity unfolded at a natural, unhurried pace. Mars was a world frozen in time since its birth, activity was foreign to its nature. Immersed in this geological stillness Aurora often had to consciously remind herself to breathe. So, this was the first time in many years that Aurora had felt the unseen, inexorable pressure of time running out.

What surprised her was that the work was mostly already done. It was as if for over a year provisions had been stockpiled, gear had been stowed appropriately, more power packs charged than would ever be strictly needed for stock standard field trips. Even the appropriate modifications had already been made to the sand sled. It was as if she had been working towards this moment through innumerable daily decisions.

She readied the sled almost habitually but fumbled as she dragged out the compressed air tanks. She was breathing hard and she could feel her heart racing. She sat down to catch her breath, to concentrate on what she was doing. A small mistake now would be ultimately fatal. Quietly and efficiently she worked through the night, painstakingly loading, unpacking, and reloading the sled.

Two months rations, compressed gas cannisters, sample bags, electron microvisor, poptent, solar powered water condenser, graphite rope, celestial navigation system, waste-molecular reprocessor, commlink boosters, flares, Buckeygel refills, spare helmet, cesium packs, spare harness, walker braces, neurovisor, rope. Now, where are they? Field notebooks, heaters, vitals monitor, med kit, night goggles, skin defrost. It all was so well rehearsed. The incremental completion of her checklist instilled a meditative calm.

Before sunrise, Aurora had the sled reliably loaded, had jotted a brief mneme of explanation to Xiao Li to be delivered after a time lag, and was ushering Denali and sled through the shed airlock into the waiting darkness.

Within an hour, the dusky gray tubes of Mawson Mars had slipped behind a ridge as Denali and she headed into the rising dawn.

ISLAND OF JEWELS

*'Liberation's good qualities, like an island of jewels -
If they aren't known, there is no way to begin to make efforts.'*

Aryasura

CHAPTER 12

Aurora

The bridge of stone, twisting its way steeply across the confluence of three impossibly steep Chasma, lay before Aurora's path like a giant question mark. This was the place where she should turn back, the place where she should finally answer the panicked calls from base and return to the end of her mission. It had been fun up to this point, almost joyous, as she and Denali had sped freely out into the waiting embrace of Mars. This was where the exhilaration should end, a brief flirtation with what might have been.

Her neuroview bellowed Terry's extreme displeasure.

"Aurora, I don't know what wank has mixed up your head, but that's all it is, wank. You won't get anywhere you can come back from because Elysium Mons is too fregging far. We all know this, we've been over it that many times, it ain't gonna work. Whatever the Ox is whispering in your thick head is total Outer bullshit. For your own sake, let it go and answer me."

Aurora opened a channel to transmit a response but immediately switched it off. Had she just given away her location? Agitated, she switched off her neurovisor entirely and a deep shiver ran through her body.

Terry was right, but it didn't matter much at the moment. She had anticipated standing at this exact spot for a long time, and her answer to turning around was more or less the same as it had ever been. That this was all bigger than her, and that greater things were at stake. Her choice was starker than ever because of August Bridges driving things this way, with full knowledge of the consequences.

"If we don't document Martian bacteria, we won't be able to preserve them."

His words not hers.

He had encouraged her, and she had taken him at his word. And after all that, August had driven the knife in.

"This is a cry for help from someone, a friend, who is suffering profoundly."

They were such best mates. Weren't they?

The whole time he'd known she'd be in his way. That's why he'd funded her, like he said, so he could come out smelling of roses when he shot her down.

That was why this expedition of hers was not about recovering a few specimens to preserve for posterity, as August had suggested. No, it was impossibly larger. Her discoveries could be used to save an entire planetary life system, to have the whole of Mars declared a reserve. And that was why she was out here, taking these enormous risks. The stakes were that high.

Denali was watching her, eager for direction. Ears perked. Aurora listened as well, to sounds pitched at geological frequencies, to an unearthly rhythm lasting eons.

She heard him calling for her. Waijungari sang out to Wheatbelt Wallaby from across the desert, serenading her to visit his camp fire for only a while. Just for a short while. He was so lonely for even friendly mateship. Come on over for a cuppa. Sing me just a little more into the universe. Don't leave me empty. You can still go back anytime you like little sister. If you turn back now you are just afraid. If you turn back later, you will have been someplace no one else will ever see. No matter how crowded-in your Dreams become after, we will always have that time together.

Her mind flattered by the sentiment, Aurora shook the reins and Denali, released to follow her lead, scrambled forward pulling her along.

Their passage across the rock bridge was like being suspended in wonderland. Mars could be a dull and dusty sort of place, the spaces long and, to the untrained eye, monotonous. Visitors often remarked similarly about the Australian outback that Aurora had grown up into. You had to develop an eye for it, and a geologist's training was a big help to see the history of the place. This Croc bone bridge was not like that. Any tourist brochure of Mars would pick out this place. It was the smallest she had felt since she had arrived. The scale of features around dwarfed her, the plunging depths waiting for her with any misstep, the canyon walls swallowing up the horizon, the unexpected colors and shadows. It had a beauty that defied description. The opening wedge of the salty crocs head of Hybleaus Chasma followed behind her, pointing the way towards the final crawl up steep terrain to the other side. As the sun set, shadows from the west end of the Chasma grew long, chasing her up the incline. Before she reached the other side, Aurora looked out, taking in the perilous path she and Denali had just traversed. There was no way the Djambi could follow them across; the rescue party would have to travel a couple hundred extra kilometers to catch up with her.

Once across the bridge, they travelled along the edge of another small canyon that had once carried a river down the flanks of Elysium Mons. Just before nightfall they pitched camp on the East side of a hill and Aurora cuddled up to Denali for a hard sleep.

The next few mornings they woke early and worked their way ever further East until the canyon of Stura Vallis ran out and all that remained before them was a long dust plain. From her altimeter, Aurora knew they had progressed some way up the slope of the volcano, but the mountain was so big and the slope so gradual that it was impossible to tell this by reckoning. They were still too far away for the peak to be more than a bump on the horizon. Their journey forward for some time would offer little variation, with the panorama behind them slowly widening as the only indication that they were moving upwards.

There was no risk of getting lost, even though a satellite positioning system did not cover their position and compasses were useless on a planet lacking a magnetic field. The celestial navigation programme in Aurora's neurovisor could site on the positions of the stars to calculate her coordinates. It seemed incongruous to use all the familiar constellations from Earth to find her way on this remote, exotic world. The evening skies of Mars were same ones Aurora had looked up at all her life - the inconceivable distances to other stars shrinking to insignificance the gap separating Mars from Earth.

There were some differences. The planets travelled a slightly different path through the night, as did other heavenly bodies. This was a consequence of Mars spinning a bit more upright than the Earth. Mercury was too close to the sun to make out. Venus had a small bluish companion at dusk and dawn. These were fine distinctions.

Dancing through the night were old companions. Orion with his great sword stalking the equator chasing the seven sisters of the Pleiades, a story shared by both the Greeks and many Australian First Peoples. The Great Bear with his eye high in the North. They were all swamped by the Milky Way, the cosmic Emu, which was a thousand times more glorious on a planet without much of an atmosphere. To be out on the sands of Mars at night was like walking on the beach of an island amidst an ocean of dazzling jewels.

"What do you think of this Denali?"

Grunt. His servors whirred as he rolled over on his back and Aurora began to scratch his exposed stomach.

Her Dad walked over and sat down beside her, his arm over her shoulder lending her warmth.

"What do you think Dad?"

"It's all right Ror. You've picked us quite a spot."

He was right. The view was unsettling off the tall cliffs of Stura Vallis and out over the other Chasma and the plains far beyond. It was clear they had gone up a fair way when the stars began to look like they are spread out beneath them. Aurora took a drag on the reheated piss her suit had transformed into coffee and enjoyed the heat fanning out beneath her breast.

"Do you think I'm doing the right thing?"

"I dunno. What's right?"

"That's not an answer. I'm scared."

"Uh huh."

"No. I really, really don't know what I'm doing here."

"You must know or why else'd you be here."

"They're coming after me. I'm putting the people I love at risk. It's the most selfish thing I've ever done Dad."

"Not the only selfish thing."

"What? What could be more selfish than this?"

"It was selfish when you left us all."

"Selfish? Selfish? You bastard. You can talk. How many times did you leave us?"

"Guilty as charged. Struth. Had to be who I was Darl. That's my point. Just like my daughter."

"You stopped. You quit. You gave up."

"You didn't. You aren't. Why's that?"

She didn't have a quick answer.

Denali sat up and leaned into Aurora for a hug. She clung onto him tightly.

"Don't worry Denzi."

He yawned.

Relaxing before the stars, Aurora let her mind rest in the tranquillity around her. Some part of what she was chasing was this peace that seemed everywhere around her. Each breath could come as free as the last. There was a joy in this constancy, which she often became lost in for hours. In that eternal now, she didn't need to have answers. Then the questions would begin again.

It was time for bed. Operating as late as they had into the Martian night meant wasting Denali's valuable energy on internal heating. Aurora climbed into her swag and hooked his batteries in to keep her warm. Then she found the spot behind his ear and switched him over into low power mode. Savouring the bust of warmth released from the condensed fats in her evenings vitabar ration, Aurora tried to find some sleep herself.

Instead she lay awake into the night. Her sleeping bag temperature, set on the far side of tolerable, sharpened her senses. Now, instead of relaxing her, the titanic silence of a dead world kept her awake. Her eyes strained open, her mind on guard against the annihilation threatened by a falling eyelid. Hallucinations began to descend; *water roared past Wheatbelt Wallaby in the distance, filled with screams.*

And filled with questions Aurora could not answer. She was completely abandoned by her better sense. The compulsion to continue was a weary madness. What the hell was she doing out here? She voiced the question aloud, earning a commiserating grunt from Denali.

The night continued to offer no answers. She thought about her plan and became dismayed as she was unable to reconstruct a whole sense of it. Every detail seemed to dissolve into a tidal rush of panic, the air solidifying around her. Aurora tossed about looking for something to sustain her against the crushing apparition and ended up taking refuge in childhood memories.

Her rubber thongs caught in the sand as Aurora broke through the spinifex and stalked up the hill. She was running towards something. She had always been running towards something. They were in the grip of drought yet again and there hadn't been a lot else to do. Out here, in the Bush, chores done, there was always somewhere else to go and somehow her soul always tilted towards the horizon.

She pretended that Jesse was hard on her heels but knew that her baby sister had predictably fallen behind. More interested in the spring flowers, clouds, and birds, than in the impossible task of catching up, Jesse had slowed to a stumbling and disinterested pace. Aurora crested the hill that had been the object of the exercise. Triumphant she turned to scrutinise her sister's performance. Far back along the red track she could make out a cotton dress bending over something in the bush. Aurora wandered down disapprovingly. Retracing ground was distasteful.

"Jesse, what are you doing with that old feral?"

The tattered and shivering gray cat glared back from its new home, wrapped in Jesse's blue school jumper.

"It's sick Rory, I'm helping it."

"Don't bother," Aurora snorted derisively.

Jesse bit her lip and began to stroke the wild cat's head.

"Jesse, you're a worry. Ferals carry disease and they kill Natives. Dirty old thing."

"But it's crook Rory."

"It's not crook, it's probably been poisoned by the Rangers. Should be too. They eat Natives."

"I don't care. I'm taking him home." Glowering, Jesse gently scooped up the dying creature and cradled it. Aurora waited for her sister's innocence to be abruptly violated with one swipe of the moggy's substantial claws. The thing was no house pet – evolution from a few centuries on hard scrub had seen to that. It was as big as a mid-sized dog. Instead the beast began to purr.

Jesse tended the ailing cat through its last days - gave it a name that even Aurora had given in to using. What was it again? Muzza.

Jesse was now a Mum. Aurora tried to imagine her sister tearing her hair out as the cute little monster ran her ragged. Sharing stories with the other mums. Juggling the intense relationship of mother and child with the competing demands of Hub, self, and family. What would that life have been like, that other life unlived? Claustrophobic, a confining prison for a restless spirit, but safe and a hundred million miles from here.

How had she come to this, outracing the entire human race to this desolate frontier? She was on the back side of beyond, but still the unachievable tomorrow called out her in notes long and low. What if she should have stayed at home, dropping out children with Jesse? What part of that life was so impossible to imagine?

"See Darl. We are what we are. Like I told you."

Aurora ignored the comment.

"That's the answer to your question."

"Come on Dad, you're just something I made up in my head."

"Same difference. We are what we are."

Aurora thought some more about the differences between her and Jesse, which used to be more symbolic than real, just the standard way siblings differentiated themselves. Jesse the fertile Earth mother. Aurora the intrepid explorer. Somehow those identifies had become fixed, and motherhood became a destination further from Aurora's mind than other planets. She recognised the irony that seeking life on Mars meant she had abandoned it in herself. Space travel required you had to burn that bridge - the risk of mutations from the radiation was too great otherwise. Aurora had happily joined the honorable tradition of Hub aunties and uncles - those who made this choice to focus scarce ecos and resources on fewer kids in a still overfull and heavily degraded world. What did it matter? She had inherited her father's light feet - hardly an ideal attribute for a mother. She was what she was.

Her toes began to go numb from cold and she realised that, somehow, she had climbed out of her swag and walked back down to the overhang, drawn back by the view. Aurora was shivering badly by the time she made her way back into the swag.

To distract herself from the cold, Aurora opened a neuroview and flew around some satellite projected imagery retracing her journey from Mawson to her current location. She noticed that the Stura Vallis landscape surrounding her, from Space, looked like a uterus, which made this place Women's Business. On this scale, the path ahead almost looked plausible. Her friends were out there following her, the Djambi turning left to drive in the opposite direction to travel round the end of Hybleaus Chasma before they could begin to catch up with her. She prayed they would be okay.

Again she lay awake, tormented by the struggle between growing doubts and an irrational fascination with proceeding forward. As exhaustion began to overtake her Aurora felt the terrible wraiths of her half-conscious imagination overtake her. Her fingers seemed to stretch into strange tentacles.

Denali twitched, immersed in his own weird cybernetic quantum dreamtime. An awareness of another consciousness laying so close to her brought Aurora back from the edge. She huddled nearer, cradling his furry body. Denali groaned. Aurora gave quiet thanks to the boffins back home whose alchemy had produced such a wonderful creature. She hugged her dog and felt a shroud of sleep descend over her. Together they shared the night, carbon and silicon, content in the safety of each other's company.

Aurora awoke with the sun already high overhead. Her body was numb with cold and sleep and sitting up was an ordeal. Her temples were throbbing. The increasing headaches were from her progressive dehydration, as precious water escaped, in drips and drabs, the closed loop of the squeeze suit. These needles in her brain somehow encouraged her. Drowning out more superficial thoughts, it allowed her to concentrate on the specifics of her mission. She methodically organised her gear for the day ahead. Cleaning dust from the oxygen harvesters - from everything for that matter. Examining her body for frostbite and pressing the Buckeygel in her suit until it was evenly distributed, with no thin spots that would compromise her insulation. She ran logistics programs through her suit's computer and reconciled her equipment inventory. She turned off the risk alerts since, according to them, it was highly probable that she was dead already.

Denali roused and gave her a lick. Crippling doubts returned in force, but they were soon overcome by a heightened awareness of her migraine. The headaches became something Aurora could hang onto. "Go forward," they seemed to say, "Get on with it. Head down, bum up. Behind is pain. Forward is purpose, clarity, freedom."

Aurora returned to her tasks and the pain receded. Apparently still alive, all checklists complete, she triggered the gas recovery program. She felt her suit tighten as the atmospheric pressure dropped to ambient levels. She stepped out of the tent and watched as it folded in on itself into a neat circular package, easily stowed on the sled. She harnessed Denali and the two of them headed off into the rising sun.

Over the next days, Denali pulled her doggedly on across the featureless landscape. After a week of this they happened along a deep scar in the land running across their route, the first of many fossae rifts they would encounter and the primary target of her investigation. Scouting the edge, she found a ramp leading steeply downward. She loaded Denali with the portable drill and the two of them walked down together. Denali was excited to be unhitched from the sled and bounded ahead, running recon as his view of the world broadcast to her own neuroview in a corner of her mind.

They stopped for Aurora to investigate promising outcrops, but she saw nothing that spoke to her of recent water. She drilled a few holes, but they came up dry and as the excursion continued in this way Aurora increasingly agitated. Why was nothing as she had imagined? The geomorphology was all wrong. The satellite images had been misleading. The sediments were abnormally dry, as if a sudden heat had vaporised every damn molecule away.

Aurora looked plaintively up the tight walls of the fossae and eons of tortured geology recorded in them, and then, suddenly, she understood. The planet had played a terrible hoax on her. Rockfalls that from a hundred miles above had looked like groundwater slumps, when examined up close, were obviously the results of residual tectonic shifts and micro-earthquakes. Instead of preserving life across the eons as she had imagined, Elysium Mons had blasted it all to buggery. Life out here was as unlikely as if she had been looking for it on the surface of the moon.

The rushing waters began to scream. Aurora wanted to claw the blood out of the impudent red rock with her geologist's hammer. She yelled out, calling the uncaring mass of it a hundred useless names.

Denali tilted back his head began to howl in commiseration. The thin air carried little sound making it barely audible, but through the neurolink Aurora could feel her sorrow being shared. How could people think of him as being just a machine?

She sat down on a rock.

It had all turned into a giant joke, her coming out here to save the planet. There wasn't much worth saving. If nothing else, she'd done the opposite.

"Thanks for checking this out for us. It'll be easier for everyone to fill out the paperwork now."

August Bridges regarded her with eyes full of generosity.

"But just because they aren't in this spot doesn't mean anything."

"It'll mean something."

And that it would.

"Ah, Denali. Where am I taking us mate?"

Denali stopped howling and switched to wagging his tail. Just like that he traversed a whole spectrum of emotion. That kind of resilience made her feel humble in being human.

"This is awful. This isn't anything like I thought. It's not going to work. We might as well go home, yeah?"

Denali sat down to groom himself.

The walls of the fossae seemed impossibly tall and her body felt, by comparison, impossibly small.

"What am I going to do mate? This is as far as I can go, and it isn't far enough."

Denali licked her and started to walk up the ramp, stopping to look back at her.

Through the neuroview she could see herself through Denali's eyes. A red dusty shape almost blending into the red cliff wall. She was sitting still so there was very little to distinguish herself from her surroundings. Mars and she were becoming one.

Just come stay for a cuppa Darl. Just a short while to keep a lonely old man company. You've got some time yet before you need to go back yonder. There's always time, if you can make it.

Aurora stood up and trudged behind Denali up the ramp and out of the fossae.

As they walked she considered her position. All the arrows in her life aimed nowhere now. The moment of first contact - the first direct meeting of life from separate planets. It was all she had imagined for herself.

A void encompassed the world, outracing the returning sunlight as Denali and Aurora emerged back out onto the surface. She felt herself sinking into it. Into loneliness. Into the lifeless crust beneath her feet. It was the only place of belonging left now that her imaginary ecology of Mars had abandoned her. Her samples ceased to be emissaries of a living planet, whispering their peculiar mysteries into her dreams. Now they were just lines on a family tree that died out meaningless billions of years before. Songlines leading to nowhere.

Funny that, Aurora thought. Just like her life.

That night Aurora realised that she had, in fact, come to the end of the line. She had counted on drilling her own water supply while out here. There wasn't any.

Desiccated dreams descended. With each breath Aurora could feel her water supply fading away, taking her life with it. With each breath she felt less. She was going to die, and she didn't care. There was freedom left to her in that.

"We are what we are Rory. We are what we are."

"Just stop in for a cuppa. What do you have to lose Darl?"

Aurora's night opened out to dreams of a distant world, seen as if through a kaleidoscope with many eyes full of tears. Strange creatures with too many heads and arms, though oddly familiar, floating impassively while she made her plea, until it became clear there was nothing left to save. Their world would disappear into their indifference. There was no point making an issue out of it. It had all happened so long ago.

In the morning, Aurora looked out the frame of clear Buckeycloth at the front of her tent. The east side of Elysium Mons was massively illuminated by the golden shadows of morning - its peak penetrating endlessly above the thin indigo clouds and smoky ruby foothills below. A divine exaltation rising forth.

Aurora sat up and felt the gravity of the majestic mountain tugging at her. In the absence of any power of her own she rose and folded the tent and harnessed Denali and they headed onwards up it. The headaches increased like something terrible happening to someone else until the pain became visible, lines of light breaking the volcano into shimmering schemata that interfolded with Aurora's soul.

From time to time Aurora hesitated, feeling the moment of her death approaching with each step. Mum, Jacob, Jesse, Zoe, her friends. All coming to an end, but then the scale of these things would be dwarfed by the intensity of the vision rising before her and she would understand that they all were what they were. Grains of sand running out into the inevitable.

And so those moments ran out, one by one, until she reached the wall. Elysium Mons was surrounded by great, slowly subsiding foothills, that would be mountains on Earth. They had picked their way up between the mountains until the only way forward was a tall cliff. The tortured stone mass jutted straight upwards, an abrupt boundary across the slowly mounting chaos of the surrounding highlands.

Aurora's concentration, focused by the razor's edge of pain cutting through her skull, mathematically evaluated the monolithic surface. On Earth, she had been an accomplished mountaineer, successfully scaling several difficult Antarctic peaks. There was climbing gear in the sled.

The world turned on its side. The ground no longer gripped at her feet - no longer pulled her soul down into sterile stone. Suddenly Aurora understood. Her moment of freedom and of redemption was at hand. She would not die before experiencing something glorious. Up there, into the wide yellow sky.

Denali looked at Aurora expectantly and then back the way they had come communicating the obvious fact that they had reached journey's end. For a moment she hesitated, considering his plea, and the pause released the pain in her head to drop down her spine and send her hurling into the dust with the weight of it. She lay on her back, gasping, staring up along the infinite walls.

Slowly she crawled her way up to her feet using a boulder resting at the base of the cliff. It was a recent break gauging by the angular edges on the exposed side of the rock. She made a mental note - she would need to be mindful of potential rock falls.

Her mind, encouraged by the practicality of this consideration, followed her eyes up the cliff face, evaluating alternative routes and judging the security of footholds. Methodically Aurora set to readying her ropes, testing the piton hammer on the rock face, packing and repacking her small backpack. She remembered the necessity of wearing a spacesuit when climbing a mountain that extended above the atmosphere. She opened the tent, climbed inside, and changed. The suit was bulky and would make climbing more difficult. She observed this clinically as the issue, when weighed against the inherent impossibility of what she was attempting, was insignificant. She collapsed the tent and stowed it back on the sled. Then she walked to the cliff and began to climb.

She looked down to see Denali pacing anxiously. Suddenly Aurora realised that her journey from this point forward would be alone. The thought was too dangerous and invited only the pragmatic response of climbing back down to reach behind Denali's ear and finger the switch that dropped him into shutdown mode. She regarded his resultant peaceful repose with pang of guilt. She would not likely return, but why should this marvellous creature, her friend in fact, deserve an uncertain fate because of her selfish and foolhardy compulsion. She set his power supply to reactivate in a few hours. If she had not returned by then she was most likely dead in any case. She input a command for him to return home upon awakening - she was certain that he would find his way, his petabytes of memory had recorded every movement of his body during their outward journey. Returning was a simple matter of playing this recording in reverse. To be sure she turned on his emergency locator beacon so that others would find him if he was close by.

Denali refused the command and just sat there, surprising her.

"Mate. You can't go with me. You can't do anything for me. You have to tell the others not to bother."

Still he sat, rooted to the spot.

"Denali," she pleaded. "Go."

Still nothing.

"I'm going anyway."

Aurora turned away and began her ascent. As she climbed Denali's white form stayed in place for a long while, until she disappeared over a stone ledge. She spied on him through a crack between two rocks and watched him tentatively circle before turning to run. She watched until he receded into a pin prick and disappeared around a bend in the valley.

The pain drove her relentlessly forward, pushing her mind ever back to the present, to her hands and body melding into the grey, sand polished rock. Even her breath became purposeful. Breathe in, know pain - breathe out, know pain. A timeless moment later, fingers numb and her frail body pushed beyond any comprehension of a limit, Aurora crawled over the lip of a small ledge. She curled into a tight ball of despondent, laboured breathing.

The damn of her world burst, and she was carried away by the sound of water rushing off into nowhere. There was no point fighting it, and as she began to flow with the world her pain dissipated. After an indeterminate time, her mind reassembled and the pain had inexplicably stopped. Or, rather, it remained, a constant but unimportant. Aurora looked around for the first time since her climb began. The clouds were below her so there was no accounting for her altitude. To her left, round the mountain to the East, she could make out the silhouette of Albor Tholus, a brother volcano to Elysium Mons. Behind her, the sheer wall continued upwards. She was too close to estimate the remaining height, but it seemed to slope upwards after a few hundred metres. The ledge she was seated on was metamorphic, a deeply folded greenschist recording the violence with which Elysium Mons had repeatedly thrust himself upwards from an immobile hot spot in the mantle.

Aurora gathered her strength and continued her climb. Her body seemed lighter; progress now effortless. In a few hours, after deftly surmounting an ever-shrinking series of indented cliffs the abrupt slopes attenuated into a long, graduated incline. The clouds below evaporated, and Aurora took in the spectacular view. There was no end to it. Her sense of scale failed her completely. The desolate landscape peppered with impacts and ancient riverbeds wrapped the arc of the world before blending imperceptibly with the translucent pink sky. The sudden, almost infinite, liberation from the awful bloody mindedness of her climb was beyond contemplation. The air, the mountain, the clouds, her body, all intertwined in a whole being that seamlessly broke and reformed in every instant.

"We are what we are Darl," Waijungari confided in Wheatbelt Wallaby. "You've come a long hard way to visit me. Why don't you sit down here and rest awhile?"

Wheatbelt Wallaby laughed.

"Okay dirty old man, but no funny business."

She critically regarded the massive head of the Goanna towering behind them.

"Don't let him worry you none. He already ate."

Wheatbelt Wallaby smiled. This looked like a good place to be. She dropped her kitbag, laid back beneath the stars looking back to where she'd been born, and felt good about how far she'd come.

"I guess I'll stay Waijungari."

"Good girl."

And with that she turned to stone.

CHAPTER 13

Calvin30

This scene unfolds with Calvin30, crowned in a beanie of looped Kenyan beads, outside on the green and dancing in your head.

Da da dada da da dada da da da da da daa dada.

How faint the tune, how high the moon, how near, how far, it's where you are.

Da da dada da da dada da da da da da daa dada

Things ain't the same they used to be, no ignorin' what's yet to come.

Da da dada da da da dada da da da dada da da daa dada

Oh frabjous day callooh callay he chortled as mome wraths outgrabe.

da daa dada da da dada da da dada da da da da da daa dada

Time to kill the monk.

dee dadad dee ddeee dada deee dddidi ddddaadiii dddiiidid dad ada aaaa dad

Amidst a free note whirl wind denoting nothing but mind unleashed, tree needles under feet, and breathing spirals inspiring madness from the circular muses of purposeless sound.

The monk sat.

da daa dada da da dada da da dada da da da da da

Why was it nobler in his mind's eye to knock off the rock we all live on than to neutralize some lonely guy so far across the ether he might be closer dead?

da daa dada da da dada da da dada da da da da da

Only this cold whole fact; that Calvin30 was a herder of men not a murderer of them. A Shepherd of Soul might lead his lambs to slaughter, but a butcher was another beast. Entirely. The manner of the deed was not the spanner in his plan. The monk was too far out to see him bleed, or freeze, as the case may be. No, it was the crudeness of the execution that transgressed Calvin30's aesthetic sense.

176

da daa dada da da dada da da dada da da da da da

Clouds coalesced and decomposed, following the flow of high blue winds far above the pine trees and the variegated lawn of wild flowers where Calvin30's graffiti painted park bench was planted.

da daa dada da da dada da da dada da da da da da

A squirrel peaked between his feet and dashed for a cone, grasping it with greedy teeth and stealing it off to a branch just outside of Calvin30's grasp. The rodent scrapped a few scales from the cone and then chided the interloper in his territory from above.

chii-chi-chi-chi-chi-ki chii-chi-chi-chi-ki-ki

da daa dada da da dada da da dada da da da da da

chii-chi-chi-chi-chi-ki chii-chi-chi-chi-ki-ki

da daa dada da da dada da da dada da da da da da

chii-chi-chi-chi-chi-ki chii-chi-chi-chi-ki-ki

A sharp squeal in the key of G at 60,000 hertz knocked the rat off his perch and onto the rocks below. It lay twitching as Calvin30 put aside his horn and stood over it. One stomp later and it lay still.

The clone scowled at the mess left on his all Nigerian leather Andres Stiltle slips, regretting immediately his rash act. Near the top of his game and reduced to wrecking good shoes, this just wouldn't do.

Then again now he'd killed his first thing and perhaps it only took getting used to. Next time he'd be more careful to keep clean.

He wiped his sole in the grass, avoiding the glazed gaze from the ghastly pile of guts the squirrel had become. The leather was still wet with it after many inspections. Calvin30 moved the shoe into the sun, and worried that when dry it would be ruined. He remembered buying them, hand crafted wonders, at a boutique in the part of the East Village still not under water. They couldn't be replaced.

To distract himself from the disaster, Calvin30 activated his visor.

The scenery softened and blurred behind the mental projections of the Earth falling away and the stars shifting sideways. From the vantage of Valhalla, Calvin30 viewed the spinning disks of planetary paths and plotted the angles. The Mirtopik deep space micro-satellite relay was mostly under his command. Months could transpire before anyone would detect that the monk had expired. Any of myriad minor malfunctions could be implicated.

But why kill the monk? Because Calvin30's control wasn't complete. A chance conversation could sink the whole adventure. Delaying news was one thing, excising it was another, and if the monk spoke to someone on a personal channel, such as that Martian scientist, then the censor could be exposed.

Calvin30 traversed down to the Terrapod and stood beside it in a panorama mosaic stitched together from shots taken by the scientific rover attached to the mission. It was unthinkably small, a few metres sphered. He called forth a mneme of the monk, a bland looking boy, one Venerable Kalsang Jampa, implacably unimpressive.

Perusing the mneme logs for a sense of the man, Calvin30 found the monk pathetically silent during his tenure on Triton. Only standard acknowledgements to system checks and spartan well wishes to friends and relatives. It wasn't completely clear whether he would be killing someone who might mind. Calvin30 shivered involuntarily. What bugged him about this guy?

What got him under Calvin30's skin was a sense that, while he might write the guy off with a flick on a switch, there was no feel of the man he'd be offing. It was all too easy. No way to bring Jampa to the party, no self-pitying lament, no source of remorse that could occur in the last moments remaining.

He scanned some mnemes of the monk at his business.

Monk wakes up, monk says prayers, monk checks instruments, monk eats, monk shits, monk sleeps, monk smiles without mania, monk cries at times with no depression. No slow fuse self-immolation of the stoic was on view. Kalsang Jampa's drama was as unselfconscious as a stone. This made him seem more unreachable than being past the edge of nowhere where he was.

What would happen when Calvin30 ended his days?

Monk dies.

And that would be all there was to it.

Was that all there ever was?

The globs of glistening goo encircling his heel print in the grass seemed to answer his question.

Squirrel dies.

If that was the sum total of a whole life, what was the point of it ending?

The glazed eyes on the limp head looked up accusingly, suggesting this wasn't the entire story. Calvin30 scowled down into them and then was caught by a laugh. That was the whole point - that people believed their life was more than less. Knowing that, and flowing that, was his power. But then it bothered him that the monk looked to be in on the joke.

A family came towards him down the path and Calvin30 kicked the grime from his crime into a ditch out of view. He grinned sheepishly as they passed.

What was the matter with him?

After they had ambled away he looked back down, and the squirrel was gone.

What the hell?

Gone. It must be there. His eyes started to panic, flicking up and down the ditch.

He squinted, thinking it somehow camouflaged in the mud. Finally, he fell on all fours and felt through the ooze.

The thing had to be there only it wasn't.

Had he imagined doing the deed? No, his slips were still slimed.

Calvin30 returned to erect, unreasonably upset. How could the damn thing just disappear? Why did he feel such primal possessiveness? What had denied him his kill?

Bushes twitched in a thicket. Calvin30 spied the culprit, a feral cat carrying his prize. The circle of life had claimed his victim - the squirrel was already half eaten. The cat licked itself over before starting in on the rest.

Calvin30 collected himself, inspired by the feline's cool insolence. There was an animal he could appreciate. How could anyone eradicate that cat and not be second rate?

Calvin took up his horn and purred a homage - his preferred Ellington standard.

> There will be
> many other nights
> like this
> And I'll be
> standing here
> with someone new
> There will be
> other songs to sing
> Another fall

Another spring
But there
will never be
another you

The cat toyed with his food, imagining its unlikely reanimation. Alive but dead. Calvin30 tipped his horn to the cat granting it credit due. If only death were not so definite then he could also kill the monk and play him too.

Some epiphanies appear only when the impossible presents.

Alive And Dead? The exegesis came to Calvin30 from entirely outside the box.

Shröedinger's cat.

Alive and Dead. The only animal he'd heard of that ever managed that trick just happened to be a cat. From his pop culture acquisition of quantum mechanics, Calvin30 knew of a freaky experiment dreamed up by a scientist named Shröedinger to show how weird subatomic physics could be.

His recipe went like this.

First, put a cat in a black box, not in a hat or a house with a mouse, but with a vial of poison gas. Next, from some radioactive matter pick an atom, any atom, whose decay will switch the trigger - when it goes the cat gets gassed. Nothing interesting from the outside folks.

Here's where it gets weird. With atoms, what you see is what you get, but what you don't see don't actually factually exist. Since both the cat and the atom are hooked together in the dark, they disappear into the shadow of their potential. So, Atom Cat gets to play it both ways - hot AND decayed, alive AND dearly departed.

Calvin30 remembered this, not because he understood the science, but because it struck him as suitably twisted. When he'd first heard of it he'd mentally put his brothers in that box and dreamt them dissolving into improbability.

If a full planet of people
and uncounted cats
die and don't in a box perhaps from some gas,
and no one outside can hear them scream,
do they sound like no sound?
It was all so extreme.

Calvin30 flushed at his fortuity in finally being able to enact this fantasy.

As everyone knew, the innards of computers used to be digital but these days they packed more switches into the same space by using quantum gates that could be both off and on, or off or on depending on how and when you looked in on them. The wizards had long since mass produced the perfect kitty killing itchy trigger finger.

It was almost too simple to link the life support in the Triton Terrapod to the stateless state of one of these illogic gates. Calvin30 stood in awe of his artistry, at how he had transmuted the crudity of murder into an endless canvas of creation.

Details, details.

He'd have to cut all communications to the pod because peeking in would make one outcome so. If the monk chose to send out a signal from his side, the experiment was still on. As far as the world was concerned, the pod would have to vanish from view. They'd have to fly up an entirely new receiver to replace the one he was about to fuse.

The risk had to remain that the monk could blow Calvin30's cover - otherwise only the fate of the monk would be in the box. But if the monk could both tell and not tell, with such enormous consequence, then everyone went into the box with him. It was too risky, of course, to make the odds fifty-fifty, and Calvin30 planned load God's dice considerably. Still, he'd have to be in the box, along with everyone else. The difference was only he would know it. The whole enchilada would become his solo.

There were the standard logistics of awarding credit. Such a stupendous career-shattering mistake for someone else to make - perhaps good old Wolf. Perhaps reveal the boy as a Rev saboteur. This could integrate nicely with the rest of his plans - although he would have to make the detective trail long enough to get the timing right. That shouldn't be a problem considering that it was going to take a while for the powers that be to realise that something more serious than a neurolink breakdown was happening here. In the meantime, the world would think of poor Wolf the way he would think of himself, as an overworked and consequently incompetent goof.

Calvin30's fingers fiddled around the pipe keys as he composed. This was a stroke of sheer genius. He warmed up into an improvisation of '*Everything happens to me.*' The cross program on the bass line would ping the connection to the Saturn up-link station to keep it open. A few standard phases needed to be reprogrammed to activate pre-programmed communication functions and to access different areas of the Terrapod's computer. He tested the programs, running up and down scales and releasing discordant squawks and fluttering tremolos. He mapped out the composition, key changes, and timing. And then he went to work.

His tongue buzzed as the notes fired and whirled cascades of floating neuroviews before his eyes. The song jerked swiftly out of the melody and into a new improvisation whenever spontaneous alteration of the program was required. As he neared completion, the song crescendoed in excitement before relaxing into a playful rendition of '*Without a Song*'.

When he had finished, he checked the time. He had spent hours immersed in the bliss of creation, but now the scene was set. What the Big Guy in the sky had said and done in seven days, a mere clone had surpassed in less than one. While the Creator had made only one reality, Calvin30 had created two for the price of one. The alpha omega and nil.

The future was both alive and dead, a shimmering wave of probability encompassing the whole human species. He had perfected the art of undermining people's sense of certainty. Now in one stroke he had consummately conquered certainty itself, casting the entire human body, including his own, into the quantum flux.

Not bad for an afternoon in the park.

His quantum self flipped off its neurovisor and looked around the park. Shröedinger families picnicking. Shröedinger bicycles and cars. Shröedinger squirrels and Shröedinger crows. Above him, Shröedinger clouds and, below him, Shröedinger dirt.

No longer would resentment motivate his Art. No longer would he wish unhappiness on the people down the park enjoying their picnics and their idle larks. Now, with precise clarity, he could see the uncertainty and hilarity lurking in every moment of their illusory reality. No need to seek it through manipulating their pathetic, tired, simple selves. Now he would feel it in the all of every minute of each entire glorious day. Calvin30 felt, as if for the first time, sufficiently complete.

A blur of calico blended through the foliage to his left.

Calvin30 leaned over. "Here kitty, kitty, kitty."

As he stroked the purring fur, the beast repaid Calvin30 by coughing up the leftovers from its feast at his feet. Cracked remnants of skull with one accusing eye spied up at him.

That creature had escaped his net, Calvin30 reflected. There was only one outcome for that being and he alone had decided it. Such a waste.

As Calvin30 wandered away he felt the eye following him and wondered if it would ever depart.

CHAPTER 14

Kalsang

Kalsang lay prone outside the pod in his over-inflated inner tube of a space suit, slowly collecting a thin drift of pink methane snow. An answer to his predicament had not come and time was running out.

Some of the aliens turned from their vigil around him, to look back towards the Terrapod, and the others besides d'Song soon followed their lead. Was this an ill omen, or a clue that might lead to his survival? Perhaps it was best not to take the actions of imaginary beings too seriously.

His attention returned to his legs, slowly burning with cold, the pain extending upwards from his feet like a flame travelling down a wick. His feet, already consumed, were numb.

The situation would have been intolerable if his legs still belonged to him. However, from Kalsang's detached perspective, the sensation was like watching a pair of well-loved trousers unravel.

Things were not so comfortable a few hours ago. Then the magnitude of his suffering would have made Kalsang writhe in anguish if his rigid suit had allowed him. Time and his contemplations had saved him. His toes were on fire? Were his toes on fire or was his mind on fire? If his toes were on fire why was his mind suffering? If his mind was suffering, then what part of his mind was on fire? If his toes and mind were one, why couldn't he stand up by his thoughts? And so on like this.

By now the suffering was just another purification that Kalsang was happy to accept. Better to face it now than after death when the consequences of unresolved karma could be more severe.

More hours slowly passed. The numbness reached his hips. His alien audience began to evaporate.

Myriad images began to swirl into Kalsang's mind as the oxygen supply in his suit dwindled. The Ice Ridges of Triton merged with the Snow Mountains of Tibet. Rainbows danced around his field of view. In the middle, seated on a jewel lotus, sat his Lama. Her body constantly shifted and broke into shards of other memories like a multi-faceted diamond.

There were his other teachers, his mother and brothers, his old meditation cell in Khyipuk, the faces of his debating partners and protectors, fragile flowers blowing in the mountain breeze, yaks and birds, starships and stars.

His body began to feel light, almost insubstantial as he observed his senses flicker in and out. He sank ever deeper into a general warm feeling.

Kalsang's body was beginning to die. He recognised the first signs, a subject he had studied exhaustively as a student in the monasteries and had incorporated into his meditations since. He was dying and, happily, he had few regrets. So lucky, even though he was just in his early thirties. He'd been trained to know that death was just part of the package of living.

Once again Kalsang patiently reviewed his situation and once again resigned himself to the improbability of escape. He checked the time left on the oxygen supply and, carefully and methodically, Kalsang began the practice of dying.

His eyes, which now refused to shut, noticed the blue globe of Neptune begin to expand until it encompassed the whole sky. A rich field of indigo permeated space. His mind began to shimmer and grow cloudy as the memories started to fade.

"Kalsang-la, Kalsang, wake up."

Kalsang looked around dreamily. Kalsang, yes Kalsang is still my name, still a name.

He felt an insistent tugging at his shoulder. He still had a shoulder. The tugging imparted a warmth that began to travel down his body, steadily thawing the numbness.

Kalsang looked up into the clear light that suddenly interrupted the ubiquitous blue. Like a proud parent Lama Wangmo gazed down indulgently at her young disciple.

"Lamala?" Kalsang murmured weakly, his features softening to return the smile.

"Dying is interesting, isn't it Kalsang?"

Kalsang's pupils widened. The habit of attention to instruction reactivated his mind. The small fact of dying did not seem to be a good excuse for disrespect to his Teacher.

"You have done what I asked, and you are dying well, Kalsang."

"Lamala?" Kalsang began to shiver as his awareness of his body began to return, *"are you real?"*

Lama Wangmo laughed and pinched at her robes. "What is real? What do you think?"

"Uh."

"No time, Kalsang. No time. Listen to me. Yes, no doubt you are dying well. Alone in your hermitage like some great yogi. In your next life, you are really going to be something. You must be proud."

Kalsang's brow registered a wrinkle of surprise. Was his teacher mocking him?

"Kalsang la," Lama Wangmo continued, "You must be congratulated. A fine culmination of a life of devotion. All the Buddhas and bodhisattvas in the ten directions and three times are overjoyed and waiting to shake your hand in the pure realms."

"How?" Kalsang's frozen mouth struggled to form the word.

"Do I need to spell it out for you?" Lama Wangmo raised her eyebrows disparagingly.

Kalsang's body twisted as the stabbing pains returned. Lama Wangmo winced, betraying her concern for her student.

"Kalsang, listen to me, your loving Guru mother.

The seeds of space grow slowly
infinite eons of swelling darkness
there is no end, but even this
wasteland of void
can bear fruit

The seeds of life grow slowly
uncounted cellular generations
evolving without direction
an accidental mind arises
this jewel from dust

The seeds of consciousness grow slowly
dull impulses of ignorance
taste of grasping and fear
forever but one day,

a clear thought
The seeds of enlightenment grow slowly
even stainless bodhisattvas
compassion hearts overflowing
rarely find suitable lands
for full awakening

My son please act quickly
our fragile mother world fortuitous
harmony of numberless sorrows
help this perfect echo
moment last longer."

Kalsang dreamily floated into the rich rhythm and comforting cadence of the teaching. Lama Wangmo shook him again, sharply.

"Kalsang, you spend all day long meditating on compassion. Everyone is your mother, your best friend, lost in a universal ocean of suffering. And then you smile because suffering is a dependent arising, an illusion, that can be overcome. This is very good, but do you ever wonder what this means in practice?"

Kalsang, with an imperceptible motion, shook his head.

"If you don't know, you AREN'T ready to die. Don't be lazy. Get up."

Kalsang shook his head, this time to gather up the unfolding tendrils of his mind, as his teacher abruptly vanished. He was still on Triton laying on his back staring up at the great blue mass of Neptune. The numbness in his legs receded as a strange warmth emanated from his bones.

He sat up. How could that be possible? His suit, which had been locked so stiff, had now gone a bit soft. The answer came to him - the CO_2 scrubbers. In routinely cleaning his exhalations they had been sequestering the expelled carbon. Now there was just enough room to move about.

No time for sitting. Kalsang pulled himself painfully to his feet using one of the landing struts from the pod. The door was still open, and he slithered up onto the open deck of the airlock. He reached up to activate the lock. Nothing happened. No matter how long he pushed, there was no response.

The returning pain in his legs was screaming for his attention, a thousand needles plunging into his muscles. Kalsang's brain was swimming from the lack of oxygen and his exertions. He slumped back to the floor, head bouncing off some metal cylinders lying on the floor behind him.

Oxygen? He rolled over and used a burst of adrenaline to fumble with one of the precious canisters. He yanked the auxiliary oxygen supply hose on his suit loose from the Velcro straps and clamped the adapter over the valve at the top of one of the tanks. The indicators in his neuroview turned from red to green as the life-saving gas rushed into his suit, which began to inflate. Kalsang scrambled to switch on the suit's pressure regulators to prevent a fatal replay the over-inflated suit scenario.

No time to relax. What was going on here? The airlock was dark. Why should that be? He tried to register the pod's status on the neurovisor. Nothing. Even the manual override for the airlock was not functioning. He crawled up a gantry and stretched to reach the view portal.

He kept a close look on his footing while his uppermost head turned to look.

Kalsang was disoriented for a moment. Why couldn't he see anything? Then he realised that he couldn't see through the portal because he no longer had multiple heads. When had he ever?

He noticed a hinge latch that he could get his foot over and managed to peek above the ledge.

It was dark inside as he expected, no need to waste energy on lights when he was out, but the standby panel lights had gone out as well, and the leaves of the plant nearest the window, still green, looked like they had cracked like glass, or ice. The fine edge of frost on them confirmed it - they had frozen. If the plant had frozen, what had happened to the TerraPod core? Kalsang's heart was hit by a wave of grief for his little friends that had lived there. At the same time, his body hit the ground softly.

He had fallen again.

What to do? Kalsang climbed back up into airlock.

He reflected on the situation. The only possibility that made sense was a total power supply failure.

A soft glow at the corner of his neuroview caught his attention. The orbiter icon. Maybe he could interrogate the computer on the module orbiting Triton to override the computer in the pod and open the doors. He held his mind on this request and the orbiter's control console appeared floating before him. A flashing warning light indicated that the orbiter had lost control of the pod's computers and that all internal diagnostics for the pod were not responding. It was strange that communication had only been cut one way. Why should he be able to contact the orbiter but not the other way around.

Kalsang studied his dilemma. His situation was dire. His pod had become a black box with no apparent avenue of communication left open. The airlock was locked and there were no other entrances. Time was running out, but where could he go? The only safe place he could go seemed to be the orbiter. He contacted the orbiter's computer, brought up the address on emergency evacuation procedures, and quickly scanned the downloaded mneme.

The contents were not encouraging. Since gravity on Triton was weak, only a fraction of that on the moon, it was possible, in theory, to insert himself into the correct orbit by using an Emergency Orbital Insertion Unit which was a modular one man rocket pack stored alongside the launch engines at the base of the Terradome. Kalsang followed the instructions and located a button that, when pressed, unceremoniously ejected the device out into the surrounding drifts nearly taking Kalsang with it.

He righted the unit, examining it doubtfully. It looked flimsy. A body harness strapped on a slight structural brace linking an assortment of rockets. It needed to be snapped together. How would they even test such a thing?

The rapidly dropping power in his suit's batteries reminded him that this absurd contraption was his only chance. With trepidation, Kalsang pulled it over his shoulders, tightened the straps, and aimed himself unsteadily into the empty sky, and initiated the launch program.

"Internal diagnostic check complete. Suit power supply on reserve. Continue?"

Kalsang's eyes selected the affirmative icon in the neuroview.

"Om mani"

"Best orbital insertion calculated."

"Padme"

"Countdown commencing."

"Hung."

"5,4,3,2,1. Launch is go. Are you sure that you wish to launch?"

What? Kalsang blinked in disbelief. What a time to ask a question like that. Of course, he bloody well wanted to launch.

The unit roared to life at Kalsang's affirmative thought, suddenly blasting a stunned Kalsang out on a course nearly parallel to Triton's surface at a breathtaking acceleration. The wall of the crater rushed towards him on a collision course. Kalsang squeezed his eyes shut, bracing for impact. He opened them in time to watch the crater rim rush beneath him with only meters to spare.

The great pink plain of Triton shot out before him as he was whipped out across it ever higher. Up he floated into the black emptiness of space as if pulled aloft by a balloon. This sense of a serene ascension was randomly interrupted by the rockets firing to tug him into alignment with the planned trajectory. Beyond these gut-churning episodes, Kalsang felt surprisingly relaxed. Nothing to do, so why worry.

Rendezvous with the orbiter was scheduled for several hours hence and, in the interim Kalsang, completed several rounds of mantras, and studied the surface of Triton as it passed below him. Triton was an ancient world of secrets, wholly unexplored except for cursory photographic mapping and some preliminary spectroscopic analysis to determine resources available to support a manned mission. No one had seen, or was likely to ever see, this elegant and remote world from the stunning perspective Kalsang experienced in these moments of free ascent into heaven.

Ahead of him grew the large, world wrapping violet crescent of Triton's twilight. As Kalsang gradually entered it, and the ground below him dimmed, he became engulfed in the utter blackness of night in the outer solar system.

"No eyes, no eye consciousness, no ears, no ear consciousness."

Kalsang flew on without any point of reference on which to attach any notion of self beyond the pale green light of the space suit's status gleaming in his neurovisor. In fact, there seemed to be little difference between his current situation and his earlier brush with death. It occurred to him that for some reason in both instances, that these moments of total dissolution were paradoxically the moments where he felt himself to be most connected with the universe, that great vacuity which contained all potentials. He settled into a mediation focusing on this realisation.

His meditation was interrupted hours later when the positioning rockets jerked him around and the main jets fired in the opposite direction to slow his motion. Minutes later his attention was drawn to a blinking red light positioned next to his feet, illuminating a smooth surface beneath him. It was then that he had the disconcerting feeling that he was standing, or rather his feet were floating, against something. As he crouched down to examine the surface beneath his feet, the light softly pulled away as Newton's Third Law of motion reared its ugly head. For every action, there is an equal and opposite reaction.

Then it dawned on Kalsang. The orbiter. He was standing on the orbiter. He activated the torch on this helmet and rotated. His outreached hand managed to grab hold of a railing. He walked himself, slowly and deliberately, hand over hand down to the main airlock door and to safety.

CHAPTER 15

Francesca

One Monday morning all her Sundays came at once.

Francesca watched once again the real time mneme she had shot with her neurovisor cam of the meeting she had just exited. If she was going to be canned for sticking her nose in where it didn't belong, which was what she had thought the meeting was going to be about, that would be fine by her, but the suckers were going to have to pay out big time. Francesca wanted to record the guy squirming as she asked veiled tricky questions hinting about the clone's secret downloads that her manager would know nothing about, but that the persons directing her manager and listening in would be threatened by. She had been on the look-out for that little tick people had when they were communicating by thought through their neurovisors with someone else. It was so obvious and annoying - anyone could tell. It would have enjoyable to watch her boss, the little cross-eyed twirp with the bureaucratic eyes and the crooked lazy grin, being forced to change his approach mid-stream, as directed by invisible puppeteers, and watch the price of her silence climb through the roof. So what if they let her go from her dream job? It was too good to be true anyway. She was expecting a golden parachute of voluminous dimensions, enough to cover her for a good long while. Then she would have headed out for a protracted period of playtime.

Only the thing was the guy didn't try to let her go. In fact, he was cheesed off about the possibility of losing her.

"You are the best operator I've had in this spot for years. You have had some good reports from the team," he said with a sigh.

That must have been Wolf. When was the guy going to cut to the chase? All this gushiness was breaking her heart into pieces, really.

"But I can't get in your way on something like this. I should have known someone with your skills would be in the running." More sighing and a particularly gross-out throat clearing.

Francesca didn't know what to say. She didn't even have a clue what the guy was talking about.

"The Academy let you in Salvador. It's a sweet job. Everyone in ComSec wants to get that one so I can't fault you, but you could have told me you put in for it." More sighing. Francesca cut in before the throat clearing.

"What? Like the Academy for, you mean the Space stuff, that one?"

"Space stuff? Are you kidding me?" The guy was getting about as agitated as she could imagine a boring guy like him could get. "Mirtopik Merchant Marine Academy. You-you lucky lousy shit. I've applied for years."

Por Dios, Francesca couldn't stand for this idiot to start tearing up. Like she cared.

"Yeah. So what? I put in for it. Doesn't everybody?"

Everybody but her that is.

"What's the chance they'd pick a testarudo like me? I don't know nobody. I didn't need to tell you shit anyway."

"No," her now ex-boss replied stiffly, "no you didn't."

So, that was cool. They were promoting her out of their way and now she was cleaning out her desk and heading off into Outer Space, like Rocket Girl to the rescue or something. Incredible.

On the way out, she passed Wolfie for the last time. He was nervous and worn out because a lot of shit had been going down in the Department lately. "Don't tell me you're leaving," he moaned. "What am I going to do with all that work?"

She handed over a stick with all the reports on it. "That's them. I finished."

"All of them?" Wolfie looked up at her like a starving man who someone just handed steak dinner.

"No, I said I finished, but I only did a couple." Wolfie grimaced.

"No stupid. I was up all last night flossing my teeth. Of course, if I say I did something then I did it. Why would you doubt me? Here." She put the stick in his shaky little hands.

"I, thank you." Then he went all teary. Jesus, what was it with men and blubbering today? Francesca started to move into the hall.

"It was cool meeting you Wolf."

She hoped he'd enjoy all the comics she'd left with a note for him in her office.

And then she was in the elevator and unlikely ever to come back. On the way out to the SkyTran station she thought she saw the clone again, except without his usual get up. It could have been any one of them because as time had passed at Mirtopik she'd seen that face in a number of different roles, but she recognised the confident gate, the subtle swagger that set him apart.

Francesca grinned and gave him a thumbs-up. She knew this was just a convenient way to get her out of the way with the least fuss, but there were lots of less generous ways to go about that. There was nothing about the clone that she trusted but she did owe him one. Probably that was the idea.

The clone looked around like he was unsure who she was motioning to and then gave her a tentative smile, and a thumbs-up back, as if he didn't know her but was just pretending to be polite and shit. She caught him out by the glint of recognition in his eyes when their gaze met.

Who gave a shit anyway? Francesca was headed off on the greatest adventure of her life and she didn't want to piss off the dude who had done it for her.

Francesca headed out to catch her flyseat on a time machine that would propel her through a day and night non-stop period of the most exhausting training in her life. Months later, she stepped off that time machine and boarded a rocket for the space station and then onto her final destination, the near-Earth orbit comet of Tsuchinshan. According to their briefing, the comet was full of valuable outer space water and came close to the Earth every five years give or take so they had to go out and mine the shit out of it while they had the chance. Her team would be relieving some of the guys that had been camped out on it as it was coming in from deep space, and would help them load the cargo, and then get everything locked down and get themselves off before the comet got too close to the Sun where it could become unstable.

Blah blah blah. Straight out of the lectures she'd been studying until her brains exploded, while her body was surviving all the slam and bam the brainiacs could throw at them, which was nothing on her really, and all the psych games thrown in to twist around their minds that she was so damn good at playing when she could be bothered. It was so easy to numb down and just work through it all that Francesca had sort of forgotten where it was all really leading to. And this was what it was all leading to; having the unlikely honor of being in the teeny tiny fraction of humans, those assholes lucky enough to get blasted off the planet and into the great beyond. It wasn't as simple and up-in-your-head as that. The reality was that she was actually doing it. Right here, right now, countdown on, leaving everything totally and truly behind her. It was so incredibly awesome, like Superwoman finding her G spot.

So now Francesca was strapping herself into the nose cone with a dozen odd other hardcores and it almost felt like sharing a Tran gondola at rush hour, but when fizz-crack-roar her head mashed down and smashed into her ass, Francesca knew this was something completely new for her. The fire and boom and the ground shrinking away looked like any one of the non-stop of neurosims that they'd put her through down to the crunch on every bone in her body. The fact that was completely different from all that was that now, in this moment, nobody could take this away from her ever. She was riding it for real, and heading into something that was absolutely hers, no looking back. All those idiots in her past could eat her smoke.

And then after a good God awful long shake her body went so feather light that her soul practically floated out of her mouth. It was the most beautiful feeling nobody had ever told her it was possible to feel.

A few hours later they were docking with the Mirtopik International Space Station and then having a good play in the zero G gym. The Earth was laid out overheard in these big panoramic windows that were unusual in this day and age when everyone went for the cheap option with cams shooting virtual landscapes through your neuroview, which meant you never knew what was real and where the ghost images of the walls kept interfering with the view. Here she was floating like Freya along the rainbow bridge fresh down from the hall of the Valkyries, stripping free from all those earthly things that had tied her down since forever, swirling like a genie dancer among the stars of the Arabian nights spread out below as the station orbited over the vast deserts that had claimed most of the land.

Francesca was sure that she had finally made it, watching her sweat beads lift off like constellations of pearl necklaces as she pushed effortlessly through her work out and the world in all its glory turned out below. The ecstasy flowing through her veins was not even limited by the ordinary distractions of lusting over the bodies of a few hot other grunts perspiring through their routines. In this magical liberty, even the old emotional traps could no longer get their teeth into her anymore. Hours and hours just evaporated into pure joy.

After a rather anti-climactic lunch of vitabars and food in tubes, Francesca and her fellow merchant marines donned pads and sparred. She was pleased to discover that with combat in space raw strength was no advantage and finesse was everything, which meant she was in her element. Kick. Slash. Spin. Thunk. She rapidly dispatched guys that she would have thought twice or three times about taking on back on Earth. Her capabilities seemed to be freed from limitation; not by her sex, not by her size, not by her strength. If she was only limited by her imagination she might finally have chance to become invincible.

Francesca imagined herself finally becoming superhuman, like in the comics and in her head, but this time for real. If she wanted to walk on the ceiling like Da Girl Fly there was no problem with that. Pick up anything and throw it like the Bitch, a little more difficult because it would also throw her, but then again, she also could do it anytime of the month.

And there was the tech they made up for combat in space; it would put Batgirl to shame. Francesca had always been good with gear because it was the great equaliser whereas the boys would forget to use it because they thought they were badass enough already, but when fighting with her this was a fatal mistake.

And of course, there was the No G dropstick, non-sparking because of the high oxygen atmosphere. After all the training, a dropstick felt like a part of her body and was a much more powerful appendage than a dick. When a dick ran up against dropstick it always lost, poor thing. Maybe that was useful in some situations, but she'd rather have a dropstick. And then there were these wrist mounted web-shooters that were actually better than the ones Spiderwoman had, that would spin out these steel-silk wires tipped with this nano-velcro that could hook into nearly anything and would let go just when they needed too because they had direct neuro-links into her arms. Having the custom micropores drilled into her hand had stung like a bastard but had been worth it.

And then there was flying, always the specialty of elite *superputas* like Andromeda who got a free pass on gravity. Up here everyone had that power, but not everyone knew how to use it. Francesca learned early. The trick was to throw other stuff and let the flying take care of itself. There was this cool neuro-app that she downloaded that would superimpose lines on her vision of the trajectories of anything she'd throw and also the anti-trajectories where it would throw her. She trained with it but then stopped using it after her body got the hang of it and it was making her go too much up in her head.

The best neuro-apps Francesca found were the ones that would paint virtual Avatars over her body. Girls on Earth would use these to pretend to have great clothes and asses when they couldn't afford them. There was an endless supply of these and she checked out the heroine range, having great fun exploring the options. Soon though these became confining and so Francesca designed one of her own, Nagualita, who was like a cross between Shamaness and Cat Woman. Just by thinking her body would change into any animal spirit, but she also got to have all the nasty gear and the hot stretch suit.

Doing this made Francesca sad and think of Elena and their superheroes. Why did she keep doing this and bringing herself down? The only superpower she couldn't have was the one to turn back time and change everything on one day, and that wasn't one being in Space could help her with.

"You okay?"

It was Raoul, who she had been ecstatic to find crewing the lunar transport when she boarded it at the end of her training. Dark liquid eyes, emotional Aquaman, a man of dreams. Too good really which was the whole problem.

She'd experimented with sex in Space with a couple of the other grunts, which was a whole other dimension in mind blowing, but she only picked the stupid ones and stopped playing around when it became apparent that casual sex wasn't a good idea when you were going to be locked up in space with the losers for the long trip to Tsuchinshan. It was a little messy extricating herself from those mistakes, but these guys were thankfully rough enough to take it and leave it.

Raoul was a whole other thing, and it pissed her off to have him see her cry.

After their training in zero-G at the Earth orbital space station the new recruits had joined seasoned Comsec, including Raoul, on-board the Lunar Ferry to the moon, where they would wait for the freighter from Tsuchinshan to drop of its precious cargo of ice and collect them.

"We're sure to have a lot of room to ourselves on the ferry," joked Raoul, in that way of his that suggested a good use for that room without actually moving to seal the deal. He could be so frustrating that way. In any case, there wasn't a lot of room.

As the Tsuchinshan freighter stayed parked, rocket after rocket arrived bringing a horde of construction workers. By the time it headed out their asses were crammed so tightly together that if she ever tried to grab Raoul's ass she'd probably grab somebody else's instead. Three days of that, sitting in those damn chairs that wouldn't recline without causing the jerkface behind you to bitch about it. And then it took another whole day to shuttle them all down to the Moon.

The Moon. What could she say about that? Who would have thought someone like her would be going to the Moon? It wasn't until Francesca had bounced across the powdery ground to the Luna City airlock with the Earth floating overhead that it really sunk in. She had to stop herself from just falling over in amazement. The quarters were tight but the view, as she dropped off to sleep, was incredible.

Raoul and Francesca got a jump on their shift by waking early, a habit they had gotten into to sneak in a little quality conversation, which was a happy way of saying they hadn't gotten started up with sex. With Raoul, Francesca was okay to take it or leave it; the important thing was spending time with him.

"Hey Geek."

She should never have told him about the comics.

"At least I read."

"Why do you mock the illiterate, mi cielo?"

His sky. She was all over that. Francesca stuffed her mouth with corn flakes and pretended he didn't exist.

"You crunch so intently, you know that?"

She crunched and smiled, spraying soggy flakes as she answered. "It's better than those tasteless bricks they usually feed us. Let me enjoy this."

"Life is to be lived."

Then why don't we stop playing games? The answer. Because playing them is way too much fun.

"Salvador. Ferriz." Stony, their butt ugly ComSec unit sarge called over as he came in.

"Who, us?"

They were the only ones in the mess.

"No, them," Stoney pointed to the empty room, "you guys sec level five?"

"Yeah. I mean at least I am," answered Raoul proudly.

"I'm nine."

Raoul tripped on that. "Wow, a licence to kill."

"Only the people I love."

"What the hell? Shovel that food down and follow me," Stony turned, expecting them on his tail.

Francesca gulped down her bowl, trying not to look at Raoul because it would be all over her if she laughed.

"I feel somehow inadequate," he said as he tipped his unfinished bowl into the Terrapod chute.

That almost did it.

They quick-stepped to catch up with Stony, Francesca dribbling milk off her chin. They followed him out by the rear airlocks where they fitted back into their space suits.

"What's the brief?" Francesca radioed to Stony once they were in a buggy rolling out away from lock. It was weird that they hadn't been given one.

"I'll tell you soon."

It must be something so secret they didn't want anyone listening in on. Francesca grinned. It always felt good when she was in on things that others weren't.

Once they'd gone through a tunnel and must've been out of range where the bluetooth could be picked up, Stony pointed out another buggy loaded up with a tank as they caught up to it.

"We're escorting that."

"What is that?" asked Raoul.

"Enough antimatter to take out a good hunk of the moon. So, you'll keep a good eye out for anyone who might want to disturb the load. We don't anticipate that, but the job safety analysis requires us to baby sit. My understanding is that we are mainly around to handle those." Stony pointed to some bucket shovels in the rear compartment.

"You need a five sec level to dig out a bogged buggy?"

"No Ferriz, you need it to know about the antimatter."

Yeah, about that? Francesca knew enough not to ask questions that were stupid because there wouldn't be an answer.

As they bumped on for hours Francesca prayed that the suspension in the antimatter buggy worked better. She and Raoul passed the time trying to wig each other out with crazy 'it's the end of the world' faces until Stony stopped them with a stern look, which was even more hilarious. Loping down rolling hills they descended into a long dark plane and turned East, skirting the edge of it.

"Mare Frigoris," Stony announced. "We're near the North Pole of the moon." For some reason, even through her thermometer hadn't changed much, it felt colder knowing that.

An hour or so later, they entered a complex of tents that looked like dunes rising out of the regolith.

"Camo," explained Stony, "Rigged so you can't see this through telescopes."

Talk about commercial-in-confidence; it looked like a military operation. Which made them the military.

Stony hopped out and motioned for them to follow, stopping first to talk to the buggy operator, a stubble headed dude who kept going on about what he was going to do with his bonus. Then they followed Stony over to a rise towards some person overseeing whatever it was they were building.

The guy greeted them with a friendly salute.

"Hey. Come up here to check this out."

The voice sounded familiar, and it took a few minutes for it to sink in that they were actually standing there with August Bridges, who was only the most famous guy alive.

"Now that you and your crew have brought in the antimatter, we get to see if this thing actually works."

What if it didn't? Raoul pulled another facing-total-and-utter-annihilation face when Francesca looked over her shoulder. She returned a contorted dead-already face. A crew commenced rolling the antimatter tank into place, bolting it onto some kind of machine wrapped around a huge donut-shaped machine. She looked back at August and thought she saw tears welling in his eyes. Hopefully it was some kind of an allergy. There was a countdown and then this weird flash, red and blue at the same time, and then, well, nothing. Maybe the thing didn't work.

She looked over to convey her sympathies to the Boss, and was surprised that, instead of being down, that he was ecstatic. He bounced into the air and hugged her fiercely.

"Hey man," Raoul objected protectively.

"It worked. It worked. We did it!"

Francesca looked sceptically beyond the embrace at the donut whatever-it-was. After the light-show nothing seemed to have changed.

"Uh. Are you sure?"

August turned around, all smiles.

"Well, for starters, we're still here."

That didn't sound too great. "Yeah. Okay, but..."

"I'll show you. Follow me," and August Bridges hopped down the rise expecting them all to follow, which they did of course.

Francesca had expected to see something more interesting closer up but was disappointed. Besides a shimmer that looked like an aurora around the rim, the donut hole itself just looked like a hole. She couldn't quite make out what August kept asking them to look at more closely.

"Watch this," proclaimed August as he climbed up a step ladder and jumped over the rim, standing in the circle on the other side. So what? He was just standing there.

"Look at the rim side on," whooped August, bouncing around like a kid who wanted his parents to give a shit.

They all backed up and bent over and saw the most amazing thing. When she looked at the ground under the rim it was lower by exactly the width of the donut rim than she had expected from looking in from the top. August Bridges' legs were prancing around down there, while his top parts above the rim seemed to hover a meter higher than they should be. It was like one of those magic tricks where they chop the assistant in half and pull the boxes apart. Except this was a better trick because when you bent to look lower the leg part went further up the body, and when you stood up the top half extended back down. August used to be a regular height, but now he seemed tall enough to play forward for the Lakers.

When August climbed back over he was all good spirits.

"That - that is going to change everything."

Then he hiked over to where the crew had assembled and gave an emotional speech, about how, because of their efforts and their discretion, they had made something that would make them all heroes for all who would follow. About how they were like the gods who had brought fire to human beings. About how now humanity would outlive even the burning out of the Sun, and how it would be the destiny of themselves and their children to inherit not just the Earth but the whole universe. And it was all due to them.

Raoul listened enraptured, but Francesca couldn't help looking around during a speech. It was an old habit from having to listen to too many idiots lecture her in her life. The thrill of what she had seen was taking a while to digest, it was just too amazing. Scanning the horizon, she picked out some dude out by the edge of the scramble zone she'd help set up to stop unauthorised transmissions. She zoomed in on him with her neuroview vision enhancer app. What was he doing? Standing there pointing his chest out in a weird way. Zooming in further she picked, the guy had a transmission dish secured to his breast. If he was legit, Francesca reasoned, he wouldn't be hiding that shit and wouldn't be standing a sprint away from where he could send out a copy.

Francesca kept her face sideways from the guy and started to slowly shuffle to the back of the pack. Like she was just trying to get a better view of how awesome August Bridges was. She jockeyed slowly around the back until she could gauge the distance she'd have to cover to intercept him on the shortest route out of the scramble zone.

He noticed her and then that was that. Francesca charged. Channelling her inner Gazelle to juice her metabolism into high gear, she cut a line to where she knew he'd run. With meters to spare she slid under his feet which smacked him into a roll that very nearly ended outside the scramble zone. The guy, unused to the low gravity, couldn't compete with a seasoned Space chick such as herself. She picked him up by the boot and flipped him, using a big moon rock to stop her own equal and opposite flip. The guy looked funny bouncing off his head while she grabbed his kicking feet holding him upside down.

By then Raoul had got there, her hero, followed by some other ComSec. The guy stopped flailing because it was clear he wasn't going anywhere. August Bridges was there too. Francesca thought he would be pissed off, but instead he couldn't stop thanking her. It was unbelievable. The only guy in the universe who really counted these days and he was all over her with admiration. As someone who had always been a nobody, Francesca didn't know how to take it. It felt pretty awesome at the same time. Raoul tried to do the talking for her, which sort of pissed her off, especially because he did it badly. She couldn't hold it against him that he wanted a little bit of her limelight to rub off on him. Who wouldn't want some of that?

And then August Bridges decided to hitch a ride back with them, like they were old friends or something. He chatted with them, but then went quiet until they were halfway back when he startled Francesca by suddenly talking. He talked and talked and talked and Francesca didn't mind listening. It was an amazing story, and especially the bit where the final message came in and August had to develop it in secret because others would have shut it down. Of this Francesca had no doubt. People could be petty little shits.

She really had to admire this guy. As far as her life was concerned people like him just didn't exist. As the time passed she noticed she felt a bit disappointed that Raoul seemed to be as totally into August and his story as she was, but she wasn't sure why she felt that. At the same time, it made her respect Raoul even more, and created this shared moment when they had both been in on something truly big.

As they rolled into Luna City, August stopped and looked them up and down carefully and asked, "You are headed to Tsuchinshan?"

"Yes, we are," answered Raoul.

"Good. Out of the way. Not a word of this to anyone. Okay? If anyone finds out it could all be shut down."

And of course, they agreed, not just because August was the boss, but because they had both gotten hooked. It made Francesca feel proud to be part of this story. It was one of the first things in her life that she could feel was genuinely amazing and not generally moronic. And August could trust her. She had kept his secret about the clone's covert downloads, hadn't she? It was a fair bet that if she had blabbed the whole project could have been derailed. And she'd nabbed that jerk before he had a chance to give the game away. So, in a way she'd had an important part to play, and, better yet, it was one that only she would ever know anything about. For the first time in her life, Francesca felt completely proud. Nobody could take this moment away from her.

As they blasted upwards from the moon towards their hook up with the Tsuchinshan freighter, Francesca wondered if any of this might in any way be of any use to Elena. She couldn't see how it could, but maybe, for a little while, that didn't need to matter so much.

CHAPTER 16

August

The glistening panels of silicon and germanium bent under the impact of the cosmic wind. The blinding radiation filling space funnelled from the panels down into the gut of the machine generating intense magnetic fields. These fields sifted and divided the more direct blast of particles entering the wide horn at the front of the ship, accelerating and colliding them, before harvesting an essential few into large magnetic 'bottles' at the cooler stern. The antimatter factory performed its work motionlessly, the pressure of the sun's might was countered by the competing gravitational pulls of the sun and the crater pocked planet Mercury below. Occasionally engines would stir to keep the orbit perpendicular to the torrent of light.

A cone shaped craft approached the factory base first, heat shields glowing. The cone settled into a circular cavity at the protected side of the factory. The precious cargo diffused into the magnetic field lining the freighters storage compartment before rockets gently nudged the ship back into space. When they had attained a comfortable distance from the factory a minute fraction of the tenuous gas held in the hold was released into the ion stream of the freighter's exhaust.

The cone disappeared in a blast of light. The brightly glowing Mercury and orbiting factory rapidly dropped from view.

As August watched his demonstration an intense sense of fulfilment washed through him. His relief was immense. Even though this event had resulted from a chain reaction powered by the critical mass of a lifetime of aspiration, even though the work itself had been nothing but joy, the non-stop effort had taken its toll.

Appearing in this neuroview to the assembled shareholders at this extraordinary general meeting was nothing less than the culmination of one of the greatest advances in technology in human history. That it had been accomplished in secrecy made the accomplishment even more amazing.

Exhaustion steadied him. Exhaustion that had become habit. Exhaustion that was possible only because of the greatness of the mission. To achieve this, he had lied almost continuously. He had lied to everyone except Calvin30 who had arranged most of the lying on his behalf. Lied straight to their faces without hesitation. Lied because the Truth behind the lie would set them free.

August had worked his charm, his hair waving with chaotic intensity to entrance each person he had personally talked to, swearing them to utmost secrecy with the authority of his unexpected appearance in the place of the usual intermediaries. Some were minor like the supplier from Gudansk not questioning why an impossible order of quantum capacitors was necessary for a telescope array retrofit. Some were illegal, taken care of at the edge of his deniable awareness by Calvin30. Some were far more serious.

"August. We are getting some questions as to why the N201-10 fusion reactor budget has blown out. I mean really blown out. Whew."

Helen Rodriguez, who had become his most trusted contact with the board following the assassination attempt, raised her eyebrows over their neuroview accusingly. She looked at him with Anya's eyes.

"I'm not sure why you are managing this project yourself August. Surely."

"What are you trying to say Helen?"

"I'm, well, August - what the hell is going on?"

"It's Gudanko's pet. I'm taking it on as a special favor."

"Hmmm. Are you trying to bomb it? I'm not sure."

August cut her off. "I don't like what you are suggesting. No, this is sensitive. Politically sensitive, so I need to run with it. A peace offering if you will."

Helen frowned. "Oh. I see. But if a takeover is in the offing surely we can't transfer assets before the deal."

"There is no takeover in the offering!"

Raising his voice was unnecessary, but the very thought of Mirtopik being swallowed up by Energyia Nova was too obscene for August to contemplate.

"August, you need to explain this to the Board."

"Okay. But hold off until the next meeting. The research has gone better than expected. We are moving beyond R&D and are creating a pilot production facility on the Moon." It was especially painful this lie, to lie in such an extraordinary way to the person who had saved his life.

"August, that is extreme. You will certainly lose your position over this. Gudanko."

"Gudanko is in on the deal. Our He-3 facilities. His engine technology. The fast-tracked expansion up in Mare Frigoris. All the extra lunar shifts for engineers and construction details. Doesn't all of this fit together for you?"

Helen was rubbing her temples, her eyes distracted by the balance sheets hanging in her neuroview. "Not really. But, I guess."

"Helen. Mirtopik isn't a company driven by bean counters. If we don't do this deal the whole thing is finished. Do you understand? And, and this is critically important. Gudanko is not to know that you know."

"Why not?"

"Do I need to spell it out for you? This is between him and I."

"But."

"Just until the next Board meeting. Helen, please."

This lie had truly exhausted him. He flattened his hair out in an act of shame. He was ready to admit defeat.

Helen frowned. "Okay August. We'll do it your way. Against my better judgement."

"Thank you, Helen. Thank you from my heart."

Illya towered behind him, shaking his head in disbelief.

"What do you care for August? Who do you love?"

Of course, now she knew that he had lied to her and this would be forever between them. Everyone would now know that he had lied, that trust had been broken, and trust was the main asset of leadership. August knew that. But he also knew that there had been no other way. If he had simply brought the information from the broadcast out onto the table it would have been questioned as a forgery, a desperate bid for him to cling onto power. The politics would have killed him long before the miracle that would occur today could come into being. He would not have lived to see it, to enjoy his place in history.

August held onto the memories of last month, as he stood in a spacesuit among the isolated crew in Mare Frigoris who had been his family for this whole journey, watching their great creation launch into the heavens. Buoyed by the fact that their project was so important that August Bridges himself had been with them, sharing meals, swapping stories with them, they had pushed themselves beyond his expectations. And he had lied to them, telling them only partial truths so that it was only when the wormhole had opened, and he had taken one giant leap for mankind into it as a demonstration, only then did he share with them the magnitude of their accomplishment.

Most of them had no idea what they were working on, but were proud of their efforts, of their service to something great. He was doing this for them. To let them share in his immortality. To everyone who had brought this moment to fruition. This was their moment.

The shareholders who were now materialising into their virtual seats had not come to be amazed and astounded. They had come to query the staggering expenditures from general accounts in the past few quarters. They were furious at his subterfuge. They had come to evict him.

The neuroview of the unfolding technological miracle only he recognised faded leaving August standing alone and exposed before the assembled wrath of Mirtopik and the world. He bowed triumphantly. "And that, honored colleagues, is the future of spaceflight."

Gudanko's posture tightened. He had flown to the Moon especially for the event, bringing with him his new management team. August knew they had come as a signal to the investors that the change of management would be swift and with as minimum of disruption as was possible. August also knew that Gudanko, even though he was eager to at last lay claim to Mirtopik, was furious at having to inherit a poisoned chalice.

"Anti-matter? This is what you have been spending on August? This is old technology, and not sustainable. It is too expensive. Those factories are old and require replacement - from this mneme they haven't been upgraded? August, can you just explain yourself more clearly? Otherwise we must conclude either phenomenal incompetence or mental instability."

The shareholders nodded. August knew they agreed with Gudanko, there was no other rational way to look at it. Some were possibly reluctant to give up on August Bridges and the dream that would go with him. Still Gudanko brought money and sanity to the table. Despite their disappointment in the failure of the Dream, August could see in their faces that they were prepared to cut their losses. There were other faces in the gallery, other eyes watching him, phantoms from his memory and promises made.

Illya and Anya and Gregori and so many others. Their suffering should now have meaning, but still the tears in their eyes were for him. Why?

A quick glance to the mood of the assembly reassured August that he still had time to get his message out. Since this was the end of an era, the shareholders were willing to allow him his finale. Gudanko would get his answer soon enough.

August took a deep breath.

Now was the moment of truth. All this while he had persisted while half not believing his own propaganda. The whole thing had become for August a noble scam he was playing on humanity. Keeping the Dream alive after the spectacular crash of the Second Wave. Preserving the fiction that kept the Peace. Keeping the faith. Justifying his past mistakes that had cost so many of his friends so dearly as he used them up to pursue a self-referential fantasy. Through it all, August had sold the idea to himself better that he had to his financiers.

Now the impossible had happened and his own good luck was harder to believe than all the lies. It was an opportunity handed to him by the gods. Now it was all finally going to happen. The gods were poised to reward their loyal servant.

"My observant colleague, you are right. On all counts. What I was talking about is the future of spaceflight. Anti-matter propulsion gave us the ability to bring humans to the edge of our solar system, but it cannot take us beyond, and it is too expensive for run-of-the-mill missions. Even if it were less expensive we could only manage to move a few people any great distance, and it is people who give value to property, and currently people are limited by the constraints of one small planet. Thus, our current unfortunate situation. Now, my good friends, I give you the future of Space."

The neuroview presentation returned to the freighter as it flew away from a shrinking sun. It rotated and, with another flash of light, slowed dramatically. In the approaching distance a strange planar structure appeared, smooth and mirrored, flashing in the sun. Cutting through the centre of the wafer was a round hole, which, as the freighter approached, appeared to contain a gray, dark disc dangling in the middle. Features on the disc, vague blotches at first, began to resolve into familiar patterns until the discs identity became easily recognisable. "It's the dark side of the moon." a voice in the audience thought aloud, the time-lagged observation restating the obvious.

The neuroview switched to a side on profile of the strange disk to provide the dramatic view of the freighter entering from one side inexplicably failing to emerge on the other.

The lights came on. August's enigmatic smile broke. He could scarcely contain his excitement.

"So, what do you think?"

The request brokered only expressions of bewilderment. August looked at his watch, which he'd arranged as a prop.

"Time's up, the package has arrived. Amanda, would you be so kind as to bring up lunar orbital camera #15 please."

The neuroview now showed the freighter from the neuroview orbiting the moon, the familiar tubes of Luna City just visible on the horizon.

Questioning eyes turned back to August's Cheshire Cat grin, waiting for an explanation.

"That neuroview was taken in real time."

Gudanko scratched his head. He smiled awkwardly, as if embarrassed for August. "With respect, I think it more likely to have sprouted wings and flew up here, out of the atmosphere, and off the Earth. A very interesting simulation, yes, but you unfortunately have missed a small factor in this little special effects show. What about the speed of light? By my back-of -envelope calculation I would guess that the signals from Mercury would be still on way here, maybe only just now would they reach us. Even if the ship is faster than light, we would still have to wait to know about it. This," Gudanko held his hands out to emphasize, "this is silly."

It was silly. August found himself giggling. The strain and stress, the doubt and uncertainty, the fear - they were all over. The others surely thought that he had finally snapped - that the long years of dreaming had finally collapsed into madness. August didn't care. This moment was for himself alone. The damn thing had worked. Even if they carted him off to the funny house what did it matter. He had done this! Gudanko's face flushed, uncertain how to handle the situation. And was he afraid, perhaps, that these histrionics would reflect unfavourably on the Com, on its share price, or on himself.

"Mr. Bridges?"

Gudanko's voice dripped with feigned compassion.

"Please, I do not mean to upset you."

Because you are clearly nuts.

"It's just that, well, we on the Board feel you have in the past done invaluable service to Mirtopik. Now, unfortunately the truth is your little simulation tells us nothing. Perhaps is time that you stepped down."

August smiled at Gudanko through his tears, at the bright light glorifying even the formerly unpleasant frame of his enemy. There was no room in his mind for malice, only wonder. August pulled himself together lest his silence be taken as surrender.

He grinned mischievously, his eyes twitching with excitement. "No, no my friend, you have it all wrong. The light from the freighter travelled no such distance; it came from only 10,000 kilometres away."

"So, the Mercury scene was a simulation?" Gudanko rolled his eyes and frowned patronisingly.

"No."

Gudanko began wriggle in his seat. "Then what are you trying to say? If it is not a simulation, then the light is just getting here. If it is a simulation than we are wasting our time with games. We've seen enough." Gudanko rose to his feet.

"I think you might want to sit down for this Vlad."

"Do not *tell* me what to do.» Gudanko›s face turned suddenly to a violent purple from the pressure of containing his emotions. He walked towards August with deliberate menace. «I speak for the Board. We›re tired, tired, and sick and tired of these pointless tricks of yours August. I call for a vote of no-confidence.»

"But Vlad, my friend, you may want to sit down."

August felt a minor anxiety, unsure whether a physical attack might be imminent. It seemed almost impossible that the cool of the Ukrainian might finally have broken.

But as soon as he reached August, Gudanko stopped. He turned to reconcile his impatience against the possible disapproval of the audience. Gudanko, now at the front next to August, faced the board and held up his hands. "We've seen enough. We should vote to end this now."

For some reason, August had to stop himself from nodding agreement.

Gudanko faced August.

"You have brought Mirtopik Com to its lowest point. It will be hard and painstaking work to rebuild, but under new management we will."

August folded his arms, enjoying the show.

"The management team from Energia Nova can bring balance and fiscal responsibility back. For too long we have engaged in fantasy and it is time to take our medicine."

August, with exaggerated timidity, raised his hand from behind Gudanko.

"Whoa. Whoa. Excuse me folks. FOLKS. You know what?" August clapped his hands loudly and clasped them together as he shook them. " You know what. We did it. We actually..."

He started to laugh again.

"The message, the message came through."

"What?" Gudanko growled, barely constraining himself, as if he might snap from the effort of suppressing his fury.

"The message from ET finally came through."

August pushed past Gudanko's trembling frame to face his audience.

"What you just saw was a prototype. It's an artificial wormhole."

"A what?" Gudanko stepped around August's flank, as if to edge him out of view.

"A wormhole. A hole is connecting two places in space-time," August said without yielding, "The light from the camera and the freighter both went through a worm..."

August tripped forward from Gudanko's sudden push, hitting his head on the lectern. ComSec officers jumped forward to intervene between himself and the momentarily unhinged Gudanko. The room was silent as the interplanetary time lag passed, and the audience struggled to digest August's pronouncement.

August climbed back to his feet, straightened his kurta, and waited for the attention of the audience to zero back in on him.

"Ah, sorry folks, I deserved that."

August waited while Gudanko shrugged past the ComSec officers, stony faced.

"Sorry folks. This is my fault. My desire for a dramatic effect has elicited a rather unanticipated response. The matter that I bring before the body today is of such propitious dimensions, such great and unprecedented historical import, that I myself was unwilling to stand before you until I could satisfactorily demonstrate its reality."

"Some months ago, Mirtopik came into possession of a transmission. Well the only way I can say it is that it was the transmission that we were all waiting for."

August paused, savoring the stunned silence.

"You must forgive my delay in informing you, but, given the charged political environment," he turned his head in Gudanko's direction, "I felt it better to use some general discretionary funds to provide a credible pilot demonstration first. Helen, our CFO, will give you a full accounting at the close of the meeting. I apologise again for the breach of protocol."

"Now, what we have created here is a working prototype of a wormhole. It is a door through an inter-dimensional string of time-space opened by a collapsed negative energy vacuum state. We construct two gates, an in and an out, very close together and use inverted quantum fluxes fed from the matter/anti-matter interactions to create a localised occlusion in space-time. As you can see I am reading from notes written by someone more intelligent than myself."

Only August laughed at his attempt at levity. He forgave his audience for missing their cue - he remembered how he had been stunned for weeks, unable to believe what the transmission contained. It had taken weeks to formulate any strategy and begin translating the alien specifications. Based on this experience he could empathise with the astonishment they were feeling.

"Pull them apart and the hole keeps linking them. What it is," August bowed to catch his breath before continuing, "what this is the greatest accomplishment in the history of humankind, a portal to our destiny and to the stars. Respected shareholders, we, you and I, have done it, together. We have done it."

August put his hands in his pockets and waited for a response. What commenced was a very hard sell. Most of the shareholders were furious at the secrecy and lack of consultation. A vote of no confidence was immediately put forward, and unsettlingly the motion was not made by a member of Gudanko's camp. It very nearly succeeded. In the end, mistrust of the dictatorial tendencies of Gudanko saved the day. The opportunities opened by August's gambit were hardly mentioned. The lynching went ahead because it was all anyone had planned, and the new information was still too raw and sat undigested. So, their plans went ahead, but with one critical difference. August Bridges survived intact.

At the close of the meeting August stalked out of the room. The ungrateful idiots had no appreciation of the nature of risk. If he had come to the board with the transmission and a proposal to build, it would have initiated a political bun fight that he would not have had the political capital to win. Gudanko would have killed it off and taken the spoils for himself, that is if he didn't get it banned by the GEO outright or sabotaged by the Revs through inept political handling. Today, August reassured himself, he had deprived his rival of the limelight and, in good time, the rest of them would see the logic of it, in good time.

Good time was a week in coming. After evaluating the facts, the Board called another emergency meeting and formally approved of August's mission, albeit with significant and predictable opposition by panarchist shareholders, while at the same time announcing a formal censure of his unauthorised use of Com funds. August was forced to relinquish many executive privileges to prevent similar abuses in the future.

But he knew they would all come around. At the end of the meeting, the imposing form of Adrian Celewiesz, the great Ukrainian banker and one-time president of the Whole Earth Credit Society, a man whose impeccable credentials as a defender of Capitalism were undisputed, stood and applauded August. The powerful man's hands resonated in the neuroview, their rhythm steady and confident, like a war drum. August bowed in acknowledgement. Soon Celeweicz's hands were joined by others, their pulse vindicating everything, conferring the mantle of godhood on August's capable shoulders. This was his accomplishment, the emancipation of mankind from their humble beginnings. As even Gudanko and a few of the panarchist's stood to join the jubilation, August bowed back to his rival, a defeated competitor who had fought a good fight. He was now in a position to be magnanimous.

The land beyond the neuroview room, the walls of Plato Crater and the long plains for Mare Frigoris, were framed in an uncompromising contrast of the blackness of vacuum and unfiltered solar brilliance. The border between the two was absolute in every shadow. It was the Palace of Light and Darkness, a celestial and heavenly abode. A place for gods and dreams but not for life. The time here was always eternity.

It was a fitting place for these scions of power and wealth, these new gods, to set their triumphant claims upon the heavens. Their future expanded confidently outward from the Moon into the stars, without limit and without compromise. After today, everything would be within their grasp. After today, nothing would remain the same.

Meanwhile on the blue and white magical planet, whose swirling face seemed out of place floating above the sterile lunar horizon, the Moon they were standing on hung in many billions of skies. Smoky and orange in some, crisp and luminescent in others, and always touching the familiar in hauntingly different ways. A glowing veil of mist against the mountain. The outline of frozen heather on the open moor. A jewel caught in a balloon of rain dropping from the tip of a fern. The desert's cool reprieve from the sun's harsh lashing. A farmer's midnight harvest of silvered sheaves. And the tidal yearning of a lover's pulse - what excuse may I find for disturbing that faint track of moon as slips past your lips?

The Moon belonged to the Earth. It illuminated the mystic of home and hillside and always it hung in the same night following the same day, through all the ages. A promise through the night for all generations to come. A holy thing.

A BRIEF FLASH OF LIGHTNING

'*Strong and healthy, who thinks of sickness until it strikes like lightning? Preoccupied with the world, who thinks of death, until it arrives like thunder?*'

~Milarepa, 10th Century Tibet

CHAPTER 17

Calvin30

The Adyar River flowed out to the Bay of Bengal and beneath his feet dangling off the end of the Broken Bridge. Little more than a collapsed footpath, chopped midway betwixt two nondescript half flooded suburbs of Chennai, it had become strangely famous enough to be maintained as 'The Road to Halfway'. A Bollywood star scene according to the hopeful tourist mneme, although not seen on any screen for over a century. More pathetic was the transplantation of the bridge upstream thither the furthest flood of the climactically altered tide. Its previous position now well below the waves from which towered a forest of wrecked architecture from an earlier era. Too exposed for drug drops, and too obscure to secure visitors, the bridge currently served as a lonely open space perfect for practice.

Fortified on all sides by the apocalyptic postcard vista, Calvin30 contemplated his position. Why he had chosen to fly so far outside his zone, to the antipole of his protected Com space, to perform this precarious mission solo? There was no cerebral explanation. Being a clone could be a critical condition here in Rev central - publicly because of said clone's connection to the Coms, but really it was the off-the-record prejudice that could kill. For protection, he'd had some reversible work on his face done, but it didn't help that the enemy knew he was coming. He had told them.

His fears cleared as his fingers worked the pads, lingering across the octaves while his soul poured free. Time passed blessedly until the crowd dribbling up the causeway attracted by the music became its interruption. Calvin30 gave a showman's nod and slowly worked past the file of idle laborers and fisher folk now packing the pathway.

He followed the lead of the green arrows in his neurovisor up the loud and busy boulevard, heading in the direction of near certain doom. Still, head down, he trod forward against the pressure of increasing apprehension. What other direction was there beside abandoning his plans? And that wouldn't do.

The pestilence of twelve million people could be felt in every molecule of moisture in the fetid monsoon heat. There was no avenue of escape, and for the most part the inhabitants of this putrid place seemed impervious to it. Their manner was unhurried, an unfocused blur of inscrutable motion. It made Calvin30 feel more desolate that those around him should not deem to notice their own misery.

Finally, the arrow poked into a door-less entry of a concrete box of a building. Calvin30 sucked in his breath before commencing to worm his way down a dilapidated corridor to arrive at his appointment.

The key, handed to him by a surprisingly well-kept proprietor for this flea trap, fit loosely in the lock and Calvin30 poked around it for some time before finding the catch. The thin door dragged across a threadbare carpet, as reluctant to grant him entrance as he was to enter. He despised the filth and took refuge in the shower he was sure to take immediately after he exited this execrable place.

Dust and betel nut spit heaped in mounds in every corner of the surrounds. Chips in the walls revealed geological strata of paint and wallpaper. A towel suspended from a tack above a leaking tap was threadbare and greasy. The rains dripped from the rafters exposed by a hole in the discolored plasterboard on the ceiling. The history of the room's past decade of occupation was traceable in the tracks on the carpet. A faded, crudely framed picture of Hanuman, the monkey-man god, was hung neatly above a makeshift altar next to a lopsided poster of a lingerie model. The room reverberated with a chaotic mix of music blaring from bicycle powered stereo systems passing in the adjoining avenue.

His neuroview faded into fuzz, which told him both that he had found the correct address and that his artifice was on track. It also meant that the ensuing discourse would be conveniently off-record.

Calvin30 sipped the insipid liquid from his water bottle and waited. If being here were not his own idea he wouldn't be here. He much preferred the anonymity of the neuronet for carrying out transactions such as this. It was difficult enough to invent a plausible excuse to leave a free-trade zone, much less travelling to the citadel of Rev power.

But instead his path had led here. Here on the outskirts of Chennai where the resurgence of communal titular ties first intersected with the burgeoning networks of small neuronet businesses. It was here that Ecos were first used to link up local currencies in a manner that reinforced intricately local economic loyalties. Calvin30 doubted whether a free transaction existed in either the city or the surrounding countryside. And just look where it had gotten them. Families moving into ruined office towers with their chickens.

True, far fewer people were starving and the countryside was a shade greener, but the squalor was simply appalling. In Shanghai, they wouldn't have beggars canvassing the central business district, that's for sure. And the shopping was a disaster. A million Net sponsored vendors in solar powered carbon-filament shacks hawking goods in dingy, recycled packaging - the homespun brands that had proliferated like weeds the world over all proudly displayed.

"I couldn't help noticing your application to travel to Chennai. What is the justification?" asked the ComSec manager with a sour face.

"I'm off to have a hush-hush tete et tete with a head of the Revs to discuss the wormhole tech and Bridge's upcoming mission." Calvin30 flashed the officer his Augustinian authorisation.

"How did they find out about that?" The man's furrowed brows indicated his disdain for surprises - a limiting predilection for a career detective.

"I'd thought that was the charge of you ComSec guys. Now I must go on the road to scout out what they know. Shame the way secrets seem to drain out of this place like a sieve." The furrows burrowed deeper into the idiot's brow.

"Errr, ah, you'll give us a full briefing when you return?

Where did they pick such a prize? A half-price sale on corn fed pricks?

"No, I'll dish you out half and slip the rest to the remaining unwashed." That half was the whole truth. "What do you think?"

The thug had hurried through the perfunctory fictions to free him to pursue his mission and so here he sat, in this cesspit, waiting. And waiting. In a cesspit.

As the day diminished Calvin30 prepared to leave when a someone tapped at the door. He opened the panel to admit a squat woman in a ripped sari. The hag was dirty and held a makeshift broom of bundled straw. Had he wondered so far from home to meet with the hotel sweeper?

"All clean, see," Calvin30 crinkled his nose at the filth around him and again at the filthier woman. "No need. No rupee from me."

"That's fine C30. I didn't come all this way for a few units of an anachronistic currency. I just want to hear whatever it was you wanted to tell me, so I can decide whether or not to have you killed."

C30 not C12? A small change in digits and the gig was up.

"General Bhattarjee?" Calvin30's tongue stuck.

This broad-bodied bag, the great Bhattarjee? The thought was not possible. Commander-Ultimate of Kaliyuga Rev? He could see it somehow, but the disguise had been too good, and in recognising her he had given up the chance to contest her bead on him. Was he dead already?

"When your friend Dr. Myren contacted us, we were immediately suspicious. C12? Such a clever alias. How could we guess?"

"Well, I am sporting spectacles." Calvin30 felt too queasy to pull off glib.

"Shut your mouth clone - I do not have the time. Your kind give me the creeps in any case. You have no mother and no father. How can one trust a creature such as that?"

"I can point to many persons, equally distasteful, proceeding from very illustrious pedigrees."

Bhattarjee locked a serpent's stare on Calvin30's fey expression.

"Save your insolence for someone with more patience. If I don't become interested in this conversation rather quickly I'm afraid your unnatural, freakish existence may face some sudden obstacles." The features on Bhattarjee's face shifted, transforming her into the visage of wrath. For terrible or worse, the venomous Bhatterjee now looked her part. Calvin30's jolted heart halted for a moment his reflex to initiate head trips - with Bhatterjee that might turn out to be fatal.

Out he blurted. "Mirtopik has received technology to enable interstellar space flight that is economically feasible."

"And this is something we don't know. Even extremely simple people know this by now. I hope for your sake this is not the only news you have brought."

"But did your informants report that the technology has the capability to terminate the entire planet?"

A flicker of engagement escaped from the General's executioner face. Calvin30, feeling a little less the cockroach being considered for extermination, released his breath. General Bhattarjee circled him, hands clasped at her back. She chewed some betel nut and spat the blood red expectorate on the floor next to Calvin30's boot.

"Interstellar travel?" Bhatterjee repeated, blood lips parting to reveal betel-stained teeth. "They've been after that one for years. And the prize is too good to consider the long-term effects. What precedent would there be for that?" Her eyes looked up and through Calvin30 to focus a rat scampering across a ceiling beam. "Why are you telling me this? We know who you are. You're Bridges' pet. Did he send you?"

"What do you conclude from two and two?"

Bhatterjee retracted her incisors. "Myren? He told us he had found evidence of a terrible technology that could destroy the planet. That the Coms were after him and his research. We had almost concluded he was a nutter until we heard from you."

Calvin30 tried to revive his composure while the General sized up the situation. Her face softened subtly, which he apprised as fear disguised.

"So, this technology that you refer to, it has a nasty side. Why are you telling me this?"

"Do I strike you as the whistle-blower type?" He tapped his Slysynth.

"The question is ridiculous. We know who you are."

"Then if my identity is self-evident, why pretend that my agenda is not similarly rendered? Would we have motivated Dr. Myren's motions to promote this meeting only for the purpose of sabotaging our project? While our message was meant to be delivered under cover, maybe it is better that we meet in the open."

"Your intrigues are tiresome clone. What is your purpose?" Her sound was pure scorn, but it was Batterjee's frown that left her dismissal undone. She could not presume his response and abhorred this vacuum.

"Why? To present the press release in person, and to proudly offer, sincerely, our sympathies to your side."

Bhatterjee's makeup transmuted into murder. Her puritan composure decomposed.

"How can you Coms be so arrogantly stupid? If the planet is gone then so are you"

"Yes. Well once we win, we win big in a game we are bound to otherwise lose."

"But if we all die?"

"Then, in that case, and the chances are largely low, from our side it would be considered a draw."

Bhatterjee, stunned, stumbled on her way back into a threat.

"This is beyond anything even I've suspected. You are evil. The Com is evil. Absolutely, absolutely, absolutely evil." The General reared back in fury. "Clone, your species must not value your lives, because your death is going to be our message back to your masters."

Calvin30 poised on the pointy end, all his senses alive in this improv. "Please reflect during the interim until I am finished."

Then Calvin30 poured forth on the wormhole and the grand opening drama, the position of the soon functional portals and the timing of the apogee of August Bridge's prima donna trajectory. He was vigilant for signs that his message had gripped in Bhatterjee's steel trap.

When he had wrapped up his divulgence she spoke, "This won't save you. Why are you telling us this?"

"Why? What is my purpose? It is so you can stop us."

With an enigmatic shrug, he left her to guess, and strode down the knife edge of his existence into the throng crushing down the street.

Dissolving into the flow of souls on the road and the false sense of escape this gave him, Calvin30 reviewed the interview. He cognized pride rising up inside. His plan had been to play the disaffected Com employee, horrified by the possibilities, confiding with the enemy. Instead he had fired Bhatterjee's ire, an emotion that was so much more inspired. And easier to maneuver.

Aware he was still in the woods, he hastened towards the jump-port before all could backfire. He found his progress impeded by the leisurely speed of the pedestrians in his path. To stay anonymous, Calvin30 paced himself to their clip, observing his surrounds like a tourist. Incense smoke billowed from the myriad altars spilling from the alleyways. Each street fronted theatrically fashioned upside-down thermometers metering the downtick on the planet's thermostat estimated from the actions of their denizens. Did they account for the incense discrepancy when they issued their Ecos?

Evening prayers, chants, hymns from a mosaic jumble of faiths echoed hypnotically, mixing with the jangling chatter of popular music and bicycle bells and horns and megaphones. Shopkeepers and bicycle rickshaw wallahs vied for his attention as he traversed their territories. On the sides of buildings holograms of gods and demons danced and battled for time against Net and neuroflick promos. A bull mounted one of the free-range cattle and nearly toppled Calvin30 together with several vegetable stalls. As he hoofed into the road to avoid the amorous bovines he was bumped by one of those ubiquitous blow-up bodied XP-Tata jalopies. If motorcars were still metal he'd have been dead meat. As it was, his ego was more bruised than his bum. The driver honked and hurried on.

Along the road at community Neuronet portals thousands queued, sipping tea from earthen cups. Rev warriors, in their off-cut kurtas emblazoned with a scatter of Net and ecoverted Com branding, patrolled the streets alert for infractions of any of many oddball Hub protocols. Their eyes tracked Calvin30 as he tacked his way past. Should they conclude he was a clone Calvin30 was sure that he would not last. A dirty mob would rip him to bits.

Balloon cradled rockets loomed overhead as they lifted from the jump-port up ahead and, as Calvin30 neared the fount of their departure, his spirits grew light. He swung into a swagger.

His performance, impeccable in every way, had put all the principals into play. Within an hour he would be aloft, powering through the clouds. From that time, it would be an even ride home to safe haven, and from then he would reel the Revs in. Bhatterjee, enraged, trailing Kaliyuga in her wake, inhaling the bouquet of blood, would follow his baits. August's fiery ascension to his fate was thus delivered to Calvin30 on a plate.

Immersed in his mind, Calvin30 finagled the angles and meditated on the minutiae of the coming months. How he would release which leaks that would lead Bhatterjee to a specific sequence of decisions, down to which ship she would hijack to press her attack. It was a deal already sealed.

To Calvin30's left he spied a line of beggars, loathsome creatures, far beneath even clones in the pecking pyramid. He noted even they had aligned themselves into a Net of some kind. Some Org coordinator was helping to change Ecos into local tokens, so the good pilgrims could convert pennies into heaven by depositing them into pleading hands. Then the beggars would duly recycle their baggies of lucre back to the Org guy, a turbaned Sikh, who would deposit the amount into their electronic accounts. Calvin30 wondered what his cut was.

Gods the weather was hot. He drained the last dregs of his dram as he regarded the beggars. A tug on his pants drew his attention down. One of those insects was pestering him for something. The crone pointed to his empty bottle and, with a frown, he dropped it to her. Catching it with a deft hand, the thing stashed it in her bag and stared back up. Her prize acquired, why did she and her smell not go away?

Hell, today of all days he could afford beneficence. Calvin30 rummaged his pockets for a few cents and tossed them to the pavement. His mouth curled as the woman pounced. Then his expression fell as she fingered her treasure suspiciously.

"Shit. My mistake. My mistake. I've something else for you. Here take this instead. Stop."

It was too late. Sniffing back at him the witch fronted up to the Org guy. The man took the coins off her and examined them officiously. Soon Calvin30 was ringed by angry faces. His ad hoc entourage wound its way down the avenue in the wrong direction. Translated through his neurovisor Calvin30 followed snippets of the conversation.

"What was it?" "A ComCoin." "He tried to bribe her, but she turned him right down." "He was most contemptuous." "Some kind of Com spy?" "What an idiot."

They paraded him, yanking his kurta, and dragging him when his feet tripped. Dark hands snatched his horn, snapping the strap and cutting off his neurovisor from its secured antennae link. Some kids kicked it along the street before taking off with it. His third eye went blind and severed from his powers; like Oedipus he fell into despair.

Calvin30 was gripped by panic, his mind spinning out of ideas as his body went limp. Murderous arms muscled him into a courtyard of sorts, barricaded round with poorly plastered brick. There he was passed roughly to the front of the pack. Having arrived, the louder shouts became less shrill and the crowd began to mill. Calvin30 dusted his kurta, willed his flustered heart to still, and brushed a waterfall of sweat from his eyes.

A Rev man, assembled in the closest resemblance to a uniform Calvin30 had seen in Chennai, scowled at the approaching inconvenience. The Org guy approached, suddenly shy, and offered the shiny chits to the officer who bit one on the corner and put them in his pocket. The Officer wiped his neck, cleared his throat and spat. Squinting at Calvin30, his interest slow to show, he tilted his head to tell them to follow.

Passing twin algal fountains flowing down the building's thermal mass walls, they entered a blessed cool gust which greeted them into a stairwell. They descended into a wide earthen room lined with sunlit water tubes, which imbued the setting with a soft, clear light. Cushions, mats and the odd metal chair littered the tiled floor, facing a stage solely inhabited by an old styled desk.

The mob frog-marched Calvin30 into a creaking chair placed on the first step of three ascending the dais. The Officer, assuming more decorum once relieved of the heat, strode to a curtain stage right and muttered to someone unseen. He glanced around, and then returned to stand by the desk.

Calvin30, lulled by the Officer's apparent boredom, began to calm down. This didn't look like a lynching. He scanned the members of the assembly and determined them, despite initial feigned ferocity, to be attending mainly out of curiosity. If Bhatterjee had wanted him deceased, she would have done the deed less publicly.

"Sri Indira Didi, senior Sabarmati clan Satyacharya for Thiruvanmiyur Hub presiding," the Officer announced perfunctorily in English.

After a time, a middle-aged woman wearing a faded sari of raw silk and topped by close-cropped hair entered and settled behind the desk while the cobbled cabal in the room assumed their seats in the dust. The Justice, Calvin30 presumed, sat quietly, her eyes scrolling his case through her neuroview. Then she spoke, addressing her remarks to his audience more than to him.

"We have a serious offence brought before us today. The use of Com currency in the Free Hubs is strictly forbidden. Why is this so? Because Law cannot be imposed beyond the understanding of the community, I will remind us and our guest. "

Calvin30 straightened and prepared to defend.

"Money. Why all this turmoil about such an everyday device? It may seem a bit trumped up. You see, money has a chequered past."

The Justice held up an Eco as Exhibit A.

"This is proper money. Why? Because it indicates effort that someone has undertaken to benefit our Mother, the Earth, which is shared by everyone of us. Not only humans, but the animals and plants that share this fragile world with us. Among many things it is an indicator of how we have reduced hazardous gases that have heated our planet. The formulas upon which this is derived are validated by many scientific Syns, and the value is agreed by the Elders and economists at GEO. This is proper money because it represents a benefit we all share. It tells our stories as well, not the stories of the elites, as it is issued by each Hub independently on the same basis. It is better than gold, for to extract that metal actually causes great damage to the planet and exhausts precious resources for the only purpose of digging something up and reburying it in a vault."

Then, with sudden emphasis, the Justice thrust Calvin30's Comscript coins forth.

"This. This is not proper money. Why? In the past this was the main form of money that existed. It does not start in a proper way with a value of benefit to everyone. It is not connected to the Earth but is instead devised as an instrument of enslavement. This money begins its life as a credit, as a debt to the issuer. To repay the debt more must be offered back than was given. For a loan this is the normal state of affairs, but the issuing of money is not the creation of value. One side invents a fiction for which another returns the sweat of their brow and the whole of their life. This had us all labouring under the yoke of many Empires, most recently the Coms. For this we would sacrifice even our precious life-giving planet."

"So, you see, rejecting this, rejecting THIS. Rejecting this is the way we have defended our freedom and protected our planet. And so, using this currency, in our Hubs, at the sacred ground where the Ecolution first took root is the greatest sacrilege."

Her diatribe was discursive, and Calvin30 recognised the vibe as on the radical side, outside the Peace by a long reach. The politically compromised line was that a happy currency ecology provided the most stability, but here that was clearly disbelieved.

She leaned over her bureau, studying him studying her.

"Who are you?" Her grey eyes belied a candid curiosity healthily dosed with suspicion.

Calvin30 responded with all the counterfeit verifiable facts composing his alias. That he was but a mere wayfaring musician pursuing his muse in the motherland of the Upanishads.

"Your Honor, surely it is me, as much a victim of this situation as she, for someone perhaps has tipped that villainous cash into my hat during my act?"

The Justice seemed unimpressed by his duplicity but did not press the point. Instead she finished her glass and proffered her carafe.

"Surely, you must be thirsty." The Officer poured a cup and approached with it.

"Much obliged for your generosity, Your Honor."

While Calvin30 drank the water, Her Honor thanked him for his frank testimony.

"The accused has admitted his crime."

What?

"There is nothing in your rendition that discounts the charge against you, mainly the use of ComCoin in a Free Hub zone. There may be extenuating circumstances, but the facts of the matter are not contested."

"Surely, you know, this whole show is proscribed under the terms of the Peace?" Calvin30 appealed.

"The Peace is interpretable. This is a Community Court following local Standards, but you are welcome, of course, to lodge a waiver in the Gov Court of Tamil Nadu State."

Her smile ambushed him.

A month or more chasing papers through the Indian civil service would seriously derail his schedule but should only be another artistic arrow in his quiver for his footloose minstrel alter ego. He dared not go there. His case could become public, Comsec could blunder in, and August might get wind of that borrowed authorisation.

"Your Honor, in my rambles I have always complied with the customs of my hosts, and so I will abide with any fine you decide."

The Justice assessed his assent while working the rosary of seeds around her neck. Her brow raised when she reached the end of a round.

"You realise Sir, that you cannot change your path once upon it, for that would make a mockery of Community Standards and the sovereignty rights of all Hubs."

This was, of course, untrue to the extent that he was not entirely trapped by the untruths of his own telling. With a word he could always consign himself to a public bureaucratic purgatory during which his ruse would be inevitably uncovered.

And this, somehow, she knew, the shrewd witch. Ah well, all the world are players and Calvin30 conceded he'd been played.

"I agree."

"Very good. That being so, to whom then do you belong?"

To whom did he belong? He couldn't say Mirtopik Com. "Ah. Your Honor, to no one, I own my own soul. I query the question."

"Mr. Calvinson. That is your name from your documents? Michael?"

"Ah. Yes. It is."

"Your Hub. This mneme doesn't say. Surely you know Community Justice is a matter of recompense between Hubs, not individuals. We must establish the negotiating parties to determine remuneration. You can then be dealt with by own Hub according to your own customs."

Of course, he had been a nitwit not to invent a Hub membership for himself.

"I would prefer not to involve them. Can't we keep this between ourselves?"

Justice Indira frowned down at him. "That is not our way. Without your Hub to take responsibility for your actions there is no jurisdiction for this court. If you will not reveal your Hub I am afraid these proceedings are over, and we will forward your waiver."

"Wait. Your Honor. There must be some other way."

Rubbing her chin, the Justice examined him, her suspicions coalescing into an opinion.

"Yes. There is 'some other way'." She blinked.

"Are there any Hubs attending who wish to take on this visitor's debt?"

The silence was ear splitting.

"Well Mr. Calvinson. It would appear that you are headed to the Courts and I can get back to my main case for the day, negotiating groundwater rights with Besant Nagar following increases in seawater intrusion there. Unless this would interest you Mr. Calvinson, if that is your name?"

"Sri Didi, we will assume the debt."

It was the Org Guy, holding his hand high above his revolting litter of human refuse, the beggars who had caused this mess. Despite his filthy flock, Calvin30 could have kissed him. Justice Indira regarded the turbaned guy with surprise.

"Mr. JV Singh. How can I possibly hold you accountable when you are the plaintiff party?"

"Sri Didi, I humbly beg your pardon. I believe that in this case it is the Community Standards themselves that are in breach and that no harm has been done to our members. Therefore, I take the opportunity to assume the debt for this man's case."

"But surely you can see the disdain for those of your jati. It is written plainly on his face."

Calvin30 swiftly subdued his features, shifting to look upon the Sikh's creatures with a demeanor of chastened humility. The beggar broad who had incriminated him expectorated while the others grinned.

The Sikh bowed. "Didi, we are simple and humble men and women, patiently accepting the injustices of our society with the grace of God. We have no grudge to bear for this man's ignorance. Besides, our atonement may be instructive to him."

"Your Honor. I am overjoyed to accept this generous sponsorship." Calvin30 interrupted, revealing his relief.

The Justice and the Sikh exchanged a glance that gave Calvin30 the sense he had just made a very dense decision.

"Very well. The fine is 1 lakh Ecos to be paid in monthly instalments by ChowpatiNet as to be negotiated. Mr. Calvinson, I release you from the jurisdiction of this Court into the care of your sponsor until such time as the two of you achieve reconciliation."

"But, your Honor?"

"Mr. Calvinson, your situation is no longer a matter for our consideration. I wish you all the very best. Good day."

Thus, with the Justice's blessing he was compressed by a crowd of grotesques who led him away from the proceedings amid cheers and jeers. Sweating and fretting, Calvin30 was pressed through a maze of tracks, down a ghat onto a littoral that filled the streets between beached high rises, skirting the tide, until they reached a derelict depot.

Once inside Calvin30 was instructed to strip to his undershirt and exchange his smart kurta and pants for a somewhat more aromatic attire. Enthroned on a limestone block his captors coronated him with a broken pot, declaring him an honorary prince of God.

Over the cackles of the masses, the Sikh educated him on a monarch's 'duties of State'. Apparently as a recipient of the largess of ChowpatiNet, he was now obliged to recompense his fellow recyclers for the substantial fee they needed to settle with themselves for his release.

"This is no issue, only return my instrument that was stolen from me and I will sing you your supper."

The Sikh smirked at this. "Please, my good friend, do not take our refusal of your generosity personally as it is evident you are unaware of the insult you give to our members by it."

"What insult do you insinuate? I have only ever treated your troop with the utmost respect."

"Should this be the case, and because of your avowed intent to abide by the 'customs of host' as you stated, you should not object to travelling some short distance in our shoes, so to speak, as a proof of this respect?"

"Is this necessary?"

"If you do not wish to play the game Mr. Calvinson, a waiver for the State Courts is already prepared."

It seemed that by accepting their charity he must assume their profession. If he aspired to escape he was coerced to beg his way.

"Time to go to work," The turbaned freak declared cheerily.

The days afterwards were a nightmare. Calvin30 was not good at eliciting donations as he sat on the roadside glowering, his clay pot crown hanging lopsided down off of his head. Any piece of plastic, metal, even paper was whisked away before he could get within ten meters of it. It was a hopeless exercise. The sum required for his freedom was ridiculously large in comparison with the paltry price offered for discarded junk. The first days he spent mulching all manner of horrible offal out of the drainage ditches and into community gardens in return for the bowls of rice and vegetables given to all raggers gathering outside the local temple.

The only alternative, waiting for an Indian Gov court docket to come open, was equally untenable. Either way he would be stuck here too long. The unravelling of a god awaited him, and he was not even on the map. There was no appealing to General Bhatterjee for his release, even if his fellow recyclers would believe him. She would likely just have him disposed of.

Calvin30 tried his hand at street theater, a difficult undertaking without his beloved SlySynth. He danced and sang and pantomimed, but all he received for his troubles were odd looks and more derision. The Sikh took great delight in informing him of the 'expenses' on his account that were mounting daily. Calvin30, terrified of being discovered as a clone, tried not to object overly much as his thoughts went into overdrive plotting possible escapes. At night he slept on the ledge of a traffic island to prevent his earnings being rifled while he slept, his exhaustion tuning out the constant bangs and bells and beeps.

And then there was that old witch - the very sibyl that had gotten him into all this trouble.

"My daughter," she pointed to a fellow destitute, young but worn beyond her years, three snotty brats in tow. "You. She." The witch latched her hands.

Calvin30 responded with some sarcastic comment that the witch considered a "Yes".

From then on, his adopted brood conga-lined behind him as he stalked down the street trying to shrug them off. He learned to accept the arrangement because the little woman seemed only happy to turn over part of her earnings to her new man. Her sole endearing feature was that she was seemingly mute. The Sikh was surprised when Calvin30 made his first deposit.

"Maybe you are learning a thing or two my good man. At this rate you will earn your freedom in some months' time."

Calvin30 lay on the concrete floor of the temple soaked to his bones, freezing as the rains drizzled off the cornices. His cough was flourishing, and he feared hypothermia as the chill infiltrated his core. Nearby him, as far apart as their mat would allow, snored the girl. The brats had packed up with granny, freeing him from midnight interruptions by those squirming vermin. His luck that, just when some peace seemed possible, the thermometer had dropped.

Driven by a visceral thirst for heat Calvin30 nestled into her, holding his shuddering body tightly against the soft warmth. She sighed and surrendered into his grip. He found himself suddenly engulfed in impossible grief, holding this disgusting woman like the mother he had never had. His sobs melded into the shaking of his gelid heart, causing him to cling to her intensely. He felt at that moment all his sorrow flowing into her comforting glow, as if she could joyfully swallow the whole of his polluted soul into the bottomless reservoir of her bosom. He wanted at that moment to stay, fused to her for eternity.

Then, wrenching Calvin30 from this reverie, the wench twisted into him, widening her legs. There was nowhere for him to go from there. Clones were created for many ends, but procreation was not one of them. He pushed her away, flipping off the mat to the gravel. Then he jerked himself to his feet and stalked away and walked the entire night.

Before falling into the dirt from exhaustion a thought occurred to him. Why was the witch so eager for her offspring to play house and share her scant earnings with him? Why did anyone do anything? Self-interest. The witch was playing him for a future meal ticket. After all, weren't they "family"?

As soon as could be organized, Calvin30 took 'wifey' out to meet the relatives. Through trial and error, he invented a suitable position for his alias and made many promises. Slowly the small change came in and added up. That week the turbaned man was more impressed.

Calvin30 widened his strategy. It turned out the town was full of desperate characters willing to divest their cash in return for any kind of promise. In only a week he repaid the turbaned man a main chunk of the compensation. Then things became more difficult. Word had gotten out about Calvin30's supposed resources and now people were coming to him. These pests greatly impaired his mission. It took time to determine that they were not potential investors, and even more time to give them the brush in a way that would not put off other possible marks. Time was running away - people at Mirtopik were going to notice the length of his absence.

The rain began again. A long storm that flushed the streets of people and stranded Calvin30 on the familiar temple steps. He watched the gutters drip forlornly. One of his 'sons' sat behind him blowing spit though something. The slaggy sound was getting on Calvin30's nerves and he turned around to snatch the offending instrument away from the boy. What he ended up holding was something far more valuable. His horn.

He embraced it in amazement. Sweet music. He was an emancipated man. In moments he could connect to the neuronet, siphon off some Ecos from company accounts, and purchase his ticket home.

His 'wife' walked over to him smiling a pathetic grin and pointing at the SlySynth and then back to herself.

"How did you? How much do you want?" Calvin30 stuttered in his limited street Hindi.

The woman stopped and gave him a confused look.

"Money. How much do I owe?"

She was becoming distressed.

"I have money now," Calvin30 pointed jubilantly at his horn. "How much?"

Her undernourished hand reached over to stroke his chest. When Calvin30 tried to push her away she angrily ripped open his undershirt. He pushed her back. Instead of resisting the woman backed deliberately away pointing at his exposed belly and the tiny letters tattooed on it like a target. C30.

How long had she known? Fear overtook him.

"Don't tell, please. Anything. Anything. Money. Please."

He was begging for his life, for her not to turn him over. He would marry her. Was that what she wanted? Anything. She returned to embrace him, but he brushed her away, unable to abide her desire. The depth of his revulsion dismayed him while she wept. He could hardly stand the sight of her.

His entourage soon deserted him, the witch and the rest of the wretches stopping only long enough to spit in his direction as they passed. They faded into the rain.

How long had they known? Who had they told?

In a panic, Calvin30 rushed to find the Sikh. He ran through the blinding rain, wild eyes imploring for direction whomever stepped into his path. "At the warehouse," they waved and dodged out of his way to avoid further contact with the madman. Calvin30, drenched to the core, burst open the warehouse door to find the turbaned calif holding court with the witch and the wife. He had come too late.

"She says you have something to tell me."

Calvin30 nearly fainted from fear. "I-I can pay. Please."

"That she tells me. That and one other thing."

"Yes." Calvin30's eyes squeezed, waiting for the axe to snap.

"She says that you are a good man."

Calvin30 scuttled on a X-Shuttle bound for LA. His ribs protruding, clothes in tatters, reeking of urine and sweat. The man at customs insisted on fumigation and an intrusive medical before letting him board.

Upon return he had to submit to intense interrogation, led with gleeful abandon, by the same ComSec officer who had approved his travel in the first place. Calvin30 dutifully filled in most of the security breaches he had provided to Bhatterjee, as if reporting on intelligence that the General had claimed foreknowledge of, leaving unsaid selected details.

Dazed, Calvin30 crawled up to his room to watch the walls crawl with his thoughts. The woman's face kept bubbling up in after-images framed in mealy rice and rats and crap. When it did, Calvin30 was gripped with a fierce desire to see every moment of her pathetic life replayed a thousand times. To see the rough, depressing weight of it grind her into the pavement of misery and hopelessness. To watch the last dull glow slink out of her eyes into a gray eternity. He wanted her to see him watching her - he wanted to see if any trace of the grotesque pity she had levelled on him in that warehouse would be left in those last moments when her own life betrayed her. If there was he wanted to see dogs chew it out of her brain.

He washed and washed and washed.

He reminded himself that it was ridiculous to be this disturbed. The woman was so pathetically beneath him. Like Bonita - so low on the totem pole of life that she could fall for a clone. Just pathetic.

When he awoke a day later, sick as a dog and sore in every muscle, he wandered down for a coffee and headed for the park to play his pipe and to pass-off promised information to Bhattarjee's operatives. It was a bit risky, following so close on the tail of his visit. His work here would be quantum encrypted, but he suspected that he was still under surveillance and the last thing he wanted to do was invite more scrutiny.

To hell with them. He needed to do something interesting to clear out his funk.

Calvin30 inspected his pipe. He was amazed to find that the damage had been minimal after the beating it had endured. The sound had developed some static and had gone a little digital but that could be tuned out. A few valves were dented but all were still operable. His password had held up although the logs revealed that someone had worked hard at cracking it.

It was time to go to work. Building up from a core of security routines embedded in some Mingus tunes, he moved into an improv mix that sent the relevant bytes of bits off to Bhattarjee regarding the facts he had to report to Mirtopik security and, more importantly, the facts that he hadn't. As usual he left out those critical pieces of information that were necessary for his plans.

The hour glass had almost poured out for Calvin30 to put in place the final granules of his plan. Despite his long respite in Chennai, it was surprising how exactly events in his absence had tracked the elaborate map he had implanted in the Com mind. The politics always moved along the groove of its own momentum to a predictable endpoint. Self-interest was a reliable slave master, which did not individuate. Ample time yet remained for Calvin30 to embark on some unpunctual construction duties in preparation for August's cathartic departure.

Boarding a builder borg body through his neuroview, Calvin30 clambered up the starship launch gantry to August's nearly finished cockpit and commenced to plant the camouflaged cam. Precision angles were vital to perfect a first-row seat of the Grand Man's abandonment.

The borg's anatomy, more ant than man, took adapting to, and Calvin30 kept clattering into things. Fortunately, none of the other borgs' pilots seemed to notice. It wasn't too long before he'd got the hang of it though, and soon he'd finagled the cameras into position. One last task to finish - he checked the other borgs' locations as they crept along the scaffolding, insectile forms backlit by the cerulean seas of the Earth beneath. He clambered his new body's awkward frame into the pilot's position and imagined himself in the place of August's fallen face. So many years in the planning, and it would all happen here.

Calvin30 could imagine every line on August's mien. The self-adulatory elation collapsing into confusion. The unstable momentums of false hopes as they faltered against the impossible facts of his calamity. The plunge into hell of a god would be such a long, delicious tumble, and Calvin30 could imagine in detail every moment. The culmination was so close he could touch it. It would be perfect.

That time was so close, so nearly certain, that Calvin30 could commence contemplation of the inevitable thereafter. After. And what then?

The hallowed almost hollowed until Calvin30 reminded himself of his monk in the quantum box. Any instant, one missive from the monk and the victory could vanish - the probabilities could collapse. Calvin30 had locked himself out of the box to cloak his crime behind an alibi of science. However, the dice rolls required to absolve him of murder had diminished to so merely impossible that the monk's demise had become received wisdom. There would always be some chance, but honestly now nearly none. It occurred to Calvin30 that he was only fooling himself.

His trials in Chennai intruded into that opening. That damn illiterate itinerant girl. Calvin30 stifled a chill. How could such an insignificant peasant evoke such a reaction?

A good man doubtlessly. Who was she to know?

To distract himself he activated his borg to crawl back towards its charging station. He paused in his passage to inspect an adjoining project, rotating in space at a span of some kilometers. It was much smaller than his expectation, its diameter only slightly larger than August's spaceship. It would be a tight fit. A thin ring of metal with unfamiliar devices, clumsy local adaptations of an alien technology, clustered like tumors outside the periphery.

At the center, framed by an angry fire, steeped in shadow, lay an eerie cratered land, the planet Mercury. The arc of the blue Earth engulfed the whole of it, suggesting a tunnel into the underworld.

It was by banishing his hero to Hades, only through tragedy, that August might rise to his godhood. And only Calvin30, faithful steward to the divine, could devise such a long-sought deliverance. August would probably only die as a man, but it was this risk was what made it real.

And after? To be truthful he hadn't foretold far beyond the fall. Calvin30 did though bestow a possible channel for the fantasy of August's return, leaving in the ship a brief epistle to steer him homeward. Perhaps, if he survived, Calvin30 could collect his broken pieces as a souvenir.

Thinking about it turned his thoughts maudlin. What would be left once August was lost?

Having downloaded from the borg, Calvin30 dialled up the aliens' transmission.

He lived it again, as he had so many times before, the horror and incomprehension of that world's disassembly. They had been such fools, so smug to believe that divinity came cheap. It was the end of the show that most rapt his attention - that soothed every recess of Calvin30's dark soul. It was the sublime grief of the Watcher, multiplied perfectly on all those faces, that touched him so deeply.

That Calvin30 could feel so One with his universe made him weep.

CHAPTER 18

Kalsang

After Kalsang reached the orbiter he had sat for days in simple amazement that he had survived. He was safe and warm. He had food and atmosphere. That seemed enough. The exquisite pink snowball of Triton rotated below him, unaware and unaffected by the abrupt exit of Life from its frozen surface.

Then it occurred to Kalsang that there were other tasks beyond survival. He thought to re-establish contact with the ground station to determine what had gone wrong. There were many duplicate communications channels by design, so at least one should allow him to reconnect. He was surprised to discover, after a sustained effort, that this was impossible. The problem seemed to be on the Terrapod side as all diagnostics for the orbiter seemed in order.

So strange, wasn't it?

Maybe the Terrapod had been hit by something, a micrometeor or some such thing. He had been lying right beside it. Did it make sense that he would have been unaware of such a violent calamity? Kalsang reviewed his memory and played back stored mnemes from his neurovisor to verify them.

There he was, walking around the Terrapod, climbing up to look in the window. It was so cold.

Kalsang mentally switched off the thermoception setting in his neurovisor and his shivering subsided. Had it really been so cold? How had he ever gotten used to that?

"What are you looking for?" d'Song asked as she tagged along behind him.

"Just this, I cannot understand what has happened. There are no markings on the Pod. It has not been hit by anything."

"What sort of anything?"

Kalsang turned around and smiled at her. Several of her faces returned snaggle-toothed grins.

"I cannot communicate with the Pod, but it appears that nothing is wrong with it. The antennae looks fine."

"Maybe somebody switched it off?"

"Huh?"

Maybe someone had. Kalsang, switched open the communications log and noted a final entry, dated just before his attempted return to the Terrapod. It was impossible to say for sure because the message was encrypted, but what other explanation could there be?

Perhaps it was routine software upgrade that had gone wrong? Such things did happen. Yes, this would explain it. And how fortunate he had been to be outside the Pod when it happened - so incredibly lucky wasn't it? Certainly there were plenty of back-up systems on board, and why hadn't he been notified? There was usually much advance notice and quite a drill whenever such changes were put into place. No, this one did not make sense.

Also, why was it the only message in the log that was encrypted?

Could such a thing be true? Why bother? He was only a humble monk, wasn't it, enjoying his retreat so so far away. He had no enemies. In his entire life, he had never engaged in any activity that could be remotely construed as political. He was not the sort to make trouble and he had no possessions to steal. His great achievement in life was to become as utterly insignificant as possible - all the better to appreciate the incredible opportunity of living.

"Maybe those people didn't like your message, Melded One."

"My message?"

The conversation drew the attention of the others and they huddled in closer to show their support until all space seemed to fill with imagined tentacles, face buds, and carapace.

Kalsang felt hemmed in so he covered his faces with his hands.

dSong warned them off. "Give him some space to think."

Her words warded off the press of bodies as they faded into the periphery of Kalsang's imagination.

d'Song was right, of course. It was the only thing that made sense.

Kalsang shook his head. The samsaric mind never ceased to amaze him. The terror of the aliens' last cry out into the universe, how could anyone react to that with a hard heart? Nevertheless, here was strong evidence, right before his eyes. The technological diagrams in the introductory sequence were what they were after. That had been the whole plan, and he Kalsang, in his pride and desire for appreciation by his teachers had made this possible. Samsaric mind? As if he could cast dispersions. The echoes were there in his own mind, for hadn't he been pleased to see the diagrams himself? Pleased to be serving his purpose to pay back the benefactors for all of their generosity. It was just like that.

Oh, he felt so stupid. Betrayal was something too ordinary to be unexpected. Driven by the greed, jealousy and a one-eyed focus on profit and power that was their DNA, how could anything else be expected from a Com?

Kalsang hung his head low. It was his great shame to be part of this. His mind reeled, the memories of the world devourer turned into projections forward to the same fate for the Earth, with the uncomprehending fright transferred from the faces of those far away and long dead onto the people and places he knew from birth, his family and the close community around his home monastery, his brother monks with whom he'd shared a common circulatory system of the crowded dormitories and open air debate grounds, his dharma sisters whose visiting smiles had made him glad and given him energy, the unexpected kindness of all the strangers he had met on his strange journey to the edge of nowhere. Names and names and names, so many. All precious to him, all doomed, and because of him. Kalsang begged forgiveness from the watching aliens for his crimes.

"I am sorry I have failed you my friends. The warning has become just the opposite."

The beings began to cry with him, for him. They were looking on him with so much compassion. How? Wasn't he the one who had betrayed the last moment of meaning for their whole world. It was too much.

"Don't cry Melded One," soothed d'Song.

Such a strange saying Kalsang thought. How could he even be imagining it?

"Don't cry. You are our hope."

"Your hope? What can I, a simple monk, do from so far away? This is not something I can do."

"Why do you think I sent you where you are?" The voice was a human one. The voice of his precious Teacher.

"Do you think your Teacher is an idiot?"

The thought made Kalsang recoil. Of course not.

Kalsang scanned the contents of his neuroview and found the mneme stored there from the original transmission. The diagrams were there. Kalsang again watched the tragedy of the death of the alien world, this time in fast motion. It was all there. What possible gain could be so great as to risk this unimaginably horrible outcome? Unbelievable.

After determining that the full contents of the transmission were indeed stored in his neurovisor he then scanned the orbiter's computer for the time of the transmission. As he had expected the mneme log had been falsified, a transmission of static replacing the alien people's warning. Another curious observation was that the orbiter's clock was wound backward by nearly two weeks.

There was no doubt now. The situation brought back into memory Lama Wangmo's song.

Make this perfect echo moment last longer.

There was no other explanation for everything that had happened. As impossible as it seemed, the responsibility to stop this madness had now fallen on him.

Kalsang knew that the first thing to do, in taking on any great matter, was to do nothing. So, he sat and focused on the empty movements of his breath. First from one nostril to the other, and then the reverse, and then together. He did this for a long time, balancing his energies so that the decisions he would have to make would be the best. Then he set his motivation. So many living mother beings depended upon him just now. No matter what was to come, he would never back down.

"Thank you Melded One."

Only when this motivation was firm did he begin to consider his course of action. There was no option to call up and inform Mirtopik Control of his plight, and they were the only ones he could call given that the craft was only equipped with laser beam communications, ostensibly to allow greater efficiency of transmission, but also to make sure that commercially sensitive information was controlled by the micro-satellite relays and could not be picked up by radio telescopes. It would be suicidal to call in if they were trying to kill him. For this reason, it was necessary to deactivate the incoming signals as well so that they could not switch off the orbiter as they had done to the Terrapod. He searched with his neurovisor, and relieved to find that doing so was straight forward, switched it off. Done.

Next Kalsang had to determine his path back to Earth. It was obvious that to stay alive he would have to return to where he had transited out from, to the Europa station on that icy moon of Jupiter.

The Orbiter was stocked with enough anti-matter to accelerate him along a direct journey back to Earth, but his provisions would not last that long. Mirtopik controlled communications from the orbiter, but Jupiter was another matter. The Jupiter Deep Space up-link was used to communicate with the Oort Array telescopes and was monitored by the entire scientific community. On a close approach Kalsang could laser his message directly to his friends on Europa, and from there they could pass the message onwards. This was his only choice, and Kalsang activated a navigation programme for a return trajectory to Jupiter.

That being done, Kalsang turned his attention to editing the computer logs as best he could to cover his escape. He hoped that his absence would not be noticed and that he was not in any way endangering his friends and fellow monks on Europa, awaiting their rotation out to Neptune.

He couldn't be sure. His actions could have been monitored by Mirtopik. His accidental escape would have surprised them, but it may not have gone unnoticed. Kalsang decided to consult his protectors.

Kalsang performed the prerequisite visualisations, slowly and exactly chanting the memorised liturgy while imagining the protectors appearing in space before him.

The air in the room began to boil with swirling clouds of black and blood. All the aliens shrunk back in terror.

"What is this Melded One? Has the sky eater followed us here?" pleaded d'Song.

"Not to worry. This is not that monster. This is only the kindness of holy beings to scare away such darkness."

The vision hardened, writhing with imagined power.

Kalsang reached into his backpack and pulled out the specially marked dice and prepared to throw the Mo, to see what future the protectors predicted from his choice.

Kalsang concentrated on his dilemma. He was desperately in need of direction. It was so important for this to be right, to save all the beings in the Earth world system. The responsibility was overwhelming.

He cleared his mind and let the problem rest there, suspending all bias and impulse.

What is the best course of action? Is Jupiter the right place? What would he do when he got there?

Hours passed. Slowly a cohesive vision began to separate, in strobe light flashes, from the ordinary menagerie of thoughts and images that ordinarily cluttered Kalsang's mind.

Off Kalsang sailed through space to Europa. Soon he was looking down on that cracked cue ball moon hanging in the shadow of an aurora-crowned dark side of Jupiter. Kalsang floated down towards the surface of Europa covered with the translucent cross hatching from innumerable thick ice plates grinding against each other as they slid over the super-cooled sea beneath. Thin metallic prayer flags flickering in the electrically charged winds from Jupiter hung from the many parabolic dishes spread across the clear crystal surface.

He was so happy to be returning. Europa, world of frozen splendors, his home away from home and of his few fellow adventurers, all plucked from their respective hermitages and flung out into the void. He felt so close to these brothers and sisters.

Kalsang descended in memory beneath the surface into the complex carved deep within crystal caverns that they had named New Shambhala station. The station was assembled out of inflatable ring-shaped tubes embedded in the ice and stacked one atop the other, green, red, blue, white and yellow, forming a cone. In the surrounding caverns, the monks had created a strange and magical world, half research station and half medieval monastery. Coloured lights shimmered off the surrounding ice walls, into which were carved intricate transparent sculptures and murals, mind-dazzling geometric patterns, animated mythical creatures frozen mid-leap, nature scenes, regional folk stories, mandalas and meditating masters floating on rainbow clouds. In the great amphitheatre within the cone was a large and lovely ice sculpture of the Amogasiddhi Buddha, his hands in the gesture of teaching, his face smiling benignly.

Kalsang saw his fellow monks as he remembered them: working in shifts, eyes blinking at their neuroviews as they maintained the Deep Space uplink infrastructure and attended to routine administrative details. While off duty, which was most of the time, they studied, debated, meditated or played practical jokes on one another. Kalsang had warm memories of the happy year he had spent there before his orders came to be the first to go to Triton. He vividly remembered his fellow monks that had been stationed with him. Geshe Tsultrim Gyeltshen, his fierce and rugged Khampa features belying a gentle spirit. Sangye Drub Tulku, famous for his bizarre antics and deep sincerity. Tashi Tsering, the quiet and intense artist, responsible for most of the ice sculptures carved into the frozen world. The sharp and inquisitive intellect of Choegyal Samten, equally at home with religious scriptures and the complex technology upon which their adopted world depended. And Zhi Lim T'ang, a very generous Chinese monk who had become his confidante. Tears ran down Kalsang's cheeks as he once again waved back to them through the airlock doors.

A soundless light exploded.

Kalsang was propelled backwards into orbit by a mysterious force. When his perspective stabilized he could see that the top of the station, which normally protruded through the ice, was missing. The contents of broken Terrapod modules formed an ejecta field surrounding the crater where New Shambhala had been. Personal effects and bits of the debris were scattered everywhere. Kalsang flew down to inspect the damage, alighting at ground zero of the explosion which had destroyed the station. At the center, the statue of Buddha was still standing, his hands no longer in the gesture of teaching but instead holding a skull cap in one hand and holding a trumpet made of human thigh bone high to his lips. Starting at the base of the statue a blood colored stain began to spill outward, slowly filling the transparent walls of the cavern beneath and extending into the seams and canyons of the surface of Europa until the moon's face burned a brilliant crimson.

Kalsang rubbed his eyes on his main head. What a dreadful vision.

"Are you okay Melded One?" d'Song stroked his second right hand lightly with many of her hands, to show her concern.

"This is not good."

It felt like the hole had been made in his heart.

Kalsang wrapped his hands tightly around himself, to ward off dizziness.

"Who were they Melded One?"

"My dear friends. They are okay."

Okay. Of course they were. Nothing had happened. It was only a vision. His friends were still there, enjoying themselves as he had left them, as certain as anything was certain.

But it was a sign, undeniable.

Kalsang relaxed into his breathing once more, sinking slowly back into his meditation. *A faint whistle blew through the stillness in his mind, drawing his attention to it. As his mental focus increased, the sound amplified until Kalsang could make out a subtle fanfare of depraved voices, howling with glee. Behind the tortured chorus, Kalsang felt a sullen presence, dark and greedy, drunk on the anticipation of great evil entering the world.*

"Demons," Kalsang thought with pity.

Then, descending out of a rainbow, Kalsang appeared in the high meadows of Tibet, standing on the banks of an emerald mountain lake. Sweet mountain air filled his lungs, a perfume of spring flowers and snow. He was talking to an unfamiliar older man who was perhaps an American. The man looked somehow familiar, but Kalsang couldn't quite remember his name. Perhaps he was a public figure of some sort. The man smiled as Kalsang opened the man's hand, and placing a jewel in the open palm, folded the fingers over it.

"Who is he?"

"I don't know d'Song."

Kalsang awoke sprawled across the floor. He lay there for some time considering his vision, letting his mind flow lightly over it without interpretation.

Kalsang threw the Mo and asked the question - should he proceed on towards Europa or proceed directly to Earth? The dice rose and fell and slowly rolled to a stop.

The answer was no. Either way the answer was no. Europa was no, Earth was no. Where else to go?

The only other place with people was Mars. Mars?

Kalsang threw the dice again.

Yes. Mars.

Was that possible? Kalsang used his neurovisor to check the trajectory. Mars was closer. This surprised him. To look at it this was hard to see. When orbiting back from around the Sun the Earth should be closer, but the transit wasn't right. Going to Earth meant swinging back from around Mars. Mars was along the way to Earth.

Did he have enough resources to get there? Kalsang checked the numbers and came back disappointed. Oh, almost, almost. The calculations, by any iteration, showed him dying somewhere between his swing round Venus and arrival at the red planet. Mars still meant death.

Shaking the dice Kalsang asked again, "Should I go to Mars?" Both faces affirmed that choice. He threw the dice a few more times, each time with the same result.

Kalsang returned to the neuroview navigation report and studied it intently. The fastest approach involved an acceleration around Uranus followed by a turn around and deceleration via Venus. The acceleration around Uranus would be crushing, scarcely survivable. He would have to reduce the temperature immediately to conserve heat. Food would not last. Water would give out after he passed Venus. The atmosphere would become toxic soon after. First, he would be crushed, then frozen, then starved, then dehydrated, and finally poisoned.

Was there any way out? Kalsang intently shook the dice and dropped them. "Death," they replied.

Why go to Mars if he would be dead when he got there? How close did he have to get for radio communications? His neurovisor returned a calculation as soon as this thought finished. It would be possible to send a single message to Mars, to Aurora, without using the microsatellites. Aurora was still on Mars, along the other Australians that he had trained with. Terry and Cath. Aurora. Of course.

Kalsang brought their faces from memory, clearer than any mneme.

His dear friend, with her copper wire frizzed hair and green eyes.

"What is her name?" d'Song asked while the other aliens wondered around examining the people from his memories, curious.

"That is Terry. She is very funny. We had a lot of fun."

"No, I mean her."

"That is Aurora. She is my very special to me. We have samaya between us."

"Do I know her?"

The question was odd, especially considering that d'Song and his memories of Aurora were both figments of his imagination.

"She is frightened."

Kalsang inspected his visualisation of Aurora. Yes, her face did hold fear, but this was not how he remembered her. Of all of them Aurora was the most fearless. Perhaps she was in some danger? Kalsang concentrated on Aurora more as her face began to fade. Yes, maybe so.

Kalsang breathed in the fear, breathing light back into her, until Aurora's image stabilized, and she began to glow of her own accord.

"Don't worry Aurora. You will be okay." Kalsang studied her and then smiled. "Okay, Mate?"

Kalsang lay back in his webbing to think about the paths before him. On one path the laws of physics and common sense told him that he would reach a comfortable and safe destination. It would lead him back to the comfort of old friends at New Shambhala and a certain audience for his critical message. Reason supported this approach. On the other hand, he had the suspicion of a broad conspiracy by unknown powers arrayed against him, a series of hallucinations, and the results of an ancient superstitious practice of fortune telling. On the path these indicated lay an improbable outcome, pain, desperation, and a certain lonely death. His mind paralysed by doubt Kalsang sang out to his protectors.

Invisible guardians, diamond visions, mysterious friends
How well do I know you?

Three great mountains rushing to bury me
deterioration, sickness, and death
How well do I know you?

Irresistible wind blowing ceaselessly
In one direction, to the end of my days
How well do I know you?

Burning candle devoured by its own light
my life since first breath
How well do I know you?

Uncertain flicker, uncovered flame
Next heartbeat or next life
How well do I know you?

Ten thousand spirits wrestling
to claim my last sigh
How well do I know you?

Irrelevant bubble in samsara's vast sea
My body tossed in the ocean of storms
How well do I know you?

Unscrupulous bandit digging up
Dusty treasures from my tomb of wealth
How well do I know you?

Fast mountain torrent carrying me
from friends' hands outstretched
How well do I know you?

Traitorous bones, inconstant blood
feckless heat deserting my breath
How well do I know you?

Other than these is anything more true?
uncertainty of appearance
fragility of thoughts
emptiness of self
this unwavering elephant path
I have followed all this life
Faith, insight, luminosity, dependent arising
Everyday your face becomes clearer
My constant guides I bow to greet you.

You know me well.

Kalsang spent the day in meditation, his mind resting on a simple image of the Buddha and admitting no other thought. When thirst stirred Kalsang from this practice he sipped some water, chewed the edge of a Vitabar, and then calmly keyed into the navigation computer his new direction.

He was headed to Mars.

CHAPTER 19

Aurora

Turning to stone did not hurt. What hurt was deciding that you didn't want to.

The world around shimmered in an uneven light. It was like looking through midday heat against the horizon. Aurora's arms, wrapped around her knees, looked to her to be wrapped in gauze. Everything was the dusty orange color of Mars.

Waijungari smiled up from below. He greeted her soul as it sank down into his patient embrace.

"Relax Darl. You and I are one and the same, see? No need to rush it. Let it happen."

Aurora almost did. She was so tired. She wanted to sink. Down into her bones. That was until she realised she was being buried alive.

The weight of Mars came down on her frozen soul like a tonne of bricks. It brought back old memories that seemed somehow fresh - memories of being crushed.

Aurora began to fight, or rather to flail. There wasn't anyone or anything to fight. The pressure closing in on all sides was overwhelming. There was nowhere to move. Her bones and flesh were being squeezed into jelly. A hydraulic force dragged her along in a tidal surge of desperation. The only direction was towards utter darkness. Even her screams could not escape, but only balled up in her throat and choked off her breath.

Not again.

Not again.

Not again.

Aurora's last conscious thought was that the only thing left to fight was her fear. Everything else was a lost cause. That was what she did, and it had an effect.

From above, floating in sudden tranquillity, Aurora watched the light in a body below her slowly dim. The rest of the world all around shone up with a light that was free of shadow. She watched others arrive and lift her body and lower it and lift it again, down and away from the great mountain.

She wanted to sink down again into solid ground and sleep. Then she would feel an ache as the body jostled with the vehicle it was in rolled over another rock.

She could hear them shouting and this brought her closer, down into the vehicle. It was irritating. Couldn't these voices shut up and leave her in peace? The more pissed off she became the closer she was drawn to the two bodies lying side by side. One was smaller and seemed to be enjoying herself while another person rocked back and forth pressing down on its chest.

The other body was less easy to look at. It looked like battered madwoman - arms and legs contorted like a dropped doll. Aurora descended closer to the frost leathered and blood bruised skin. It was disgusting. She fell with a panic into the pinhole opening inside the tangled iris. Back within the body she felt the irregular beating of a heart. And she could hear again, but faintly. Once again there was meaning in words.

"She's dead Terry. Stop."

"No."

"It's not helping."

"Don't tell me what to do anymore Pip. She can't be. Shit."

"I'm sorry."

"Sorry? Why are you sorry. It's my fault."

"It's not your fault Terry."

"Who the hell are you to tell me it's not."

"The rocks were unstable. She was standing too close to the cliff. It just happened."

"Who told her to come out to help? I knew better."

"When you stop feeling sorry for yourself Terry."

"Don't."

"You aren't the only one who loved her."

"Oh Christ, Pip."

"Xiao Li. Xiao Li. Please don't leave us. You look so lovely. I can't bear it."

It couldn't be. Xiao Li, dead? My friend.

Aurora felt her will to live slip. Then the voices faded into a bland buzz and all feeling dried out. Above her body again, it was like watching a play through a telescope. She couldn't quite follow the plot but felt obliged to keep watching. The unfocused faces of the actors were still familiar. There was a faint, unpleasant smell about them. They were the last blemishes on the general softness of the universe around her. Pleasure and pain, and the distinction between the two, faded into a thick haze.

Dancing lights that tasted of ozone captured Aurora's attention and she followed them on their random paths through the smoke. As they travelled, random scenes lit up under the torch light. First, she was back in the vehicle with the bodies, watching the landscape unfold ahead of them. Then she was outside while it picked its way through a deserted valley like a lost ant.

Then she was outside the wreckage of a spaceship strewn across an adjoining valley, some past disaster. Lying around were many mummified corpses, tossed among the rubble. The lights flickered over to a corpse clothed in a space suit and slumped against a rock wall an unusual distance from the impact zone with decaying footprints trailing back to the wreckage behind it. The body had scratched a word on the rock before it had collapsed.

"Home."

As the lights flickered away to some other place Aurora noticed a movement, a thin vapour in the shape of a man, still scratching and re-scratching the word in the stone.

The lights slowed and began to sputter. The empty red plains of Mars sounded like wind rushing over a chimney. The embers of the lights winked out, not into darkness but into a clear absence of light. Aurora's life before began to wind past like an old movie.

It was the day they finally processed Dad's corpse. She'd missed the funeral, but she had at least made it back for this. The body was lowered into the digester, where its molecules could be efficiently devoured by microbes, fungi and worms, turning a complex, enigmatic, self-destructive but endlessly generous person, into high grade compost. The sparse saline fields of wheat surrounding them awaited another meal.

Aurora kicked a can across a salt scar. Dad was gone, together with his grand exuberance and endless stories. He had been an oasis in this dry and gutted land, pointing out the small things that had shared their wonder with him. Dragons lurking under the rocks. The tree that still stood, full of life and breath, a century after the soil beneath it had died. The sky filled with the geometries of gods. Dreamtime Beings, the ones he was allowed to tell her about, which lived in every outcrop and streambed. Despite the occasional drunken rages that mortified him, Dad had somehow made the balding country of her birth come alive. Now he was dead and his magic songs along with him. What was the point?

A wedge-tail eagle flew high overhead as a dot swooping across the clouds. It winked in and out of the empty sky over the empty land. Her eyes followed it. Into the sky, into the stars, free from the dried and futile life beneath. With it, her spirit flowed.

The sepia tinged memories ran out. Nothing but light was left. Then she saw, or rather felt, a familiar presence. Somehow, he had arrived when everything else was leaving. The presence steadily resolved into someone she had known and loved, and whose arrival was not expected.

Kalsang?

CHAPTER 20

Francesca

Francesca sized up the intruder as he slunk into the change room and rummaged through compartments and duffle bags full of the players' gear, looking like a dog left alone in a meat locker. She had to look twice to decide if her eyes were deceiving her. This snowball in hell was a stupid place to be in the first place, and no place to be a thief. Where did he think he could escape to? What did he think he was going to find? A nico fix? A pocket-sized nuclear bomb? From the panicked look on his face that would be a good guess. An enchanted potion, misplaced by San Orisha, that was going to turn him good looking? He'd need that, or maybe just start with some self respect and a hair-cut. Balls of fluff and tissue and pens and other useless crap liberated from their fast-holds by his fumbling? If that was what he was after, then he was onto a good thing.

It was a fun to watch somebody thinking they were being so sneaky when they weren't, but maybe this was more serious than just some harmless klepto. His anxiety had a dangerous edge of desperation. Wings grew from his temples, spikes down his back. The Archangel pick-pocketing souls? No. The guy was too pathetic for that kind of fantasy - too soft in the face, like a an over nervous eco-scout earning his merit badge in interplanetary espionage.

Francesca recognised him as a player from the opposing GravBall team. He was a mediocre player, good enough, but generally out of shape and not that aggressive. Even with her twisted ankle that had forced her out of the game and into the showers, she was certain she could take him.

He turned around, eyes wide like a gecko, the one last moment before she could slip her headlock of steel around his slippery neck.

"Can I help you find whatever it is that you misplaced in one of our pockets?"

If the thief's face were an armadillo it would have curled itself up into its own anus.

The man looked around her. Was he looking for an exit or trying to preserve her modesty? Francesca appreciated the thief's good manners while intending to take full advantage of them. I made her pause though. She hadn't thought the thief would be a nice guy. A shy bandit. Cute.

Her pause created an opening. The thief's embarrassment suddenly gave way to panic, and he grabbed one of the uniforms while pushing past her to make a bolt for the docking bay hatch. Whap! Two meters from freedom he suddenly shot forward, propelled by her kick to his lower back. His face cracked into the wall. Francesca gritted her teeth. She could practically hear the sparks shooting through the guy's skull. The thief rolled on the floor, blood spheres pooling off his forehead and spinning off across the floor. What a mess. Oh well, he might be a nice guy, but that didn't give him a get out of jail free pass.

Francesca floated expertly down on her feet like Queen Insecta about to devour another husband. Her toned legs folded and clicked with entomological precision as she confidently swam over to inspect her prey, which lay waiting where she had landed it. Maybe she had gone a bit overboard.

"Whatya' think Capitan Klingon? Ready to give up? You don't look like you want any more, do you?" She licked her mandibles and prodded at the dude with her toe.

Time moved forward in single frames as the *porco graso* spun over and pulled Francesca's foot out from under her. His adrenaline jump-started hands somehow managed to grab a fire extinguisher hanging within reach on the wall, and the idiot blasted her with it.

Reaching through the cloud of white powder, her mighty claw gripped the bastard's spacesuit collar and lifted his weightless ass off the floor. Francesca's elbow crunched into his face, followed by a sharp uppercut jab to his throat. As the man GASPED for air, she emerged from the smoke transformed into some kind of devilish ghost.

It pissed her off what perverts with jellyfish guts thought they could get away with dumb moves like that just because she was a girl. She grabbed him by the hair and hurled him into a set of lockers, which burst open showering them in a cloud of stuff.

Following the thief's momentum Francesca spun around to target him with another kick but then tripped, giving the man a second chance to collect himself. She looked him hard in the eyes to see what he was thinking. The thief was still avoiding looking at her naked majesty. Was this waste of space still actually ashamed to fight a woman even though she was kicking his ass. Surely such chivalry should not go unpunished.

But then she noticed that the man's modest eyes were actually focused on something else. They were tracking the spinning arc of a plastic card on a neck cord that had been knocked into cartwheels from the lockers she had opened with his face. The thief sprung off after it off with a cleaner jump then she remembered from his lame gravball attempts. The guy had found what he wanted, and his excitement propelled him past her to the prize and onwards towards an open hatch.

Francesca grasped at air as the man's boots slipped away. As she spun into position to push off the ceiling, the man snagged a bench that had broken away in their fight and launched the improvised missile at her.

She knew what the game was now. The man's interest in the key card answered all her questions. This guy was looking through their pockets for keys that weren't his. Probably he was some Outlander nut looking for a quick ride home and didn't realise this was the hard way to go about it. Whatever the reason, the guy wasn't really leaving her much choice except to pound him senseless. She had experience with guys going Out. Even on the short ride out to Tsuchinshan she had to grapple one guy back in through an airlock while Raoul re-bolted the inner door. After they had restrained the nutcase Raoul had held her tight. She was an even bigger nutcase for letting go.

What was she doing in the middle of this fight going all dreamy? Snap out of it. In that lost second the man scrambled through the hatch and up the docking shaft with Francesca's fingernails scratching his heels. As he pulled up on the first rung of the gantry ladder, Francesca's talons wrapped around his ankles and she sank her fangs into his calf tendons. His blood tasted like fear. She felt like one of those mean rattlesnake rats back in Cuba that once bit her sister. Too bad she didn't have their venom.

"Vaffancolu!"

"Italian blood," Francesca mused as she licked the red round her mouth, painting a death mask on the skeletal white of the extinguisher dust still caking her face and body. Stimulated by this thought, she surged forward straight into the heel of his boot. Her nose fountained balloons of blood as the man limped out of her clutches, fleeing this insane vampire bitch who was now definitely bent on devouring his ass.

Higher they raced along a refuelling conduit towards where the freighter was moored. The man looked over his shoulder as Francesca closed the distance between them. At last he reached the refuelling dock and shot downward out of a panel in the ceiling towards the freighter door. As he frantically fumbled with the key card, swiping it again and again through the groove on the door panel Francesca dropped out of the ceiling, ready to suck every last bit of pulse out of him. The man turned to face her, his back against the stubbornly unyielding door. Oh Jesus, not another crying guy.

Francesca folded up her Dark Angel wings into her back and advanced.

"Look, put down that card and I won't beat the holy living shit out of you. Cause I should, you know. I still have your footprint in my face."

She wiped her bloody nose across her cheek.

"So, what you gonna do? Take our ship, huh? Why you want to do something stupid like that? You can't even get the door open, what you going to do when you get inside Buck Rogers?"

"A spetta, a spetta, per favour, please, don't hit me anymore, please, firmedi, stop please."

The man was beaten.

Francesca felt a bit disappointed, like a child called home from play. She had been enjoying the fight, the taste of blood, but she didn't really like violence. It was the rush and the feel of the power in her awesomely toned body that she liked. Fighting in the buff had been amazing too, exercising her inner kick-butt Xena warrior princess. And God knew it needed the exercise, especially after being packed up in a flying tin-can for the last month. Oh well. She tilted her head to accept his surrender.

"What's your name?" she asked to reduce the tension and stop him from doing something stupid.

"Ah. Marco. Marco Uliassi."

Marco slumped backward against the door, or rather slumped backwards against where the door should have been. The door had opened as he turned to face Francesca, which had been funny. The idiot had given up cornered against open air. As the absent door failed to support his weight Marco fell backward, tripped over a railing, and fell slowly down the ship towards the nose.

Francesca dove to catch him, but then the man had managed to get tangled up in the travel bungees. His flailing foot had released the catch, which had sprung him down to the cockpit in a flash, taking all the hand straps with him. Now Francesca would have to swim down, because there was like almost zero gravity here. She propelled herself calmly downward, pushing off the walls, but then misjudged one launch angle, getting herself stalled floating in the air midshaft with nothing to grab onto.

"Mierda!"

Francesca went into spasms like some netted dolphin trying reach something while Marco the mad thief recovered himself and began inspecting the apparently unfamiliar controls.

"You won't get anywhere weirdo," she shouted down from her invisible cage of empty space. "The key just gets you in. You'll need the pilot's neuroprints."

Then Marco started talking to someone who he'd obviously connected to through his neurovisor. He could have just thought it, but Francesca had noticed that people liked to look like they were talking to themselves even when they didn't have to.

"Raffaello? Raffaello? Raff? I'm in but I need to go fast. Testa di merda. You are supposed to be there. Pronto? Ah."

Francesca watched him following instructions from his unseen collaborator, deftly taking the controls, typing in keys and downloading mnemes into the ship's computer. Boy, she had gotten this one totally wrong. This was obviously more organised than just some crazy guy freaking out. Their ship was actually going to be hijacked. Why? Did this have anything to do with the all that stuff with August on the Moon? She made up her mind that it did, which made the guy into a terrorist, which made him seem less nice.

Francesca twisted hard, working her way to the wall centimeters at a time. She saw Marco snapping himself into the pilots webbing while the airlocks hissed close and the warning strobes flashed the missing crew to their stations for the unexpected emergency launch. This was going to be bad for her.

As her fingertips finally found a surface, the ship began to shudder violently. She finger-walked her way to a railing and then flung her way forward but it was too late. The walls ran into her too quickly as the ship retros fired and as she bounced back her feet became entangled in the webbing she had been aiming for. She swore as she clawed at the webbing but in vain. The main boosters fired. At this close range it could have been bad news for the people on Tsuchinshan. This was her last thought before the g-forces swung her in a violent wide arc and banged her skull into a bulkhead.

She came around sometime later, her head throbbing, tied up with the same webbing that had caught her. Oddly enough, she was clothed. Was she wearing Marco's shirt? Such a prude terrorist that guy. And where in hell had he gotten these pants? They were totally ridiculous. She figured out after thinking about it that they were pressure leggings from the medical kit pushed up to her thighs. And then, to top it off, he had stuck her legs through the bottom a silvery sack of some kind and cinched it to her hips with a bungee strap. She looked like some escapee from an Oompla Loompa asylum.

Francesca easily squirmed out of the poorly improvised knots and looked for a way out of her enclosure. Marco deserved points for effort with the way knots had been piled on knots, but he had neglected to pull the rope tightly enough, perhaps out of some misguided concern for her comfort. It was a pity that she was not civilised enough to reserve the same consideration for him when she would catch him. The door was locked, of course, but the vents were large and unsecured. Rubbing her wrists to restore circulation, she angled a jump towards the nearest one and caught it with her fingertips. Unscrewing the lid with her fingernails she slithered her way upwards to freedom.

The vents turned out not to be the free ride advertised. The screws were on the outside and they proved surprisingly resistant to being kicked out from the inside, especially given the slipperiness of her body in low gravity and surrounded by vent work that was mainly silicon nanomat, designed for minimum friction to air flows to conserve energy. Nearer the ship's Terrapod things got particularly gross, with bacterial slime mats that had broken free from the main fermenter sliding out from wherever she pressed a hand, semi-suspended fungal spore masses attaching to her skin and colonising it, the nearly unbearable heat of compost that kept the further interior of the craft liveable, and the pungent reek of shit being deconstructed into useful pieces. Through the translucent walls of neighboring conduits, unimaginable horrors sloshed and squished, the internal organs of some giant beast.

Francesca thought about Raoul and felt particularly attractive. She suddenly felt quite shut off from him, with thousands of kilometers of cold space between them. She hoped he was okay. The other guys too, but not as much. There was a lot she should have said and done but hadn't. What kind of idiot was she? Where had all that defensive armor gotten her? Her Impenetrable Shield and useless Lasso of Truth that she never used on herself where it needed to be used? Scuttling around like a pathetic cockroach in these pipes of shit, that's where. Scuttling, that was the word for it. Trying to keep ahead of the merciless thoughts by one handhold, one butt slide, one squashed foot unstuck from an unexpected crevice, one wiped face momentarily free of gross sludge, one frantic scratch at the unreachable itch that she imagined was a colony of insects feeding between her shoulder blades, one scream!

"Hey. I can hear you in there."

Francesca froze.

Marco tapped on the wall. "Right here? You're there right?"

It was more stupid not to acknowledge him.

"What do you think?"

"I don't know. Maybe I'm going Out myself. I've been hearing a lot of noises."

"You don't have to yell. This wall is so thin I could almost break through it."

"But you can't?" He sounded worried.

"No idiot. If I could I would have already strangled you."

"Look, I don't mean you any harm."

"Is that how you feel about the crew you left behind on Tsuchinshan, living for months on half rations until they get rescued? What about the crew you maybe killed blasting off from so close?"

There was a long pause, like *El Cretino* hadn›t quite throught all the consequences of his actions.

"Uhh look, Signore. You are hungry, ci? I put some food and nanosorbs and some clothes I found back in your room. If you can get back to them, you can make yourself comfortable."

"Screw you." The offer had invalidated in one hit any heroic notions she still held about her struggles of the past day, like a torpedo shot beneath the bowline of her barely floating ego. Too deflated to argue further Francesca began the hour-long crawl back to her original confinement.

Exhausted, Francesca slipped back down the vent and squirmed out in a slimy placental mess back into the makeshift prison. In her absence, the room had been made up. Sleeping web had been secured in one corner, a clean pair of overhauls and a work shirt in a stuff sack was tied to it. A ration kit loaded with vitabars and other stuff floated free in the room, and most importantly a water cube! Francesca latched on, sucking down the water with great gulps. The most painful part of her confinement had been being immersed at times in various liquids but being afraid to ingest any of it. 'Water water everywhere.' Wasn't that how it went.

Consuming a Vitabar whole, Francesca checked over her new provisions. Nanosorbs and vac, thank God! Emergency oxygen and first aid kit, with scalpel and scissors removed of course. Exercise bungees installed. A spacesuit in case of total depressurisation. Even a few green plants from the Terrapod Atrium and a view screen on saver with pretty pictures to look at.

Marco had gone to lengths to make her comfortable, which must have required some courage on his part, never knowing when she might get back. Or maybe he had just re-screwed the vent while he worked. Or maybe he didn't because what was the point if she came back and he couldn't let her back in. Maybe he was just one of those OCD guys and couldn't help himself. Whatever. She decided to accept his peace offering, at least until she could get her hands on him. The only thing he hadn't returned she noticed, was her neurovisor, which she understood because she could make trouble for him with that, but which also meant that her stay was going to be impossibly boring. She wouldn't be able to read any of the comic mnemes stored on her neuroview. At least she could work out.

Francesca rubbed nanosorbs over her body, the microtubules magical capillary action sucking the greasy and gummy grossness off her body and leaving a film of a sand-like nodules that were easily slurped up with the vac for later recycling in the Terrapod. It was a bitch when it got in your eyes though, which set her off blinking like some mad person with a tic for a while.

When she was fed, cleaned, clothed, and rested there was a tentative knock on the door.

"Come in," she said hopefully, standing to the side of the door ready to pounce.

"Signore, I must respectfully decline." Marco wasn't as stupid as she'd hoped.

"If you aren't here to finish what you started, what are you doing here?"

"Uh, I'd like to talk to you."

"Estupido. You are waiting for my permission when I am your prisoner?"

"Ci. All right." There was an irritatingly long pause.

"You want to talk, but then you shut up. Good, get lost."

"Signore. What you said. Do you think that I killed anyone?"

This guy was unbelievable. The asshole steals our ship and then wants absolution for it.

"What am I? Your confessor?"

"No. No. I guess."

"Look, if you didn't kill anyone - I'm not saying you didn't. How couldn't you risk their lives by leaving them on an unstable comet? Especially as it gets closer to the sun - that thing could outgas anywhere. What are they going to do? You should have thought of that maybe?"

"Ci."

"Talk to whoever that was telling you how to snitch our ship, or someone else who cares."

"Ah Raffaello. Ci. We used to be friends."

Francesca saw an opening, a wedge she might work on between Marco and whoever was directing him, that she could use to get some information. "Used to be? Why are you helping him if he isn't?"

She could hear Marco tearing up.

"Ma famiglia. I have a family, you see?"

And then she got the whole story whether she was even remotely interested in hearing it or not. Basically, just as she had thought, the Revs had picked up on August Bridges' amazing invention. Okay maybe it was copied from the aliens, but they sure would've had to invent a pile of new tech to make it work. Anyway, the Revs reckoned it was going to destroy all life on Earth, or could at least if all the stars aligned, as if everyone hadn't heard that line before a million times. So they were going to take it out, using the perfectly democratic method of the shooting it down with the comet impactors on-board this ship, the ones they would shoot into the other side of Tsuchinshan to loosen up the ice they wanted to mine.

Obviously, they couldn't count on Mister Mushy here to do the job right, so they had launched this other dude on a one-way ticket to a rendezvous spot, and then he was going to take it from there. That was as far as Marco's knowledge went, that this Souren dude was on his way. Marco had served with his old amigo Raffaello under the same Rev assisting with famine relief somewhere in Central Europe. The Revs were active in that sort of stuff, keeping connected to the Hearts and Minds to make sure the Coms didn't get the upper hand as they had managed to in Russia and in the Sovereign Economic Zones.

Marco had been convinced into stealing their ship and driving it to the provided coordinates. The point where she lost respect for him though was that this wasn't about protecting his family like she thought. It sounded like the guy was completely homesick and although he was doing this out of some misplaced sense of duty he was just feeling sorry for himself because it meant he might not see his Momma and brothers and sisters and long chain of relatives again, or at least for a long time in the case that he went to prison.

"Wait a second. Let me understand this because, to be honest, I completely don't. Your family isn't under any threat at all. It isn't the money because the wage on Tsuchinshan must be outrageous and you've just pissed your pension up against the wall by stealing the ship and the civil and criminal penalties will impoverish you. And isn't this a bad move if you are homesick because you won't be seeing your family again if something bad happens or you get locked up? So that isn't it. This makes no sense Marco. You, you are a stupid person that's what I think."

"No Signore. I am stupid, of course, but you don't understand at all. I put my hand up for this mission, for my Rev, my Net, my Hub, the whole of Gaia. If I fail in my duty, what then?"

Aaargh. A fanatic. Even more intolerable. "I take it back. You are worse than stupid. You have actually swallowed that panarchist bullshit."

"Ci. I believe, and it is good to believe. This mission is to prevent the end of the world. It is worse if I turned it down, so much shame. I couldn't face my family."

"They probably wouldn't give a shit," Francesca laughed, "What the hell are you even talking about? You think your family will be more worried about their own shame or your life? End of the world, how cliché - how do you think anyone could accomplish that?"

He couldn't say, which was typical, and even more typically because it was top secret. How many times had that one been used? Too many times, that's how many.

That was as far as the conversation went. Despite Marco's tired attempts to resurrect it, Francesca had had enough. He was a fool and that was all there was to it. Despite all the truth of the past excesses, climate catastrophes and a million other large and small disturbances in the Force, she was tired of living in a world where leaving on a light switch was the hard road to Hell. She had never herself signed up for the Campaigns, wearing the resulting ostracism as a badge of Honor. That this guy was basically flushing his life down the toilet for a struggle that was so far over most people couldn't remember that it had happened in the first place. There were more real things to real about - real pain, like what the families of the workers this bozo had marooned would be going through. Like what Raoul was going through, not knowing if she were dead or alive.

She had more important things to think about now, like preparing for this Rev guy, probably Kaliyuga Rev if he was as Indian as his name sounded. Chances were he wasn't going to be a pushover like poor Marco and she didn't want to be an easy target. Jamming the door lock from the inside and donning the spacesuit Marco had left her, a tight fitting Buckygel number, Francesca re-entered the belly of the beast to explore her options.

Some days later, through the vents in the corridor inside from the airlock room, she heard the kind of singing that could lead to ear bleeds.

> "Kya acha laga ta hai
> Acha laga ta hai
> Bhi ala ru ko sapana
> Sucha laga ta hai"

Although she could not see him unloading his ship, Francesca could already tell a few things about this guy. For one, he thought he sounded good, which meant he was the worst kind of narcissist. Two, he was very careful about everything he did. There was no banging around and rushing or swearing, and no panting and ass scratching, only a cool efficiency in the sounds of his movements. So he was dangerous. Three, he was an asshole. She picked that up from his first conversation with Marco. It went like this.

"Bongiorno. I'm Marco." There was a pathetic hopefulness in his greeting.

"Macro. Hi Macro, I'm late. I'm late because you were late. Nearly an hour late and if I hadn't readjusted my trajectory to take that into account I would be dead. Now do as I say, or you will be dead."

"Ci. Ci."

"And stop the Eurokutta. Speak so that I can understand you. Clear?"

"Ah, yes."

"Not 'YES'. Try speaking a civilised tongue. 'Jee haan'. Do I have to spell it? Surprise me and don't be a moron."

Typical. It never ceased to amaze Francesca how arrogant some Indians could be, as if they had always been the center of the cultural universe on Earth. Power, no matter how it was earned or how ephemeral, always turned people into dicks. A narcissistic, calculating dick. The guy had a very bad vibe. Francesca was glad she was not waiting around in the room for him to come knocking.

"I'm heading to the cockpit. You secure these Macro."

"It's Marco."

"Whatever. Your instructions are in your neuroview. Those there need to be loaded."

"Ci." Points to Marco for unexpected self-respect and for not mentioning her existence.

Mi madre muerta. She had anticipated these movements and had planned her next step, but the reality was hard to face. This was how it was - the path from the airlock to the cockpit for her meant squirming back through the guts of the Terrapod, at least that is what she had memorised from a map on the inside of one vent she had explored. Clambering up a side vent she followed the pulses of air up the main Terrapod oxygenator, a slowly tapering rubbery tube with side channels that split and funnelled away like the blood vessels of some enormous beast.

As her journey became increasingly claustrophobic, Francesca psyched herself up to the task by imagining herself into Shrinking Violet, overcoming her shyness to navigate into the circulatory system of her beloved Leviathan to save him from his own death wish. She pulled herself forward gently so as not to disturb his breathing, mindfully finding footholds on his bronchial arches and branches. Somewhere in here she would find his noble soul to save it from itself, and, while she was there, rescue his heart from that power-hungry bitch Kinetix.

He would see then who really loved him.

The airway narrowed further into a self-sealing valve that let the air pump into his heart but kept the blood and gunk from flowing backwards up it. Her boyfriend had a strange anatomy, but what else would she expect from the severe mutations he must have suffered from that radioactive meteorite.

She pushed further into the darkness of his core, wriggling hard to push through since she could not shrink further, her atoms having reached the limits of how far she could compact them.

Stuck. The valve pursed tight around her hips, regardless of how hard she kicked and pried her fingers under the tight belt around her waist. She could feel the black ooze of destiny close in around her, revealing itself by the way it slowed her movements although she could not see, her headlamp failing to penetrate the goo.

This was how it was going to be. She was going to breathe her last breath in here, balled up somewhere deep within her lover Leviathon's breast. Perhaps she would kill him by clogging his arteries before his fight with Regulus that should have finished him instead. In the end that was all she would be - a fatal clot in a heart that still belonged to another.

That was good. She should write some of this stuff down.

When the distraction from her fantasy wore off, Francesca started to panic. She punched at the valve with her padded fists and cursed and shouted inside her helmet, but it was completely futile. It began to dawn on her that this was the end of her life, and she could fight her way forward no longer. The crowded backlog of fears began to work its way through her brain, ballooning her brain with frustration.

Elena called out to her again, begging her to come back to her rescue, condemning her for her shameful powerlessness, cursing her for reaching such a stupid end and not coming back and fixing something that couldn't be fixed.

Overwhelmed Francesca flopped, limply acquiescing to an inevitability that washed over her like a wave. At that exact moment the air pressure that had built up behind her spat her through the valve, like being farted out of some enormous ass. It took a few minutes for Francesca to recognise her sudden freedom and forget about almost dying.

Her next step was made for her as her foot was drawn into a peristaltic pump vent that was working the nutrient rich sludge into a nearby reaction chamber. Francesca remembered that there should be only one such vent in this chamber and that a maintenance hatch she was aiming for should be within arms' length. She pirouetted, running her fingers along the wall until she found the clasp, and then turned it. The hatch opened, and she surfed through on a belch of brown. Francesca hauled herself over a handrail and closed the hatch, a bit too loudly. She was through. Down the corridor, she could hear Souren's singing.

As bad as his singing was, she was grateful for it. It meant she didn't have to worry about being overheard as she crept down the corridor to the cockpit. As she advanced she was relieved to hear Souren dressing down Marco.

"You loaded the impactors as instructed?"

"Ci."

Francesca could see the shadow of the Indian's head shake in annoyance.

"You had better have done them correctly as this entire operation is completely dependent on them."

"Ci. I lowered them into the tube and locked the hatch. It was not too difficult."

Francesca peaked quickly around the corner to get a look at her adversary. He was pretty much as she expected from the singing, the typical thug with a tank-like build, but with longer hair than she had imagined, greased and wound into a bun on his head. And then, as she was pulling back, she spied something else. One the ledge of a console just out of immediate arms' length was her neurovisor. She could get it, but she would be seen. Looking back up the corridor she planned her flight, mapping each hand and foot hold to give an optimal flight path.

"I should not tell you," Souren continued, "But seeing as you have no one to tell it to out here."

"Ci. Is true what you say. Except for the woman."

"What?"

Francesca took her queue and whipped forward, gripping her visor as nimbly as she could with her spacesuit glove and propelling herself off the console back up the corridor.

Souren reacted amazingly quickly, almost grabbing her foot as she fled, but the extra seconds he required to determine where to jump next allowed her to out distance him down the hall and into the airlock, where she lowered the outer door between him and her at the last possible moment.

She fitted her neurovisor, it seemed to take forever before its thread-like worms burrowed into her brain. Then, with her mind lit up with the ship's schematic, she lowered her helmet's face shield and activated her oxygen in anticipation of Souren doing the obvious next step of voiding the airlock and jettisoning her out into space. As the alarm sounded, she activated the magnetic soles on her boots, and grappled into one of the two maintenance jet units.

A few seconds later she was sucked out the doors into space and frantically pulling the jet pack onto her shoulders, firing it just in time to avoid falling into the rocket burn of the ship. Along the ship's hull Francesca flew towards her target, the manual Fulcrum release. Because the ship was still accelerating, the Fulcrum about which the ship normally rotated to provide artificial gravity had been tucked in. If it was released now, it would mix up things inside that ship like shit in a blender. It could be enough to ruin the launch and throw off those impactors from hitting their target. That was the best she could hope for at this point.

Her neurovisor interpreted her thinking into a schematic mapped over the contours of the ship with colors grading towards her target along the spectrum from blue to red. When she confirmed the red blinking target as her destination, her backpack fired her on a least distance trajectory to reach it. As the jets nudged her towards her destination the tutorial began. Near the end of the lesson she became aware that there was another person enrolled. It was Souren.

"What the hell do you think you are doing Francesca?"

Now he knew her name and what she was up to. She declined to answer because she had more urgent things that needed doing. She had just touched down on her target and began prying at the panel she needed to get under, which as not easy with padded fingers.

Souren continued. "I need to tell you what I am doing so you don't do anything rash. August Bridges has developed a device that punches holes through space-time."

Yes, that was the one. And she'd been there when it switched on. An alarm in her neuroview beeped, warning her that her time was limited.

"We have credible information that the device is unstable, that it could destroy the Earth."

Yeah. Breathing *could* kill us too. How many times had atomic particle colliders been accused of the same thing.

"I am here to destroy it before it is used."

If it is so dangerous and their proof is so good, why don't they just stop it through the International Courts then. Blowing it up seemed a bit drastic, but people never wanted to bother with the paperwork.

"If you stop us then you are murdering the planet."

And there it was, the ever-present charge of Gaiacide, the threat used to pull all good children into line. The truth was any change to the status quo upset these ecofreaks. If she was going to take sides it was going to be with her boss, August Bridges, who had given her existence meaning.

As she broached the panel and began unlocking the Fulcrum, guided all the way by the neuro tutorial, Souren lost it.

"Listen you crazy bitch."

His true colors finally shining through.

"Your choice then, the ship or your boyfriend?"

My what?

Francesca peered down the ship and saw a man walking up to her from the airlock. She knew it was Marco because he was advancing like a penguin that had just peed its pants.

"Signore. Please."

"Jesus, what are you doing out here?"

"Please, I have to stop you or that Indian, he'll kill me." Francesca stopped herself from laughing. He was shit scared that was for sure.

"Christ you're an idiot. What are you thinking? I'll just knock your butt right into space. Get back inside before you fry out here for no good reason."

"Francesca, please. I'm afraid."

Francesca knelt to resume her task of working a metal bar underneath the release lever.

"No shit. I don't have time for this. Move your waddling ass inside or you'll be toast that's for sure."

Francesca gave Marco a sympathetic look. She'd kind of gotten to like him. Then she bent over and arced backwards hard, throwing all her weight into forcing the lever open.

The lever gave way. A crack began to open in the ship's shell about thirty meters away and the sharp blast of the Sun's light on the other side poured through it as the Fulcrum separated and moved away, connected to the ship only by thin nanoalloy cables that would cause it and the ship to begin orbiting around a shared center of gravity.

The Fulcrum cables went tight and then all hell broke loose. The cables strained, and the centre of the world instantly shifted. Francesca was glad she had set a line on the ship so, as she tumbled away, she knew that she could still make it back. As she fell twisting streaks of light arced past away from the ship and into the night. The impactors had been launched. Maybe she had been successful but there was no way of knowing.

As she spun she saw that poor Marco had not made, or been able to make, similar safety provisions. As they fell away in parallel paths Francesca made an incredibly stupid decision. She unlatched herself.

As Batgirl Francesca straightened herself, steeling her nerve, and her bat-jet boosters fired, rapidly depleting limited fuel as she shot through the distance to rescue yet another hapless citizen of Gotham. It was discouraging that they still needed her. Why couldn't they get their little loser lives together and take better care of themselves?

She grabbed onto his belt and glared at his eyes lolling around their sockets in terror. She blasted around to find the rapidly vanishing pinprick of light from the bat-light she had linked to the end of the safety line connecting her abandoned Utility Belt to the spaceship. She dropped all her fuel at once, betting on maximum acceleration to bridge the distance. There would be no second chance.

Stretching her body and hand and fingers as far as she could, Francesca just barely managed to catch the light.

CHAPTER 21

August

Venturing forth on the wings of destiny, I face the rising sun. Long the patient and faithful father - the original god from the birth of man. Only so close but not too far away we were nurtured by your brilliance yet bound by your sphere. Now your children have grown, have matured. In this fateful moment, I, your son, will lead your offspring to their destiny among the stars.

August stood proudly at the stern of his vessel, *Icarus,* as it passed through the wormhole. He was amazed by how uneventful the passage was. The hole, or rather the glare of sunlight passing through it, had slowly grown in the distance until it just exceeded the diameter of his ship. The only difference on the other side was that radiation from the now imminent Sun had triggered the protective shield to block off the forward portal.

This disappointed him. August's speech, composed on his journey up from the Moon, had prepared his imagination for a poetic confrontation with The Celestial Father. Now his moment to represent Humanity in this ultimate coming of age was marred by a technical oversight.

August repressed his impulse to indignation. Now was not the time for any emotion other than to appreciate this propitious moment in history - his moment of immortality. August steered the ship wide of the wormhole portal, happy to feel the helm turn under his command. The engineers had wanted to do the whole maneuver on auto-pilot, as if August Bridges were just along for the ride like some test monkey. August was happy he had insisted on performing the honors himself. This was his triumph, the culmination of his vision. A god must, after all, fly under his own power.

His thoughts activated the mneme in his neuroview that would send his carefully chosen words back to Earth where they would echo for posterity. The idea of racing his own words back home was a stroke of genius that he was pleased to have thought of. In one gesture he would prove mankind's mastery, not only of Space but also of Time.

As he cleared his voice, August thought of the preparations for a welcoming parade that had started even before he boarded the Icarus at the Luna Orbital Station. He had been training for weeks to build up the muscle mass to prepare himself for this moment. August Bridges would surprise everyone by leaping out of his limo and striding confidently down the street.

He was already savouring the moment of his re-entry into the world, the triumphant return from exile - the bastard son of Zeus freed from Hera's curse.

The ghosts stood out amongst the cheering crowd. Illya, the giant, towering above the people around him. And Anya and Gregori were there as well. They just stood there looking irritated, as if nothing was happening and August the Conqueror, with all his glory, was only a lack of breeze on a muggy day.

August cleared his voice and practiced his address. It would be broadcast live within minutes.

"I speak to you from Mercury, the God of Story, and I am here to tell you the strangest of stories. Where I stand is an impossible place for a man to be. With the radiation of the Sun so high out here, I would have been destroyed by cosmic radiation before I returned. And yet here I stand to bring a story from the Gods - a story of freedom and of passion."

Now that the ship had turned with its back to the Sun the forward shields began to open again. August smiled at the sight of the blue planet seen through the hole in space where a tiny blue dot should be instead.

"The time has come for a new beginning of time. Until this moment we have counted the weeks, the months, the years by our captive journey around a single star. Since the beginning of our species, the beginning of our form of life, time has been a circle always running into itself until, for each of us, it runs out."

August noticed a change from the direction of the Earth. Two small pricks of light appeared to the left of it.

"From this moment on, time will move like an arrow piercing space to connect the most impossibly distant points in our galaxy and eventually our universe."

The small points of light were diverging slowly from the Earth as they grew brighter. August was annoyed at the strange phenomena distracting from his speech.

"We will ride on these arrows, penetrating the impossible distances with our Dreams."

August lost his train of thought. The lights seemed to be pulsing as they grew bigger. What were they? An alarm glowed.

"Mr. Bridges. We are live in one minute," a producer's voice reminded him.

"Yes. I have my speech ready. There is no need."

The lights flared, now much larger than anything else in the sky.

"What the Hell?"

Calvin30's panicked face came into his neuroview.

"Boss. You have to get out of there!"

"What?" The clone's command so contradicted the sanctified moment that August's first impulse was to tell him to go to hell.

"Get off the line."

"Boss, Kaliyuga has locked missiles on your mission. They will arrive in five. You have to steer clear."

"How?"

"You have scant seconds to escape. The cockpit doubles as the lifeboat. The rotation from the Fulcrum should fling you to a safe radius. The latch is on the deck next to the pilot's webbing. Pull off the panel and push the flashing button."

The clones warning was accurate.

As his lifeboat fell away, The *Icarus* main ship dissolved behind a brilliant flash of light that August watched in dismay. Then there was a second flash, much closer, blinding him for a moment, violently shaking his escape craft. When he recovered from the shock, Calvin30 had dissolved into static. August froze, paralysed by disbelief. This couldn't be happening. He must be dreaming. He tried to wake up. Nothing changed. August impassively regarded the glowing remains of his ship flaring and evaporating into darkness. It couldn't be happening.

Adrenaline kicked in, and his body began to shiver. He grabbed his arms to keep them under control and laughed. Finally regaining his composure, August realised he had little time remaining and he had to act. He tried to open a channel to Calvin30.

"Okay. I survived. I'll come back through the portal. Just give me a homing signal."

There was no response. Communications must be down now that he had fallen out of range from the hole.

"*Icarus*. Re-activate autopilot. Return through the wormhole."

"Mr. Bridges. I do not have those coordinates."

"What the hell?"

"Mr. Bridges. I do not understand what-the-hell." Would you like me to perform a search for what-the-hell?"

"No. No!" August pounded on a wall before pulling himself together.

"Icarus. What are the coordinates for the wormhole?"

"Mr. Bridges. I do not have access to that information. My communication links have not been restored. Can you focus your eyes on the area of space you wish to return to?"

"August looked out the blast screens and then the outside cameras, trying to locate the lights on the wormhole, or even some embers from the rest of his ship. It seemed that he might have been flung away from the Sun so that the apparatus had been swallowed up by its fierce glare."

"*Icarus*. Locate any man-made items in space."

"There are 149,137 man-made items in space. Would you like me to provide you with a list?"

"Not in space. In my vicinity."

"I cannot locate any such items."

"Towards the Sun?"

"My instruments cannot detect anomalies within the solar interference. Can you suggest another approach?"

August switched communication with the *Icarus over* from vocal mode to thought mode to speed things up but met with no more success.

"Can't you do anything to help me?" he pleaded.

"I am fully stocked with a range of provisions to allow survival for four months. I also have a full range of entertainment and personal development solutions. However, I must warn you that radiation limits will be exceeded before then."

"Damn you."

August's mind raced through possible scenarios. He brought up the recorded images of the ship being hit by the missiles.

"*Icarus*. Compare the constellations from this shot and project coordinates based on the current position of the constellations."

"Done."

"Return to those coordinates."

"Returning to most probable location." Which didn't mean they were returning to the right location. August wandered lost in a soup of probable locations while the *Icarus* informed him of the increasing improbability.

August was watching the rerun of his ship exploding for the hundredth time when his rage began to ignite. This was too professional to be pulled off by mere Revs. This thuggery smacked of Gudanko. He had overestimated the pig. He had presumed that the fat slob would be honorable in defeat and would never stoop to such underhanded tactics. August roared out at his rival for daring to mar this sacred occasion.

Do you hear me Vlad you sack of shit? You better hide.

August became increasingly hysterical as he realised that there was a diminishing hope of escape. The blast furnace of the Sun at this proximity would wear down his radiation shields before he was a fraction of the way back to Earth. The blood drained from his face as the realisation sunk in. August Bridges was going to die. He might be remembered forever but, the fact was that very soon, he was going to die. He tried to call home, to complete his speech, to reassure the world and to leave an impression of dignity and bravery that would last for all time.

"Hello. This is August Bridges. Can you hear me?"

There was no answer to this question.

The same question repeated for hours.

The same absence of answer repeated for days.

August lay in the pilot's webbing, mouthing a vitabar and mumbling into the static in his mind, revising a speech that would never be delivered.

It was clear that the communication systems had been wired only for proprietary laser link, which required an exact knowledge of his location, given that there was no micro-satellite relay in this region of the solar system. August Bridges was going to die, sometime soon, and no one would know the moment or manner of his passing.

It was absurd. Impossibly absurd.

And more maddening than that he did not know how his loss would play out in the media. Would his passage be considered a success, or would the technology be branded unstable? Was it possible, for all these years of sacrifice to come to nothing.

At the edge of dreams in the random times when sleep overcame him, August could see the crowd waiting for him. The waves of adulation carrying him away. The victory that he alone had accomplished. The totality of his vision coming to fruition, but the ghosts were always there too, spoiling the scene with their presence, and then he would wake to nothing.

He called out into the static for many more days, each time with an ever-shrinking expectation of an impossible rescue.

Then he saw the ship flaring its jets. As it slowed it decelerated passing over him and towards the sun, a manifestation of divine grace so improbable that he burst into tears.

OCEAN OF STORMS

*'The ocean of suffering is
immense, but if you turn around,
you can see the land.'*

Thich Nhat Hanh, 20th Century Vietnam

CHAPTER 22

Kalsang

In the beginning there was no beginning, only a mere moment when the impossible density of potentials squeezed out of nothing and the universe opened like a lotus blossom. Between now and then lies only a sequence of such moments, each one running out into the other. The lotus blossom opens still.

The realm of stars lies beyond the furthest distance of our imaginations but does not exceed our reality. Each quantum of our existence is inseparable from all that has arisen and all that may arise. Ten directions and three times are insufficient to contain it.

Somewhere, perhaps in the middle of a wormhole linking two planets in an inconsequential star on the rim of an unremarkable galaxy in a cluster of many, all comes back together as the forces of physics and being align. Unending beginnings, exploded stars, lost things, rain, and broken hearts. All there, reflected in a perfect mirror, an exposed neuron in the mind of God.

The small circumstances of our lives continue, scrambled by the inevitable decay of memory into lonely parcels - like misdirected love letters cherished more for what they represent than for what they were. Yet, despite our faulty memories, we do not achieve our escape. We remain imprisoned within these moments.

And so we suffer.

* * * * * * * * * * * * * *

Was his decision a mistake?

The question bubbled up continually within Kalsang's mind. Had it been rash to follow the dictates of intuition rather than the propositions of logic? Saving the Earth was hardly a personal, spiritual question – billions upon billions of sentient beings' lives were at stake.

The bubbles rose with greater immediacy now that he had turned down the oxygen in the cabin atmosphere to maximise his time alive on his suicide mission to Mars. Kalsang gulped in the thin air. After a while he managed to settle his breaths into a steady pant which made his lungs ache.

He asked his imaginary friends for council. "Am I doing the right thing?"

The aliens crowded together and conferred. d'Song, as always, spoke for them.

"Melded One, the last time we did not listen to our hearts and this was what destroyed us."

"How so d'Song?"

"We took the easy way. We learned the secrets of the Channel Between Worlds and we set about building it because of our desire. Our greed made our hearts difficult to see."

That didn't answer his question. Now he was asking hallucinations for advice? Better to doubt everything from such a deluded mind. There was still time to choose another way, wasn't there?

The only thing he knew for sure was if he stuck with this plan he would die. Even if everything went right, he would die. Somewhere between Venus and Mars. He would die slowly like this, aching for breath, freezing, hungry, dehydrated. He would die in just this way and he didn't know if it would make any difference. The radio beacon could malfunction, the Mars crew could fail to recognise the signal and, finally his message, for whatever reason, might be ignored.

So what, Kalsang wondered, had made him so set on this course?

A slight change in the angle of his swing by with Uranus would still take him to Jupiter. Every molecule in his body urged him to take that option when the time came, but his heart stayed firm with the decision even while his mind kept repeating this question like a mantra.

Was he mistaken?

Oh, the animal he was had a clear answer to his dilemma. The simple choice was self-preservation. Animal instincts always had an easy answer. He was used to ignoring them, but that didn't mean they went away. If anything, they seemed to grow subtler and more pervasive over time. The Buddha was right. They offered nothing in the way of freedom. Undeniably. And the logic and blessings of his Teacher firmly blocked this choice.

Still, flying against the force of these instincts was such constant effort. Only a lifetime of experience swimming against this current kept him from going mad. And there was nothing so clear in this case. The Buddha had nothing to say about going to Mars instead of Jupiter. Perhaps there was another way that he could not see yet. Perhaps he could figure out some way of meditatively slowing his metabolism more. Perhaps he could survive.

Probably not.

Was he so used to denying himself that he was choosing death over survival just to spite those instincts? There was too much at stake for such selfish considerations.

"You are thinking too much Melded One. How can you ever solve a problem that way?"

"d'Song, thinking is the benefit of being human. Animals can't."

"The animals of our world did not build the Channel Between Worlds. That was done by our thoughts, our powerful imaginative minds. There is much wisdom in the animals."

She didn't make sense here. Weren't animals inhabitants of "lower realms," inferior intellectually even to ghosts? They were objects mainly of pity and protection, although some could be Buddhas and so should be respected, but d'Song's challenge gave him a new way of thinking.

Kalsang's imagination wandered along this line of reasoning, back to the Earth as he reflected on the hard choices filling the lives of his old friends, the wild animals of the Tibetan Plateau. There they greeted him with a chorus of thousands: the yak's bellow, the snow leopard's yowl, and the bray of the wild ass. Numberless hungry eyes stared back at themselves in the mirror that reflected the universe. All these mother beings he was striving to save, their voices joined by the accompaniment of a chorus of the aliens.

Kalsang listened to their song.

> *Alive. Our miracle today alone*
> *Striving hot against the cooling blood*
> *Our weary flesh feeds the living world*
> *Red tooth and claw churned back to mud*
> *All Time is turned by a billion worms*
> *We take our stand and face the daily flood*
> *From the gut we defy easy choices to die*
> *Beyond our undying need*
> *what is left within your fading bones?*

In their song Kalsang found his answer. He was thinking too much about a future that he had no control over whatsoever. All choices were nearly the same in this respect. His ignorance was as complete as any animal. What did an animal do instead? It lived. It made each decision as the moment arrived and took the consequences as they came. They had a kind of contentment that made them alert to the unseen. They had the wisdom of not second guessing.

CHAPTER 23

Calvin30

Gudanko cut an unimposing figure, conducting his calculations calmly established in his seat at an understated desk. He was the least noticeable feature of his office. The place was decked out in faux-Kremlin *Ancien Regime*, perhaps by some long past occupant as the decor completely contradicted Gudanko's character. The cost of refurbishment meant he had kept it.

The accountant's features were interrupted by the umbra of an Orthodox steeple and the cobweb gantries of the Dnipropetrovsk Cosmodrome cast through the mid-morning sun darkened polarised glass. Silhouettes of spider-like robots, casting spasmodic shadows as they crawled about the vast spaceship yards, completed the picture. It said something that the dramatic background failed to recast Gudanko as an antediluvian titan presiding over his fellow denizens of the deep. Instead his presence transposed upon the grandiose scene a pedestrian sheen. No place encompassing him could be that special. This was his unique power.

Calvin30 had had ample time to assess the man since being motioned dismissively to this seat over half an hour previous. Gudanko's fingers tapped out a steady cadence on the keys projected through his neuroview on the desktop. Otherwise the only other acoustic was extremely measured breathing. Calvin30 shifted in his lethargy. He reminisced a vision of August to keep cognizant. Master August's inconstant buzz would keep anyone awake, the opposite of this incessant bore.

Calvin30 missed his old boss. Missed him missed him missed him. August had sailed away leaving in his absence a wake of grey. Calvin30 could not even savour the memory of dismay on the Great Man's face as his divine grace collapsed. It was such a shame, the consummation of well-nigh endless toil stolen from him. That miserable misfired missile missing the wormhole and clobbering August's ship instead, cutting all communications. That bitch had extinguished his climactic moment. And now he had nothing from all of that. No rapture. No options. Just shit. Even the possibility August would survive to strive with eight more lives was divided by near infinity.

Across the desk Gudanko paused, a sudden metastasis that flipped open Calvin30's eyes and flicked on his switch.

"Thank you, Oksana. I will need a few minutes to complete some business and then I will meet the Minister."

How did those few minutes before a Minister rate him, Calvin30 wondered?

"Mr. C30."

The prefix affixed to his initials took Calvin30 aback.

"We have something to discuss regarding the circumstances of the death of our Chief Executive."

"Well," Calvin30 offered, "there is a full accounting in the ComSec report."

"Indeed."

"As I reported, I was sent to Kaliyuga to confirm what they knew about the wormhole. It was a reconnaissance mission. I often performed such functions for Mr. Bridges."

"Was it wise to reveal details of August's mission to his sworn enemies?" Gudanko still had not looked up to acknowledge his clone.

Calvin30 bent to receive the rising gaze halfway. "Sir. I see that you must have read the report. What you say is correct and prearranged. There was a need to corroborate my credentials with what they already knew."

Gudanko said nothing so Calvin30 carried on. "I am continually grieved that despite my warnings, inadequate heed was taken, and measures were not in place to shield Mr. Bridges."

"No. It was unforgivable." Calvin30 strained to discern any sign of satisfaction in that colorless pronouncement, but the new CEO's self-control was impeccable.

"Yes, well, there is a matter not so well documented in your report. Why is it you were gone so long?"

"I was detained," Calvin30 explained." Tortured." As if he were a machine that had been tampered with.

"Tortured?" Gudanko's composure leaned towards interest. "You have not documented that Kaliyuga has engaged in any direct physical harm to your person."

"I didn't see the significance and ComSec did not ask."

Calvin30 waved the bait. A verifiable instance of torture would lend credence to attempts to have the Rev officially listed as a terrorist Org with the Indian Gov, who then might be enlisted in the battle against it. Given the lack of a clear confession from the conspirators in August's assassination, this information could prove useful. Then again, who in the world ever cared what became of a clone?

"Is there anything you would like to add now?"

Calvin30 was, for a second, genuinely unhinged by the question. His humiliation felt too imminent for him to manipulate skilfully. By keeping mum and playing dumb he'd hoped to find some freedom from the whole thing.

"No. Nothing new."

Gudanko tapped his fingers with disinterest, "There are details that are missing from the record. This you have already volunteered."

"Well, originally I was arrested for offering Comscript to a beggar."

"That is a severe accusation," Gudanko interrupted, pre-empting his clone's testimony, "doing so would violate the Peace. No Gov could enforce that."

Calvin30 encouraged the diversion. "Perhaps I was not literally arrested."

"Explain."

"It was not an official Gov action. I was judged in a Hub Court by a mob."

"A Hub. You were not a member? You must have had some choice in the matter?"

Calvin30 redirected before Gudanko could intrude any further into stressful territory. "Their leader was an ideologue and I was disclosed as a clone."

"And the name of their leader?"

"Yes. Her name was, I believe, Sri Indira Didi." Calvin30 mentally removed her as an item from his who-to-do list. This much could not be doubted, that Gudanko would be thorough in securing his Com's honor.

"Thank you for answering my questions Mr. C30. Besides espionage, what other services do you perform?"

"Sir. I am an asset of Mirtopik Com. My series originated there, my copyright papers are clear on that. As an asset I can perform any service not precluded by U.N. Resolution 146731-A on Clone Franchise."

Gudanko returned to his neuroview, as if he had forgotten his visitor's existence. "Technically these days' clones are free to go, yes?"

"Go where?" Over the rainbow?

Gudanko looked casually through an opaque gaze.

"Anywhere. Go anywhere."

"Sir?" Was this hypothetical personal?

Gudanko scratched his skull, as if confused that his lucid words could be misheard.

"Mr. C30. We have arranged a severance package that should see you cared for. Oksana will go over the details with you."

"What?"

"This isn't personal. We have concluded a productivity review and generally clones, perhaps because you take your employment for granted, have not achieved the performance that we want to target."

"But a clone has no home other than the Com." Without any warning the bomb had thumped down leaving no room to drop and cover. Calvin30's position was completely obliterated, and he began to panic.

"Your asset value has been mostly depreciated and we can write down the rest." Gudanko concluded as close to cheerfully as he could. "Enjoy your freedom Mr. C30."

Gudanko could have had the decency at least to laugh maniacally as the trapdoor sprung leaving Calvin30 tumbling down the shit shoot. Instead he motioned dismissively towards the door before returning to his work. Lacking other options Calvin30 left the office.

One door closed, and its customary predecessor declined to crop up. Calvin30 walked over and over around the block until people began to watch. An ill wind from India blew, exposing his suddenly thin skin, allowing him to realise the lack of insulation resulting from his sudden unemployment. A clone without a Com was open game for anyone. He scowled as his thoughts flashed back on his makeshift 'family' in Chennai and how low he could cower in order to belong. The recollection of clinging to that dirty girl filled Calvin30 with alarm. A piece of him still looked back on that indecent incident with longing - it gave him the creeps that he could sell himself so cheaply. Just a few weeks on his own and he'd gone off the deep end sleeping with the plebes. Now, with no hope of home, how low would he go?

Ducking into his collar, Calvin30 started out toward the most unattended direction and hoped nobody noticed. What an imbecile to believe his own spiel. The only one undone by all his Faustian foolery was his own lonesome. A miniscule shift in coordinates and all his plans had gone to shit. The wormhole was still working whilst August likely wasn't. Not the scenario he'd been aiming for. All because he'd ordered that Comsec Salvador, that whore, into his own line of fire.

He walked down into the Ukrainian underground. August might yet persist, but not in any position to redeem nor rescue him. Calvin30 folded his fists up his sleeves to ward off the cold and shivered while he waited for his train. He ought to board any old line now since they all led to nought. Nothing to do now but fiddle until the world was inhaled into a sinkhole in the sky.

Conceivably what was eating at him was conceding that he had a conscience. The demise of the Earth had been entirely collateral to the demands of Art. The high stakes had seemed to vindicate his artistic vision, but now that that anointed vision had been lost, there didn't seem to be any point. As if this day wasn't claustrophobic enough.

As his train careened to his stop, Calvin30 considered his options. He could flop on the tracks now and be flattened. Why not? Or, could he somehow choose to accentuate the negative? What unique magic was singular to August anyway? Was he missing the transition to his solo act because of this fixation? Putting in a bit of distance, could the hole in the sky be a prize in disguise?

Calvin30 lipped the reed on his pipe. Was that it then? The hole was the thing. How hadn't he seen it? August's insane dreams were only a small piece of the infinitely unfolding futility this thing could release. A global population of pipedreams would be pulled towards that hole-in-one. One had only to flip forward even Gudanko's timid imaginings to see where things were going. A colossus of hubris - unleashed upon the Earth. The new perspective was majestic, but did he, Calvin30, have the chops to compose a symphony worthy of such a cacophony?

Minding the gap into an empty car his tune continued as the train groaned, locomotioning down along the tracks, wheel within wheel.

Later, back home in LA, Calvin30 looked down from the bar stage, but not as usual at the decrepit regulars. His focus today was populated with a disco light display of breaking news from his neuroview. A spinning Pandora's panorama.

Gudanko had just proclaimed August's push into space was misplaced, and that wormholes offered an unparalleled transportation revolution. Why worry over Mars when the Seine could irrigate the Sahara? When highways between the Free Cities could bypass any Syn eco tax? When your cold goods could be stored in Antarctica?

The resulting Rev Campaigns came unspooling like stories written on toilet paper pulled by a toddler. Gone were predictably deliberate, strategically selected short lists of campaign actions, the staid invitations for Coms or Govs to negotiate, the steady advance of the Campaign - the call for activists, the 'War Links', the 'What's New On The Front' reports from field commanders, and the neuronet opinion polls reported live into the battle grounds.

There was a desperate move to lock down the now empowered Coms - strikes, bombs, boycotts, neuro hacks, data scrambles, guns and roses and Holy Moses. The latest GEO convocation was disarray on display. To outlaw wormholes or pilot 'a study of the costs and benefits'. To be or not seemed to be the question of the day. The world was vibrant with a dizzy frenzy.

The action had never been this fine and sifting through too many prospects was arduous but, at the same time, Calvin30 relished some sublime storylines as if they were fine wine.

Rocky Mountain preppers issuing a call to arms against the alien wormhole horde staged to infiltrate their obscure rathole cabins. A Parisian selling a device claimed to deflect 'the holes' from passing through the psychic space of your place. The Mayor of Shanghai folding enforcement of trash controls because it would all be dumped into Space forthwith. Some Indonesian armchair conservationist figuring out loud how wormholes might flush out forest fires. The New Yorker suing Mirtopik for damages to his time-space continuum. Villagers in Tunisia filling in their well to prevent infidels from flushing up through it. Adelaide decommissioning desal plants while evaluating drawing water from Darwin. The fashion mnemes promoting conspicuously consuming lots of crap to be coming back as the new black. Real men, it was now proclaimed, shouldn't have to wait for Space.

All that with a steady drip drip drip of anger pooling to a level close to over spill. People were just itching, once again, to make a killing.

Calvin30's panorama dipped and scrambled in time with the Miles Davis electronic jangling jambalaya he was playing that was beginning to irritate the regulars.

Someone from the audience bought him a shot.

"Hey buddy, anything to stop the shit you was playin'."

Calvin30 took the tip and vacated the center stage. It was time to find another dive to jive in. He lilted out a new lick, dialling a friend, who had been waiting for his call.

"Clone?"

"Myself alone and on the phone. Free to be me for thee my dear General Bhatterjee."

Chapter 24 - Kalsang

Sometime while in the crushing jaws of the Uranus swing by, where Kalsang's small capsule picked up the critical momentum to fling it into the inner solar system, his endless loop of misgivings ceased. The deed was done. Kalsang knew where his course would take him. The fate of the Earth was as it had always been, certainly beyond the control of a mere monk.

His spacecraft, *Garuda* was what they had named it, the winged mount of the Buddhas, a symbol of compassion. *Garuda, granting freedom from hope and fear.* That was how Kalsang felt now, freed as he was from the burden of making his decision. The *Garuda* finished its final maneuver and his body became light.

"So close, isn't it?"

The external camera feeds revealed the last piece of land Kalsang would ever see - Uranus' strange moon of Miranda. The *Garuda* had almost grazed its surface. The claw mark canyons and buckled valleys that ripped this lonely and magical world nearly in two were marvels. They flew past pinnacles with impossible twisting geometries and over cavernous crevasses that seemed to reach nearly the core of the world. It was as torturous a landscape as he could have imagined, suggesting visions of the cold hells he and his fellow monks had contemplated to make them aware of the potential of suffering from an untamed mind. Looking ahead to endless nothing where he was sure to die, Kalsang almost longed to land on it.

Then, after the painful crush of the gravitational sling shot, his long journey into silence commenced.

The incessant whispering of the demons became quiet as the pale green of the sideways rotating Uranus faded behind him. Kalsang almost missed them. As awful as they were they had been his travelling companions for so many days now. Perhaps they had been lured down by Miranda, attracted to the similarity of that tortured landscape to their tormented minds.

Cold hell. There they might have departed to join the miserable inhabitants of that world, cracking and dripping supercooled fluids from their bodies into the ruptured ground. Due to his monastic training Kalsang found himself grieving over their imagined fate. More likely they had drifted ahead toward the Earth as if pulled by a magnet towards the growing potential for misery there. Most likely his mind was growing too tired to still hear them.

Then there was a more concerning absence. d'Song and the others had dissolved into whispers, into the figments of his imagination that they had always been. Even though they were hallucinations they had been his companions, and he caught himself missing them.

A long lonely road lay ahead, and it made Kalsang shiver. Back in the Triton Terrapod, before the excitement and the alien visitation, before the terrible choice and the intercessions of his guru, and after the novelty of his hermitage had worn through, why had he not felt lonely then?

Of course, he had had the constant scurrying from the on-board biota to keep him company. The gentle kindness conferred by the simple presence of other living beings, wasn't it? Now they had all sadly died and Kalsang wondered how long he would be able to survive in the chill and dim darkness without them. He could feel some part of his heart begin to freeze - perhaps part of it left behind with the demons on frozen Miranda.

In groaning unison, they accompanied Kalsang's song.

> Lost worlds in the deep sleep of Ages
> Dim bodies in the graves of dead suns spin
> Forlorn my bones fuse with this nameless mass
> Beneath the frozen wind, sound, vibration,
> Am I not a part of this Dark Matter
> Universal skeleton and flesh and skin
> Roaming endlessly without friends?
> How is it that I too am not so alone?

CHAPTER 25

Aurora

"You really screwed it up this time mate. You probably can't hear, but I'm gonna tell you anyway."

Nine words and Aurora felt each one like an itch that could not quite be reached.

"Xiao Li's dead because of you. Straight up."

When she woke from her coma this was all Aurora could remember from it. Terry telling her that her best mate had died, and the fault was all hers.

There wasn't any getting around it. Since her eyes had opened, after an initial burst of excitement of which she was only slightly aware, her friends had avoided her. As if they didn't have much to say to her. As if what she had might be catching. Their approach to her, even from the ordinarily effusive Freya, was clinical. The truth was they were coldly furious. The unforgivable sin was going Out and someone else dying instead of herself. Especially Xiao Li, especially Shel.

And they pushed her to get back on her feet. They'd lost too much in getting her back to let her fall off into the oblivion she craved. Terry told her as much since she was doing much of the pushing.

"Time to get up off your backside again Aurora. No lying about."

Aurora complied. She couldn't whinge. Not after what had happened. She switched on her muscles, like they were machines under remote control, and strained to stand. Her feet were on fire and slipped out from under her when she tried to stand.

"Get up princess."

Terry hoisted her back into the pilot's webbing rigged up to hold Aurora upright for the physio session.

"Having only three toes isn't an excuse either. You cost me two fingers and I can still do more than pick my arse." Terry held forth her right hand admiring the missing last digits on her ring and pinkie fingers and the scarring from the frost bite.

Aurora looked at her own hand. For an instant her fingers seemed to extend out into strange multi-colored tendrils before returning to normal. She shook to clear her head and resisted the urge to slump. If she did that Terry might just leave her hanging there. It wouldn't be the first time. Better to get this over with. She focused on her foot instead, learning to lean away from the missing toes and keep her balance. It was so much effort for so little return. She didn't really want to return anyway. And then her foot dissolved into flippers tipped with more weird tentacles. She felt light, like with a few flicks of her feet she could swim through the air.

"Get out of your head."

Terry gave her an annoying shake that didn't stop until Aurora made eye contact. The bitch was enjoying this. Why hadn't Terry just let her die? Why did she have to keep bringing up Xiao Li? Like she was trying to guilt Aurora into staying alive.

Exhausted, but too ashamed to cry, Aurora slipped one time too many and Terry shouldered her down into her cot.

"Okay, where were we?" Terry began once she'd returned with a cup of tea and drank it herself. Aurora just wanted her to go away.

"I know this isn't doing you any good Aurora, but I find it gets it off my chest to let you know all the shit you stirred up. Where were we?"

Whirling gyres of sand devoured the world. The Djambi containing Terry, Xiao Li and Phillipa rolled steadfastly forward, more to avoid being bogged in the rapidly drifting fines than to travel towards a destination.

"Please don't come. Leave me," Aurora pleaded silently.

"We almost did turn around there and then. Biggest fucking sandstorm of the year coming on up off the plains and we'd just found your track after going a long way in the wrong direction. Pretty stupid trick crossing between the Chasma like you did so we'd have to go around. Bet you thought that was smart."

"It was like that most of the way. Driving blind. Shel wanting to help but useless, Pippy telling us what to do, but doing nothing. And then the damn tin can broke an axle."

Aurora imagined Terry laying there. Short cropped blonde hair slick with sweat - the back of her squeeze suit stained orange by a day on her back under the Djambi, straining to weld things back in place during a break in the storm.

288

"So, there I was. Shel handing me oxy when I asked for arc damper and me telling her off for trying to kill me. I'm just finishing that last weld and fuck me, but this tongue starts slobbering over my faceplate. I roll over and who is it crawling in under there with me? Denzi! Must have banged my head ten times backing out I was that excited. Shel and Pip are just standing there hugging each other, and I ask them whether they want to get a room or are we going to download the dog and get on with finding you."

The rest of the story followed a familiar track as Terry had kept repeating it to be certain that it sunk in. By now Aurora could imagine it as if she had been there.

The three of them had followed the feedback stored in Denali's brain until they reached a cliff. Terry had found a ridge that swung around up to the place where Aurora had apparently climbed. She didn't remember any of that. The sun was setting by the time Terry, dragged by Denali in the sled, had rode up the narrow ridge and seen the emergency strobe on her backpack flashing. Terry had found her nearby

"Sitting stock still like you were taking in the sunset on a Summer's day. Only it was colder than I'd been in my life. My squeeze suit wasn't built for those pressures and those bruises haven't gone away either. At least you had the sense to put on a space suit, I'll give you that. You'd think you'd planned the whole thing bringing that along."

"Terry."

"I'm not done yet Aurora."

Aurora bit into her lip. She somehow needed to hear this, but she didn't want to.

"So, anyway, the sun was falling and if you hadn't already frozen I was going to. There wasn't much choice in it. Rigged us both up with rope and started lowering us down over the ledge. We were almost to ground, not ten meters up, and Shel runs up to help. Well that's it. Useless rock had been sitting there a billion years waiting for my boot to knock it loose."

Aurora felt Terry's hand on her arm, a steady grip that seemed to hold her mind in place.

"That's how it is. Now you go out and do the stupidest riskiest dumb thing in the history of the solar system and you're still here. Shel gets hit with a rock - in this gravity you'd hardly call it falling - and it does her in. Could have happened anywhere. That's all it is Aurora. When it's your time it's your time."

"I'm, I'm sorry."

"Don't beat yourself up over it Ror. Shit happens." It was the first kind thing Terry had said to her since she had woken up. Somehow that kindness only pushed Aurora deeper into despair and she felt now even more of a fool. Once for causing her best friend's death and all over again for thinking she'd had some control over it. As if through her repentance could bring Xiao Li back. Only she couldn't. So there wasn't even any point left in wishing herself dead. She wasn't even deserving of self-pity. If she tried this logic on Terry, she knew what she'd get back.

"Silly bitch."

Aurora laid down, with the reasonable excuse that the session and trauma were all too much. At the end of the day, she preferred to be frozen again because there wasn't any point in doing anything else.

Wheatbelt Wallaby wandered alone in the Dream. The Drought had left nothing to eat and had scalded the land free for such a long time that nothing would ever come back. Her belly felt as if it had swollen into a mountain and her throat was so thin she could barely breathe. She wandered the endless Red Plains without hope, looking in vain for anyone who had not already turned to stone, who still felt need. She saw her beautiful sister, frozen in the place where she herself had tried to freeze. On the side of the big mountain. The Dirty Old Man had kept her instead.

"Why? Take me. I came to you. I wanted you."

"Sorry Darl. I like you heaps but she's prettier. Nothing personal. Just the way it is. Thanks for bringing her but."

Aurora opened her eyes. They were keeping the lights low near her cot, but they still seemed painfully bright. Someone was sitting with her. Someone always sat with her. Aurora supposed they took it in turns. It wouldn't be a good look just to prop her up out in the utility shed. Somewhere out of sight and out of mind, which is what they must prefer. That's how she'd felt about Jules at times. And then she'd felt guilty about being so ungenerous. To be honest Aurora wished they'd get over the pretence of concern and just leave her to wither away. This was all too painful.

Wheatbelt Wallaby saw something glimmer on the horizon and she headed for it, expecting only another mirage. As she approached, she was amazed to see that a spring had miraculously broken through the dead skin of the world. Overcoming her fear that the water might again overwhelm her she bent over the spring and drank.

The person rostered on for the next pity shift was Phillipa. Aurora was appreciative that she didn't expect much in the sympathy department with the woman. If it were Chandra, with her professionally neutral kindness, Aurora would have lost it. With so much self-indulgence running through her head, she welcomed spending time with a straight up bitch like Phillipa. At least she always knew where she stood.

"Aurora. I need to bring you up to speed with things."

Phillipa couldn't help herself.

"While you were unconscious some very good news came in. The ET monitoring programme has been successful. They've captured some new tech that creates tunnels through space. So that means all our work here has been meaningful. Settlement will be happening soon, and we've laid the ground. I thought you'd like to know."

Aurora's adrenaline levels coursed, and she heard her heart beating in her head. Was this true? If it was then her whole ridiculous trip had been hopeless from the start. Any life left on Mars was doomed. Her mind replayed August Bridges explaining to the world that the way had been paved by his old friend Dr. Davidson. His good mate. Wasn't she though? Now he could now tick Elysium Mons off the list of potential hiding places for life.

"There was also an awful tragedy. August Bridges was killed testing the wormhole himself. A terrorist incident."

So there was karma. Aurora felt inexplicably sad. Even though she despised him, August was still one of the most significant people in her life. The initial attraction that had sparked in their only meeting used to irritate her. Somehow now it felt like opportunity lost. Now the only person she could be angry with, besides herself, had been taken out of the picture. There were more details. Phillipa kept going on long after Aurora in her chronic fatigue had tuned out.

"Xiao Li."

The mention of her friend drew Aurora's attention out of the fog. She looked up to see tears in Phillipa's eyes. They looked out of place.

"I, I loved her you know."

There was strained passion in Phillipa's voice, and Aurora suddenly liked her more. Phillipa turned her head away to recover herself and started to leave the room.

"Phillipa?"

"Oh yes. One more thing. Your monk friend, I believe his name was Kalsang. Communications with his module went dead while you were gone. My sincere condolences."

The bitch walked out.

"Dad," Aurora gasped. Was there any point in living? The pain was too much, and Aurora dropped off the map and into it.

All the water remaining in the world ran out, down an impossibly small hole, back into the hidden spring where life had begun. Parched, Wheatbelt Wallaby followed it but found the spring had dried up. She dug down into the dirt, sucking at the retreating moisture with a ferocity that exhausted her. She continued sucking down the cold dry sand until her body filled with it and began to blow away.

Something rough and rubbery pulled against Aurora's cheek. She could hear a familiar panting in her ear. A warm wave radiated from this sensation through her body, pulling her world back together. A raincloud of love scattering showers.

"Thought I'd bring 'round your old mate Denzi. He's been whinging the place down to get to you."

Aurora open her eyes and tried to thank Terry, but she felt too overwhelmed. The lovely roughness kept tickling at her ears. Aurora smiled but her mouth wouldn't mirror it. Her body came back into her sense of being and she lay in it, enjoying the licks and the solidity they brought to her heart.

"Hey, Denali. See it's Rory here. You're a good boy. She's alive because of you, you know. We were just going to turn and run when you found us."

Aurora managed to drag her fingers weakly through her friend's fur and then lay there with his snoring weight rumbling against her. Aurora felt, for just this moment, entirely grateful to be alive. Her mind descended into a warm blankness from which she had no will to emerge.

"Hi Aurora. It's me, Shel."

"Xiao Li?"

"It's okay. I'm all right."

Aurora would have sat up to greet her friend if only she could put her billion pieces back into a body.

"But you're dead."

"That's not entirely true."

"Am I?"

"Not so lucky."

Xiao Li reached over to embrace her and found Aurora's body for her in the process.

"Why not? I mean, why me and not you?"

Xiao Li laughed in her captivating sing song way, which brightened any day. "Jesus isn't finished with you Ror. She has a lot of work for you to do yet."

"And none for you? That seems kind of arbitrary."

Xiao Li laughed at the joke, which Aurora wasn't quite sure she'd made. "No. Plenty left over for me too I'm afraid."

"Are you an Angel?"

Xiao Li considered the question. "Only, I guess, in that part of you that is."

"I'm sorry Shel. I'm horrible for doing this to you. It was unforgivable. I only wanted freedom for myself, not for this to happen."

A great river of sorrow welled up from underground and blanketed the dry land, wicking down into the hissing soil. Life was returning to the dismal world. Forests of algae matted along the shores and a mist rose from the sea and thickened, trapping heat and fattening into clouds.

"It's already gone Ror. We are free."

"What am I supposed to do?"

Xiao Li smiled kindly, her tears mirroring Aurora's.

"What am I supposed to do?"

"Right now, my love? Nothing."

The clouds opened, and the rain poured in filling every crevice in the thirsty dirt, gluing the world together with a deluge of love and pain. Wheatbelt Wallaby rolled in the mud until every part of her was caked with it.

CHAPTER 26

Kalsang

In the mirror of the universe, Venerable Kalsang Jampa sat watching the unremitting stream of hours pass by in darkness.

Time passed without any reference points to quantify it. No regular motions dominated the heavens. Devoid of any element of circularity, the Wheel of Life flattened into a line extending only from one moment to the next. Everything was a decision. Sleep when you choose. Eat when you choose. Awaken when you choose. Breathe when you choose.

Even the unavoidable journey from birth to death had become a motion from darkness to light, as the Sun in the forward portal slowly and imperceptibly brightened. The line of time, in its usual dimensions and direction, lay only in Kalsang's memory as he hurtled homeward from his post at the frontier of the solar system.

For months Kalsang trained himself to subsist upon less and less, to prolong his life to its furthest extent. The essential elements in this struggle were water and air. Water would run out first as an accumulating amount of it was lost or irretrievably contaminated through breath, phlegm, sweat, and voiding without a terrapod ecology to cleanse it. He monitored his body as he carefully regulated his daily ration of the vital fluid. If his dehydration was too severe his kidneys would fail. Kalsang's skin became thin and his throat eroded raw by the steady friction of dry breath.

"d'Song?" He would ask for her, the odd short name eliciting a rationed amount of hope falling into a survivable amount of despair when she failed to reappear. That too was important, for it reminded Kalsang that he was still human.

"d'Song?" he asked again.

The long avenues around him were silent as he swam through them. No phosphorescent street lamps glowed and the dim light from the sun burrowing this far underwater tinged the shadows blue. No creatures remained to cross his path, which made no sense since the city was a productive reef. He pulled open many doors. Ascending the hallway to his old apartment, he used all his hands to open as many as he could. The kaleidoscope of sight from his faces took in the desolation of endless vacant homes.

Where had they all gone?

"d'Song?"

He spied a toy at the foot of a ramp, a doll, floating in a clump of grass. He was sure it had been hers, and his two middle hands held it close to his heart.

Kalsang awoke to an alarm going off in his neuroview.

He focused his mind and his neuroview projected forward into the darkness, following the red arrow of the alarm. Soon a white speck increased into a lumpy body.

What was it?

The specs flew down before him and he read them carefully, his excitement growing. It was an asteroid, but one made almost entirely of ice, a captured comet perhaps?

While on astronomical charts of the solar system the Asteroid Belt appeared as a planetoid crowded swath of space, the true scale of distances between each made it very improbable that one would pass close enough to his path to be approachable.

Kalsang quickly forgot his dream as he eyed the floating iceberg greedily. There was enough water there to ensure an adequate supply for his full trip. He rejoiced in his life being so fortuitously spared. But then the calculations in his neuroview just as quickly erased the hope they had delivered to him. The trajectory corrections and loss of speed and fuel to reach the asteroid would so lengthen his journey as to make the trip to Mars untenable. It was a false reprieve. Kalsang watched, with whatever dismay his lethargy would allow, as the asteroid slipped from view and off the radar.

After that Kalsang's hopes drifted like abandoned spirits in the wake of the asteroid's trail, leaving traces in the mirror that reflected the universe. As they faded, Kalsang heard them sing, accompanied by d'Song's soft voice.

Crossing the arid infinities of Space
Waters of the firmament are thin
A few molecules in a hundred kilometers passed
Oasis atoms drifting in the boundless desert
Lost in an endless quest for the slightest taste of wet
Ghosts stretched thin across the void
How like my mind when grasping at the mirage of true existence?

CHAPTER 27

Francesca

Once Francesca returned through the airlock she'd locked Marco, who was thankfully too much in shock to talk or resist, into the store room. She stalked warily down to the ships' cockpit, stepping over the myriad items that had ripped free when the Fulcrum had suddenly switched on the gravity.

Rather than a hidden enemy ready to pounce upon her, she found Souren hanging with one leg in the pilot's webbing. He must have been attempting to tighten the straps when one side gave way and tipped him out at a critical moment. His head hung next to a blood smeared console where it must have collided. Ouch. She knew how that felt. Francesca pulled Souren down and tied him tightly before dragging him back to the storeroom imprisoning Marco, so they could enjoy each other's company.

"Tell me if he dies or anything. Let me know, okay?"

Marco nodded hopefully.

Back at the helm, she patched her neuroview into the ship's computer and dialled up ComSec. It took a while but finally a harassed looking woman with Command patches faded up in Francesca's head.

"Who am I speaking to?" she demanded.

"ComSec H45E013, repeat ComSec H45E013. Salvador," Francesca signed in.

"Corporal Salvador. Congratulations, you killed a great man today."

Francesca's heart sank. Had she been too late? Tears welled up at her failure.

"The worm hole's blown?"

There was a pause. "I am not at liberty to disclose information like that to terrorists."

What did she just get called? No, no, no, that was all wrong. The injustice of the accusation stung Francesca. Of course, what else were they to think? The Revs had a long record of installing operatives higher up than her.

"I'm not a terrorist. I stopped those guys."

The Commander regarded her sceptically. "Guys? We only have one 'guy' working with you Salvador. A Marco Uliassi. No history of this kind of action with him, and certainly not with your level of training."

"Yeah. He was useless, but good enough to get the Indian in."

"Did you say Indian, Salvador?"

This was getting too complicated. "Sorry Commander. Just download my mneme log and see for yourselves." Francesca sat back and opened her intentionally recorded memories for ComSec to rifle through, back to a point. Flashbacks flipped up in her mind as Comsec did their thing in her head. All the time she kept thinking, "Jesus, don't let August Bridges be dead.

When ComSec had finished their scan, Commander Bitchface appeared again.

"It looks like we had it wrong."

And a big load of thanks for putting your ass on the line to stop the bad guys? Nada.

"The wormhole survived."

Thanks to who? Awesome news anyway. Francesca's relief didn't last.

"Then why'd you say I killed August Bridges?"

"That's true, you did. Forensics have re-calculated the altered trajectories resulting from your Fulcrum engaging. The impactors missed the wormhole, their original target, and contacted Bridges' spacecraft instead."

Francesca was in shock. Had she actually killed August Bridges, the guy she admired over pretty much everyone? Without responding, Francesca downloaded an optical of the wormhole's coordinates through the ship's telescope. She would be getting a better view than anything ComSec would have seen from the Moon, especially since her flight path was sideways to the Sun so her instruments wouldn't be blinded by it. She was probably close enough to fly in for an up close and personal.

After some flicking around, there it was, unmistakable, the machine she and Raoul had seen come to life that amazing day on the Moon. Rotating like a magical ring with a small blue ball, it had to be the Earth, shining through it no matter which side of the ring was facing towards her. And, to the side, a bunch of debris sparkling like a cloud of glitter. Like tinsel on the Christmas plant in their balcony garden when she was growing up, marking out another year of family tragedy. Even more sad because it was pretty. Francesca wept.

"We're sorry, Salvador."

Then the ComSec guys commenced with their assessment of the ship. It wasn't long before they gave Francesca more bad news.

"Corporal Salvador. We hate to tell you this, but you don't have enough fuel to get back to Earth."

And merry Christmas to you too.

Francesca closed her eyes to try to do whatever people are supposed to do when someone casually tells them they don't have long to live. Get mad at God? Then she had a start, and asked in a hushed voice, trembling because bad news always came in threes.

"Raoul? I mean the other guys. What about them? We blasted off straight on anti-matter right next to the station. Did anyone get hurt?"

"We're talking Tsuchinshan?"

"What do you think?"

"Oh, only a few injuries there. Luckily they were all in the gymnasium on the other side of the complex."

"And?"

"Okay. Well this guy. Corporal Ferriz contacted us wanting to send a message to you. We had him marked for a suspect until you cleared things up."

Francesca cheered up. If she was going to die, at least she had something to live for.

"Do you want me to send it through?"

Did people have to be this stupid?

"Here it is."

The mneme opened and magically Raoul blossomed in the air in front of Francesca.

"Nobody died *mi cielo*."

Then he sat there, looking out towards her soul. She could feel that he yearned for her, the same way she yearned for him. She saw it in the sadness in his eyes. Why hadn't they just gone ahead with everything? Probably because everything always led right away to nothing and he was the same as she was. Afraid. Everything had remained unsaid where it was safe from being spoiled. And now it was too late.

"Ahem."

There was a long wait before he said anything else. It wasn't like Raoul to be at a loss for words. His beautiful eyes were red, and, for once, Francesca was happy to see a guy who had been crying.

"Baby. I don't know if you are okay. I don't know what I'd do. Anyway, I wrote this poem for you.

> There is no need to name this thing.
> Whatever it is.
> Nameless it is free, boundless,
> a rainbow without residence,
> drawing light from the dark rains
> and painting with the weave of Open Sky."

It was a message straight from his naked soul to hers. She felt uplifted, like Shayera Hol whose wings had never carried her as high as her love for Green Lantern John Stewart had. It wasn't her fault that his duties as the first mortal Guardian of the Universe had come between them. It was his. Men could be shits like that.

"Come back to me mi cielo."

Francesca reached out to touch him and he faded.

"It's not happening my friend."

Her beautiful Raoul. If he offered her a ring now she'd take it. She'd never thought that about any guy. She had the crazy idea that maybe she should offer him a ring. After all, if she was going to die they might as well get married. Maybe she could order one that looked like the wormhole ring. They could disappear into it - into their own parallel dimension. Maybe, if she drove the ship into this wormhole that was where she'd end up. Some place with him where all the other crazy shit in her life didn't exist. No, if she did that she'd only end up back on Earth.

Francesca's eyes popped open. Was she that stupid that she hadn't seen her way to escape when it was floating right in front of her face?

"ComSec. Do I have enough fuel to make it to the wormhole?"

The guy didn't answer, and she was about to ask again.

"Affirmative Salvador. Just enough fuel but you'd come out the other end on ancillary power. Not enough to get back to Earth."

"But then you could come get us, right?"

"I guess so. You'd have to have enough power to get into the correct orbit. I'd have to check."

"Check? What do you have to check? You're telling me this is our only chance and you think I'm not going to do it?"

"Well. I suppose so." I suppose so? Francesca wanted to hug this guy, but then she wanted to kick him. He was sitting on a pile of experts and it took a *testarudo* like her to figure out something so obvious. Francesca thought her way into the navigation console of the ship and ordered it to calculate her path through the wormhole.

While she was doing it, the guy interrupted again.

"The reason we advise against that idea was that your craft really isn't designed for the intensity of radiation near Mercury."

This guy was all good news.

"You mean like we're going to die if we do that?"

"It's possible."

"Coño. If there's any possible remaining to me I'm doing it, right? Everything else is impossible."

Another maddening pause that was way too long.

"Okay. We found a sequence that might work, but we will have to carefully maneuver your craft. You can't travel outside a very tight corridor or you won't make it back alive."

"Do it already will you?"

And that was that. The fulcrum pulled in, making everything spill around for a few minutes. She neurochatted with her prisoners for them to web up, and she clipped herself in for a ride.

As the anti-matter drive engaged and the g-forces started to pull, she let her friend Marco in on a little secret.

"Hey Marco, do you know your friend Souren there planned a suicide mission for us and didn't tell anybody? Don't worry, I'll probably get us home, but I just wanted you to think about who you pick as friends. I always like ones who don't try to kill me." That should make for some warm feelings between the two of them.

The crush of acceleration continued for what must have been a day. By the end of it Francesca felt the areas that weren't sore, instead of the ones that were, because they stood out. Half way there they twisted so the ships ass-end was pointed at the sun and the portals now contained a view of a blue dot that was the Earth. She hadn't expected it to be that small, which made her feel very, very small herself. Reminding herself how close to the edge they were focused her mind on the present.

But it didn't take long for the present to turn into the past. She was pissed that the guys at Mirtopik hadn't patched Raoul through yet. Apparently, the communications system had been damaged when Marco had blasted off. She'd tried chatting with Marco over the intercom, but he was too boring, and she didn't want to spend what could be her last hours being that bored. Francesca filled in that time thinking about True Love instead.

True Love was real. Tia Yuricema had told her Franceleeta that everyday as she flipped out the fried tostones from the pan in preparation for their daily routine of watching neuro-soaps. Tia loved proving her point, freezing the action to point out a particular look and embarking on prolonged neurolink journeys to archived reruns, actor bios, celebrity news, banner-ads, and accidental porno mnemes (which were clearly not True Love) to prove her point until Francesca BEGGED for her to stop.

"Well. You know it is True."

"Yes Tia, you told me."

"Do you know why it is True?"

Francesca knew the answer by rote and communicated this by dulling her eyes and looking bored.

"Because the Lord God would not have made so much evil in the world without creating some things so perfect the Devil himself would hide his face in shame should his eyes fall upon them. There, see the Look he gave her."

"Bah."

Francesca bared her missing teeth in mock fury until Tia relented, at least until after the next programmed break. Francesca didn't really mind the obsessions of the old woman. Where else did she have to take refuge. She loved her weekend visits, especially missing Momma peeling herself out of last night's binge and trying too hard to be cheerful to hide the bruises on her soul.

It was far better to sprawl out on the pull-out sofa and live in a world where the passion of this week's hero could outshine last week's betrayal. That other actress had been a bitch anyway. The one he was with now - she would be True.

Francesca lingered purposely on other good memories. Reading the latest editions and combing the comic archives with Elena, enjoying their favorite heroines and latest adventures.

Sentimentality was addictive. Francesca clung to these crumbs of what could have been. And then this insanity would turn back to Raoul. Why had he not made a move? She could see that he thirsted for her. Of course, that would have made him just another one of those guys whose biology made sex into something like eating. Raoul was different. He was so much wiser and more self-controlled. His maturity accentuated his manliness and made her desire him more.

On the other hand, she hated him completely for it. It was unfair to torment a girl by constant attention and flirtation without delivering the goods. It had driven her crazy, but she was proud that she had held back and not given in herself. If he could play it cool, then she could. She could definitely do that. And who cared. Maybe their time had run out.

Round and round in her head. Francesca could not will him into her life right now and even if she could he was not a magician to make a broken person whole. She would destroy him before any happiness could come of them being together. She could see it happening because she knew what a total nutcase she was. And what man would want a woman who had so much anger in her? Would even Raoul, with all his depth and compassion, want to bring that chaos into his life? That settled it. She was happy that nothing had happened. For sure she would feed on the life force of any True Love that happened into her life until she had eaten it all away. Such a man as Raoul deserved True Love in his life, and Francesca knew it could not be her.

It was better for them that way, like in her comics and Tia's soaps, which kept going and going nowhere. They were true because happily ever after never happened.

Haruhi Suzumiya was under continual observation by galactic powers for her ability to bend time around herself, a power of which she was almost completely unaware. It should seem ridiculous to her that days never reached nights and that the same school uniform was always fresh and that her perfume never faded. Poor Kyon, always coming up with excuses for her when all she really wanted was the truth to set her free.

In the end, it only made sense that she would destroy the boy for the devotion that had kept her imprisoned, even if it meant she must battle the universe for her place in it. If she knew what was good for her she would follow her heart and not his.

But comic book stories also had to wrap up, for good or for bad, in a fixed number of scenes. Then you had to buy the next one. That was why Francesca escaped into them. Life was not like that. One thing just bled right into the next thing. Which brought her back to Raoul and her, something which would never nor should ever be.

Francesca went off her food. After days of winnowing away like this, one memory in a string of memories finally brought her back to her senses.

Tio Luis used to drop in, following day long SkyTran rides all the way from Manzanillo, to preside over Santeria rites, initiations and funerals, since he was the main Ifa for her Hub. He always brought small trinkets and toys that she and her sister treasured.

Tio and Tia had split years ago, and he had remarried, but they still had an affection for each other that was clear. Perhaps this was the shadow of the True Love Tia yearned for.

The coming of the Fall was augured at one of these impromptu gatherings. Tio Luis, in the thrall of possession by Orunmila, the spirit of prophesy, had gazed at her casually from under his trance, and declared.

"This one will run a long way. She'll run, and she won't know any rest until she dances in the clouds."

Tia had yelped like she had been bitten and had swung her niece behind her dress as if her physical intercession would be enough to block the curse. If not for her Tia's clear distress the event might have faded from her mind. Tia didn't smile so much when Tio came to visit after that and then he had died.

That dreamlike memory of the curse, which was never mentioned again by the family, served as her salvation. They might have thought it was beyond her kid brain to comprehend but it had caught hold in her picture of herself. The curse became an impenetrable force field, separating Francesca forever from True Love. The curse was who she was fated to become so why try to trick herself that she could go beyond it. The Fates had written it in her bones, to run and to fight. There was no point fooling herself that there was any other way.

Her Tia had protected her back then, but not in the end when it really counted. Those soaps that told her Tia of True Love were also loaded with a paranoia that betrayal lurked in every heart. So, when Francesca told her of the horrible stuff happening with Elena, her bitch of a sister had already gotten in and poisoned Tia's thinking.

"You shouldn't do this to your sister Francesca. Don't tell me these lies. Hector is right to turn you down. You shouldn't act like a little slut."

Before Francesca could lose herself again in more stupid dead-end memories, the anti-matter drive kicked in and she spent another day with her ass being squeezed through webbing. As was usual for her, she welcomed this minor pain in her ass because it distracted her from all her larger pains. But it was still pain, that's what it was. So, was the purpose of her existence only to suffer? It seemed like that almost all the time. In his own way, Raoul was a pain too, the very worst kind, because that pain tried to fool her into loving it. Into craving it. She'd spent her whole life not being fooled, so why was she letting it happen now. It didn't make sense.

Finally, the wormhole ring slid into view, a magical sight. She was about to fire full guns to go home when the guys in mission control stopped her.

"Salvador. The mission crew have identified a problem."

That was totally predictable. "What is it? I'm about dead out here."

"Well, it turns out that the anterior diameter fin to fin of a Persephone 34G transit craft is 5 centimeters larger than interior diameter of the wormhole."

"You are telling me my ass is too big to go through that thing?"

"Apparently."

Apparently, you are an idiot for just now looking that up.

"That's it? I'm just gonna die."

"Well, probably not. With exact firing we could get you through but there would definitely be structural damage to both your ship and the wormhole generator."

"So what."

"Well we don't really know what happens if that happens. The alien technology behind this isn't well understood. Massive forces are involved."

"You are telling me I might blow up?"

"We don't really know. We would position the jet fins to intersect the wormhole ring at a point of maximum structural integrity."

"What are you saying? Like what are my chances?"

"Well, we don't really know."

Useless. Why do they build stuff they didn't even understand? Of course, Francesca had helped bring it into existence, so who was she to dish out about it? And how were they to know this wide ass clunker she was driving had to fit through it?

"And we might blow up the universe too?"

"We don't think so." Which was so reassuring because the universe was a pretty big thing to blow up.

"Like, how long do I have to make up my mind?" Because she had to weigh her life up against all the rest.

"Not too long." A tick down clock appeared in her neuroview. Like the kind that super villains always had on hand to tell the good guys how much time was available had to bust the evil plot.

"Why?"

"If you don't go before then the orbital window will be lost for us to collect you."

"And if I wait for the next one?"

"Well." What was it with starting into bad stuff with 'well'? Did it make it any easier to hear? "Well, you would die from radiation poisoning before then."

"And if I miss the window?"

"Well, since we jettisoned excess weight to get you here, you'd probably starve before we could intercept your ship." This was like picking up from a pile of shit-out-of-luck sticks.

"And there is a chance I could blow up everything?"

"Well, theoretically anything is possible. Unlikely though. We think."

Seeing as she was in no rush to end the universe, maybe or possibly or whatever it was, Francesca dialled up the exterior neurocams to check the hull for one last check of the debris field. That was when she spied it. Further out from the debris field, a small piece travelling towards her. She zoomed in and her heart jumped into her throat.

"He's alive."

"Sorry Salvador. Please repeat."

"August Bridges. He's alive."

The signal to Mirtopik had gone dead. It was probably because the wormhole had interrupted line of sight laser communications and she needed to compensate for the effect. They'd programmed it so she just had to push the button hovering in her mind. Instead Francesca realigned her beam to contact August Bridges' little pod.

"Hola, Mr. Bridges. You there?"

"Hello," said that voice, she would recognise it anywhere, "this is Icarus. Can you respond?"

He sounded frightened and shook up, not like the confident August Bridges she knew at all.

"Icarus, this is Persephone." Oh, to hell with it. "Mr. Bridges is that you? Is it really you?"

There was a pause, like maybe he wasn't sure who he was. Maybe the shock of the blast had rattled him that much.

"Yes. August Bridges. Who else who I be? Who are you?" Francesca sensed fear, like maybe he thought she had come here to finish off the job she'd started.

"I can't believe this. It's really you. Don't you remember me from the Moon?"

"I repeat. Who is this? Why are you blocking my wormhole?"

That's right, it was his.

"God, I'm so glad I didn't kill you when we shot at you." That sounded amazingly bad.

"You shot me? The Persephone is a Mirtopik model. Did someone send you to finish the job?"

The little craft was slowing down.

"No, no, no, don't do that! You have to go through first before…"

"Then move out of the way so I can pass."

Out of his way? The clock was winding down. "I get it. You think I'm here to kill you. I know it makes some kind of sense, but that's not the way it is. I'm the ComSec on the Moon who knocked that guy with the cam. I stopped them. Do you remember?"

"I, I don't know. Just move aside so I can pass."

The clock ticked lower into completely too late territory. Shit. "Look, if I move there isn't time."

Mr. Bridges appeared before her in a mneme, likely to check out her body language, so she reciprocated. He had the shakes and looked pale and wiped out. She felt awful for doing that to him.

"I do recognise you," Mr. Bridges nodded.

This struck Francesca as stupid, a mneme could be borrowed by anybody. She could be anybody. She almost told him so but didn't because that would be even more stupid.

"You have to get over here or we run out of time."

"Time? Why?"

Why? Really? August Bridges must be worth a thousand of ordinary people. He was someone exceptional. Someone whose existence would move people out of their shit. Someone admirable. If she died, before she stopped breathing no one would remember her. Souren, people probably didn't even know he existed, or wished he didn't. Marco had a family that he didn't deserve.

"If I go through you can't go through. Mr. Bridges. Seriously. I almost killed you already. You gotta go now or you won't have a chance. Trust me."

August looked at her uncertainly. "Can I trust anyone?"

"What other options do you have?"

August Bridges frowned and vanished. The little ship jumped forward, making its way carefully through the debris field and then accelerating away. The clock kept ticking. The little ship rapidly closed the distance to the wormhole. The clock kept ticking. Francesca was so happy. August Bridges was going to make it after all. The clock kept ticking, and he was mostly there, and the clock kept ticking down to the last.

Alarms sounded. Francesca was determined. Better not to risk disaster. Better that she might have to die so he could live. It was a sacrifice she would be remembered for. Time was out.

Francesca thought of Raoul and never seeing him and never having a shot at True Love and how meaningless her life suddenly appeared. Against that certainty the slim chance of the universe exploding seemed kind of absurd. Without really thinking Francesca fired the programme, engines gunned into action, and they shot forward edging the little ship out.

She had to be with Raoul again. The thought of not seeing him provoked a thirst that was intolerable. She was like a ghost craving for a second chance at life. She had no other choice.

"What are you doing?" August Bridges screamed. "No. You can't take this away from me. You can't!"

The larger ship went through wormhole with a small shudder. Suddenly the full Earth was there before Francesca as if she had never left, and the moon, and safety, and Raoul. The little ship was not there. The wormhole ring, when she looked back through it, was now just filled with empty space and faint stars. The lights lining its rim had gone out.

Francesca occupied herself erasing the mnemes from the ship's computer of her encounter with August Bridges. Her ComSec training was good for this at least. She knew she could not so easily remove the stain in her soul.

CHAPTER 28

Kalsang

The cabin of the *Garuda* grew slowly warmer. Kalsang welcomed the change from the temperatures, which had previously been set at the lower limit of endurance to conserve energy. The feeble trickle of energy from the solar panels increased to a steady stream as the Sun ballooned in size and brilliance. His persistent cough abated.

How wonderful. It felt like the first months out on Triton where his mind had been truly free for the first time in his life. Except that this time he knew the end was soon to come, and this made him apply himself to his practice as never before. Whenever he felt like daydreaming or falling asleep he would loosen or tighten his mind like tuning an instrument. Soon his body lightened as wave upon wave of bliss descended and his contemplations achieved a new level of lucidity.

d'Song and the others reappeared. It was good to feel them near, waiting respectfully while his focus on them resolved. It was good to not be alone.

These perfect days quickly passed, and as the Sun grew beyond familiar proportions, the temperature approached the upper range of where environmental controls in the *Garuda* could keep the cabin cool. Kalsang became aware of the change as steady rivulets of sweat drained from his body requiring him to drink more frequently to avoid dehydration. And so his meditations became disrupted.

"Your star is very bright, Melded One. Are we headed to your home world?"

"Not so far. To another planet."

"Oh," she sounded worried, *"You have a Channel Between Worlds?"*

"No. Definitely we do not. Not yet," Kalsang hoped.

d'Song wiped one of her brows. Could she feel the heat as well?

As the heat grew beyond sweltering, Kalsang began to wonder if he would last as long as necessary to contact Mars. There was no possibility of that now, the *Garuda* being on the opposite side of the Sun from there. He set up the communications so they would broadcast his message should he die too soon. Without his being there to tell them, there was no way for those on Mars to know the importance of the message. His message could be overlooked as an anomaly, some routine technical download, or a hundred different reasons. Of course, his presence was no guarantee.

"I don't want to fail you."

"Fail us Melded One? We have been dead a very long time."

"The message that you sent."

"The message that WE sent?"

What did she mean by that?

"So many might die if they build it. I made the wrong decision."

"You made a decision. You likely could not stop them anyway Melded One. Why are you doubting now?"

All the other aliens nodded their agreement with her.

He didn't have an answer. d'Song was right of course. He had very little of his precious life left. To spend it second guessing that which could not be changed didn't make sense.

"We are dead. You are alive."

For now.

"Stay alive Melded One."

Stay alive? As long as he could? Stay alive until he successfully contacted Mars and could talk to Aurora or Terry or whoever would listen. Stay alive.

Kalsang drank some more water and tried to relax, folding his robes on his lap. His head began to nod.

He saw a man digging desperately at ground while the sky behind him was on fire. Electric sparks flew up from the soil as he dug, tormenting him. He recognised this man, but he wasn't sure from where. He felt an impulse to wrap his robe over the man's shoulders to protect him.

Sweat dripping into his eyes woke him. Kalsang rubbed it away and tried to return to his meditation, but with limited success. It was so unbearably hot. How was he going to survive the coming months?

Kalsang's training kicked in. He reminded himself that no matter how unbearable his condition was, the suffering of many other beings, at this exact moment, was greater. He turned his attention to the fantastic realms he had many times been instructed to visualise - inconceivable hells and molten surfaces where numberless unfortunates lived and suffered. After he had learnt to look beyond his fear of these nightmares told by old monks, Kalsang had become a bit sceptical. When he asked directly, none of his informants claimed to have first-hand experience. Perhaps the only purpose here was to frighten the novices into doing their religious homework?

As he matured, Kalsang had begun to appreciate a greater purpose behind the Buddha relating these woeful tales. No matter how difficult his own circumstances became, he could always move the focus from his own sufferings by developing compassion for others. Also, if the mind could realise the endless bliss of Enlightenment, was overwhelming suffering beyond its capabilities? He didn't think so.

In Kalsang's imagination, the atomic flames of the swelling sun became pregnant with the agony of a billion billion beings. Their cries were joined by all others labouring unprotected from heat. Animals crawling in the deserts, ghosts sweltering under the rays of a full moon, and human beings whose minds were on fire. Their anguish took form in his mind as a song.

Inside the trillion crushing suns,
Fire so fierce that flame freezes adamantine,
Brilliance so dense that it hardens to darkness,
Eruption crushing eruption crushing eruption
Every atom in agony, torn and torn again
Here all my elements were born
In this most common of places.
How unlikely there that I was not.

In this way Kalsang controlled his mind.

CHAPTER 29

August

Above August's refuge, the sky burned blue, a blaze of sodium and oxygen stripped from the small planet's crust by continual clawing of the solar furies.

This blaze, reflected in the mirror of the universe, matched that which ignited in August's mind. At first it burned slowly, at the edge of his awareness, allowing him to steel his nerves through the challenges of landing the ship in the correct spot on an utterly alien world, in digging through the sediments with the wrong tools to find the pink, organic rich ice, which was buried much deeper than reported, in lugging it by hand aboard his ship to feed it to the terrapod located in ship's heart. Sparks with the brilliance of welder arcs shot up from the charged ground as he had dug, rattling his heart. Without the anger he might have given up a thousand times, but he had fought through it.

Anything was preferable to the despair that had overtaken him that moment when the wormhole closed, and he had followed through the ring the sparks left by the vanishing ship, not homeward millions of kilometers to acclaim and immortality, but only a few millimetres to a lonely abandonment.

That stupid, terrible woman. She had shown him the way to the wormhole. She had stirred hope of rescue when his hope was almost gone, and he might have easily faded into shock and depression. But, instead, she had done the cruellest thing - dangled the possibility of an easy escape before him and then slammed it in his face. And for good measure she had done so by breaking the wormhole, his greatest accomplishment. At that moment, August's vague anger at Gudanko exploded at a new target. That bitch. He could still hear the echo of her encouragement.

"Don't stop Mr. Bridges. There's no time. You have to trust me."

And he had. Her concern for him was so apparent, so urgent. As if she valued his life over her own. Her appeal had overcome his paranoia. She was his salvation. His Angel. And then he had run towards her with all his heart. She was willing to sacrifice herself for his deliverance. That came through in her voice. It seemed the closest thing to love he had felt in his life. She believed in him and his dream. She was his protector.

And then that terrible moment when she had turned and ran, taking everything with her as she went. It was at that moment that August learned to hate. He could have died then, consumed with fury, if he hadn't noticed familiar handwriting scrawled on the side of the box stating, "When all else fails set your sails."

Calvin30!

August had torn the box from the wall and ripped it open. Inside had been a new neurovisor. August had carefully removed his neurovisor and held Calvin30's gift up to his forehead, waiting impatiently for it to insert itself.

The clone had appeared in space before him.

"Hi Boss. If perchance you find this early, see it as advance precautions for a happenstance, which might yet happen. But if this moment finds you trapped on the other side of the rabbit hole, here is the key to save your soul."

An animation of the solar system had then appeared imagined in space between August and Calvin30. The picture of a ship, his ship, was floating near the orbit of Mercury. On Mercury, a flashing beacon attracted the ship to land in a crater near the top. As Mercury continued around the Sun, the ship stayed sheltered in the crater until it had rotated to the opposite side of the Sun near the orbit of Venus. Then the ship had launched up to the anti-matter station, refuelled, and then shot off towards Venus. Swinging around that planet, the little ship then whipped off towards Mars.

"If you are stranded then that crater is the only place in the Mercury space that is nice to land. Not too cold and not too hot, just right and, moreover, there is ice."

Ice? August remembered this from some earlier briefing. Even though Mercury's tilt was the smallest of all the planets, that tilt meant that the permanent shadow in this one crater near the North Pole could protect him from the Sun's radiation. That shadow amazingly preserved ice left from ancient comets. Ice meant water, which besides radiation shielding, was the vital thing that was in short supply on his small capsule. Food had apparently been well stocked. When Mercury's rotation caught up with Venus, he had enough shielding in his ship to make a quick dash into a swing by gravitational boost from Venus that would allow him to escape the radiation zone in time.

Of course, why hadn't he thought of it himself? It was perfect. The clone who had come through for him still stood there, frozen in the neuroview, as if waiting for August to thank him.

August Bridges had never felt more gratitude towards anyone. Because of the clone he might live to win another day. He would rise from the ashes like the Phoenix and surprise them all. Even better, he now knew his enemy's true colours. Gudanko was finished. August planned to publicly emasculate the man, to send the slug crawling on his belly forever in exile from the Coms. The thought brightened August's mood and re-ignited his fantasy. The crowd began to roar again.

August pulled out the vodka that he had saved to commemorate his victory. Pouring a thimble full, he toasted the frozen image of Calvin30 as he had every day since this ordeal began. When he left this hellish place, his bottle would be finished.

One day the work of stockpiling enough water was over. Then the long wait began as the fires in the sky burned ever brighter. Then storing up hatred became August's sole preoccupation. Each breath took him closer to the day of his revenge.

Through a portal August could see molten metal glowing on the horizon of his small refuge, reminding him of how slight the margins of his survival were. If he died, as was likely, Gudanko would have stolen it all from him. There would be no brave new future with August's steady hand upon the prow. No interstellar dynasties to bear his name. No legends bestowing immortality in his lifetime. No victorious return to the Earth. No parade.

The passage through fire would soon be over August reassured himself. The universal heir would return from his long march, hardened and strengthened. Gudanko would be vanquished and all his ill-gotten gains returned to their rightful owner. August encouraged these fantasies, embellishing them with graphic visualisations of potential fates that would befall Gudanko and his ilk. The more claustrophobic August became, the more horrific the imaginary rough justice he meted out against the man he hated.

He was not only going to depose Gudanko, he was going to murder him, disembowel him. He was going to torture him slowly, make that smug idiot feel the pain knowing that his life was slowing, inexorably, slipping away with August Bridges controlling the rate and the moment on his extinction. It was too bad that his enemy was too insensitive to feel real pain. Not the slow, deepening pain that August was facing. There would be no way of avenging that agony.

August turned in his webbing, trying to sleep, to find even a few minutes of release, only he couldn't. Each breath was a reminder that he would not relax until his revenge was achieved.

Enough.

Enough.

Enough.

August reluctantly realised that his anger was wearing him out. He did not realise this all at once, but in increments of desperation. There had to be a better way.

The search for escape led him in many, iterative directions, which seemed to wind tighter and tighter circles as time went on. He tried to apply himself to a regimen of self-improvement, but his attempts were pathetic. The heat and discomfort quickly derailed any such pretensions. An inexhaustible library of neurovids and music were a temporary oasis for the mind, until they began to rerun in his subconscious. And above all he drank huge volumes of water, so much that he had to accelerate the filtration cycle and began to taste his own urine. He tracked the passage of weeks by the length of his hair, which by now had regrown past his shoulders. His depression advanced like an army.

Who was August Bridges anyway?

A spoiled only-child of the Portland suburbs. No noble lineage and no significant childhood trauma to impel him towards greatness. Even with effort August found it hard to evoke much feeling for his parents, or for the split-level townhouse he had been raised in. August had reinvented himself so thoroughly, in such spectacular fashion, that his true heritage had seemed incidental.

Mom died in an accident, flattened by an unbalanced SkyTran container flipping off its rail. It happened on one of the few times Dad had managed to coax her out from the house. August had not been able to attend her funeral as by then his exile to the Moon had begun. Not that it mattered. Mom had effectively left them almost from the beginning. It was painful to remember her just sitting there, and by doing nothing demanding everything. Not taking her medication because she preferred the vacuity to the responsibilities of love. It made him furious imagining himself doing the same thing.

Sitting, just sitting.

Mom.

So what if he had to reinvent her in order to fall in love with her? He had publicly romanticised her and her Siberian immigrant pedigree into a picture of stoic dignity. So what if her only life achievement after immigrating was to marry her high school boyfriend, a latter-day dentist. She had no dignity to bestow, but he had inherited it from her nevertheless. And of course, it was this conceit that had led him to Russia to discover his 'true' heritage and his destiny.

August thought long, trying to recover anything in his upbringing that would prepare him to survive his current predicament? The only advice he remembered from Dad, delivered with any passion, was not to lend out his tools. Dad's approach with anything complex was to, in his benignly bland manner, let it go its own way. August reflected on the irony that it was precisely his own inability to let time pass without elaboration that was now driving him crazy. Dad might have handled this.

A month later, August dragged himself through a stupor to disengage the ice excavation gear and dislodge the ship from its footings in preparation for his rapid escape to the shadow of Venus. The heat hit his ship like a punch as he flew out of Mercury's protective shadow. The air rippled, and the walls became hot to the touch. August had to put on his spacesuit and turn on the internal refrigeration to stop from cooking. It was unendurable, but, hour by hour, he felt it recede as he rocketed away from Hell.

By the time his small ship limped its way to the anti-matter factory, August almost lacked the energy to maneuver the ship up to the maintenance entry, angling it so the factory's shadow would shield him during his foray.

August fidgeted nervously. This was it. The smallest wrong move and the most explosive substance in the cosmos would evaporate him instantly. The blast might even put a dent in Mercury. Sweat collected in his spacesuit gloves. As he stepped out of the Icarus he was already panting.

The gantry leading from his ship to the refinery as a long thin straw, which looked as thin as a needle sticking out of the factory. August could barely fit down it. The claustrophobia was overwhelming. Steadily he crawled, hand over hand, controlling his panic. Exiting the other side of the needle, he pulled himself into a larger cylinder with the walls all around him covered with canisters labelled with bright warning stickers.

Warning. Do not handle manually.

August selected one of these bombs surrounding him. He wrapped webbing around it. He pushed the release on its bracket. He tugged. He tugged again, and again harder.

The canister popped out towards him. He pulled himself quickly out of the way. With light tugs he slowed the canister. It stopped, centimeters from another tank, and slowly rebounded. Moving into the gantry needle the cannister bumped the entrance, and a red light flashed on. It turned off. August started breathing again. Hand over hand he pushed the bomb up the needle. Sweat covered his eyes.

The canister was safely bracketed in the Icarus fuel mount. A display in his mind told him this was so.

All was well.

Edging away to a safe distance from the anti-matter factory, August aimed himself towards the calm clear light of Venus and fired the engines. He blacked out as the g-forces kicked in.

When he awoke, Mercury was a small circle behind him. He had escaped. To be on the move again made him giddy, and he was in high spirits for the first time since the disaster.

For a while everything seemed possible, but the heat continued to work on him. With each passing day, the mirror of his life reflected more harshly upon him. Recalcitrant ghosts began to dance within his mind.

August scowled at Gregori, lounging in the corner of their cramped shared space. Such a fool the man had been, to choose someone like August to be his closest friend. Such a fool for the clown to entrust his tears with anyone, least of all someone as selfish and driven as August. To have offered up his wife in whom he could see no fault. What kind of idiot would trust so much.

"It's okay August. That's what men do."

"Don't you forgive me. It was your fault anyway. You never had the balls to stand up for yourself. You were weak."

"Give it up August. You think it was about you? That's a laugh. She wanted to hurt me. Me. You could have been anyone."

August hurled his rage at Gregori, who simply evaporated in response.

"She loved me. She needed a man not a clown," he shouted and pounded the wall where his friend had sat.

Condescending laughter bounced around the cabin.

"Whatever you want to think man."

"She loved me."

The light from Venus now filled the ship from the forward portal like a minor Sun. August pressed his cheek against the pane, wishing himself to move faster towards the light. He was sure he could not endure one more moment of the torment in his mind. Then that moment had passed, and he was sure he could not endure another. He was gripped by the urge to leave and found himself already dressed in his space suit and waiting in the airlock to prepare to jump. Before the airlock door opened, the radiation alarm went off, requiring a manual override that August reluctantly declined to trigger.

The light grew stronger as Venus approached, a soft reflected light. The planet was so close in size to the Earth that August almost felt as if he were staring down from his bedroom skylight on Luna City.

They were laying together on the best bed they had ever shared in the luxury suite that his new wealth had purchased. Anya had her back to him. August's eyes traced the length of her spine to the point where the small of her naked back converged with the beginning of the solid anchor of her hips where his fingers liked to rest as he held her when they made love. The line of the sheet covered just enough to provoke his desire to unveil his lover.

"I told myself that you might learn to love."

The tone told him of the finality of her decision.

"Nyusha. I don't understand. We will be great together. There is nothing we won't accomplish. All of our dreams."

"It is all your dream August. It is only yours."

He could bear no more. His hand pulled back the sheet and he embraced her. She did not retreat from him, but there was little passion in her response. Instead she held his arms, watching him carefully until he had finished.

Her eyes were painful to meet, and August rolled away, allowing her to climb from their bed to the shower. When she had cleaned and dressed, she poured some tea for them from the samovar and they drank without saying much.

"It was a mistake August. I am going back to Gregori. He is a kind man and does not deserve this."

"Fine. Go then, but you are leaving everything."

"Ah, my dear, you once looked like that to me, like everything, like a great man. But August, you are only a man trying to be a great man. I am sad for you because I know you will achieve everything that you say you will do and more. In the end, in the end I am afraid you will not be missed."

That hotel room door had continued to close on his soul ever since.

August was sobbing, and he couldn't remember why. Why hadn't Mom come out of her room all day? He'd just come back from his friend's house, a friend whose parents spoke to one another. The absence of Mom, so familiar to him that it had seemed almost comforting, now seemed unbearably shameful. August knocked hard on her door and didn't stop kicking it until he heard her cry out.

His fists left blood on the ships' wall, and his knuckles had a metallic taste when he licked them.

Suddenly the ship began to shake violently as the gravity of Venus gripped it. August had enough sense to climb into his webbing and buckle himself down.

The ship's walls blazed as it fell into the upper atmosphere and the air inside began to boil. As he dipped beneath the fathomless clouds, the frail walls began to buckle, and August realised that his ship, designed for interplanetary travel, could not possibly survive such a path. His faith in Calvin30 had been so unquestioning. Why would the clone, who was so meticulous in his planning, fail to account for such an obvious detail?

Again, what did he really know about the clone? Why had he had taken it for granted that his henchman would always be there for him? Was it just his desperation to prove Anya wrong? Because the bitter truth was that the clone, like everyone else, had his own mysterious agenda and how pathetic was it for August, with all his glory, to only have his lackey to depend on? The truth was Anya could not have been more painfully prophetic. It was the clarity of her insights that had drawn him to her so why could he discount her final word on him?

No one would miss him, after all he had done for them. The acids of Venus would consume him, August Bridges, liberator of the world, and leave no trace. He would not be mourned.

August's fury shook him harder than Venus shook his fragile lifeboat. It was all he had left. It continued to crush him even after the ship emerged from beneath the ocean of clouds and shot back out into the stillness of space. His anger left him no room to rejoice his unlikely escape. What was there to rejoice in a life wasted?

"August, August."

August twisted his neck as he sat up, as if jolted awake from a dream. Had he fallen asleep? It was Illya's voice.

"August."

There it was again. August could feel his blood pounding in his neck. He wasn't dreaming.

"Who do you love August?"

Again, another shadow, darting across the floor before melting into the wall. And more laughter. August squinted to make out a face near the head of the shadow. Deep eyes, his father's eyes, looked back at him with pity.

Hatred welled up in him. The eyes of Illya, his true father. They were supposed to nurture and protect him, not abandon him, not block the path to his destiny. With murder in his mind August began to stalk the shade, lashing out and hitting the walls and floor as it faded out of reach at the last moment. He chased it though the hours, waging constant war. Nothing else was clear in his mind, only the cold intent to rid the world of this demon. He would kill it before it killed him. The air slowly cooled as August fought, until the effort overcame him, and he fell into despair.

The small red eye of Mars from the forward view portal looked down approvingly on the crumpled warrior who had fallen in battle.

Time passed.

The silhouette of a man wearing flowing robes entered the capsule and swam through the air towards him. Through blurred vision August saw a smile and then felt the careful brush of a hand across his brow.

"Illya?" He whispered, hopefully.

"Ah good. You are waking up now," said an unfamiliar voice.

PATH TO GROUND

*"Though primordially we are not separate,
not recognizing me, you experience me externally."*

~ Yeshe Tsogyal, 8th Century Tibet

CHAPTER 30

Kalsang

Kalsang tasted the soup of ashes. As his mind dried out, the desire for each labored breath of depleted air had to be weighed against the ever-growing pain in his ribs and diaphragm. The decision to release his hold on life grew from this indifference as his mind fell into itself, a prolonged and monotonous descent.

Encircling the dying monk, the interior of the *Garuda* looked like an infestation of roundworms. Hoses, ducting, and optical cable dangled from the ceiling, flexor and tensors wriggled and arced out of the walls - all testament to the numberless repairs improvised to keep the cramped living space alive. The scene was imbued with an intentional incompleteness. Cables and webbing pulled out in economical lengths. Screws turned only deep enough to catch, and hose brackets clamped lightly. Every effort undertaken had been only just adequate with no energy squandered.

The *Garuda* was not a Terrapod. The interior walls were hard nanogem alloys, not tissue membranes exchanging heat and gases with a robust fellowship of living beings. In place of an organic self-regulating physiology were millions of electrical circuits, mechanical pumps, filters, and chemical plants with trillions of possible combinations for malfunction. The walls had buckled under pressures they were never designed to withstand, blessedly in reinforcing angles.

The outer skin of the vessel was pitted and burnt, blackened by the passage through the ochre vapors of Venus, which had been a necessary trajectory required to slow the ship down enough to be captured by the gravity of Mars. Metal fins and instrument booms extending over the edge of the heat shielding on the in drawn fulcrum had melted down to nubs. Blast shields had welded over the windows they protected.

The small dun shape of the Garuda was insignificant against the encompassing void. Whole planets were reduced to mere specks of reflected glory amidst the glare of the forever noonday Sun. And then, incomprehensible amidst such astronomical stillness, there was movement.

The movement, a punctuated flicker, suddenly emerged from the imperceptible and grew steadily bigger. Periodically it was surrounded by a burst of halo.

Small rows of lights became discernible from one another, one of them urgently flashing red. A long sash of silver grew in its wake. Closer, thin spider arms adorned with dishes and prongs, extended towards the Garuda in greeting. The movement had become a ship. Prominently displayed across the ship's bow appeared the name 'Icarus MTP100X'.

Inside the ship was a living man.

Kalsang's eyes opened. He turned his neck, somehow overcoming the inertia of lethargy. Bright lights twinkled in his neuroview. His pupils tracked the lights and squinted, bringing up a panel of messages and a static filled external view from one of the cameras that had somehow managed to survive the heat of Venus. A vessel was docking to the *Garuda*. The airlocks had coupled. Atmospheric cross-checks were positive. The new ship was under autohelm. Emergency protocols were activated. Authorization to open the door was requested.

The effort to focus his eyes and process this information exhausted Kalsang. His eyelids drooped. His diaphragm constricted, and a whiff of bottled oxygen dripping through his face mask to his lungs allowed his eyes to open again.

The airlocks hissed open. Air, pungent with oxygen, seeped into Kalsang's carbon saturated lungs. His mind collapsed into a dizzy spiral, and he slept with deep, labored breaths. When hours later he awoke, his mind was invigorated by the newly arrived possibility of survival.

Kalsang's sense of smell awakened with him, and the stench of putrid faeces made him gag. The reflex injected enough adrenaline into his muscles to bring him to his feet. Numb hands wrestled with the clasps in his pilot's webbing, eventually releasing him to fall against a wall railing. Carefully, Kalsang walked himself down the rail to the open airlock. He breathed through his mouth to avoid his sense of smell.

Faded shadows of d'Song and others motioned for him to follow. With measured exertions Kalsang pulled himself after them, through the airlock into the foreign ship. He looked around the sewerage stained chamber and saw them clustered around something, d'Song's face full of concern. They parted before him as he approached.

The man was laying naked, nail marks gouging any skin within reach of his twitching hands. He floated in a cloud of his own shit. Kalsang's heart nearly burst, not only at the wretched sight of suffering, but at how grateful he felt to see another living person. A spontaneous prayer arose in his mind.

Oh, my brother my brother my brother
So long we have travelled
too long we have travelled
Time beyond memory
Inconceivable winds of fate
Blowing through vast space
Have cast you upon the shores of my gaze once again
Oh, my brother
The recognition is instant
This face you wear is my own
The taste of your tears is not different
The suffering cut into your bones a perfect match
Oh, my brother
I have missed you so
As my heart touches yours
No longer alone
To see you is a perfect refuge
From my long exile
I return home

Impelled by a surge of compassion, Kalsang pushed off through the air to the man's side, and began to brush long tendrils of slimy, matted hair from a translucent brow. The man groaned and called out, and then fell unconscious again before Kalsang could summon the strength to answer. Aware of the futility of his efforts at cleaning the man, Kalsang looked around to locate a better tool, and spotting a vacuum hose tucked under the galley, pulled the hose out to the man. Kalsang noticed an open container of vitabars. He paused from his task to eat one.

Warmth spread from his shrunken belly as he chewed down the bar. A heavy feeling overcame him, and he swooned. As he slumped back his eyes rolled past the man and he noticed the man was crying.

The man's body shuddered, sobs forced out through utter exhaustion, like an abandoned baby fighting off sleep. Kalsang struggled to keep his eyes open as his gaze floated past the man. Such a pitiful state. Resolve strengthened within him to do something to help. Anything. He vomited.

Kalsang pulled his way along the wall back to the vitabars and sucked on one, taking care this time to extract the necessary nutrition from it without overwhelming his shrunken stomach. He sat and watched the man sleep and, after some time, when his body had gathered enough strength, Kalsang pushed off from the wall towing the vacuum hose through the air behind him. With deliberate motions, Kalsang vacuumed the shit cloud away, and wiped the man's festering skin with his robes before rubbing in a nanoid disinfectant that he had scavenged from a first aid kit.

Shuttling between sustenance, sleep and his project, Kalsang's vitality slowly returned. As he rested against the galley wall, chewing another Vitabar, Kalsang studied the man. The man's features were bold, and symmetrical, and oddly familiar. Long aristocratic fingers. The hair was a mad tangle, curling out at uneven angles like the tentacles of an octopus. He must have a strong constitution to survive the horrific ordeal he had been through. Strong blood. It felt good to see him clean, some dignity restored.

"Melded One, who is he?" asked d'Song.

"His face is familiar, isn't it? Yes, I have seen this before many times, but I cannot remember where."

Kalsang drifted into sleep and awoke to find the man had gone. He floated to the middle of the room and looked around. Few hiding places were available. Doors to all galley stores, closets, and observation cupolas had been pulled roughly out from their hinges. Crawl space vents were barricaded - wedged behind bulky cargo containers. Passenger webbing cut off from the floors had been strung across the airlock Kalsang had somehow managed to push his way through. How fortunate it had not held.

For the first time Kalsang noticed the desperate chaos in the cabin. What demons the man must have battled. Eliminating the monsters' hiding places had not been enough to diffuse them. The man had fought them. Partially healed savage rips scarred the Terrapod wall membranes, spilling out fungi, plant roots and disorientated invertebrates. Hydroponic fluid oozed out into buoyant spheres. Frantic fingernail scratches clawed at instrument panels. Ominously Kalsang noticed a stash of weapons, improvised missiles and spears, wrapped in webbing and tied to a handhold.

The *Garuda* was the only place the man could be. Kalsang headed back to find him. There was no telling what this wild man might do to all his careful repairs. Even though the man's ship was well stocked for a crew of one, the resources of both ships would be needed to see them safely home.

Swimming through the airlock passage, Kalsang visualized the man's face. Certainly, he had seen him before, but where? The *Garuda* was a dark cave full of dangling shadows. Kalsang had turned out the lights at least a month before to save the energy. How long ago had it been?

As Kalsang entered the cave, a hand grabbed him roughly from above, rotating him up off his feet. Something sharp jabbed into his throat.

"Do you know who I am?" demanded a hushed voice.

It was a rather odd thing to ask, the logical question would be to ask Kalsang for his identity. But, he did know this man, he remembered.

"Yes," Kalsang responded haltingly, "you are the man in my dream."

The spike in his throat pulled back for a second. "Don't lie. You don't know who I am? Then why are you here?" The force behind the spike returned.

"I am not sure."

"Bastard. I told you to leave me alone. You don't exist, understand? You don't exist. Why don't you listen? WHY?" A bubble of blood formed and drifted off from Kalsang's neck.

"I am bleeding."

"Shut up. Shut Up. You? Bleed? I'd have killed you a hundred times already if you could bleed, wouldn't I? You're such an asshole Illya. I killed you myself so many years ago – how could you bleed?" The spike plunged deeper and turned and Kalsang fainted.

As he regained consciousness, Kalsang felt the man hugging him tightly, wet cheeks pressed against his and weeping. As he pulled himself back the man cried out in delight, before pulling abruptly back into the shadows of the airlock.

"You aren't dead?" The man tentatively asked after a while.

"No." Although Kalsang realised in saying that that he wasn't quite sure.

"You aren't my father?"

"No. Certainly not." The question would have struck Kalsang as funny, if not for the weary menace in the voice.

The man advanced warily out from his corner. "And you bleed?" He said this looking at the red stains on his hands as if they might disappear if he took his eyes off them.

"Yes. Isn't it?" Kalsang touched his neck and held forth a blood-wet finger and traced a red line in the man's open palm.

"Oh." The man groaned, holding Kalsang's hand to keep his balance.

"You need water?" Kalsang asked.

"It all tastes like piss. Oh. Yes, that would be good." The man's answer had the tone of someone comfortable with receiving service, an important man. Kalsang hauled himself up on emaciated arms, and crawled towards the airlock, but his advance stalled at the entrance. He gasped for breath. "Sorry my friend, you need to help me get it for you."

The man looked up from his hands with a blank expression.

"I would get your water, but too little body power," Kalsang pointed to his bony legs, hanging out from his robes like loose pieces of string.

The man rubbed his hair, and then looked at his hand again. "You cleaned me?"

"Yes. Isn't it?"

"I see." The man looked up from his hands, and his red eyes searched into Kalsang's. Tear tracks through residual grime crossed his checks, and feelings of loss and distress reflected in Kalsang's heart. The man shook his head dejectedly. "You, you need my help?"

"Thank you."

The man wiped the tendrils of hair out of his eyes and swam, pushing Kalsang before him, back through the airlock. The man lowered him delicately down into a passenger webbing. Securing the tethers too firmly, the man headed to the galley to take a long drink. He pulled the hose out almost to its full length so Kalsang could have one also. Then he left the hose dangling as his attention turned to fitting a neurovisor onto his head.

"We must be almost back to Earth. Not so bad, eh? And what happened to you my little friend? Lunar overshoot? They must have used autopilot to join us up before collection. Now I must get us on a new course before Gudanko can. Wait a second." The man's eyes twitched with disbelief. "That can't be right." He looked to Kalsang for confirmation. "Where in Hell are we?"

"Perhaps. Ah. Almost to Mars, isn't it?"

Suspicion returned to the man's eyes before they twitched back to his neurovisor. "No. It can't be." Kalsang could see the man's eyes scanning some virtual hole in the bulkhead that apparently moved as the man turned his head. The man sprang about madly, looking wildly around the 360-degree view relayed to him by the cams embedded in his ship's hull. "The Earth. Where is it?" he asked accusingly, casting a quick glance over his shoulder at Kalsang. "Where in hell? Wait. I see something. A planet? We're on a course towards it. But it's not blue, it's red. It's red." The man ran his fingers through his hair and his body slumped away. He said nothing a long while. "It is Mars?"

"Isn't it?"

Collecting himself the man dragged over a box of vitabars. They shared the meal in silence - exhaustion had rendered words a luxury. And then they slept.

When he awoke, apart from d'Song sleeping in a corner, Kalsang was alone again.

He sat in his webbing and said some prayers, waiting for the man to return from the *Garuda*. In his weakened state there was little else he could do.

His webbing began to pull taut and loose items spiralled down out of free fall to the floor. Shortly thereafter, the man stepped lightly through the airlock gantry, with a satisfied look on his face. He had dressed himself.

"Your fulcrum's big enough to give us some gravity." He said, bouncing his boot slowly off the floor.

"And your ship there," He pointed back down the airlock, "it is a Mirtopik craft. So, what is it you haven't told me my friend?"

The man lay down on his webbing and stretched into it. The contrast between the self-composed person before him and the pitiful wreck that Kalsang had first encountered was heartening.

"My name is Kalsang."

"Glad to meet you. I'm, you say you don't know me?" The man again ran his fingers through his limp hair. Kalsang did know this man, even outside his dream. Yes. He was very familiar, as if he had seen him every day, only he didn't know him. So strange.

"I have seen you before, and in my dream."

"So you said. And what I need to know is, who sent you?" The menacing tone slipped back into the edges of the man's voice.

"Ah. I am not sent by anyone. Just like you, I am trying to get back home. To Earth."

"Why should I believe you? Mars isn't a stroll to the corner shop. You would need to match my trajectory exactly for us to meet."

d'Song danced behind the man, making silly faces while Kalsang was trying to focus.

"What are you looking at? Why are you smiling?"

"You are not helping d'Song."

She poked out ten tongues at him and disappeared.

"Nothing. I am from Tibet."

"No, I want to know who you work for."

"I work for Mirtopik Com and my monastery. I am coming from Triton, from the Neptune array."

The man studied Kalsang and then shook his head and laughed with disbelief. "The monk. You're the goddamn missing monk. That's too, it's too incredible, unbelievable, impossible."

Something changed in the man's face, as if he were quietly relieved of some burden. Kalsang sat up in his webbing and smiled weakly. "It is just like that."

Kalsang felt a spaciousness that expanded out around them in every direction, an endlessly stretching dark balloon. Kalsang closed his eyes and felt the great expanse of emptiness emanate in all directions from the combined beating of their hearts. This void was not the same as the one that had, over the past months, consumed him with its absence of dimension, a gray noise with no source. Now it pinched inward and unfolded outward from a new central coordinate, a new center of meaning, the impossible reality that now he was one of two.

"Are you okay?" the man asked with concern.

"Thank you." Kalsang answered. *Thank you for being here with me.*

"You really don't know who I am?"

Kalsang opened his eyes and met the man's stare. "I'm surprised you don't, but, I realise I haven't exactly looked myself lately." The man ran a towel through his hair, fluffing it. He pulled the towel off with a flourish and smiled like a politician.

Kalsang shook his head doubtfully. The gesture deflated the man's hopeful smile. "Yes, are you are named August Bridges?"

"Ah ha." The man reclined back in his webbing.

And so it was. Kalsang was pleased to have remembered. But, who was August Bridges? Then he remembered.

Amazing. There was no doubt that this was the same man, but it was extraordinary. August Bridges was so powerful. How could he be here? Kalsang felt sure he was hallucinating, and it didn't instill confidence watching d'Song and the others wandering about in the background. That the ship was full of aliens was more likely than this. There he was, the very face Kalsang had imagined had tried to murder him to hide the truth of the message from the stars. The very man. It was too unbelievable, but there he was.

And here he, Kalsang, was also. Isn't it? He had survived. Equally impossible.

August, the man at the center of the whole mandala, was sitting here, with Kalsang, an ordinary monk, in the middle of vast empty space.

"Lamala?"

But even the omniscient mind of his precious teacher could not bend space and time to make something as extraordinary as this happen. Could it be possible?

Trying in vain to fit the impossible into the reasonable, Kalsang fell naturally into the routine of analysing the situation using Buddhist logic. His mind, his Lama's mind, mind itself, although able to shape reality by the labels it applied was not autonomous from that which it labelled. So, there was no separate omnipotent mind. On the other hand, the materialists might say they were tiny points in an unimaginably vast objective frame and, if so, August and his meeting was too improbable to occur. Isn't it? They were so insignificant. But the universe was not like that. The universe was composed of its parts, all equally insignificant. No universe existed separate from those parts and, so, equally dissolved into insignificance. Instead, everything arose together, in non-dual dependence, a symphony of liberated energies dancing together from time without beginning.

But the reality was too enormous to wrap up like this in mere concepts. Kalsang felt the cause, and his part in it, binding the whole galaxy, passing through stars and lifetimes to manifest in this moment. Tentacles sprouted from his legs and new heads opened out of his neck like birch buds popping in early spring. His body was interchangeably human and alien until he became uncertain of the distinction, blending with the many faces and limbs of enlightenment. A single heartfelt intention was bearing fruit in a continuum of being that stretched from so long ago and far away. Centuries of momentum made the impossible inevitable. Kalsang was the name currently attached to one part of it. August was also attached, in another way. As the wave travelled through their lives it had crested in their having tea, here in the middle of nowhere.

"You are looking very handsome Melded One," teased d'Song.

Kalsang had not felt more whole and alive in a long time. He smiled warily at August. What were they creating now he wondered?

Chapter 31 - August

Uselessness hung heavily on August. The sluggishness of his exhausted body had been a helpful counter to his derangement and hyperactive imagination. Now that his body had begun to repair, and his insanity had subsided, his increasing reliance on the comforting regularity and relaxed presence of his unlikely shipmate began to bother him. It was shameful, in fact dangerous, to feel not wholly in possession of his fate.

August devoted the first efforts of this new phase of his rehabilitation to clean the Icarus. The automated scrubbers, with the assistance of gravity provided by the Garuda, had rapidly cleaned the air, stripping away the filth and stench and replacing it with a dry, antiseptic odor. The walls required vacuuming and scrubbing, and every crevice harboured new challenges. He found the action therapeutic, as if, as the monk had suggested, the offal and grime on the walls were the stains on his soul. If only it were so easy to wash those away.

He became possessive of the project. He shooed off the monk's attempts to pitch in until the inscrutable little man dutifully retired to his hermitage on the other ship. The actions of cleaning, the friction of hands and scrub brush on the walls and floor, were like painting reality back into his surroundings. The sweat and resistance returned his body to him, exorcising the wraith that had until recently inhabited that zone. Sometimes his thoughts broke in, like a drunkard invading a prayer meeting, and the brush became a weapon of vengeance, obliterating his enemy. It was not difficult to image Gudanko's treacherous essence into the slimy ooze fleeing before him.

Engrossed in his task, August lost track of time. When he stood back to admire his progress he was surprised at how much of it he had made. There remained very little of the open wall that he hadn't scrubbed clean. Ignoring the protests from his stomach he approached the darker crevices.

Prostrate in an open vent he felt a hand grip his leg.

Now what did that monk want? When August slid out of the vent he found himself alone. The monk was nowhere in the Icarus. Perhaps he had imagined it.

Returning to his work he heard movement and a sharp bang behind him, as if the monk had knocked over something big.

"Hello?"

No answer.

Suddenly August felt compromised in his position, laying with his arms and head stuck in the vent and his belly exposed without. What if an assassin was hiding elsewhere in the monk's ship? It was a stupid thought, but enough to make him jerk and scramble out of the vent. The room was empty.

"August."

Illya's whisper sent a shiver through him. August scanned the room for something sharp.

"August."

Wielding his brush, August advanced into the aft cabin.

"Who do you love?"

August stopped and shook himself. Was he going mad again?

His heart beating, August dropped the brush and scrambled as quickly as he could through the airlock, back to Kalsang, back to sanity.

Kalsang was sitting there, ensconced in his meditation, eyes half-closed and working his beads. August, convinced Illya was following him moved as close to the monk as possible, huddling into a protective presence. Kalsang opened his eyes and smiled at him.

"August-la. Are you all right?"

Kalsang looked up but his eyes went somewhere else in the room and he smiled cheerfully. Why did it sometimes look as though the monk was relating with some invisible persons lounging about the room with them? Could he see Illya?

"Is there something August?" Kalsang inquired in a calm voice.

"No. Nothing."

"Okay, okay. I will make us something for tea." Without further ado the monk stood and left him, chasing the shadows before him as he went.

Feeling alone again, August cast his eyes around for something to do that would distract him from his ghosts. The monk had left his neurovisor behind. He had noticed that the monk often took it off when he meditated. It occurred to him that this was an opportunity to find out the truth behind his little friend.

When August had first heard that the monk had disappeared off the grid he was in the thick of construction on the worm hole. Still the news brought him low. He had grieved for the brave soul who had made ultimate sacrifices to bring his Dream into fruition. Perhaps, he had told himself, there was yet hope that the man had survived despite the loss of communication and was on his way home. It was this hope he had shared in the requisite press release to the shareholders. A generous donation had been made to the monk's monastery to sponsor prayers for their lost comrade. Now here they were together. The timing was right, but it was too incredible. It had to be checked out.

Keeping an eye down the airlock corridor, August warily donned the monk's neurovisor. He grunted from the shock - inserting another person's custom fitted neurovisor was very painful. As icy electric fingers dove into his brain, August coughed and threw up in his mouth and, with a concerted act of will, swallowed it back down.

A neuroview emerged, fuzzy and shaky, but with the standard Mirtopik mnemes still recognisable. August thought his way through the security workarounds Calvin30 had schooled him in and scanned the opened field for summaries.

Visions flickered through August's mind like half remembered memories of dreams. Long and complex sequences recording various ship malfunctions for later reference. All manner of recorded visualisations of strange religious iconography and memories of other monks talking or mumbling prayers or performing monotonous rituals. Silly and sentimental neuropics of animals and nature landscapes downloaded from the neuronet. Targeted recordings, marked by Mirtopik's deep space science division, zoomed in across an alien landscape of pink ice and strange dark geysers.

His heart pounded as he suddenly flew upwards from a jerky and panicked panorama of a coral and black streaked world receding below towards an improbably small fleck of white growing into what he recognised as a deep space transporter, the same model as the Garuda, at the end of the trajectory. He recognised the world below as Triton. So, the monk's impossible story was true.

August steadied himself from the rush and his gaze snapped back to monitor the airlock for Kalsang's return. He took deep breaths before he re-entered the neuroview, reminding himself to keep part of his attention on look-out down the airlock corridor.

To confirm his discovery August sought out some of the uncleaned extra-terrestrial transmissions that he remembered pouring over as they first downloaded, recorded in his memory in loving detail. There they were, unblemished and complete, not chopped and tagged by the commercial-in-confidence people as the rest of the world would have seen them. They were all there down to the last fateful transmission in the file catalogue.

Something was wrong. He couldn't put his finger on it. Long shadows fell down the airlock passage indicating the monk's movements.

August concentrated hard on the list scrolling past in his imagination. And then he saw it. The dates were all wrong, recorded weeks or months before he had first seen them. He zoomed in to confirm when they had been downloaded. Perhaps there was some technical delay of which he had never been briefed. The log confirmed that they had been transmitted to Earth first on the day they were recorded and then, inexplicably, a second time on dates that matched what he remembered, and a third time for the 'official' download.

Kalsang's long shadow strolled across the threshold into the room. August reached for his forehead and then paused. The neuroprint requesting the downloads. It was Gudanko's. August recoiled with shock as his hands gripped the neurovisor preparing to pull it off before he was discovered.

Returning fingers gripped around the lip of the airlock and August ripped the neurovisor out, hurling it towards the monk's webbing, which launched him backwards.

Pain powered through his body as it jerked into an epileptic fit, doubling over, his teeth cracking against each other as they sliced through the tip of his tongue. Firm, smooth hands pulled him downwards as he fell into darkness.

Sometime later he awoke, his vision blurry and his mouth aching and dry from the gauze packed into it. He was tucked comfortably into the monk's sleep webbing. Kalsang hovered in the middle of the cabin, legs crossed and hanging in another webbing.

August squinted, sizing up his newly unmasked enemy with respect. The sophistication of this plot was astonishing in its scope. He had no idea where it was heading or how the monk was involved, as he surely must be.

Imagine rigging the Triton array with a dual transponder and to slip this past even Calvin30 for so long. August grinned despite himself - the little smart ass had finally missed something, and a security breach of this magnitude was an unforgivable mistake. Gudanko would have had plenty of lead time to prepare, to undercut his position, to poison the Board in advance of any new discovery, which explained perfectly the loss of confidence and threats to kill off the ET programme. Once the goods had been delivered, when August's grand bet had paid off spectacularly, they'd brought in the assassins. When that failed, the evil toad pulls in his conspirator, this harmless looking monk, to cross the solar system to clean up for him.

Of course, the Triton station had failed nearly a year past. To meet him here on such an exact trajectory, could it all have been planned from that far back? August groaned, and the monk pulled up next to him to replace the gauze on his forehead. Why, thought August, doesn't he simply finish me off now when I am incapacitated or, more to the point, before when I was more a wreck? Why help me?

Perhaps the monk simply needed his company for the long road home, but there was something else. August prided himself on being a good judge of people and the monk did not seem to have an insincere bone in his body. More likely he was also a pawn in this game. Perhaps they both simply being collected together, to be secretly dropped into some unnamed lunar crater when they arrived back home, conveniently disposing of two birds with one stone? How had the monk survived in the first place? Any sensible scenario eluded August. He decided to bide his time.

As the hours unrolled along the long passage to Mars, August became convinced of the monk's innocence. After watching him carefully, it occurred him that the monk seemed peculiarly guileless, more so than perhaps any person he had ever met. Even Gregori. More than that, this assumption came with a certain convenience. The demons of his own mind still lay waiting and were presently a more imminent threat. August allowed himself to relax and enjoy the rare luxury of a companion.

He regaled Kalsang with his story, his personal hagiography. August the visionary who rose as a humble servant among the Nets repairing the damaged Earth until he saw the chance to touch the stars. The conquering of Mirtopik and the launching of the remote listening posts to Europa and Triton. The collection of alien civilizations that had earned him respect even while living in the exile, an injustice that had been so ungraciously imposed upon him by his former comrades.

Kalsang proved to be a poor audience. He was polite but yawned and looked around out of boredom.

His mother. August had mentioned her as a footnote. Suddenly Kalsang was all questions. What was her name? How long had she lived and how had she died and how had he felt about it?

"She left us long before she died, and I have not visited her grave," August snapped.

"But I think you were a good son to her," Kalsang added hopefully.

"Yes, I was a good son. Yes, I have been. But she could not be a good mother."

August, red faced, had sulked for hours after that exchange, but was drawn back to the telling of his autobiographical epic. Some monk's bad manners should not interrupt the important task of practicing the reclamation of his legend.

Later, as he recounted the days in Siberia and the creation of Mirtopik, the unprecedented union of Net and Com that had catapulted him into space, Kalsang had the audacity to bring the story back to Illya.

"This man? You say you killed him?"

"Not myself, no, but I feel responsible for it. He killed himself really." August pushed on without explanation.

"And your friends from the Net, where are they now?"

Gregori and Anya, where had they gone? August had no idea.

"Why should I know?" he grimaced, and then, in a resigned voice, explained, "It has been too long, I do not know what has become of them. I should not care. You see, they turned against me. They were not my friends in the end."

"That is how it is," replied the monk with a sad shrug.

Backing off, the monk became a less active listener, allowing August to finish his stories uninterrupted, and this was preferable.

As August arrived at the end of his story, delivered in increments over days that had no boundaries, August noticed a focus return to the monk. As he mentioned the last transmission, the Golden Prize, the grand glory of his career and especially the building of the wormhole through space to Mercury Kalsang's inscrutable face turned pale. Why?

Those fleeting expressions surprised August but gave him an idea. Could Gudanko's betrayal also be the monk's tragedy? It didn't add up. Why would Gudanko kill the goose that laid the golden eggs? Unless the monk knew too much. Turning off the lights would not have damaged the assets, but it might have covered up some collaboration. What would have been significant enough to trigger homicide? Nothing made sense.

August continued, describing his ascent to divinity and the moment of treachery, where his rightful place at the prow of this grand new era had been taken by a pretender. Now, there was an opportunity to help right this wrong and return custodianship of this incredibly powerful technology to a true leader of vision and responsibility.

August sat up to his full height to emphasize the point, his hair straining to retrieve its former stature, weaving a spell to draw Kalsang out from behind that damn neutral civility. He appealed to the monk's sense of mission, which must surely sit behind a monk's decision to give up women and pleasure and life and go into exile.

As his center of gravity shifted, August began to slowly pivot backwards in the webbing. The pivot occurred so incrementally that August did not notice his predicament until too late. He finished dangling ridiculously in his webbing with his back to the monk, his hair grazing the floor. When Kalsang reached to help him, August brushed him angrily away and the gesture pushed him back into a bulkhead where he banged his head. Sputtering in indignation August roared, "Gudanko doesn't know who he is playing with."

He noticed an expression of concern flash across the monk's placid face. He had managed to touch something there. Steadying himself, August smiled awkwardly as he pulled himself together.

"There are dangers with the technology that this man does not fully appreciate. Only a responsible person should oversee it. Someone with a truly altruistic vision such as myself. Not this man with blood on his hands." August sighed theatrically. "Perhaps it is more than any man should be responsible for."

Kalsang's expression shifted into an intent gaze that felt like it was shining light into some dark corner of Augusts' soul that no one cared to look into anymore. August smiled weakly back. The monk raised his eyebrows to some unseen audience.

Days later it became clear to August that the monk was a threat, but not in the way he had first thought. The man was a thief. That naïve front was a ruse, which had lulled him into a false sense of security.

After his initial paranoia had relaxed, August took great comfort in this unexpected friendship. It felt like stepping out of a time machine dialled back twenty years. After his first attempt at reclaiming self-importance had fallen flat, it was a great relief to communicate with another human being as an equal. Kalsang and he shared silence together. There was simply nothing else to do. In that simplicity was much peace of mind. That was before August discovered the little fellow had a hidden food stash.

August had earlier done the math. They couldn't announce their arrival at Mars because Gudanko would be controlling those communications. His return to power depended on stealth and there was only so much food. To put himself in charge of the final allocation, to ensure his survival if the existing reserves proved too short for two people, August had carefully hidden away a portion. The rest they carefully rationed between them. It seemed like a perfect plan as the monk was so trusting and apparently had survived on very little on his journey up to this point.

"What are you doing there?"

"August-la?"

"In there. What are you doing?"

He could see Kalsang was unfamiliar with lying because, despite his words, the truth was written all over his face.

"Oh, it is very dirty back there. Isn't it?"

It wasn't.

"Are you eating that?"

"This?" Kalsang held forth the vitabars concealed in the folds of his robe. "No." He was bold, August gave him that.

"Then what are you doing?"

"Food stores are there." Kalsang pointed to the main pantry. "All should be in there, but it is not."

And what could August say to that? Admit that he was withholding vital supplies from his companion.

"Yes. I didn't realize."

"I am taking for later. Same as you, isn't it?"

August went back to do a quick count of inventory and checked his watch. More was missing than he had expected, especially given the small numbers of bars the monk had been carrying. Then he remembered how on past days his count had often seem to be off by a few bars that he had put down to bad memory, but it wasn't. The sneaky bastard had been slowly shifting supplies right under his nose. After helping Kalsang move both secret caches to the pantry, his worst fears were confirmed. The count still short. The monk had been eating his food.

"Kalsang. Are you sure this is all?"

The monk shrugged. "Someone must have eaten them."

And that was nothing August could object to, after all he himself had been eating extras.

After that the battle for resources was truly on. Both sharply monitored how much the other ate, drank, and even breathed. Portion size was a daily negotiation.

"I am heavier than you are, I need more," August objected.

They both looked on their neuroviews to check the metabolic requirements for each, each estimating different numbers to the other's detriment. Surely this scrawny monk didn't need that much. August went looking and discovered that Kalsang had squirrelled away some of his "eaten" bars.

"You were peeing too long August-la. Maybe you are drinking more than your share."

"Do you have to breathe so heavily when you meditate?"

"Only when I need to purify extra contamination from you. Besides when you sleep," Kalsang mimicked August thrashing around gulping like a fish. "and then you rush about wasting so much energy, isn't it?"

"This is my ship's food."

"This is my ship's gravity."

It went on and on, their distrust escalating. The damning moment came when August discovered Kalsang sending surreptitious signals through the Com channels.

"What are you doing?"

"I am trying to contact Mars."

"We can't do that. I told you." August grabbed Kalsang roughly. Kalsang resisted with surprising strength. They bounced around the cabin in the low gravity, each losing control of their momentum.

When they finally came to a rest Kalsang panted, "my friends are there."

August threw a flashlight at Kalsang, who ducked. "We already went over this. If they find out I am alive we will never make it back to Earth."

The monk folded his arms and did that annoying telepathic conversation with his invisible best friend. Then he relaxed into a determined gaze. "Okay."

The days passed in a grudging mutual standoff where they both stuck to being fair because neither could get away with anything else. Just to be on the safe side, August downloaded his memory of the monk's neurovisor security signature into his neurovisor and remote linked both, allowing him to eavesdrop on what the monk was seeing in his neuroview. Calvin30 had shown him how he could accomplish this trick with Mirtopik issued equipment. It had proven handy on several occasions.

In some time, the rusty sphere of Mars had grown large enough to see major surface features such as the great valleys and volcanoes. They had both sat down to rest after a particularly difficult repair. August noticed Kalsang's eyes narrowing into space before him, a sign that something was active in his neurovisor. August made an excuse to retire to his ship.

As soon as he was out of sight August tuned in.

"Cee zed triple ot forty-seven delta. Cee zed triple ot forty-seven delta. Emergency beacon one one five hundred echo Charlie. Transmission received by Mirtopik Mars One – name change courtesy of the Richy Rich dickheads that bought us out. Repeat transmission received."

August clenched his teeth. That treacherous lying snake.

The woman's voice continued, "if this is a real emergency you are transmitting on the wrong damn channel and are a biggest pack of wallies this side of Venus because you are on a sequence carrier for deep space communications and this is a dirt track at the end of nowhere, not a relay satellite." Behind the voice appeared a dusty and greased streaked face of indeterminate gender.

"If you aren't dead yet, show yourself because nobody was looking at this bloody thing and wouldn't be unless they were looking to do maintenance on some dodgy wayward nav sat like I was doing just now."

"Hi Terry. So good to hear you too."

"Kalsang?"

"Hi Terry. This is your friend."

"For real? Kalsang? You're shitting me."

"Yes Terry."

"It is? Nah. Can't be."

"Ta daaaa."

"I'm dreamin' or something. Kalsang. Holy shyte. Kalsang. But. Kalsang? Fucking oath. You're still alive? It was all over the news that you'd karked it. Jesus what a sad day that was. Christ, I don't fucking believe it. Kalsang?"

August heard metal dropping to the ground with a bang. "Ah shit, my foot. Who cares. Kalsang?"

"Please Terry. Please, please to be quiet. I must be a secret," responded the monk in hushed tones. "I am so very, very happy to see you too."

"Kalsang. It really is you?"

"Yes Terry. It is just the little cheeky bugger you know well coming back to haunt you again."

"Hah. You are that. This is your best one yet – come for my birthday, have you?"

"Yes, your birthday Terry. You look to be very beautiful this time. So young. Maybe your watch is running backwards," the monk giggled.

"Yeah," the woman was laughing, "You stitched me up there. Stupid taking the bloody thing into space with me and you kept changing the time on me while I slept."

"And you," the monk's voice was quivering with repressed laughter, "you, you kept yelling at us for being too late. Ha ha."

"Yeah ha bloody ha. I had to go all the way to Mars to get away from shit-stirring monks and their piss weak jokes." There was a pause while the woman blew her nose.

"And I had to almost leave the solar system to get away from a foul mouthed, wrathful Aussie. You are such an angry person Terry. Your face goes too red. Tsk tsk."

"You didn't come all this way to wind me up. Christ Kalsang you look like death warmed up for a party. How did you survive?"

"It was very hard Terry. So, so, so hard." The monk choked back a sob.

"Ah shit. Kalsang. Nah don't do that mate. Shit, I'm going all teary. Yeah."

"Yes Terry."

"Hey, don't worry about people hearing. I'm out in my shed. Why don't you want anyone to hear?"

August, listening in, leaned forward out of interest. Perhaps the monk would reveal more clues about Gudanko's schemes.

"Somebody is wanting to kill me Terry. Shhh, you must promise to me. Don't tell."

"Kalsang, we're all friends here."

"Aurora, Julia?"

"Ah mate. Bad news. Really awful bad news actually. Julia, she passed some while ago mate. Xiaoli, well." August could hear the woman choking back tears now. "Xiaoli had an accident. She's gone too mate."

"Oh, so terrible." They both went quiet for a time.

"I'm sorry to be the bearer of bad tidings. Rory too. Mate, she's in a bad way. Going Out. We've been doing it rough lately."

"Oh, too sad. Too sad. Julia was a very gentle person. Xiaoli, she is so, so bright."

"Yes," sniffed Terry, "yes she was. Hey, I have you going on orbital fly by. You're just shooting through, are you?"

"I cannot stay. We."

August clenched his teeth, expecting the monk to expose him.

"Meaning I. I, I must need water, and also food."

August considered forgiving Kalsang for this indiscretion. The communication had apparently occurred in confidence and more supplies were critical.

"Hmmm. Can give you that, but it comes with a passenger."

"Aurora?"

"Yep. Rory needs to get home fast."

What? They couldn't do that? In frustration, August ripped out the hair he had wound round his finger, knocking his neurovisor in the process. The neurolink became distorted and began to drop in and out.

"Maybe this is a problem Terry, isn't it? I will help Aurora for sure, necessary, but I am also in trouble."

"Look Kalsang, I can't see the problem. Why can't we just broadcast your situation back to the authorities? I'm sure they'd sort you out."

"Yes, but you, I understand you are now Mirtopik Com."

The neurolink began to shrink into tunnel vision as August ran his thoughts over the controls trying to correct it.

"Didn't see that one coming. Bought us for a song and dance and a wad of cash, which I s'pose everyone needs. Some of those Com arse-wipes have it in for you?"

"You cannot direct broadcast to Earth Terry."

"Ah, too right mate. In olden days with radio fine, no worries, but it's all laser now. They'd control that."

"Yes. Isn't it?"

"We're looking at putting Rory in hibernation and launching her into the flyby path of the next shuttle come 'round. She'd be drifting for months. The gods must be with us thank Christ. You couldn't have come at a better time. This way you'll get her home before they sling past. No one should be the wiser. I'll have to drop in extra emergency rations, which will have to slip past the hard-nosed bitch running things down here. I can, nah, yeah. Yeah, should be right."

August was furious. He had to stop himself from marching in on Kalsang and confronting him. Now he not only had to manage the monk, but also to play nursemaid to that same deranged woman who had only made his life difficult. How was he going to manage this? His hand, in an involuntary reflex reaching for his hair, upset his neurovisor again.

"So, who's trying to kill you mate?" Terry whispered.

August strained forward to hear the answer as the neurolink crackled and went dead.

It took some days for the monk to front up to him about the new passenger. August knew that Kalsang would eventually have to, and he enjoyed the brief sense of power that came with toying with him, eliciting small lies around the edges of the truth, making him break his vows, if the little liar even worried about them anymore.

To his disappointment this game didn't last long. Kalsang unapologetically blurted it out while they were working on sealing a breech in his Terrapod. Then the shoe was on the other foot as August had to put on his own show of mock horror and disgust. Kalsang merely waited him out, and then there was nothing more to say and they finished the job.

Still, August's feigned anger seeded the real thing, and over the following weeks he fell into a foul mood that nothing would dislodge. Even though the trade was a good one, a guarantee of life in exchange for a lifeboat, August was not looking forward to serving as a nursemaid to that woman who was trouble at the best of times when she wasn't Out. If Kalsang wanted to keep his little friend, then he could look after her. August had more pressing things to worry about, like the details of reclaiming his empire.

He imagined that she would smell, as if they would be transporting a corpse, if only bringing with her the staleness of sickness. Anyway, he was still healing himself from admittedly the same kind of madness. He didn't have the energy to support anyone else.

The bottom line was she was uninvited, or at least her presence was not cleared by him. And which ship was more well suited for her to stay in? Not the monk's tight quarters. In fact, the little man had taken to sleeping in the *Icarus* already. How would it hold three?

When the hour came, and the small coffin capsule dropped into the *Icarus* freight airlock, August was not pleased. The capsule was heavy and cumbersome as he and Kalsang struggled to heave it out of the lock. He strained his back. And then opening the box was complicated. A latch snapped back on his fingers, causing blood to pool under his nail, a wound that was not going to heal quickly.

Both he and Kalsang labored to pull open a sliding panel, which should have opened automatically. They unwrapped a cold buckygel stocking sitting inside the box. And there she was. The woman was enveloped in a web of wires sewn into and out of micropores all over her body. She jerked as August administered the adrenaline shot, and then they could see her softly begin to breathe.

Kalsang wandered off and August sat with Aurora as she lay sleeping. He turned over memories of the only time they had met. She had seemed much younger then, prettier. With nothing more to do he studied her mneme logs. Her story was incredible, and he admired her insane tenacity, a trait he could identify with. Something in her face, lying there, seemed pure and unfettered. Unlike him.

"Who do you love August?"

He had always seen Illya's question as a condemnation, a curse aimed at a man who was too cold for love. Now he saw the pity in it.

At that moment, a seed of an answer to Illya's question was planted in him. The seed's future was precarious, for it had landed in the sterile soil of the heart of a man with an enormous ego. Despite the odds, it might slowly take root, allowing August to fall in love. He didn't notice that it had happened. How could he notice it when he had never fallen in love before? He had played at love, believed himself a lover, stolen love from others, consumed women. However he had never fallen in love. And he would not realise that he had until, days and weeks and months later, when he understood that his thoughts had rarely been far from this person. From Aurora.

CHAPTER 32

Aurora

Denali crouched on a sand dune and howled as the strange round clouds slowly lifted the Beloved away into the sky.

He had smelled the Beloved being carried off, through half closed sleepy eyes he saw Her being lifted in. His ears pricked up. Although he had scratched on the hatch they had ignored him. The smell was bad. Something was very wrong - with Her - with the Beloved. She was hurt. When They left She was not among Them.

Now the Beloved must be going up too, following the strange clouds. Away from him. So far away.

Denali whimpered his confusion and dismay.

The strange clouds shrunk until all four became one and then, after a burst of light, became nothing.

Denali dashed around a field of rocks hunting made-up prey. He had never seen prey, but he knew what it was. He pounced and dashed and chewed on his paws. He put his mark on rocks, so She could find her way back. To Him. The Beloved. He sat in Her sled and waited and slept and waited very long and slept.

Grease Smell Friend looked through the hole in the hatch and opened it and called for him. Denali half wagged his tail, whimpering.

"Hey cobber. You lonely too?" Grease Smell Friend wrapped her long soft padded arms around his shivering body and groomed him and scratched his stomach as he rolled over.

"This place is really starting to suck."

Denali grunted and stretched to expose a larger area of his stomach.

"Come with me mate. It's cold out here."

Denali stretched and got up. As they walked across the dirt he looked backwards towards the place in the sky where the strange clouds and the Beloved had disappeared. Then he followed Grease Smell Friend inside.

* * * * * * * * * * * * *

There was no meaning anymore. The forces buffeting Aurora's body mixed with the random sensations and memories rearranging in her mind like pieces of shattered colored glass rolling in a kaleidoscope. Blinking moments of flame and orange ground falling away flickered quickly behind the horizon of her attention. The sudden silence replacing the after-burn blended with the remembered silence of the vast red plains. Waijungari reached out for her, grasping for what had been denied him, keeping parts of her while the rest of her plunged noiselessly out into darkness. Flashes of adulthood, childhood, dream, hallucinations of strange creatures with many heads, the roar of rushing ocean - all came jumbled in no particular order.

Her disembodied perspective, floating in a chaos of water, watched fragments of experience spinning past with random debris. She saw them carry the empty husk of a body, distantly recognised as her own, out of the dry dust, down fantastic walls of stone, into and out of hatches, airlocks, doors, plastic membranes. Soft hands plying her rigid muscles and the tender sensation of a polymer tongue licking her cheeks - moments of human and robotic tenderness that temporarily pulled everything back together again. The irregular pulse of her madness. A pulse. It was all that remained of her, this kindness of others was all that remained. A pulse. Punctuating the endless emptiness of being into which she was dropping. A pulse. Fading gradually, returning unexpectedly, by turns more tentative, becoming softer. A pulse.

Aurora had almost fallen completely into the long quiet when she noticed the eyes. Brown eyes with flecks of green, familiar in a very distant way - a background detail of a memory accompanied by a wince of distaste. The eyes, intently staring into hers, were masked in hardness but there was something of herself in them. She mirrored their intensity back - a force of exertion her body had nearly forgotten. This force became her new centre, a passion. An ocean of life welled up under unstoppable pressure. As her gaze penetrated the hard mask, the eyes flinched and jerked away.

Aurora screamed.

From her fog she recognised she was in a new place. Two men exchanged glances. One retreated and the other came forward. She recognised in him an old friend although his exact identity was obscured. The recognition brought a happiness. A pulse.

"Aurora?"

"Ka-ka-kals."

"Okay Aurora," said her friend with a golden smile. "You are going to be okay now."

"Thank you."

"It is okay now Aurora. Please you rest."

The other man came over and looked at her hesitantly. "What are we going to do with her?" he asked with purposeful dispassion.

"What to do?" shrugged her long ago friend, raising his eyes to confront the brown green gaze of the other man. "What to do August-la? Ahh."

Aurora turned her head weakly to watch the other man stalk away and felt she did not like him but that she felt drawn to him. A pulse.

Many moments passed like his. Aurora wasn't sure how many. It was as if time had only tentatively come into being - like a random old acquaintance who might leave again at any opportunity. With time came pain, an ache. It was this long ache without beginning or end that held her together. Ache held her muscles to her bones, her movements to her muscles, and her mind with her body. One was the slight ache of simulated gravity that pulled her toward the floor and allowed her to haul her emaciated self from one side of the cramped living quarters to the other, over and over again - this ache held her insides together with the outside. There were others.

"Do you need some help?" The irritating man, August, always asked her in the same doubtful tone.

"If you don't care, why do you keep asking?" Aurora grimaced as she pulled herself steadily forward into the ache. She had only recently recovered her speech.

August shrugged, "have it you own way." As he once again went glowering off, he paused to look back and for a moment Aurora saw disappointment in his face. So he would ask again, soon, with the same feigned lack of interest, and again she would tell him to bugger off. She began to look forward to it.

Occasionally she let him help her, and she enjoyed his graceful movement as he positioned her in the physio equipment. August had a way about him that told her he was confident with women. The way he placed her foot into the webbing. The way he steadied her hand to practice her grip. It was sexy, which was an out of the hat feeling for her. Her first reaction was to resent him for it. She had made her own way, thank you, further than any man. But she found herself succumbing to the feeling. Wouldn't it be fine to just let herself go? Kalsang was sleeping or meditating. August's face was so close. She looked into his eyes.

"August Bridges?"

"Yes."

The dream ended abruptly. Aurora scrambled away like she had been cosying up to a death adder. How could August be August Bridges? And Kalsang Kalsang? The only two persons she knew for sure were dead. Besides Xiao Li. And she remembered seeing her too.

"Are you okay?"

August, August Bridges, reached over towards her. Aurora reacted as if he were a zombie about to grab her. She hit him with the extinguisher they had been using as a dumbbell and, panicking, looked desperately for a place to hide. She pushed past August, holding his head and disoriented, and leapt into the airlock corridor. On the other side Kalsang was standing up to greet her, smiling in a way that seemed suddenly menacing. August was coming behind her, Kalsang in front. Ghosts. She was surrounded. Then she spotted the emergency lock-down levers on the airlocks for both ships and pulled them in turn without thinking. Panels slammed into place, almost catching August's arm, which he jerked back at the last second.

Their heads hovered there, looking through the view portals from either side, while Aurora held her knees and hyperventilated.

What was going on? Nothing made sense. Did souls go to heaven in space ships? It seemed a slow way to go about it. Kalsang, there was some logic for his presence, but August Bridges? That was just weird. It was a dream. It had to be. A dream. A dream she could deal with, but this was too long and drawn out to not be something else.

"Aurora," said the intercoms, two voices saying her name at once.

"Aurora, what did I do to frighten you?"

"Aurora, please you be peaceful, okay?"

"You lot can't exist. It isn't possible."

Aurora sat there, determined to wait them out, while they took turns telling her the most unlikely tales. Kalsang, making his way back home from a failed station at the edge of the solar system hooking up with August, who'd been camped out on Mercury after surviving a missile hit. And the both of them picking her up like some hitchhiker on the way back to Earth. She was surprised her imagination could cook this up.

She waited and waited. August Bridges? The feelings she was about to give into. She didn't want to think about that. She didn't even want to imagine that. The smarmy asshole who was behind every disaster in her life. Twisting her words to mean the opposite in front of the whole world. Pretending to be her friend. The guy leading the charge to bulldoze the remnants of life of Mars, of a whole planet, when they didn't even know if it existed or not. If he had just backed off, would she have? Would Xiao Li still be alive? She couldn't bear to think of it.

Aurora fainted into her exhaustion but awoke from sleep to find herself still in the dream, and hungry, and feeling alone. She saw her Dad tapping on the portal, inviting her to leave. She opened the latch into Kalsang's ship and sat down beside him while he meditated, hugging him and weeping. She could feel August's eyes following her as she did.

"I can't take this Kalsang."

"It's okay Aurora. It is just like this way. Please relax." And he took her hand in his and leaned into her. The simple gesture made her feel protected.

"I am happy you are alive," Aurora said, "even if you are just in my head."

Kalsang gave her a comical look that was reassuringly typical of him. "Thank you. I am happy to be alive here with you."

After that Aurora tried to let things be as they were. She unlatched August's door and he didn't eat her head, but her guard was up, and she insisted on doing her exercises alone after that. She sensed that this hurt him, but he kept up a good front. He didn't deserve that much from her, but as the days passed she began to suspect he was less an evil man and more the idiot she had first pegged him as. Too much of a wanker to realise his own impact on others. Aurora found she couldn't really hate him, which was disheartening.

One night she dreamt about them together.

They were floating, enclosed tightly together in a wicker basket, beneath a dozen variously colored weather balloons they'd somehow cobbled together. Below them stretched Antarctica - a frozen empty mass bordered by mountains whose names she knew. It was freezing and the only thing to do about it was to hold to the warmth in each other. She didn't want to be anywhere else in the universe until the basket scraping against the gravelly ice interrupted and they disembarked, heading separate ways.

"What do you think of him Dad?"

"You could do worse, Darl."

She woke without memory but with a sense of sadness and loss. As her eyes opened she fought back the daily panic, twisting around searching for landmarks to steady herself and seeing only walls.

Pulling off the sleep webbing holding her along the wall, she rotated her feet slowly down to the floor, pushing lightly from a brace until the nanohooks in her stocking gripped the carpet. Kalsang and August were hanging from the walls opposite her like sideways bats, still sleeping. With tentative steps she made her way to the nearest view screen showing the Earth at normal magnification and reached out to trace her fingers in circles carefully around the vivid blue planet. It felt bigger than yesterday and the day before and the day before that. The display announced that they were now one month away from arrival. Halfway back to the Earth from Mars. The voyage so far had seemed like a dream, but suddenly it seemed they were progressing to a destination. Aurora flattened her palm against the Earth's projected centre and closed her eyes.

Wheatbelt Wallaby wandered up into the stars trying to pick her place among them, with the other sisters. You would think with all that space it would be easy for her to find a spot not taken, but it wasn't so. There wasn't much of any place to rest.

"Can you feel it?" a grating voice disturbed her reflections. She ignored August while contemplating the oddness of her thoughts and feeling the distance that still lay between her and her planet. She ignored him until it became apparent that he wasn't going to leave of his own accord.

"I can," he continued, taking Aurora's dismissive shrug as his cue. "I felt it a little on the Moon. The distance I mean. I thought I understood a little about Outlanders, but then I was still too close to the Earth. Anytime I could just open a skylight and see it. So brilliant - so serene. You could almost reach out and touch her. Every month, for a few days, we would pass through Her magnetotail and the static electricity would stand my hair up on end. Any day I could climb on the Ferry and, in a few days, be back. After I was lost out there. I've never felt so lost. I can really feel Her even though it's only a picture. I can, can't you?"

It was true. The small blue and white ball drew Aurora in, tugging together the pieces of her 'self' from their random places - calming the endless sea inside of her. She pressed her palm deeper into the Earth's power and felt her body jerk involuntarily.

"You can feel it can't you? Can't you? Scientists can't measure it - such a subtle force - ground down the whole goddamn Second Wave. Such biologically sentimental creatures we humans are, but not for long - not for long. If we can reach other Earths."

"Leave me alone!"

Of course, he took this personally.

"Hey. Where am I going to go? It's driving me crazy locked up by myself for months. Now I finally have some company but with your brooding and our monk friend there distant and muttering away, what kind of company is that? It feels more alone than when I was alone. All I want is some companionship. Can't you just give me something? Anything damn it?" August bent over hyperventilating.

"I, I'm sorry. It came out wrong."

"Okay. Okay." He sighed and steadied himself against the railing. "You think? I, I don't get it. I get it, believe me, I do. I'm barely holding myself together too. But I need to talk, to be with you." He started to tear up. "I just need to."

Aurora reached over and hesitantly stroked August's back, feeling the bones protruding through his depleted skin. "It's okay." She ignored her first impulse to pull back and pressed softly into his back. Even that light pressure moved him away in the light gravity until he slid into the wall. He felt so delicate, as if her hands would push through him like a tissue. Funny she hadn't noticed that, he'd seemed so strong when he was helping her. He shivered and tightened himself.

Aurora ran her fingers up and down August's back, exploring the ridges and depressions, as with the plains and cliffs on Mars and the long scrubby fields of home, she felt stories there. The thin frailty of his skin scarcely containing the life within it. What he said was true. She felt in his vulnerability, his exposure to the void around them, that in that way his story was the same as hers.

For a few moments, it seemed that Wheatbelt Wallaby had found an open spot in the universe. Her star, while alone, could only wander, but the line connecting her to another star contained a story, and a story contained all the rest.

"Thank you."

She felt him tense up when he said it, like he was unfamiliar with the words. She dropped her hand and left him.

Kalsang walked in with a handful of vitabars. "We should have breakfast together?"

They sat chewing quietly, their minds intent on the rationed morsels, as they reverently watched the Earth light beaming down on them.

Their days fell into a routine as the voyage meter slid past three quarters of the way home. Aurora felt increasingly grateful to wake up into the simple narrative of three travelling companions. Two men. Kalsang, unfailingly kind and attentive, but who was remote in his self-possession. August, brittle and abrasive, but who was, in a way which was not entirely unwelcome, drawn to her. Kalsang and August and Aurora. Mates. Of a sort.

The intense blue and white presence of the Earth continued to grow subtly in the neuroview, and Aurora felt herself come together bit by bit. The effect was not subjective, she felt it in her body. They were becoming by small increments more whole as the planet grew before them. It was a scientific phenomenon. As August had said, it happened with everyone, but nobody knew why.

Aurora was coming home and that meant she was getting better. The moods of her shipmates also began to improve as they continued. The tension between Kalsang and August seemed to dissipate. The relief of being able to predict their healing in this linear way, from moment to moment, produced a background of pleasant euphoria. Her recovery was accompanied by Kalsang's peacefully murmured prayers - the first sounds she heard as she awoke and the last sounds into which she would drift as she fell asleep.

August, with the spark coming back to those brown green eyes, could be quite the larrikin, although Aurora kept her guard up against his charms. That she found him attractive in anyway was still too disturbing. How could she contemplate any connection with August Bridges? Any man on Earth would have been preferable, and she hadn't let them in either. Even extending an olive branch of friendship seemed at times to be going too far.

Aurora watched August while he slept, snoring lightly. She wondered at his ordinariness, the fragility he had shown her before reburying it, and the warmth that was somehow developing between them. Aurora had hated him but somehow had never been able to dismiss him. Aurora decided that what she had always found impressive about August Bridges was that he never would quit.

Up in the sky, Wheatbelt Wallaby wondered about her star sisters out there, in the Pleiades and back on Mars. Would she ever catch up with them? It would be good to hang out and be beautiful together. To have people admire them. Spending too much time with the brothers was starting to grate.

As tomorrow became tangible, the mood began to harden. The shell of the ship became more like a prison and the distance between them and getting home became increasingly intolerable. The space within the linked ships seemed to shrink, rations became insufficient, and the smells were intolerable. Arguments broke out, some even started by Kalsang. This was a well-documented phenomenon but anticipating it didn't make Aurora feel any better.

She increasingly retreated into sleep as the depression began to bite. As she slept, the events of the day merged with her dreams as her mind shifted seamlessly between worlds and times. She dreamt about Dad dying again and awoke back in her webbing, yearning for the clarity of the darkness. She was afraid, and the feeling did not sit well with her.

She walked to the galley and dragged a cup of coffee from the beverage hose. Kalsang was there, mashing his vitabars into strange conical shapes and lining them up on a console.

"Torma," he said and added no explanation.

She reached over and flicked one of the little towers off the console. Kalsang reached over and flicked her on the forehead. They traded expressions of mock anger, and Aurora blinked first.

"Karma," he said in a serious voice.

Aurora reached across him, grabbed the flicked bar out of the air as it rebounded off the floor, and stuffed it in her mouth.

"Torma," she mumbled.

Kalsang giggled as Aurora, issuing sprays of crumbs, failed to contain herself. She spat out the remains into her hand and made a show of reforming the squishy mass into a cone and placing it back on the console.

"Hmmm," Kalsang inspected the result, "needs work."

"It does, doesn't it?"

"Okay for now. You are just beginner". Kalsang rolled his eyes.

"You got that right."

They sat and regarded each other with affection. Then Kalsang stood up, grabbed her by the ears and touched his forehead to hers. "We are going home," he said before heading off towards the toilet.

"Yes. We are." Aurora took a drag of coffee from the hose, leaned back and admired the blue planet hanging on the wall console. "Yes, we are." She mostly felt happy, for want of a better word, being around Kalsang. There was no possibility of rejection, and more importantly, no hint of clinging. He loved purely, and it made her feel safe.

August was in another category. When Aurora finished her coffee, she stood up out of her webbing to stretch and looked around to see him standing in the doorway watching her intently, as ever.

"What're you looking at?" Her false annoyance was ruined by an involuntary blush.

"You."

"You must be desperate. Can't you look at other girls for a change."

He grimaced, which turned into a grin and held up his thin pale hand up over his eyes and pivoted his head to indicate that he was surveying the competition. "You are different to all of them," he announced.

Aurora mirrored his grin. "Thanks mate. That's the best compliment I've had in centuries. Could that difference you mentioned be you're starved for choice? I'd imagine in your day you've had any woman you wanted."

And it was true. August, even dragged through the muck like he'd been, still retained redeeming features. For one he moved, even in low gee, with an easy confidence that was the more powerful for being understated. At the same time, he could come off as a big dag. Even matted and unkempt his hair looked that stupid that the threat in him was muted and it was difficult maintain barriers against him. It didn't help that Aurora's libido seemed to be flickering on after months in deep freeze and years in captivity. So, there was that.

"Seriously, that's all it is, isn't it?" She felt sorry to point out his delusions, but she'd seen herself in the mirror, especially after the wear and tear of Mars. Of course, these days he wouldn't claim any prizes either, but he would recover. "As soon as you set foot back Earthside I imagine you'll be swarmed."

"That's true," he agreed casually, yawning. "But still, you're different."

"How's that?"

"You don't want anything from me."

"You're not far wrong." But of that Aurora wasn't entirely sure. On some level, mostly physical though off and on with other parts of the package, she was starting to want something from him with a confronting intensity that she was sure had something to do with having just come back from the dead and also being truly starved for choice. There was no question her body desperately wanted his to be in it. This had been the case for weeks, and with a growing force. And all she had to do to get there, as was generally the case with men, and definitely the case with August, was to get out of her own way. Unfortunately, for many, many, many reasons that was a horrible idea.

August sensed her ambiguity and shrugged indifferently in a way that said, "you don't want anything from me, but you still need me." And then he snort-laughed, which was obviously not the effect he was looking for.

Aurora laughed too loud back. To hell with pretence, this was the first good mood she'd had in awhile.

Then they sat back in some webbing smiling with each other for a while, chatting a bit about life, not too full on, and in turns quietly acknowledging the Earth hanging between them on the wall.

"How do you know him? The monk? Kalsang?"

"Kalsang. We're mates. He's as good as they come."

Her answer seemed to annoy August. "It doesn't look so big," August said waving towards the Earth as he got up.

Something about the way he said that was like a splash of cold water. The arrogance. Whole planets were trifles to this man's ego. It brought back in a rush everything about August that Aurora hated. How had he gotten off the hook about his decisions on Mars? Just because she was tired and needed to pretend, didn't excuse her acting like some schoolgirl. Someone she loved had died because of this man.

"I do need something from you."

"Anything."

"Answers."

"Sure."

"First off, with my broadcast at the AGM, do you use people like that often?"

August gave her a thoughtful look. "I use anyone and everything that comes my way to get where I need to go. I don't make any excuses for that."

"Were you ever serious about protecting indigenous life on Mars, or was it just something you pulled out to use me?"

"I did think about it. I still do."

"And yet it doesn't stop you."

August looked annoyed. "You know the most about this right? Has anything you've ever reported directly confirmed any part of your theory?"

That hurt. "It's not just my theory."

"Sure. But did you find anything? After everything, years, millions spent, anything?"

"No."

"We have standard xenobiological sterility protocols. You yourself conformed to those when you were on Mars."

"Screw you. It's not the same thing. We are scientists. The kind of people who come through that space hole of yours. Who's going to control them?"

"Over some hypothetical?"

"I'll give you a hypothetical. What don't you know about this wonderful invention you've downloaded from the other side of the galaxy?"

August flinched, and Aurora knew she'd struck a nerve. "You don't know, do you? There is technology in there that human science won't understand for maybe hundreds of years. You've just gone and whipped it up following the recipe, haven't you?"

August began slowly pulling his hair, an action she'd noticed him doing when agitated. "Something this important, you can't expect us to just sit on it?"

"So then, maybe you've doomed us all. Did you think about that?"

"It's operating technology, I'm sure the aliens have investigated it."

"Have investigated it? Been careful? Like we have? I'll bet there's more chance of that thing blowing up in our faces than there being life on Mars. Can't you see? We shouldn't muck around with things we don't properly understand."

"It doesn't work that way. It's the nature of life to expand."

"Keep it in your pants mate."

"What? Look, I want to do all this the right way. Humans will do what they are going to do. Even with the Ecolution, do you think that people are going to stop degrading the only world we can live on? We are only doing it slower. We have this very small window to point those attentions off away from the Earth. After that we won't have enough resources left and we will be stuck."

"That's what you were thinking when you wiped out our scientific budget on MASO. That that was a good way to protect life on Earth by killing off life on Mars?"

"I did no such thing."

"Of course, you didn't. Someone who works for you did."

"No. Listen to me," he commanded. "I did no such thing. And I would not have made that decision."

"Then, how?"

"I continually told people that Mars was the first-place people would want to go with our wormhole, so we needed to be prepared."

"What do you think people were going to read into that?"

"Your budget should have been increased, not cut."

"With all the big bucks floating around for Mars, or were you spending them on something else?" She had him there.

August put on a show of considering what she said, but Aurora could see the effort that involved.

"People sometimes take what I say and run with it."

"You think?" All that power. How could he be so blind to the responsibility that came with it.

"It doesn't matter. In the long run we will have done things right."

"My Dad used to say, 'In the long run we're dead.' That conversation of yours almost killed me and it killed my friend."

"Wait a second. You're blaming me? Me? I read your mneme logs. Wait. Those were your decisions. Not even yours really. You went Out."

"Piss off."

"No. Aurora. That was horrible. I don't mean to say that. Look, it was an accident. And you were sick."

Aurora dropped her head. All these reasons, so familiar to her and they didn't help.

"I'm sorry."

What for? For her madness, or for his lack of accountability. She wasn't sure which was more tragic.

A small hole appeared in the middle of the holoscreen of Earth with a loud bang and an alarm sounded. The skin of the ship resounded with a clatter that reminded Aurora of a summer hail storm pounding on a tin roof.

"Micro-meteors!" August shouted.

Aurora scanned the reverse side of the room for the exit hole. She reached down in a corner and held up a small pebble. "It didn't make its way through. See the dent?" She pointed at a black mark on the wall. Kalsang bent over to inspect it with her.

"What are you two idiots doing?" thundered August. "Into the Safe. We can't clean up if we're dead." And as if to prove his point another hole banged open in the floor right next to Aurora's foot.

This was real. Adrenaline fired through her as time both speeded up and slowed down. More cosmic bullets swished by, one grazing her shoulder and opening a gash. Kalsang pulled her to the floor with him, forgetting that the micrometeors could just as easily come from below. He had blood on him too, although Aurora wasn't sure if it was his or hers. The hiss of escaping gas was loud. Her lungs were already struggling in the rapidly dropping pressure. The cocoon of illusion separating them from the vast and deadly vacuum around them had been punctured. They might die in seconds.

August motioned them over. Together they yanked open a thick nanogem alloy hatch on the bulkhead. While August bravely held the hatch for them they squeezed into a cramped space that forced their bodies to curl into one another. Imminent death retreated with a twist of the latch locking the hatch down behind them.

It was dark. The Safe had only been designed for one person. There they waited until the banging from the micrometeorite shower ended as abruptly as it began.

Kalsang was all right. It was Aurora's blood not his. He moved sparingly and tucked tightly into the corner, taking up little space. His soothing rounds of mantras seemed build a protective shield around them. August was something else. After hours bundled on-top of one another he was completely wearing on her nerves. His hair angled into her face and got up her nose. He twitched and squirmed and whinged. He even went so far as to imply that they were somehow invading his space, taking up his oxygen, since they were on his ship. As if they happened to be in the Safe on the Kalsang's ship the story would be different.

After a long time spent mushed against August and contemplating murder, the all clear alarm sounded and August, with exaggerated movements, pulled out the evacuation suit capsule from its compartment. What he discovered when he had it opened caused him to howl. Only the helmet remained in the capsule, the rest of the suit was missing.

"Shit," August yelled and turned to look at them accusingly as if hiding essential survival equipment was a favorite pastime of theirs. "The suit. It's gone!"

"Yes," replied Kalsang in a neutral voice, "Isn't it?"

"There isn't enough atmosphere in here for all of us to stay much longer." August carried on like a pork chop depleting what atmosphere was left.

"I think the both of us would be happy to leave you to it," Aurora snapped and then she did a crazy thing. Whether it was from desperation borne of claustrophobia or from the sheer stupidity of anger or some sense of doing the right dumb thing, Aurora grabbed the evac helmet and jammed it over her head. The silicon sleeve sealed tightly around her neck, nearly choking her, and she looked through the heavily scratched and fingerprinted visor back at August. The inside of the helmet stunk of stale perspiration and fear.

"Someone? You've been wearing this haven't you?" Aurora glared at August bitterly. "You didn't put it back. This is your stuff up." Then she realised he couldn't hear her.

August tried to pull her back, but Aurora kicked free and crawled into the Safe airlock shaft. The hatch snapped shut, almost catching August's hand.

One quick hiss later and Aurora felt her skin bruise all over as her blood pressed out in the near vacuum. She almost fainted from the pain but, somehow despite her panic and confusion, she found her way into the space between the Icarus and Garuda, there she activated the coupling airlock. It hadn't been punctured by the micrometeors. Lucky. As survivable air pressure returned she swooned. Coming to was agonizing. It felt as if her body had been beaten over every square centimeter. She banged on the stuck latch of a storage locker until it opened and the two space suits within fell out at her, flailing about her like drowning rag dolls.

Painfully, Aurora inched her way into one of the suits and swore as the neck couplings failed to match to the helmet she had donned in the Safe. Pulling the neck seal of the helmet she was wearing over her head was murder, but she finally managed to pry it off together with a clump of her hair. The new space helmet went on easily. After her neurovisor patched into the suit's computer, and after checking the diagnostic panels appearing in her neuroview, she purged the airlock and stepped back into the mayhem of their living quarters.

The micrometeors had made a dog's breakfast of the place. Rapid pressure drops had sprung latches on storage lockers and the contents had spilled everywhere. Optical fibre and wires from burst panelling wove around the room like snakes. Worms and insects from the Terrapod roamed the air. Much of the debris was clustered around puncture points where it had been pulled by the sudden vacuum. Most of the holes were already plugged this way. Lucky again. If they hadn't been Aurora realised she would not have survived the vacuum. She'd been so stupid.

Aurora stuffed the spare space suit down the Safe airlock for August or Kalsang to use.

"Special delivery," she croaked, throat hoarse, as she slid down the wall and collapsed.

August emerged. He gave her a concerned, though perfunctory and painful, pat on the shoulder before turning to inspect the damage, shaking his head as if the raw chaos around them was somehow the result of shoddy workmen. Aurora watched him with a feeling of profound disappointment. This man had spent his life living off the sweat of others, casually screwing around with lives he had no idea about and was in person the biggest pain. Of course, her honest complaint was that she had been idiot enough to be drawn in by him. Although the effort was incredibly painful, Aurora struggled to her feet to stand by him. In the process she lost her footing and fell awkwardly in the slow gravity.

He caught her. She struggled against his uninvited assistance, but he held firm and she gave in only to the practicality of it.

"I can handle it."

August looked at her sternly. "I can't believe you're still alive." His voice cracked, and his eyes were red. Had he been crying?

"Give me a few minutes. We'll see". Aurora attempted to steady herself by slumping over a railing and broke into a coughing fit. "Stop that."

August stopped hammering her on the back. "Oh, is that hurting you?"

Answering was wasted effort and Aurora let it go.

"Sit down. I can take care of this now." There was deep concern in his voice, but she was in no mood take orders from him. Aurora pulled herself up as much as she could and glared at him. "Like you took care of the suit in the Safe?"

He huffed but dropped it. As she bent over to place a pressure cup over a hole, the black spots in her eyes ballooned and she began to pass out.

August carried her carefully back to the Safe airlock. "What's going on?" Aurora slurred.

"The monk can work better than you," he replied dryly before laying her carefully down and closing the airlock.

Kalsang greeted her warmly when she got inside, helped her out of the suit, and gently and very lightly massaged her back and head with warm, healing hands until the black spots dissipated. The casual kindness of it made her cry. Before he suited up himself he showed her how to link her neuroview into the Safe connect point.

"You will need to communicate with us through August's suit because it is from his ship. This suit is from my ship," he explained before he pulled on his helmet and crawled into the airlock.

Once again Aurora was alone, but this time it was not her preference. She watched through August's helmet cam as they worked, slowly and methodically, to clear and patch the leaks. Kalsang once stopped to push through extra provisions for her, but the two men did not return to the Safe to eat with her. The reason for this was to conserve the limited air supply of the Safe. Aurora felt excluded. Out of pride, she refused to talk to August through his link and from his side he did not seem to be aware that she was looking through his eyes. After many long hours of this isolation and ever-growing loneliness the memories began to trickle back. Her friends - Julia and Xiao Li. The blur of her rescue. She thought about Terry telling her about how Xiao Li had been killed trying to rescue her. She cried.

While idling and chewing a Vitabar, she patched into August's link to check up on their progress. She winced in annoyance as his voice came into her head over the neuroview. She sat up when she realised August was speaking to someone other than Kalsang.

The man he was talking to was an odd-looking character, and somehow familiar. He wasn't much to look at, thin and balding and over-groomed, but there was something about his eyes that somehow drew Aurora in, as if he was her trusted friend holding intimate secrets even though he had no idea she was looking in. His voice was fluid and friendly and calm. His words seem musical, falling and rising in a melodic cadence and seemed to rhyme more often than was normal, like he was speaking mystic poetry. August's voice, even though speaking to the man in dismissive terms, gave away a hint of enthrallment.

"You were expecting me to call?" August demanded.

"Don't be so surprised Boss," responded the man with nonchalant deference, "I stocked your craft with enough kit to make it the long way back around. The physics of that track is exact enough to make a guess. So, yes."

"You let me hang out here for months without contacting me. Do you have any idea what I've been through?"

"No Boss. It isn't possible for me to imagine. Do you think I planned that sabotage? Would I connect with you until you came within a safe enough range for a clandestine laser line? I assume that's why you did choose just now to occasion a call? Otherwise you'd have signed in from Mars via the Mirtopik grid."

"No one even tried." It was a strained comment. The hint of dejection in August's voice made Aurora feel almost protective of him. There was loneliness in his power, a vulnerability that she hadn't previously guessed at.

"We did try but no reply. With no signal back from your ship you were just dead and buried up in heaven Boss. No loss to Gudanko though. You can guess how efficiently he slid into your office. High drama for your funeral but few tears the day after. Hard to get in, easy to go - ride with the tide - you know the score."

"What is the score, Calvin30?"

The number at the end of the name identified the man as a clone. That explained where Aurora had seen his face, although unlikely his in particular. Clones. Their very existence told her how far Coms could go and why they couldn't be trusted. Along with a wrecked planet. Little things like that.

"Gudanko's playing things his own way these days. Space isn't the place he's facing. The man is planning to Swiss cheese the planet for increased efficiency. A logical follow on from a fellow of his methodology."

August's eyes squinted, and Aurora could hear his breath tighten. "That goddamn fool."

"So, Mars has been spared. That crazy lady paleontologist will be pleased at the reprieve."

Aurora sighed. Maybe her work still had a chance to succeed.

"He's insane. We shouldn't muck around with things we don't properly understand. Someone told me that and it's got me thinking."

Aurora smiled and willed August to leave it at that.

"Boss, I'm at a loss."

"Think about it. Even bringing anti-matter down to the Earth to power something like that would be incredibly risky. Even if everything goes okay, we will just eat our future faster. Efficiency isn't the way. We learned that 100 years ago."

"What would you then recommend?"

Be content with less, voted Aurora.

"The technology will never be safe on the Earth. It's our only home. We need to talk to the Revs."

"That good oil is on the boil."

"Right. Good. Then somehow you have to move us down to the planet."

"You will not feel this a satisfying fix Boss, but Gudanko will need to rescue you."

August's eyes blinked at that. "What? That is insane. Gudanko cannot know. Not now. I absolutely forbid it."

Why August would be so alarmed stymied Aurora. Was the man's pig-headed pride so big that he couldn't stand to have to rely on his rival, even in a life or death situation? She almost said something.

"August. You know I cannot entreat to fly the fleet. I have no pull for control. Think this one through. Gudanko will just have to see in your face that he's taken your place. If he thinks he holds all the cards he will carefully deal, but out of his hand he may throw them away."

"Are you saying if he can't control our fates he will see us dead?"

"Umm, yes." The stranger seemed momentarily puzzled by the comment. "There are many ways. It is easy to die in space."

"So, the only way to survive is to put our lives in the hands of the man who wants me dead?"

A puzzled frown winked across the stranger's face and Aurora realised the cause was August's mixing of pronouns. The man didn't know about Kalsang and herself. He was quite sharp to pick that up.

"You are right - I don't like it - but we can get out of Gudanko's clutches better when we are on the ground."

"More room to move Boss."

August's helmet turned to scan the room and picked up Kalsang pulling debris away to patch a leak. The monk smiled and gave a thumbs-up.

"Calvin30?"

"Ah, August. There is someone with you."

"You didn't know about that? Have I surprised you?" August seemed genuinely pleased for his lackey to be at a loss for words.

"August? How?"

"I thought you knew everything Calvin30? How is this? My crafty friend does not even know what is going on in Mirtopik Com? What do I employ you for?"

"Who is he?"

"The monk. That monk from the Triton array you idiot. The one we lost. Well guess who found him?"

August was clearly enjoying himself. Beyond the expected shock of the near impossible, Aurora noted, there was something else that struck her as odd. Did a flash of terror cross the stranger's face? "Incredible, isn't it? We were out by Mars and this guy just appears out of nowhere. How is that possible? What do you think?"

The stranger was shaking, visibly unnerved by Kalsang's presence. What was that all about?

"What did he say?"

"What did he say? What did he say? You don't know? The infallible Calvin30. Do I have to tell you everything? Nothing much actually. That he survived the destruction of the Triton array and found me by accident. Can you believe that? Do you believe that?" August challenged.

The stranger shifted uncomfortably, and then slowly his smile returned. "No Boss, I do not see how it is so. It is impossible. The probability is infinitesimal."

"Do you think he is a plant by Gudanko? Ha. And you think you play a long game Calvin30? The man must already know. What do you think?"

"I, I do not know. It makes no sense but makes more sense." The smile stabilised and the stranger's face began to soften.

"It makes no sense but makes more sense?" August mocked his subordinate's uncertainty. "Really? Find out."

"Yes Boss. And what then? What if he is from Gudanko?"

There was a long pause. Aurora felt sure August was on the verge of saying something she would never forgive.

"He's not."

"And how would you know amigo from foe?"

August grinned. "He had an excellent reference."

Aurora felt a rush at that, something between love and pride. He'd listened after all.

The clone scratched his head, working through the puzzle.

"Phantom referrals seem out of the frame Boss. How else can this be explained?"

August looked around. "I don't know."

"And should the worst contradict your trust. What then must be?"

August looked again at Kalsang and his vision narrowed.

"We take care of it."

"As is our way, I'll make that play."

August nodded.

The strange man's lip curled and then the link faded out.

It took Aurora some minutes to take in that last bit, but as she did the tight walls of the Safe seemed to close in on her. August had irritated her and tormented her, but she hadn't thought he was capable of anything evil. The more she thought about it the more it was obvious. How else could a man get to his position of power? Were the vulnerable moments they had shared just part of the same game? She didn't know what to believe.

After what seemed like impossibly long hours, her confinement finally came to an end when August slipped into the Safe to trade places.

366

"How are you feeling? Are you able to go out?" he asked.

She wasn't. She hadn't been able to sleep. Every inch of her body was bruised and depleted. She felt betrayed and frightened by one of the two men that had become her entire world. She had to warn Kalsang.

"We'll see how I go. I've had some rest," she lied and pulled on the suit that August had just exited.

"Are you sure?" He seemed honestly concerned. He seemed to be.

"Well I'm not going to spend much more time cramped in here with you." She winked at him, a nervous gesture since what she had said was exactly the truth.

August seemed taken back by this. "Uh. Come right back when you need to." At that moment, he certainly didn't seem like a Com sociopath, but looks were deceiving.

"Rightio."

Aurora steadied herself on Kalsang's waiting shoulder. She motioned for him to walk with her over to the airlock of the *Garuda* where, once the space was re-pressurised, she and Kalsang could speak without helmets or the potential of being monitored. She told him everything she had overheard. Kalsang sat down to take in the news, then looked up at her thoughtfully.

"I have something to show you," he said. Kalsang carefully extracted his neurovisor and handled it to her.

Aurora braced herself as the tendrils slid painfully through her skull. She watched the neuroview mneme in amazement and horror. There was no way to put what she was seeing into a meaningful context. A whole world had been sucked dry, ripped to pieces and suddenly, blank, nothing, erased from the universe. It was the most terrifying thing she had ever witnessed and there was no context into which she could fit it. More frightening to her was that it scarcely penetrated the numbness in her being. The scenes unfolding before her made it clear how much her heart had itself been sucked dry and emptied out.

Her focus shifted back to Kalsang at a time when it all became too difficult. She didn't know what to make of this.

"What?"

He held his finger up to her lips.

"I do not know Aurora, isn't it?"

He was crying.

"I really do not know. It is too impossible. All I have ever done is what my teacher told me. Go here, do this. Easy like that. Even to Triton. Easy. Now August-la has built this terrible thing. All because of me, isn't it? Now what can my teacher tell me? What?"

Aurora became dizzy as the enormity of what he was asking fell on her. Her whole world and everyone she knew. She couldn't save hypothetical bacteria on some inhospitable rock; how could she do anything about this? And here she was swanning around with man who had created this horrible machine. It made her sick. It was all too much.

"I need help. You are my friend. So sorry."

The gravity of his request was communicated through the weary sadness in his eyes. "How?" Aurora mouthed, panicking. Kalsang bent forward and caught her falling head. Cradling it in his palms, he pressed his forehead against hers.

"What to do?" he whispered, in a tone strangely soothing in its despondency.

"We need to tell August. He will help." Aurora wanted this to be true, but of that she was far from sure.

"No, no, no," Kalsang's face contorted as he squeezed her hand, "August cannot be trusted."

An alarm sounded warning that the ship would be soon be slowing in preparation for arrival into the Earth's orbit.

CHAPTER 33

Calvin30

The vessel identified itself as the S.V. Senji Maru, a scavenging ship, the kind that cleared the lunar earth orbital lanes of lost bolts and ejected boosters and performed salvage operations.

Following the mission parameters uploaded into its robotic brain it recognised its intended target and pursued it, unsheathing the laser welding tools from among the arsenal of instruments at the ends of its octopoidal arms. There was no option of avoiding it. The momentum driving the Garuda/ Icarus towards Earth precluded steering. The electronic brain mapped the target schematic to the rotation of its quarry and, once locked on, took aim on the digitally highlighted sections. And then, in two quick bursts, the communication transmission and sensory arrays on the Garuda and Icarus were disabled.

The action was silent and exact. The only indications were the sudden disappearance of the outside view in the Garuda's external monitor and the subtle winking of a red diode on the pilot's console. Those two simple changes effectively transferred full control to the attacker.

The monotone of Vladimir Gudanko droned through the onboard phone.

"Hello August. What truly wonderful news it is that you have survived such a terrible fate. It is completely unbelievable. The Board and I extend our profound sympathy for your plight and look forward to seeing you as soon as possible. We have arranged this escort for you back to Luna City. It is imperative that you stay locked on this ship's beacon to avoid losing your way. I will be transiting to the Moon to greet you personally."

That whole scene would play out on automatic, according to a schedule laid down to the letter from long before August had flown up the rabbit hole in the sky. In fact, it had been the de facto back-up plan from the get go. All this was from a time that was by now almost irrelevant. The game had grown enormously since then. In those innings, August had once been King. In the new age dawning he might be more a pawn - an essential pawn nonetheless.

Calvin30 dispersed the pieces with his fist. Together with his pipe, this chess set constituted the greater part of his personal non-fashion assets. As a rule, his position was unassailable, but this time his inspired gambit, sacrificing his castle to promote August back from lost pawn, was in peril.

The pattern began with Queen Bhatterjee. Moving her into position was the lynch pin, and to execute this move he'd sold her Rev on the following logic. To correct their currently criminalised reputations as murderers of a now posthumously revered August Bridges, Kaliyuga Rev had been given a target. That Bridges yet lived the neuroscript transmissions from the Garuda sent to Bhatterjee confirmed this. How much she missed him was in her hiss. And why should she care that her maximum foe had fallen into the talons of his rival who would surely dispose of him on her behalf? Only this. Perhaps out of gratitude to his rescuers he might breath hidden truths of his horrible experiment. And, of course, August's reappearance at the side of his supposed assassins might rehabilitate their tarnished image. So, the plot hatched that the Revs would snatch August from Gudanko, with Calvin30 thankfully driving once again as irreplaceable to the cause.

Calvin30 pondered the pieces scattered across his apartment's Persian carpet as he bent to collect them. There was no hope in spotting a pattern - white and black casually intermingled, bishops on queens and kings under their castles. Yet Calvin30 caught himself trying to spot it.

That mental trap of mapping order on chaos mirrored his current impasse. Calvin30 was joyous over August's arrival. The appearance of his boss's face put all the other pieces in place. All the pieces minus one that is. A fatal unforeseen gap had appeared in his perfect playbook. Unforeseen because it simply could not be - the thing that pushed through his worst dreams and upset his rest - the impossible actual improbable fact that made him want to scream - was that goddamn monk.

That cat was so far out of Calvin30's box - in fact nowhere near to its proximity. Not only that, but he'd popped out of that hat at the point of optimal pain. Had the monk returned to Jupiter he could have encountered any number of stopgap fates. The most likely a collision with the altered path of a satellite and the colony on Europa, a contingency Calvin30 had been monitoring. That plan had obviously fallen flat.

Calvin30's disgrace was consummate. Such an unjust juxtaposition of tough luck. Conceivably it was a bad dream, but dreams have the courtesy to break when you wake. The night was too warm and his skin too clammy in his pyjamas. He played his SlySynth on Alto into the bleary dawn trying in vain to find some better way to replay the monsters who were living well and happy in his head.

Off and on Calvin30 dozed in ill-repose - awakening through the morning - compulsively re-imagining each moment of his talk with August over and over and over again in his neuroview. Again and again and again and again he dissected August's words and scrutinised the implacable presence of the monk, this ghost of a chance, his face, his expression, his impossible happenstance. Slowly, a picture forming in his mind became increasingly clear. What August had said was true - that the monk had not yet spilled the beans.

But that didn't restore his carefully played chessboard. The monk's absurd reappearance had replaced Calvin30's inspired plays with some horrid order ouroboros. No matter where he began his rumination, he ended up eating himself.

Where the hell was he?

The dawn was waking the walls of the run-down barrio where he was wandering. Calvin30 looked for landmarks and concluded he was lost, loitering some place below Hollywood in what looked like La Brea. He checked his neuroview GPS and located the Tar Pits close by. Oh, how appropriate. And, to top it off, he noticed with disgust he was still pimped out in his pyjama top.

The gates at the Pits were open early for an event and Calvin30 displayed his instrument to be waved in as the entertainment. He detoured from the group, attracted to a statue of a tar trapped elephant calling to his unstuck family. Poor fellow - off for a prehistoric afternoon wallow and ends up a fossil. A baby elephant, fearing its father's fate, screamed, bereaved, but the mother appeared merely annoyed. Brother, can't you tell the difference between mud and tar?

Stuck in the muck in a truck with a mammoth. Stuck. That's where he was. As outlandish as his plots had spun, Calvin30 hadn't travelled this far by leaving loose ends laying. Any longer lapse in action could give traction to an unpleasant reaction. He had to pull the pin and call it a day. And yet he and they stayed. Stuck.

Even an artist knows enough to not stray off the canvas, Calvin30 reasoned. Jazz itself was the tension between freedom and a frame. Going solo outside the set notes was a no no. And yet tempting.

Fulminating on the pachyderm's Palaeolithic stupidity, Calvin30 funnelled his parallel pathos into his horn - churning his ennui into the circular fire-breathing of Roscoe's 'Dragons'. Softly crescendoing into the cycle, longer and stronger, he concluded his solo in didgeridoo mode.

If only he could similarly keep August and the monk out of trunk reach, but what sort of ooze could glue one and exclude the other? No tar seemed to tug at the monk, ostensibly not even death as Calvin30 had seen. That was too eerie to consider without despair, which placed August as the trappable variable. Then he was back to where he began. Calvin30 could not cook up any perception of what he had put August through out there. How could he conceivably fathom what he had done to the man? His creation had escaped him.

Calvin30 halted. The Moon was higher than the Sun causing his shadow to be confused. Half of it somehow slipped through the crack of dawn. Heading counter to the course of things was also natural. Perhaps that was the point. Maybe the game was about more that hitting your marks and watching them fall. Perchance it was a dance.

At that moment, the call came through. Great gears had begun to grind. The ocean was in motion. A Comsec goon on the phone informed Calvin30 that Gudanko had presumed to fly him to the moon, and Calvin30 could not refuse. He bid his adieu to the mired mammoth and meandered back to his apartment with the demeanour of a man abandoning his plans.

Some Terran rotations later he was again swinging down round the dark side, descending into Luna City. In his neuroview as the *Senji Maru* he cradled the hitched spaceships and crew, drawing them into his path, carrying them in palm of his hand. It would be so easy to crush them in his fist, a technical glitch that would finish all his risk, but would also leave him not much to live for.

From his seat in aisle twenty-nine, Calvin30 spotted the signal. The first of the offloading month-on-month-off miners being delivered could be picked out from their reflective livery. One dude four rows up winked his retinas at Calvin30, who checked his *bona fides* through a neuroview data match. After that, a sizeable proportion of his fellow passengers appeared to pulse red. Now he could perceive the sleeper Rev force that had infiltrated the incoming miner shift. There were nearly thirty. The download also included a signal he should ping when he had managed to tag August's coordinates.

In return, he warmed up his sax ad libitum into a soft little ostinato that trafficked back to the infiltrators the ComSec codes they needed. Queen Bhatterjee's black knights had almost reached the white side's undefended back rank.

His illicit melodic linkup attracted a lingering look from an old fan. Down the aisle from his seat Calvin30 gave a wily smile to this VIP on the passenger list, one Francesca Salvador. She frowned in response, perhaps sensing that her passport up was for her comeuppance. Calvin30 had never forgiven Francesca for her part in interrupting his front row angle on August's falling Angels. For pilfering that perfect moment of his, and worse, the witch had selfishly ditched August. She had swept out her tracks too, the wicked bitch, with just one little slip, a last unclipped snippet that let Calvin30 guess. Speaking to herself who would she have solicited forgiveness from, if not August? Today she should pay for her unseemly duplicity. After studying her romantic history, he had readied this up and coming reunion. It wasn't a fair bargain - his bottomless pain for a simple broken heart. She'd gotten off lightly. Possibly he was going soft.

He tripped up for a tete é tete.

"I can place your face. From Deep Space?"

"Uh, yeah. The guy with the music stuff. Thanks for those. I enjoyed them." He could see he caused her to be nervous. And so should she be.

"Music can take you places you'd never otherwise see."

Francesca considered this cautiously and acquiesced. "That is totally true. Thank you."

At least the harlot had gratitude, a virtue in others largely lacking. "When I listen closely, I can linger on the misery of the human soul and, in that, find salvation."

"Yeah. I suppose."

"When you listen skilfully, you can even hear your own heart breaking."

"Is that so?" Francesca blew her hair, exposing the effort of her composure.

Calvin30 quickly licked his lips. Ladies in love. Like the Titanic powering towards the ice pack. She would sink so deliciously swiftly. It was a shame he would be too busy to sit in on the show.

"I have to go now," she suggested.

"Where?" he asked, puzzled.

"Down," She said as she turned towards the lock where the disc landers were kept. She glanced at her ComSec insignia. "They want me down there right away for some reason."

"Mucha mierda!"

Francesca's face screwed up at his wishing her much shit, theatrical lingo for luck en ole espagnol. Then she signed off and left.

Soon after Francesca left, they were shepherded into the landing discs where she had headed. Calvin30 noted one disc had already flown as he climbed into one chauffeured by pilots.

While his disc driver drove, Calvin30 chose to forgo the view to take in a quick tutorial on how to fly. Something he would need to know this afternoon. Disembarking through the back pad at Luna City he split from his soldier provocateur shift workers under instructions from Mirtopik head office and strolled along the path that his neuroview highlighted before him.

Calvin30 greeted Gudanko, who was sitting unimposingly in the ingress lounge of the forward landing. He noted the reduced gravity suited the slim man's posture, somewhat releasing the tightness in his spinal coiled spring. Out through the view portals sat the *Senji Maru*. Gudanko's eye twitched.

"Your ship is fifteen minutes ahead of schedule." Gudanko smiled mildly. "We decided to delay going in without your participation. You are still interested?"

"I wouldn't miss it for the world." Because there was no place in any world that would miss him.

"You will go in first to assess the risk. We are unsure what a man in August's condition will do as he has been alone so long. Men in solitary confinement become strange. While unjustly in prison I saw several them. When they came out they either crumbled or they fought. It would be sad to see a man like August crumble."

And how handy to have on hand one disposable clone?

"It would be a tragedy," Calvin30 agreed.

With ComSec standing by at an accommodating distance, Calvin30 tapped on the *Icarus'* airlock door and it opened. Then he made his entré.

The outer opening closed and an inner one opened to admit Calvin30 into a dimly lit space. Before him stood his man, August standing grander by far than his anticipated state of delivery. Clean and with his scrambled hair dampened straight. The sight of him brightened Calvin30's mind. Behind August, grinning like the idiot he couldn't be, was the entity of the monk, disturber of uncountable sleeps. And grasping the monk's hand, wary in her eyes as if congenial Calvin30 were the veritable Devil, was a woman?

"Anymore of you in here or is this it?" Calvin30 quipped. With the situation sliding from the sublime through the ridiculous it was a question worth asking.

August, enjoying his minion's double flip, came forward.

"No, my friend. This is it." And then August contributed significantly to Calvin30's shock by hugging him. Paralysed by the surprising gesture, his arms locked to his side, Calvin30 stumbled through. "Good to see you too."

From his embrace August whispered, "what else don't you know?"

"Allow me to introduce you. Calvin30, my assistant. This is Venerable Kalsang Jampa, formerly of the Triton Array and, of course, the indomitable Ms. Aurora Davidson of Mars."

Calvin30 awkwardly waved. The woman from the AGM, why not? Perhaps a piece of the wormhole had twisted off and gotten stuck in August's ship, promiscuously pinching people out of his past.

"I am so glad to see you Calvin30. I am assuming that we have touched down at one of the mining terminals for transhipment to Earth. How did you manage to slip us by my old friend Gudanko?"

"Actually Boss, he is expecting you outside."

"What?"

"In our previous discourse, I believe this was discussed."

August fumed but soon ran out of room to manoeuvre on the matter. Calvin30 halted him with a redirect before he started to panic.

"It may be better if I stay with the others in this place while you go out and face-to-face. Then we will muster out after you so that your oppugner will become confused and flustered by your surprise passengers."

The practicality of this counsel - sharing his confusion to achieve his purpose - helped Calvin30 recover. As August turned to go, he stared at the mystery woman and she returned an uncertain smile. What was the essence of that exchange? A quick scan of her visage through his neuroview verified Aurora against her spitting image. Apparently, her position should be in a stasis canister midway to Earth on a medical evac. Somehow, she had happened to hitch her wagon to August's star bringing with her fresh resources. They both looked better than worse for their wear. Knowing August, would he have taken advantage of all that the woman had to offer? The droop in his strung-out look suggested he hadn't.

After August exited, Kalsang calmly called to Calvin30, "we are happy you are helping us."

As accustomed as he had become to that voice, from evaluating every mneme ever catalogued on Venerable Kalsang Jampa, listening to the monk live made Calvin30 leap in his skin.

"That's what I do." In answering he had the odd sensation that any insincerity in himself was instantly sensed. "I help people follow their hopes." Wherever that may lead.

"Isn't it?"

Unsure how to respond, Calvin30 turned his attention through the portal to August and observed the confrontation. Gudanko, standing cautiously close at the front of a formidable phalanx of ComSec goons. August striding out with his regal mane swaying, regarding his mundane opponent with disdain. The two leaders squared off and August, although the captive, still had the number of his fastidious nemesis. Gudanko addressed his opposite, who became agitated. No doubt the Ukrainian had offered terms of surrender, a proposition August was tossing down with much dust.

Focusing his sights on Gudanko's unperturbed features, Calvin30 blinked and set his tag. To the Rev agents currently tracking Gudanko's neuroview broadcast, that guy was now August, the target for the taking.

"Are we to leave now?" The monk had the timing right.

"Ah, yes."

Their appearance poked past the impregnable reserve in Gudanko's nerve. Calvin30 could see his metrical mind ticking over, computing the improbabilities as incomprehensible. August picked up the improvement and stopped posturing.

"Oh, that's the rest of my party. See, the wormhole works my friend. I told you." August's smile went wide enough for eagles to fly in it.

The extent to which Gudanko was stunned by this stunt could not be surmised because, at that moment, an explosive blast of smoke dissolved the scene into chaos. Firefly smart darts flew between ComSec protectors and indeterminate Rev invaders.

"Ditch your neurovisors or you'll be hit," Calvin30 broadcast to his associates, as he glad-handed August back into his group and behind the craft. Aurora and August were quick to flick their visors, but Kalsang clung to his as expected. The mneme of the alien scene must be in its memory.

"Drop it or they'll drop you," Calvin30 shouted as a smart dart tracer whizzed its winding way into a ComSec defending their position.

Kalsang frowned down at the ground.

"It'll be locked, no one can look in. We can locate it later using your cerebral signature."

To push the point, a smart dart found its mark in Kalsang's space suit bracelet and began to burrow in.

Calvin30 wrestled the visor away from Kalsang and hurled it. On cue August yanked the monk back from clamboring after it. The smart dart extracted and arced off after its target.

"No!" The renunciate lost it, but more barefaced was Aurora chasing the displaced headset into the haze. Nail chewing commenced as August threw himself into the mess to rescue her. Aurora fought fiercely to free herself from his heroic intervention.

"Let go of me, you gutless wonder!"

"What are you doing? Are you mad?"

"We need that! We need that you moron!"

"You see the darts? Do you want to get caught? Anyway, we can find our way without them," August waved toward the visor on Calvin30's brow.

"Why is he able to keep his?" Aurora snapped.

Calvin's lips formed a reply, but August slipped the response in first. "Because they both think he's on their side."

The debate ended as the battle line crossed over the lost property, pushing them back. Then the mayhem in the room turned around the captured pin.

"They've taken Gudanko. They've got the Boss." Calvin30's neuroview murmured, melding with the Rev rodomontade, "we've acquired the target. Proceeding to extraction point nine."

Calvin30 still holding Kalsang by the hand, hauled him to the wall and pulled off a pre-loosened vent grill. Pulling the gravity reduced man was as easy as walking a child.

"That shaft will shift us straight to the back-landing pad."

"The rovers are out front," August objected, "the back is only used for visitors' landing discs."

"You oughtn't doubt me Boss. The discs from my ship should be still in the stalls. The airlock was rigged by the Revs to blow so it will slow anyone following. What do you think?"

"Brilliant."

Aurora interrupted the tender moment. "We are not going until we have our neurovisors back." The lady was as red as her fellow Martians. Kalsang enforced her right flank. August was flummoxed by this filibuster and stalled.

Then one of Mirtopik's best called over to them, and there was no place to go but into the wall. Calvin30 shooed them down the flue before refusing to enter after them.

"Hurry up. You need to be there when I arrive. I'll handle these guys."

Before Calvin30 re-secured the screws, he glanced through the shaft after them and met the gaze of the monk who looked positively distraught. That sight gave him some strength.

"You," Calvin30 inhaled the word while resolving the rest.

You will die.

CHAPTER 34

Francesca

Why did people have to be such complete and utter pains in the ass? The guy whose nose she had just had to break could have avoided it completely by leaving any of the fifteen times she had told him to get lost. Of course, he couldn't because people were paying him to keep asking and he had to eat. This was what Francesca told herself the first fourteen times before deciding the last time that if he asked again she would have to deal with it.

"What's the story Francesca? Come on?"

As if he didn't already know that stupid story. About how she single-handedly defeated the terrorists trying to blow up August Bridges and had risked her own life to go after him and then had braved going through the wormhole thing to return. Everybody was telling that story, so why did they have to keep asking her? So she broke that guy's nose, and now that would be the story, about what a machismo she was, how in some freakish way she was now some symbol of returning virility for those long-time limp dick Coms. See, even our women have balls. They even got into all her personal stuff, like who she'd hooked up with and why and where, which was all news to her because she had totally forgotten it. Now it was all over the neuros, repeating in people's brains around the world like some sorry dream she couldn't ever wake up from. She just hoped Raoul wasn't watching any of that, although she knew, she hoped, that he would see right through it. He knew who she was, and he could give a crap what people said.

Instead of all this, Francesca could have told the truth about the reality of what happened to August Bridges, that she had his blood on her hands and staining her soul. That she'd screwed him over and then hammered the nail in. But she couldn't. It wasn't the story everybody wanted to hear anyway.

And hitting that guy was ridiculous because she had been dining out on that bullshit story he'd only wanted to hear her repeat. She was like this Queen of Shit now. Everyone was lining up to give her stuff for lying. Amazing hotel rooms, food she never thought would touch her lips, free money, hot guys giving her whole-body massages with happy endings, famous people who never knew she was alive before asking her opinion. She heard some chicks were even dressing up like her, which was funny and really sad at the same time.

All of this in exchange for handing over her self-respect, which had been the only thing Francesca had ever really had to trade. It was like the Cheetah, Wonder Woman's enemy, selling her soul to that Plant God in exchange for immortality, which before Francesca had always felt was a good deal - like getting everything for nothing.

Today she felt like it was something.

Francesca had been trying to avoid the paparazzi crazies by taking the laundry exit when that guy had popped out and hounded her down the street. Now that he was down all the other seagulls were flapping in out of the sky to see what was going down.

Good luck that there was a volantor cab in the area, and just in time she got out of there. Off on her way to the Mirtopik Needle. Now Francesca could afford a flying cab, and wasn't that worth something? High above the dried-out town and all the little people who didn't have a bullshit soul that was worth anything. The Queen of Shit. She couldn't say some part of her wasn't enjoying this. The part of her that felt like she'd done this before, like in some past life when she'd been Cleopatra, not like everyone else, but some interplanetary version with many heads and tentacles and shit. Maybe with those wild aliens who sent that neuro of the wormhole. Why not? Those feelings must have been from another life because people falling at her feet wasn't something familiar to her this time around.

The cab hovered down the Bat Cave entrance, into the ground under the needle, going almost as far down as the needle went up. Stony was waiting for her when she climbed out.

"You look like shit, Salvador."

And she did. Hardly any sleep and too many Margaritas hanging off her hips. "You're one to talk, asshole."

Stony grinned. "Always insubordinate. You haven't changed."

But the sad truth was that she had. "Are they going to let us go?" The question almost got stuck in her throat before she could say it.

"Yep, Salvador. We got in. They needed extra detail to watch some Rev chatter because Gudanko is headed up to Luna City to greet the Tsuchinshan crew in person when they come in."

Thanks to all the Saints who never gave a shit about her before. "Why is he doing that? Seems like a lot of trouble for a boss that big."

"You want to ask him? Or just thank your stars he is because that means we can get up there to see them in too."

"Just like that they let us go?"

Stony picked his teeth, like he always did before telling people stuff they wouldn't want to hear.

"Not just like that. Some media guys want to see the reunion."

Francesca had to stop herself from helping Stony get the food in his teeth unstuck with her boot.

"Settle down. It is getting us up. You want that, right?" Stony extracted his gross treasure and inspected it proudly.

Francesca chilled. She was going to see Raoul and she could lie once more to get there. After all her story was his story too because without him the story would be true, except that August would be back and alive telling it, not her.

That night they left. Shooting to the moon on the same ship she and Raoul had travelled in months before filled her with nostalgia for him. In such a short time they would be together again. It seemed unreal. Some family members from the crew were travelling there with her. Some wanted to thank her for some reason, which Francesca felt uncomfortable with since she hadn't actually done anything to help anybody. Mostly they wanted to take pictures with her. One woman kept looking at her strangely, which prompted Francesca to make a sign against the Evil Eye. One of those things her Tia had left her.

That creepy clone dude was also on-board. If there was a guy deserving of the Evil Eye, it would be him. Probably no point, as Francesca doubted it would work against the Devil himself.

Towards the end of the flight she heard him playing that horn of his and wondered what shit he was getting up to with it. She gave him a hard look that she instantly wished she hadn't because he took it as an invitation to come up the aisle towards her.

He pretended not to know her at first, as if he was dragging out of some long-lost memory or something which was about as convincing as some decked out pimp pretending he had honest feelings for her. She went through the routine of admiring his music, which got her thinking about how he'd used his playing to hack the deep space network and what he might be getting up to.

"Music can take you places you'd never otherwise see."

Which was like him confirming it for her. She played it dumb and said something non-committal. On the guy went about salvation and suffering and heartbreaks. It was like he was trying to send hidden messages in normal conversation, the way he spun hacks out in his playing.

"Is that so?" The sooner she could get away from this guy the better.

He looked at her with psycho eyes, which made her think he was going wipe her out for killing August, or at least let her secret out. Despite her tenth-degree ninja juju training she started to sweat. *Dios mio.* She felt so bad about what she'd done she'd almost wished he would do something to make her pay. She gave him the shrug with the legit excuse that ComSec had called her down early, which was true anyway, but Francesca felt like she was lying about it for some reason.

Reading between those lines, she was sure he was on to her whole horrible secret, that she would have fooled exactly everyone except for him, and he was covering for her for his own weird clone reasons. The way he had rigged the Deep Space network through his music it was almost impossible that he didn't have a front row seat to the whole thing. The guilt this thought brought was crushing. It was bad enough that she had finished off August, the main man that she admired, but what made her feel like a totally useless asshole was that she was more worried about being uncovered than what her betrayal had meant to him.

Francesca wondered if there was any way to kill the clone without people finding out, the way she had with August. Even thinking about that made her sick. If it hadn't been for the clone, she wouldn't have connected with Raoul. She was truly grateful for that, but only that.

Enough of this head-trip. Francesca needed to clear her mind in order to practice flying this disc, so it was a good thing the pilot was a good-looking enough guy, which is what she needed to keep her attention on his every word and away from her shitty thoughts. Flying down from the Lunar Transfer Vehicle parked in orbit around the moon was done in a disc, an honest to goodness flying saucer, covered with a clear buckeyball dome for protection. The thing was designed to maximize visibility. It was evacuated to avoid the possibility of a catastrophic depressurisation, so you had to suit up. The flight down was awesome, and soon any memory of the clone and all the other memories he brought up were lost in her sheer marvel at everything.

Francesca imagined herself as the goddess Diana, the huntress returning from her hunt, descending in her throne into the open moon.

She was glad she insisted on driving the disc. Part of her training had been in piloting these things, if only in the simulator. She was damned if she wasn't going to take advantage of her new power of celebrity to have some good old-fashioned fun. With judicious blasts of the retro rockets, Francesca dropped the flying disc down among the broken peaks of the Montes Alpes, falling into valleys and frog hopping at the last possible moment to avoid collision with the lunar ground, and then bounce, up again into the luminous Earthrise.

But at the same time, Francesca knew she couldn't enjoy herself as she much as she once would have, because now she was the Queen of Shit. With Elena she had excuses, but not anymore.

"What the hell Salvador?"

"Just having fun Stony."

"Well get it over with. We have work to do."

Francesca was buzzed when her disc skipped down at Luna City and she bounded into the waiting airlock. To hell with everything. She was going to see Raoul as soon as she finished this shitty little job, whatever it was.

What it was a total full-on lock-down. Stony was in fine form, personally checking every encryption setting. Elite ultra-tuned Ginyu Force storm troopers were everywhere. And something big was going down in the deep space landing pad section because it was all blanked out, even to her grade. The security was more intense than even when August Bridges was building the wormhole. Just thinking that name made Francesca blush in shame, but there was a reason all that had happened, and a reason she was here, and that reason was named Raoul.

Why they put all this security on a routine transfer of the crew coming in from Tsuchinshan was hard to figure out. Maybe they had another terrorist on-board, but it would have to be Bhatterjee herself to need all of this. From her side it was totally boring, just checking things other people had checked already. With the part of her brain that wasn't mindlessly repeating procedure she began to think about the clone playing his sax on the way up. It seemed to be a weird thing to do.

Maybe his solo would shed some light on things. Francesca ran the same filters she had on the Deep Space stuff and, sure enough, it was in there. Subtle deviations off the notes that looked like static but held another coherent signal. She couldn't break the encryption yet but noticed an odd echo signal crawling around the notes coming from somewhere else in the ship. Most of the other guys had been miners, not ComSec, but there was definitely a two-way thing going on in there. She had to tell Stony.

One of the ComSec guys told her he'd gone off to the ancillary launch pad. "Why's that?"

"Oh, to secure that transhipment of asteroid miners. They aren't being let in while the op is on."

So, the blanked out main pad wasn't about Raoul. That meant her lover to be might be just standing around down a short corridor that was completely open to her. Francesca's heart went pow.

"Hey, where are you going?"

"I've got something I need to show the Sarge. A possible security breach. Probably not, but I need to get it looked at."

A few quick loping steps down an 'under repair' gantry and she was there. The whole gang. And there he was, waiting for her like in a million dreams, grinning radiantly, boring into her mind with his smiling wise eyes, completely welcoming. And there, tight beside him, defending the space between them with psychic laser beams, was that woman with the Evil Eye from the flight. She was friendlier now. She was also, as she announced herself, Raoul's wife. Her name was Jolene, a name he had never felt it necessary to mention in all the months of close quarters.

"Oh Francesca. We are so happy to see you again."

Raoul stood by impassively, watching it happen, his sad lovely eyes with every word retreating by parsecs into the forever distance of never was.

"Raoul has told me so much about you that I feel you and I have a lot to talk about."

Raoul's wife was so gushingly thankful for her husband's rescue that Francesca could scarcely stop her soul from vomiting all over the woman's intentionally too revealing dress. He hugged Francesca carefully, not the warm soulful hug that used to wrap her damaged soul in a cocoon of light. Like a brother.

Tactfully excusing herself from the party, as soon as it would not be too obvious and rude, Francesca wandered away into the greater Luna City compound to find a dark place to match the congealing blackness of her mind. Unfortunately, there seemed to be no such place to be found. Un-monitored space was at a premium in this cramped mining compound that some marketing genius had named a City. People were everywhere. Francesca returned to hyperventilate in the airlock by the discs and resisted the urge to race out of it. There would be too many alarms if she did. That, and her desire for privacy at this painful moment, exceeded any urge to end herself. She let her actions numbly follow the least-distance avenue of escape and, donning her spacesuit, she took refuge in a familiar place by hoisting herself into the vents. She completely forgot what she had come to tell Stony.

There was no need to go exploring to find greater solitude because this was it, so Francesca curled up into a ball just inside the vent opening and wept. Out leaked the pain and inner desolation that had stored within her for many years. Softly, but not constrained, like a confluence of many rivers meeting on a level plain. She did not sob. All resistance in her body washed away on an even tide of sorrow. She succumbed to her feelings and the rising flood, within an hour, crested leaving her strangely refreshed in its wake.

But when the tide began to ebb it turned red, drawn back to the gravitational centre, the central fact of the whole shitty mess, which was that Raoul was a complete dick. He had gotten inside of her mind and played her as she had allowed no man to do before. It was a complete invasion and the asshole thought he was just going to walk away from it all, with her heart tossed casually into some poetic bullshit collection jar. He hadn't even had the honesty to sleep with her, which was the slap in the face that she could not abide. She would have figured it out if they had because she wasn't a fool, but the slippery creep had made himself, instead, into some Saint of her imagination, some unattainable dream of perfection on which all her hopes could collect. Francesca's thoughts turned casually to murder.

A red light began to blink on and off and on and off in Francesca's eyes. She ignored it for a while, until her irritation drove her to open the priority channel that beckoned in her neuroview.

"The prisoners have been taken by the Revs. Down to the H2O extraction tubes or up through the arboretum. Split two teams in those two ways. Raj and I will check the back-landing bay just to be safe."

Shit, shit, shit, shit, shit. That message in the clone's static - it had been important. Francesca was sure of it. The latest complete screw up in her career full of screw ups. She thought to call in, but the shame of the whole thing caught in her throat. How could she explain why she was hiding in an airlock vent?

"Roger that C30. How did they escape?"

Francesca's interest perked. C30? The clone?

"They tagged the captives right next to me. I moved into a vent and the darts were thwarted by the cover. Afterwards they dragged them off with the group who took Gudanko."

"I gotcha C30. We have recaptured Gudanko - they dropped him and ran. You say they still have the prisoners. The boss wants them bad."

"Doubtless you'll collect them. To button-up the back-door Raj and I will block off the South lock."

"Copy that C30. Tango Uniform."

Tango Uniform for Thank you? What a bunch of try-hards, playing super soldiers after being cooped up on the Moon for so long picking their asses. Here is the question of the day - if they were so hot why send only two guys to the only real escape point? Their incompetence annoyed her, mainly because it distracted her from what she wanted to rush out to do, which was to go kick in the teeth of the man who had pretended to be someone she could have loved. She shifted herself and her stony heart back down toward the head of the vent deliberately, like the assassin she had become.

"Assistance request. Raj has been hit. The terrorists. Past the last advance to the landing locks. Come quick."

"Roger that UOR C30. We are on our way."

This meant they were coming right to her. Adrenaline gripped Francesca as her muscles tensed and she flipped around ready to spring out of the vent. Four figures dashed underneath. Francesca launched down on the last one to pass with a fury. Her anger burned from her breast and she burst into green flame. She snagged her prey around the neck, wrenched hard and the figure rolled over her back with a disconcerting absence of resistance, so gently that, for a second, she had the sensation that she had grabbed a pillow in a spacesuit, not a living person.

Keeping the momentum of surprise going against her more numerous adversaries, Francesca laid into her downed victim's solar plexus with a solid thud. As she wailed into his gut with a third and fourth vicious kick she got a view of the downed man's face. It stopped her in her tracks. He seemed so ridiculously relaxed, like he was lounging at the Copacabana or something and not getting the absolute shit beaten out of him. Their eyes met, and she could swear that he was actually feeling worried about her, like she was some long-lost friend who had gone bat-shit crazy. For some reason that look both enraged her and disarmed her, like a bomb blowing up inside of her backwards into her gut. She stalled.

Arms grabbed around her back and began to pull her away. The arms were weak though, like her own skinnies after she had returned from her long voyage off gravity. Francesca easily broke the lock and turned to face her attacker.

The face looking back at her stopped her cold. What? She could have sworn she was looking into the eyes of a guy who totally couldn't be there.

"You."

The ghost of August Bridges levelled a shaky fist at her. She stopped breathing. He recognised her all right, after coming all the way back from his deep space grave to get her. Then just when Francesca, frozen in terror, thought he was going to reach into her heart and pull it out, someone else grabbed her and pushed her hard off her feet.

Even though she could have flipped her attacker, she was too freaked out to do anything. Francesca crossed herself as the woman who had pushed her came at her wielding an air canister. They locked eyes. Francesca knew that face too, but how? She thought the woman must have recognised her too because she suddenly put down the bottle down and backed away. A thought of Elena flashed through Francesca's mind, of how she had failed her. And for no reason that made sense she felt the same way towards this stranger. Like she was letting her down.

"Don't get in our way again," the woman shouted, and Francesca fell back. Her broken heart suddenly seemed too heavy to bear, the shock and the guilt of seeing August, the strange hold over her of the downed man, and now this woman for whom she felt strangely accountable. As Francesca sat there she was caught up in a giant wave that had come straight across the galaxy to sweep her away. A tsunami so impossibly big even the Silver Surfer would get rolled.

Then the clone ran in and over to a panel.

"I'm exploding the lock."

Pop. Out they flew. The instant decompression spewed them out onto the ground. It took a few moments for Francesca to orient and, as she did, she spied the four figures taking off towards the nearby landing disks. The first two were already strapping in while the second two scrambled for the one furthest away. She pelted after them, in long vaulting strides, targeting the slowest whom she recognised as the man she had downed. He was bent over and hobbling. She peeled him away just before he could step up to the disk after the clone, and as she yanked him down the landing disk dome locked in place. The rockets fired but, instead of lifting away, the disk pivoted towards them as if the pilot was trying to fry them with his boosters. In fact, that was exactly what the evil toad was attempting to do.

Francesca noticed a twisted piece of panelling laying near them, which had been the outer airlock door before the explosion. The panel was laying on the lip of a small crater, with just enough room to crawl under. She tugged the man after her with little resistance and managed to wedge them both under just as the booster rockets bore down. The panel buckled under the pressure but did not give and, thankfully, deflected the heat. Otherwise they would have fried.

When she was sure the attacking disc had finally lifted off, Francesca dragged the man towards the last landing disc, so he wouldn't be out exposed to a second attack. The man caught on to her intent and ran as fast as he could manage. When they had entered the landing disc webbing she strapped him in. She noticed he was bleeding from his mouth, but otherwise gave the impression that he wasn't particularly bothered. He smiled kindly at her and mouthed "Thank you." What the hell for?

Francesca turned her attention to the landing disc controls. She lowered the dome and rocketed off in pursuit of the others.

A few minutes later she heard the clone over the security band. "Team 5. Team 5. The lock is blown. One of your guys I didn't recognise dropped down on them. The fugitives ran him down with a disk plus one from their own side. I've taken up pursuit so watch my sign. No need to follow along with the last disk. They can't survive out here and there is no place to hide. I'll follow hanging back, so you can track us."

"Roger C30, this is Comsec. Not sure who you're talking about though with that extra man getting the drop on them. Not one of ours. We're all accounted for, even Raj here with one nasty lump. Come back in before you are out of return range. We don't want to lose you too. Over."

Francesca frowned. Nothing added up. There was no other landing disk on the pad that she had seen. And the clone couldn't confirm that she and her captive were dead because they weren't. She smelled something foul. She looked around and saw no one following them. The only conclusion was that it was the clone who was the person who tried to pulverise them. That made no sense, no? The clone would have absolutely no idea who she was and, because of that, had no reason to want her dead. And the guy next to her didn't seem the type to invite murder. Well now that clone had made a terrible mistake because she was definitely in the mood to want him dead, and when she caught him it would be more than just wanting. Francesca concentrated all her rage on this outcome and jammed her foot on the accelerator.

She glanced at the man she had just alternately beaten and rescued. He smiled back at her like nothing had happened. Like getting pummelled and blasted was just one of those things. It was weird, but what was weirder was that August Bridges look alike? Some actor brought in for the re-enactment? Maybe, but that actor was very good because she knew that face. How could she forget it? And why would ComSec be chasing after an actor?

Could it all just be some kind of set-up, even the whole drama on Tsuchinshan and her fight to the finish that hadn't stopped anything? Was it all some elaborate scene in some Campaign between the Coms and the Revs that she had gotten herself mixed up in? Her head spun. Francesca generally reserved contempt for conspiracy theories as being the ramblings of old men trying to stay relevant. Well, she decided, conspiracy or no, the clone had to pay and as someone still on the ComSec payroll, nailing a traitor was something still in her job description.

The man next to her eased into another position. He was definitely in pain. She opened a link to his mind through their neuroviews.

"You okay mister?"

"Not so good not so bad. Are you okay?"

No, Francesca wanted to say, not okay for a million reasons, but what was it to this guy anyway?

"Why not?" she shrugged, "except for your friend trying to kill us."

"Yes," he answered calmly, "what to do?" As if someone trying to kill him was one of those things that just happened in life that you had to get over, like storm damage to his house or something.

This confused Francesca way more that it should have. Someone trying to dust her was not someone who was going to get off lightly. She cut the conversation to focus better on vengeance.

The flaring nozzles of the two landing disks in front of her wove back and forth before the rising slopes of an upcoming lunar mountain range. They dipped down over the lip of a large crater, and Francesca followed, cursing as she swerved to miss a larger moving conveyor feeding into some kind of rock crusher. Huge robotic tractors underneath them raked the surface of the crater, feeding the recovered ore into even larger automated haul trucks travelling in tandem with the tractors. She soared over their silent continuous labors and turned parallel to the helium 3 processing plant kiln, a long glowing tube. More robots, with spinning weather vane hooks locked arms around the recently filled red gas tanks filled by the processing plant and trundled off down a train track towards a long ramp dug down into the lunar surface.

Woom! A large cone faced container shot up and off of the ramp into the sky, until it was lost in the light of the Earth rising up over the horizon. Woom! Another one lifted off and slid on by. Bang. The anvil of insight collided with her numbskull brain. Of course, the ramp was a mass driver, a great magnetic catapult that slung the processed helium-3, and anything else that could fit in a cargo container, back off to Earth. It would be one hell of a gee hit to start with, but then you would just sail down. No need to get a ticket for the Lunar Transport.

Francesca tipped over the top edge of the ramp in time to see the two parked landing disks. Standing outside one of the open containers, two were confronting the one. No doubt they wanted to know where their friend was. The distraction gave her a cover to sneak her disk over the edge and touchdown on the track blocking the container's exit. The fugitives had just boarded the container when she broadcasted over a closed ComSec channel.

"We have them now C30, all three of them. They are in a container on a mass driver by the processing area. We have landed on the tracks in front of them."

An angry voiced shouted back. "Are you mad! They don't have a link for you to talk to them. They will crash into you and you will all die."

There was some logic there so Francesca bluffed back. "Roger. We have cleared off of the skip and have set the engines to leak fuel, so the thing will explode."

"Idiots. Orders are to capture not kill. Gudanko will crack your heads."

Francesca smiled at upsetting the wise guys rhyme. She must have really gotten under his skin.

"We thought..."

"Wait a second. How did you? There hasn't been time. Who's on the line?" It was clear he had seen through her ruse.

Why lie. "Francesca Salvador, ComSec level 9 reporting."

There was a pause. "Well Francesca, your penchant for popping up in inopportune places improves your probability of rapid expiry. Thus, to bypass any superfluous corporeal compromise of your position, I propose you should forthwith fly!"

The lights up the ramp began to pulse. Francesca couldn't believe it. At the last moment before there wouldn't be another, Francesca tugged hard on the controls and banked their disc into a ramp walls as the container shot forward. The landing disc bounced back upside down and skidded to a halt next to the next freight container being mounted on the tracks.

She was trapped, pinned down by the caved-in dome and pinched by her seat up around the steering column. The hiss of oxygen leaving her suit from a rip told her that she had only minutes to live. Then she felt hands working her body loose from the wreckage, steadily and without panic, until she was loose and being pulled from the wreckage by her passenger. Her mysterious companion helped her into another container, which had apparently also been kitted out for people. But why?

Her breath returned to her as the cabin pressurized. Another minute might have been too late. The black spots dissolving from her eyes, she accessed the container's computer through her neurovisor and found a way to have the container loaded for launch on the last heading. Then Francesca removed her helmet. Her companion also removed his. He was young, about her age, with a shaved head. It was probably the exhilaration of barely surviving, but the fact was he looked beautiful. He stood there looking straight into her black soul without flinching.

She turned away and shook her ratty hair. Just what she needed today of all days. The container jolted as it moved onto the launch ramp, and the man nearly fell into her. Francesca caught herself on his arm and steadied them both.

"We should get into the webbing?" he suggested.

"Yes. Right now."

Just as they strapped themselves the sirens began to shriek. The man reached over to pat her arm and Francesca pulled away.

The g-forces came crushing down on them as the container launched. They almost knocked her out. They stopped as suddenly as they had started, and the absence of gravity filled her frame. Her eyes in contrast felt like they were weighed down by lead. She fought the desire to sleep. What if this guy was a murderer or something, like the clone?

"What is your name?" he asked.

"Francesca," she mouthed.

"Tashi Deleg Francesca, I am Kalsang."

He smiled kindly at her. Francesca decided for no good reason that she could trust him, and she let herself fall asleep.

She was safe.

THE CRY OF WILD GEESE

Lakes and pools adorned with lotuses and the beautiful cry of wild geese,
Everything unowned within the limitless spheres of space.
Taking these with my mind, I offer them

~Shantideva, 8th Century India

CHAPTER 35

Francesca

The days travelling from the Moon tiptoed by softly. It was strange and wonderful to take a break from her usual place on the pointy end of the arrow of time. It was a luxury to breathe without purpose, to feel removed from grit, grief, and guilt. And Kalsang, the name of her strange new companion, had somehow set this up.

"Was that really August Bridges with you guys?"

It was the first thing she'd asked him, even though part of her didn't want to know. If he was it was wonderful, a reprieve for her soul from a dark fate that she'd sealed by abandoning him. If he was it was terrible, because one person in the universe knew exactly what a self-serving callous bitch she'd been. That recognition and accusing finger he'd levelled at her in the airlock. Who else could it be?

"Isn't it?" Kalsang answered nodding his head affirmatively before answering her second question with his name.

That was as much as she could get out of him. He'd silenced her with a finger and a confidence that unsettled her. And then he'd insisted on silence while she unwound through all the possibilities. That they'd patched up the wormhole and somehow brought him back. It wasn't impossible. But so many things didn't line up, such as the terrorist attack and why Gudanko would want him captured. It could have gone on and on but Kalsang stopped her.

"We need time to heal now Francesca." He had tears in his eyes as he spoke, and in them she saw a pool of pain. And that was that. She felt compelled to do as he said and tried to give herself space to do something she had never let herself do before. Heal.

For his part, Kalsang spent most of his time silently in meditation. He seemed so strong in his quiet spirituality. This became enormously attractive to her. So deep that Raoul's deceitful similitude of peace would have only covered the surface molecules of where this man must go. So deep that Francesca forgave Raoul and quickly had difficulty remembering even his name.

It seemed strange that in this cramped space with Kalsang she would find the breathing space that had eluded her all her life. It felt so wonderful she wanted to dissolve into it. There was something about this man that was so right, in the way everything about men before had been so wrong. She felt herself falling for him.

But even in this peaceful place of refuge she was still pulled all over by her thoughts.

Wasn't this the story of her life? Flying on a magic carpet made of toothpicks bound together by fishing line and fantasy - just another balseros trusting unpredictable currents to carry her makeshift raft to a place where she might stick her toe into the golden sand of the promised land. The search for True Love was the only quest she would never grew weary of because it was blended into her genetic fibres.

The Earth, projected from the forward cams, hung in her neuroview like a pinata promise. If one were handy, she might catch hold of a passing comet and break the big blue bubble open to spill out any sweet things inside. The inside of the Earth seemed a proper place for True Love to hide, at the heart of things. Searching on the outside had been futile from the beginning. Perhaps she might see a future with her beloved divined in there. Francesca looked longingly down through the thin layers of cloud and soil separating her from her goal. The distance seemed only as short as the distance between two hands.

The Earth, a tiny island of blue in an ocean of black. The whole thing probably contained only a few spoonfuls worth of True Love. Still it was there, she knew, because maybe she, Francesca Xavier Salvador, had actually found a piece of it.

CHAPTER 36

Kalsang

"Is this your Ocean now, Melded One? It is so beautiful."

Taking d'Song's lead, Kalsang looked out over the heads of the other aliens crowding around the portal. He could make out oceans and continents, which slowly appeared like a reunion of long forgotten friends. There was North America and Africa and Antarctica and Australia and all the brilliantly translucent blue oceans in between and China advancing over the horizon out of darkness. They passed over great drowned cities and endless patchwork fields. Kalsang held his breath as the mountains began to grow. Spilling out from them the thin glimmering line of the Tsangpo, the Brahmaputra. Lhasa was down there in its folds and the great resurgent monastery of Ganden and somewhere, in the east, in Golak, in small yak hair tents and stone houses were his mother and uncles and their families lived. He could almost breathe the sweet mountain air. Slowly it rolled into the distance as they advanced over the blank steppes of Kazakhstan and the fairy lights of what must be Western Russia. The call of the land was so intense that he felt like bursting from the capsule like a dandelion seed and floating down of his own accord.

He turned his head down and looked at his new friend.

"She likes you, you know?" teased d'Song.

"I am a monk," Kalsang responded, making it clear that that was as far as that thought would go. He watched it almost dissolve and directed his mind to the broader predicament. His neurovisor lay somewhere behind them on the Moon. He was unable to go back to it. By some unlikely coincidence, he had survived and was returning to warn humanity of their great peril. Would people believe him without the evidence? His thoughts clung to his neurovisor, wondering what would become of it. To be as effective as his situation demanded he had to let go of that, to concentrate on the present moment. To be aware.

Francesca was resting which was good. He sensed in her an enormous potential for joyful freedom, but a deep burden of pain could drown her instead. She would go either way. He prayed for her and, from her, out to everyone else living in the world below.

What a pity they could not see their home the way he did. They all couldn't share his immense sense of relief from returning to their own mother after such long periods of absence. He could see vividly how lovely, how irreplaceable, their magnificent world really was. It was their true refuge amidst the unimaginable and unendurable sterility of the stars. The knowledge of its potential destruction made its awesome fragility even more manifest. Kalsang shivered.

A song rose from his heart:

Infinity of fortunate moments delicately balanced in this perfect sapphire blossom
Winds carry the fragrance of memory up to me
Scent of fire, air, earth, and water
Yesterday I looked up through the clear skies of awakening
Today I look down towards the solid ground of realisation
Holy naked jewel realm
I prostrate before the throne of 1000 Buddhas
My friends don't you recognise
the single face of all our mothers?

CHAPTER 37

Aurora

Wheatbelt Wallaby came blazing down into the open sky as the world swelled up before her. The great Waugal, the rainbow serpent, was alive and well down there, writhing and playing, sending waves dancing throughout the great sea on the top of the globe. The whole Dreaming of Yulbrada, the Earth, rang out with a billion songs calling her home. She wanted to add her own lines, to sing herself back into joyous existence, but her mouth opened, and nothing came out.

Every cell in Aurora's body opened to the healing before her, but her mind remained closed to it. It was stunning to be so close to home after so long an absence. She looked over at August who was looking back at her. In the rush of life returning to them he turned to embrace her with an incredulous laugh.

She wanted to. Her body wanted to. Her heart maybe even. But how? The loss of Kalsang to their pursuers was the only thing in her mind, the loss of Kalsang and the impossible mission that it was now solely her responsibility. Because they had melded, she knew Kalsang couldn't have died as the clone had tearfully informed them. That was an odd way to think, but it made sense somehow. That fact didn't change anything.

The whole situation was impossible from the beginning. The evidence was still back at Luna City in Kalsang's neurovisor. The only chance of getting it back seemed to be to stick with August and his creepy lackey. Of course, without Kalsang could they even get it open?

Perhaps she could somehow win August over to her mission for when he regained his place in the order of things, as was inevitable. Perhaps the good in August, the vulnerable lonely person who had been laid bare before her in their long journey home might somehow be reachable and be open to her influence. Perhaps. The truth was she was starved for choice.

She questioned her spurning of the honest reflex of August's hug. There was something obviously still left in them for her, as inexplicable as that was. Anyway, he needed her.

Thinking this way left an opening for Aurora to roll with the momentum of the moment in a completely unexpected direction. As August turned away she reached for him, pulling him back and kissing him with a passion that surprised her. As he reciprocated she fell back before the fierceness of his lips. When he was finished, she let go and looked out through the remainder of the flames as their re-entry completed.

CHAPTER 38

August

He had been so tired – so tired that there had seemed to be no point in continuing. His constant efforts to survive had depleted him and, as they left the Moon, he had been ready to give up. Surrender. Let it all get away from him and try to find some small place to repair. Now life flowed back into August's veins as the parachutes deployed and he fell away from Aurora's embrace back into his webbing.

The force of gravity returned, straightening his body into alignment and returning his sense of direction. Everything was clear to him now. He had survived the great trial and returned from utter defeat and certain death. He would once again stand tall on solid ground and return to battle as a wizened warrior should.

He gazed forward as the clouds welcomed them and the landscape unveiled below them. Only possibility spread before him in all its varied richness.

Most importantly he felt Aurora by his side. It was her kiss that had awakened him from his slumber and he intended not to disappoint her. Anya's curse had finally failed and now he had found a way to replace her in his mind. Aurora was different. There was a clarity in her and he felt no need on her part to mold him into being different that he was. Her honesty would support him, allowing him to not make the same mistakes by isolating himself again. He had a new chance to prove himself, to become truly great.

Gudanko had done him a favor. He would have created many enemies in the way he would be pushing the new technology, and these enemies would be potential allies. There was a chance of re-aligning himself with old friends and making amends. He promised himself that he would cultivate these relationships this time and not simply use them as stepping-stones. He would make everything right by promoting the responsible use of this new power.

The Earth, with all her majesty, called up to him with a tender voice that made him weep. August vowed to create a royal future for Her, one in which the mistakes of the past would be overcome, and she would become the dignified, life-nourishing center of a new galactic dynasty.

He looked for affirmation back to Aurora, but she was looking away.

CHAPTER 39

Calvin30

As their capsule touched down, Calvin30 noted they were floating. Their landing spot was chosen to be far from any place anyone would suspect - to allow them to wander in the wilderness for a while. According to plan they'd be sustained on their path by caches positioned in anticipation of their passing.

That path was pulsing with potential. Kalsang was hopefully pushing up daisies where Calvin30 had ploughed him under, though he wouldn't count him out until he'd danced on the dome head's bones. He was proud he had finally seen through the deed, an action he'd completed without proxies. Perhaps it was a test he'd been given by the cosmos, to prove his place in the annals of chaos.

Groaning under their own gravity it was obvious they would be beholden to his lead. Motivating them out of their current languor would take some kind of carrot.

For August it would be that kiss, which Calvin30 hadn't missed. The sight of hope igniting in August's chest, the re-firing of his passion, his over-puffed belief in his personal myth. And how perfect that the woman was using him. This was breathtakingly beautiful.

Unreciprocated love and deceit. That was real tar baby. Black as night and as bottomless. August, that fantastic fool, was going to sink into an abyss so sublime that he'd drag the world down in with him.

The hatch flew open and fresh air flowed in. Around them the rolling motions of an ice-free Arctic Ocean and nearby a beach. Moved to his core, Calvin30 produced his pipe and blew out of pure gratitude.

Oh, what a wonderful world.

GLOSSARY

Alignments: Credited improvements to ecological performance by an organisation in a manner that reinforces global ecosystem repair and stability.

Buckeyball (also Buckminsterfullerene): A unique soccer ball shaped molecule of pure carbon named after Buckminster Fuller, an avant-guarde American architect, systems theorist, author, designer, and inventor who designed the geodesic Dome and was the first person to suggest the use of a global currency like the Eco. Some fullerene materials (Buckygel) have near perfect thermal and electromagnetic insulating properties and so are incorporated into materials used for the construction of space suits and radiation shields on spacecraft.

Campaign: Globally coordinated actions by many entities and actors against commercial interests with the aim of forcing them into alignment with the dominant economic system of the 22nd Century, which values ecological stabilisation and repair.

Com: A liability limited corporation, although in the 22nd Century most Coms are multinational (or multi-world) entities.

Comscript: A form of money used by Coms for commercial dealings. Use of Comscript is illegal within many local communities and ecological-commercial networks.

Comsec: The security department for a Com.

ComSyn: A dynamic ideation of the evolving status of a corporation projected electronically into a person's brain to facilitate timely and informed executive decision making.

Dreaming: A term invented by Western anthropologists to describe a deep concept from Australian First People spirituality wherein country and individuals are continually woven together by story as an act of continual generation and co-creation.

Dropstick: A baton shaped weapon which discharges current from the tip at high voltage.

Eco: A global currency based on formulas quantifying the universal economic benefit from activities which promote repair of global and local ecological systems.

Ecolution: A revolutionary movement which, by the 22nd Century, has fundamentally restructured human political, economic, and spiritual institutions to restore ecological and climactic balance to the planet Earth.

Ecoversion: The capture of a publicly traded Com through the acquisition of shares by panarchist entities (Hubs, Nets, Sys, and Revs) which are aligned with the Ecolution.

Fulcrum: A heavy compartment containing the engine and fuel tanks of a space craft connected by nearly unbreakable nanofilament cable to the living compartment of a spacecraft from. The living area pivots around the fulcrum thus simulating gravity.

Gaia: The living Earth wherein life participates in homeostatic regulation of the climate and environmental conditions to optimise conditions conducive to life.

Gaia Ecological Organisation (GEO): An organisation which oversees the restoration of Gaia, the living Earth. The GEO coordinates the activities of large-scale institutions aligned with global ecological, hydrological, chemical, and geological cycles, and also sets the formulae and standards for accounting for impact and repair of Earth ecosystems by organisations and communities.

Garuda: A bird-like spiritual being with many descriptions in Hindu and Buddhist mythology. In Vajrayana Buddhism, Garuda can be depicted carrying Avalokiteshvara, the enlightened deity of Compassion, and symbolizes the freedom and wisdom of mind which transcends conditioned existence. Kalsang's spacecraft is named the Garuda.

Gov: A vestigial political institution which has evolved from existing government forms. Govs coordinate resource sharing, infrastructure, and other public institutions operating within specific geospatial jurisdictions. Govs are significantly influenced by other entities (Hubs, Nets, Coms, Orgs, Revs and Sys) whose jurisdictions intersect in a Gov territory.

Helium-3: A light, non-radioactive isotope of helium with two protons and one neutron (common helium having two neutrons). Helium-3 is an important fuel used in fusion reactors in the 22nd Century because the fusion reaction releases charged protons, which can be efficiently converted to electricity.

Hub: A local community institution in the 22nd Century wherein individuals develop their sense of place and primary identity.

Icarus: A figure from Greek mythology, Icarus was given wings glued together with wax by his father Daedalus and warned not to fly to close to the sun where the wax would melt. The ambitious son ignored his father's warning and crashed to the Earth. August's spacecraft is named the Icarus.

IndraSys: A global, Indian dominated Sys which aligns global economic activity with the protection of biodiversity and related benefits. In Hindu mythology Indra is the King of Gods, while in Buddhist iconography Indra symbolises the interdependence and co-emergent emptiness of all phenomena.

KaliyugaRev: The most aggressive Rev and principle enemy of the Coms. KaliyugaRev believes that space flight is heretical as it distracts humanity from the difficult task of restoring balance to the Earth.

Local: A unit of currency used by Hubs for day to day economic relations. Locals are Hub-specific but can be converted to Ecos based on a Hub's positive environmental activities. Locals have the function of binding individuals to the Hubs and rewarding Hub loyalty and identification.

Mass Driver: An electromagnetic catapult that is used to provide the thrust for a non-rocket space launch.

Full Melding: The attainment of maturity for the Aliens. Prior to Melding the brains and associated nervous systems of their multiple heads are not fully coordinated and develop alternative perspectives. With Melding an Alien's concept of self has developed to accommodate these multiple perspectives within a singular identity so that they all function in harmony.

Maa Al'hyat Sys: A Sys coordinating economies which protect and repair hydrological cycles, particularly within arid regions. Maa Al'hyat is the largest such hydrological Sys originating from the Middle East, and thus is primarily an Islamic organisation.

m'Hoomuun: A sister planet to the Mother Ocean within the Aliens' solar system, which independently developed an environment suitable for life.

Microdropper: A solar powered atmospheric water generator (AWG) that extracts water from ambient air and funnels the moisture to a newly planted tree's root.

Mneme: Encoded packets of feelings and memories, which are stored and transmitted from one brain to another via neurovisor technology. Mnemes can also be composed by computer.

Mo: A divination technique employed by Tibetan Buddhists involving rolling dice following meditative visualisation and chanting of mantras.

Mother Ocean: The home planet of the Aliens. The planet is almost entirely covered by ocean.

Nanobot (Nanoid): A product of nanotechnology wherein a microscopic robot is assembled molecule by molecule. Nanobots facilitate many targeted chemical, industrial, and biological processes with minimal energy and resource investments.

Nanoprocessors: Miniaturized computers assembled similarly to nanobots.

Nanoweapon: Weaponised nanobots that have been outlawed in the 22nd Century due to the impact of their devastatingly targeted capabilities on individual leaders.

Neurolink: A communication connection made between two brains via a neurovisor.

Neuronet: The integration of the Internet with the neurological systems of human beings via neurovisor technology.

Neuroview: A vivid internal subjective experience of an individual, like a dream, which is projected into the brain by neurovisor technology.

Neurovisor: The principal communications technology of the 22nd Century which connects electronic technology directly into the cerebral cortex of the brain.

Net: one of the dominant Panarchist economic institutions of the 22nd Century. Nets are commercial networks which connect constituent Hubs and operate in collaboration or competition with other Nets or Coms. Nets use Ecos as their primary currency.

Org: Non-profit entities which coordinate and deliver most essential services in the 22nd Century.

Oort Array: The Oort cloud is the furthest belt of objects orbiting the Sun out beyond the orbit of Pluto. The Oort Array is an array of publicly owned space telescopes which are located in the inner edge of the Oort cloud and are dedicated to cosmological observations rather than the interception of extra-terrestrial communications.

Panarchist: A political philosophy wherein individuals nominate their political membership within exclusive networks, as opposed to geographic location. Panarchy is also an approach to economics, which uses the lessons from system theory and studies of ecology to understand human economic behaviour. In the 22ⁿᵈ Century, Panarchy has become the dominant global political philosophy in competition with older capitalist and socialist ideologies.

Pleiades: A bright cluster of seven stars visible to the naked eye and located near the vernal equinox, marking the beginning of spring. In ancient Greek mythology, the stars represent Seven Sisters who are pursued by Orion, the hunter. The story, associated with these stars, of sisters fleeing unwanted attentions is also found in the oral histories of various Australian and North American First Peoples.

Pod: An Alien matriarchal extended family grouping led by a single female Queen from whom the children of a pod descend. Pods also include selected male concubines, including Alphas which have decision making status and Betas which do not.

Proximity Malaise Syndrome: Also Outlanders, Going Out, Outers, etc. A psychological syndrome which increases in intensity the further a space farer travels away from the Earth. A small number of persons, mostly hermit meditators, are apparently immune from the effects. Women are generally more resistant than men.

Quantum Computer: A computer design which takes advantage of the strange ability of subatomic particles to exist in more than one state at any time to improve processing speed, energy efficiency, and information security. This technology has also been used to provide the conditions for artificial consciousness to develop in machines.

Rev: Activist organisations which are at the vanguard of the Ecolution, pressuring the Coms into ecoversion and compliance with the terms of The Peace. Revs use either legal or extra-legal means to achieve these ends. While some Revs have a registered legal status, others such as KaliyugaRev are outlawed.

Second Wave: The Second Wave of Space exploration wherein humanity, led by the Coms, established outposts and the Moon and several other planetary and satellite bodies. The motivation for the Coms was an existential imperative to develop Space in a bid to provide a future for unconstrained market expansion. The cost of the Second Wave proved prohibitive and led to the wide-scale decline of the Coms as global powers.

SkyTran: A prominent form of public transit in the 22nd Century. A SkyTran carriage, or fly-seat, is suspended below a fixed rail suspended between poles like a ski lift. A fly-seat on a SkyTran can select alternative directions at intersections, and installation of SkyTran poles allows traffic to travel through urban landscapes with a minimal structural footprint on the ground allowing reuse of old road ways for urban agriculture and other purposes.

Squeeze Suit: A restrictive body stocking impregnated with 'buckygel' which maintains 22nd Century Martian explorers' skin under Earth atmospheric pressure while protecting against loss of heat, moisture and cosmic radiation.

SpaceX Terminals: Floating offshore space ports connected by rail to selected cities in the 22nd Century.

Syn: An organisation focused on developing solutions to complex problems such as Gaia restoration, which operates via the neuronet through the coupling of big data, artificial intelligence, and networked human minds.

Sys: Powerful, macro-scale institutions of the 22nd Century. Sys are the glue which holds the Ecolution together by coordinating economic activity with specific global environmental systems and cycles. Sys are an amalgam of messy human political, economic, and cultural relationships with clear scientific principles and an adaptive legal structure. The Sys undertake the role of referee in mediating Net and Hub identity and exclusivity with the overriding imperatives of global repair and stability.

Tata XP car: Vehicles with inflatable bodies composed of steel strength textile skin resulting in a greatly reduced weight with resultant safety, energy efficiency gains, and reduced price.

Terrapod: The use of technology mediated living ecosystems to dynamically maintain survivable environmental conditions during long term space travel.

The Peace: An agreement brokered between the Capitalist Coms and the ascendant Panarchist institutions wherein the Coms were left free to pursue unfettered markets through the development of Space while the

Panarchist bodies enforce ecological constraints to economic growth on the Earth.

The Surge: The mass migration of Aliens from the Mother Ocean to the sister world m'Hoomuun through the development of wormhole technology.

Tides: A demarcation for time developed by the Aliens which, as a marine species, first tracked time through observing the tidal movement of ocean currents.

Tsuchinshan: A near Earth comet whose orbit approaches the Earth every 6-7 years at a close enough distance to allow access by space craft. During these passages it is mined for water for use in Space development.

Upside Down Thermometer: A dynamic register of a Hub's positive contribution to the repair and stability of the climate and an indicator used to set an exchange rate for local currency into ecos.

Volantor: A Vertical Take-off and Landing (VTOL) vehicle which redirects thrust from turbo props to travel both vertically and horizontally.

Waijungari: A Dreaming hero of the Ngarrindjeri people of the Southern Murray River region in South Australia. Escaping a jealous husband whose wives he had stolen, Waijungari ascended into the sky and became the planet Mars.

Wheatbelt: A region of Western Australia that extends north from Perth to the Mid-West region, and east to the Goldfields-Esperance region. It is bordered to the south by the South West and Great Southern regions and to the west by the Indian Ocean, the Perth metropolitan area, and the Peel region.

Wormhole: A theoretical passage through space-time that could create shortcuts bypassing the need for long distance space travel. Wormholes are predicted by the theory of general relativity.

Yulbrada: Yulbrada, the Earth, in the languages of several Australian First People inhabiting areas ranging from Southeastern Australia up to the Northern Territory.

ABOUT THE AUTHOR

Samuel Winburn has spent a very long period writing Ten Directions, his debut novel. He was born and raised in Alaska before relocating to Western Australia two decades ago. He, therefore, has had the privilege of inhabiting both Ends of the Earth. He has been active in the development of the profession of Environmental Accounting through his work building a successful environmental accountancy, teaching at local university, and co-founding the Australian national professional organisation in that field. He is especially grateful to have been an instigator for a United Nations award winning non-profit to empower local school kids to become climate leaders.

Samuel has been attempting to practice Buddhism since he was a teenager, having the exceptional good fortune to study under wonderful Tibetan meditation Masters.

If you want to engage with Samuel, you can do so via this book's Facebook Page (Ten Directions - @directions10) or via his web page www. samuelwinburn.net. Please consider leaving a review on your favorite online book community.

ACKNOWLEDGEMENTS

This book, so long in the making, is truly a collaborative effort including the input of friends and family who radically changed the story over the years through their helpful insights. To my children: Aurora, whose name entered these pages before birth, and to Django, who insisted that I add an alien with his name to make things balance. My chief inspiration is contributing to a better future world for you two.

To my high school English teacher, Sue Zimmerman, who read my first complete draft and suggested ways to tie the characters together and insisted a love story was essential. To John Croft, for all the inspiring Dragon Dreamings and for the Gaia House library, which you lovingly curated and shared with me – those books informed much of my book. To David Michie, for many years of helpful advice from a seasoned pro to a perpetual newbie. To Elaine Lewis and the Maia Maia team for brainstorming and road testing many concepts in this book at local primary schools – who would have thought we could do that? To Sandy Spicher, who suggested edits to my opening chapter and who helped me put out the call to engage other commercial editors. To my story editors, Marta Tanrikulu and Mary Dedanan, your comprehensive advice in restructuring my story was invaluable. To Susan Kornfield, my number one fan, whose advice immeasurably improved the opening chapters and whose unsolicited praise was extremely motivating. To Nadia Nelson, for your careful reading and ideas about reincarnating aliens and getting rid of the fish people. To my good friends, Durstin Selfridge, John Argus, Kym Flannery, and Jason Hart, who read my early drafts when most of the writing was crap – I owe you. To Barbara Kingsolver: we may never meet but Poisonwood Bible inspired a complete beginning-to-end rewrite. To my Mom and Dad who couldn't understand all the technobabble, thus forcing me to remove most of it. To my beloved Kristy Watson, who copy edited the book and who was not afraid to hit me over the head regarding sloppy writing. The remaining errors are where I chose to ignore your advice. To Alfredo Jimenez for your awesome book cover. To my dear friend Uzy Samorali of Unleased Design, for your expert work on my author's website.

CPSIA information can be obtained
at www.ICGtesting.com
Printed in the USA
FFHW020713240119
50283752-55303FF